THE
LAST
BLOODCARVER

THE
LAST
BLOODCARVER

VANESSA LE

ROARING BROOK PRESS

NEW YORK

Published by Roaring Brook Press
Roaring Brook Press is a division of Holtzbrinck Publishing Holdings
Limited Partnership
120 Broadway, New York, NY 10271 • fiercereads.com

Our books may be purchased in bulk for promotional, educational,
or business use. Please contact your local bookseller or the Macmillan
Corporate and Premium Sales Department at (800) 221-7945 ext. 5442 or
by email at MacmillanSpecialMarkets@macmillan.com.

Library of Congress Cataloging-in-Publication Data

Names: Le, Vanessa, 1999– author.
Title: The last bloodcarver / Vanessa Le.
Description: New York : Roaring Brook Press, 2024. |
Audience: Ages 12–18. | Audience: Grades 10–12. | Summary: Nhika,
a young woman hiding in the fringes of society, must use her
forbidden healing ability to cure the only witness to a murder.
Identifiers: LCCN 2023001104 | ISBN 9781250881526 (hardcover) |
ISBN 9781250881519 (ebook)
Subjects: CYAC: Ability—Fiction. | Magic—Fiction. | Murder—
Fiction. | Fantasy. | LCGFT: Fantasy fiction. | Novels.
Classification: LCC PZ7.1.L3915 Las 2024 | DDC [Fic]—dc23
LC record available at https://lccn.loc.gov/2023001104

First edition, 2024
Book design by Meg Sayre
Printed in the United States of America

ISBN 978-1-250-88152-6 (hardcover)
1   3   5   7   9   10   8   6   4   2

❧

FOR MY MOTHER,
MY FATHER,
AND MY BÀ NGOẠI.
MAY I MAKE YOU PROUD.

SNAKE

HORSE

MONKEY

SHEEP

ROOSTER

NHIKA'S APARTMENT

DOG

CENTRAL

DR. SANTO'S MANSION
DRAGON
CONGMI MANOR
TIGER
THEUMAS MEDICAL CENTER
CAT
OX
PIG
RAT
BUTCHERS' ROW
THEUMAS

— ONE —

SOMEONE LIKE NHIKA, WITH HER FIDGETY SMILE
and frayed satchel of snake oils, didn't belong in these streets.

In the Dog Borough near the harbor, she never would've stood out in this attire, with her cropped sleeves and bare hands. There, residents traded silk for cotton and wool, and the cog-work of their automatons crackled with rust and crusted sea salt. Here in the Horse Borough, women wrapped themselves in tight silk dresses and men in boxy robes, concealing every inch of skin with long gloves and high collars. It was the fashion, stemming from the fear of people like her.

The myth of them, anyway.

People watched as she slipped by, this little soot stain in a city of silvers and blues. Eyes didn't linger; they gave her as much space as she wanted. Paper-vendor automatons raised newspapers on segmented arms as she passed, so clean that her warped reflection greeted her in bronze. Today's headline was about the death of Congmi Industries' founder, all the buzz in Theumas despite being week-old news. This tabloid had made a grasp at relevance by adding a bite of scandal to the headline: ACCIDENT OR ASSASSINATION?

Nhika checked the slip of paper in her hand again, nervous about getting lost. In a planned city-state like Theumas, she shouldn't have worried. Every road had been numbered, the cross streets alphabetized, but she would look a sorry scrap of rags and tinctures if she showed up at the wrong door.

In the Horse Borough, the city was flatter, spread out. Not so layered—no boxlike homes stacked atop one another. Every building demanded its own space, tall and painted, the awnings curved in the style of pagodas. It wasn't hard to find her client's home: one of many town houses, so even and identical—differentiated only by the wrought iron number nailed above the door. They were a simple kind of elegance, with a tiled roof and multiple stories and a balcony at the very top. With a breath, she approached the door and knocked.

There was no immediate response. Nhika looked both ways up and down the street, feeling exposed on the doorstep. So, she waited as folks around here did, crossing her arms and tapping her foot and trying to look like, maybe, with a shower and a haircut and a complete change of clothes, she might've belonged.

At last the door opened, just a crack, caught on chain locks. Through it, half a man peered at her, eye narrowed. He knew who she was from a glance and ushered her in hastily, undoubtedly wanting her off his doorstep just as much as she did.

"We have a back entrance," he muttered. His voice dripped with disdain. Nhika had a great many retorts to use against him, but a sharp tongue had never made her any chem. No, she had other talents for that.

"My apologies," she said, brushing past him. If he noticed her sarcasm, he didn't acknowledge it. They didn't exchange names. Their interaction would not require them.

His home was smaller on the inside than it looked, the furniture made of dark, lacquered wood and inlaid with nacre. She caught sight of a wall-mounted rotary dial, too. Few were rich enough to afford their own home telephones. As she observed the twin place settings, the double armchairs, the two pairs of shoes by the door, she understood why the house was so small despite the man's obvious wealth. She understood why he was desperate enough to hire someone like her.

It was a home meant only for two, and one must've been on their deathbed.

"Where is the patient?" she asked, holding her bag of tinctures close as though she were a home doctor.

"Upstairs," the man said, squeezing the thin scraggle of hair on his chin. "Follow me."

Nhika trailed the man to the stairs, glass clinking in her bag. "Now, I'll have you know, I don't believe in this homeopathic nonsense," he insisted as they climbed, each hardwood step creaking underfoot. "Whatever you use, your salves and whatnot . . . I want to know the *scientific* premise."

She'd heard this disclaimer in some variation from all her clients. Nhika couldn't blame them—coming from a technocratic city like Theumas, of course he had to renounce homeopathy for that shiny, modern medicine. But, with a contemptuous smile, she understood that somewhere, deep inside, he did believe. He wouldn't have sought her out otherwise.

Or perhaps the physicians had already written off this patient as a lost cause, and he was desperate enough to hope that ginger and ginseng could do a damn thing against death.

But of course they couldn't.

That was Nhika's secret—well, one of many. She didn't believe in this homeopathic nonsense, either.

They came to a bedroom on the uppermost level, its curtains flung open to look out onto the balcony. A woman slept alone on the wide bed, wrapped beneath the heavy comforter. She looked almost like an automaton in the making, with a skeletal frame and catheters hanging out of her. A large boxlike machine sat at the opposite side of her bed, slowly eating its command roll as its cogs worked, dripping fluids and medicine through her lines. The heavy breathing of its bellows filled the room.

Nhika approached the bed and the man sucked in a breath through his teeth, as though about to change his mind and usher her out the door. Perhaps he just now noticed her Yarongese features: her golden-brown skin, dark irises, and hair the color of coffee rather than ink. Growing up in Theumas had wrung some of the island influence out of her, but that didn't deter clients from their paranoia. Nhika glanced back at him, awaiting a verdict, and he held open a palm to let her approach.

She took a spot at the bedside to inspect the woman. The patient held a placid expression, her eyes closed, and Nhika might've thought she was napping if not for the mottled look of her skin. Even for a Theuman, she was unusually pale.

This position was eerily familiar—a memory pulled from years ago, her at the bedside while her mother lay beneath a thin sheet. Only, there weren't so many catheters and machines, just Nhika's hand in hers, and her mother had never looked so sallow, not even in death.

She blinked out of her thoughts. "What's happened here?"

"It began as chest pain, and one day she collapsed. Since then, she hasn't been the same—weak, in pain. She's asleep now from all her medicine, but the doctors say it's only to make her comfortable. Not cure her. They say there's no more hope, but . . ." His gaze swept over the woman, his expression forlorn. "I don't believe that. We had plans. It's not over."

Nhika inched closer to the woman. "And what do the doctors think it is?"

"A disease of the blood, probably from her mother's side. But her mother was never like this." The man straightened his robe, clearing his throat with the air of a scholar. "If I had to guess, I would say it's those invisible micromes, some form of onslaught on her heart. We'd just gotten back from a trip out of the city. Perhaps she contracted something there."

He said this haughtily, and Nhika realized he didn't know a true lick of microme theory. He was just repeating words he'd seen in the papers, or perhaps from the physicians. She could say whatever she wanted, and he'd probably believe her.

Nhika rolled her neck. This would be easy.

"I'll be doing my own exam now," she said.

"No gloves?" he asked, the curl of his lip betraying his suspicion. He wouldn't have asked that question if she were Theuman, but a touch from a Yarongese like her had become a dangerous thing among the superstitious.

"I can't feel a pulse through leather and, as you might've noticed, I'm hardly in a position to afford silk," she said. Nhika bit back the bitterness; he was not the first to question her bare hands.

With a hesitant nod, he permitted her to work, and she feigned a brief physical exam. Then she extended a hand toward the woman's neck—slowly, to show she meant no harm. With two fingers in the cradle of the jawline, it looked like she was taking a pulse. And she was, but it was so much more than that.

With the interface of skin against skin at her fingertips, the limitlessness of her awareness exploded forth, racing first across the woman's vascular system—every vein and venule, branching and collapsing in waterways across the woman's body—and then her nervous system, snapping from synapse to synapse as electrical impulses did. Nhika layered herself into the woman's skeleton, wove herself into the vibrant workings of bone and marrow, and then the muscular system, her consciousness picking through corded tissue and wrapped sinew.

Nhika felt the ghost of the woman's pain mirrored in her own chest, bursting against the rib cage. The pain expanded with her empathy and she quelled them both, but not before she learned the source of the injury. There was a mass of damaged tissue staining the woman's heart, starved of blood.

Nhika gleaned all this in a matter of seconds, less than it required to take a pulse. When she drew her hand away, she knew every ailment this woman had, could see the history of this woman's body etched in the unfurled tapestry of her anatomy.

But she didn't reveal any of that, because then even an idiot such as her client could put two and two together. Even an idiot could realize what Nhika truly was, something far worse than a sham healer.

Instead, she opened her pouch of tinctures—all just a couple drops of aromatic oil in water. Placebos.

"For the pain, I suggest some licorice extract, either taken in tea or directly as drops. As for the micromes, I would suggest—" *What did she have in excess at the moment?* "—eucalyptus, applied topically on the chest for a week."

He nodded, and then seemed to remember he was a more discerning gentleman. "What does it all do?"

"The licorice has a certain structure of carbon rings that synapse with pain receptors to alleviate them," she said, waving a hand as if the details bored her. Now she was talking out of her ass, too, drawing from words she'd seen in stolen textbooks. "And the eucalyptus, well . . . It has natural anti-micromial properties. With my titer, it's stronger than fermicillin."

"Stronger than fermicillin?" he repeated, and suspicion snuck into his voice. Had she pushed his ignorance too far?

"Fermicillin is made from mold, you see, so there's lots of processing to make sure it's safe for human consumption. It's diluted, so to speak. But eucalyptus oil is all-natural, so no need to dilute its anti-micromial properties." She gave him an innocuous smile, ready with the lie. "It's a secret the drug manufacturers would kill me for divulging."

That seemed to satisfy the man, and he nodded again, as though she had made any sense at all. "How much do I owe you?"

She pinched her chin, trying to discern how much she could swindle from him. While he seemed desperate, an exorbitant price might only deepen his doubt. So, maybe something middling, just to get her to her next rent. "I want to see your wife make a full recovery, so I'm willing to lower the price for such a critical case." Nhika looked back over the woman, corpselike in her bed. She could heal her, truly, if she wanted. For a moment, she had almost considered it. But her stomach flipped with hunger, and she remembered that she couldn't spare the energy.

"Fifty chem for the eucalyptus regimen, and I'll lower it to twenty for the licorice," she decided. Nhika watched his expression, half expecting him to accuse her of conning him for chem. But his eyes held only resolution as he traipsed to the bedside, taking the woman's hands into his.

"Honya, love, I've found something that might help. It's not over."

His frostiness had left him, replaced only by tenderness, lips in a half smile and eyes soft. Nhika almost expected his love alone to melt the paleness from the woman's lips, to return the rosiness to her skin. She looked away, biting the inside of her cheek. When her eyes landed on the nightside table, she found the woman's doctor's note, a misdiagnosis of hematic disease alongside a question: *Would you like to donate the body of your loved one toward the Santo Research Initiative?* The man had marked *No.*

As she watched the man and his wife, sympathy wheedled its way into her chest, but she dug her nails into her palms to silence it. *Nhika, no. Don't fall for that.*

But the man clearly had no one else.

Neither do you, and you haven't the energy for this.

He'd pay her enough for a big dinner.

And if you get caught?

She'd healed blocked vessels elsewhere in the body before. She knew she *could* do it.

You're going to heal her, aren't you? Curse your wretched little heart.

Nhika placed a hand on the bedside, calling the man's attention. "If you would, there is just one final physical examination I'd like to conduct, just to make sure I'm not missing anything."

He blinked, the words slow to catch. When they did, he stammered, "Of course."

"For the patient's modesty, may I have the room?"

"I'm her husband," he tutted.

"Well, then, to preserve the secrets of my trade." She flashed him a tight-lipped smile. He seemed to weigh it, but only for a moment, before relenting.

She walked him out of the room, closed the door behind him, and drew the curtains over the windows. Once concealed from snooping eyes, she settled at the bedside, turning her gaze to the woman. "I pity you, poor thing. Having to be wed to a fool who loves you."

Then, eyes closed, she took the woman's hand.

They connected, and she was once again privy to all the layers of her anatomy. Wading through the nausea of the woman's medications, Nhika teased her influence toward the heart, where she tasted the acridness of dying tissue. There, she found the offending ailment: a narrowed vessel, obstructed by a clot.

This, she could work with. When she was young, her grandmother had taught her on fat deposits and scabs. Then, her father had formed a blockage like this deep in his leg. Now, Nhika stretched her control first to the vasculature, where she wrapped her influence around the clot. All she had to do was force the clot to degrade—after her grandmother's tutelage, it was second nature. However, she didn't burn the woman's energy stores; her patient would need those to recuperate. Instead, Nhika burned her own, feeling the core of her abdomen heat. The fire carved a path up her chest and through her arm, warming the place where skin touched skin. She felt a surge of power as her energy, raw and healthy, flooded into the patient's bloodstream.

It took a moment to reach the site of the heart, but as it did, her influence strengthened, a fist tightened around the clot. Nhika leveraged that influence, willing the clot to shrink: cells bursting, fats shriveling, proteins dissolving. It followed her command as surely as a trained muscle, the blockage withering to rot as her own energy burned.

Next, she flitted to the damaged tissue of the heart, finding it warped compared to the rest of the anatomy. It stood out like a wrong note in a smooth melody, discordant every time her influence passed by. She didn't salvage what had already died, but the muscle clung to its livelihood, and she bolstered it: scaffolding the structure of the heart chamber, reinvigorating it with electricity.

At last, Nhika pulled away, not daring to expend any more of her own energy. But she'd done enough for the woman to recover. She drew a deep breath to regain her grounding in the world around her, her senses slow to return as they trickled through a wall of nausea. The silk sheets came first, crisp underneath her, and then the firmness of her feet against the floor. Her chest deflated with fatigue and she felt the knot of hunger in her stomach expand, reaching her skull as a headache.

She smoothed the hair out of her face, her palm coming away with a sheen of sweat from the effort. "Your husband owes me a great deal," she huffed, mostly to herself. Through her fatigue, Nhika smiled; it had been a while since she'd healed another. This was what her ability had been meant to do, after all. It was not, however, meant to be used in secret, hidden away behind placebo oils and false examinations.

She stood shakily, drawing out tinctures of licorice and eucalyptus and leaving them at the bedside table. As she turned to leave, the woman gave her first indication of life, a noise in the back of her throat as she flinched. Nhika felt a bite of jealousy—that this illness had been so simple to heal, where her mother's had not.

She went for the door, but when she turned the handle the man was already there, opening it from the other side. They blinked dumbly at each other for a moment, and Nhika narrowed her eyes, wondering how much he'd witnessed. He only stepped past her and into the room.

"How is she?" he asked.

"Seems like you were correct about the micromes. The tinctures I left on the table should work. I'll leave a card with instructions for their use."

"And how much do I owe?"

"Seventy chem," she said. As she watched him draw out his wallet, her eyes narrowed.

Gloves. He wore gloves. Did he have those on before?

No—she'd seen him hold his wife's hand without them. And now that she scanned him over a second time, she noticed how his collar had been tightened around his neck and how he'd put shoes on, even though they were indoors.

He handed her the chem and she snatched it a little too quickly. Nhika backed toward the door, but he held out a gloved hand to pause her.

"Won't you teach me how to use the tonics?" he asked. He was stalling. Had he called the constabulary? Did he suspect what she was?

No, of course not. For people like him, her kind didn't exist anymore. He would be calling the constabulary on a myth. But then again, he had been superstitious enough to hire a yarb doctor.

"You'll find it intuitive," she said, inching toward the door. He stepped forward. Would he grab her?

When she reached for the handle, he drew a kitchen knife from the folds of his robe. His arms shook, his grip poor. Nhika scowled, her fingers flexed in anticipation beneath her sleeve.

"What's this?" she asked, forcing disinterest. Underneath it, she hid the quiver of her hand, knowing she might have to use her gift in a way her grandmother had never approved of.

"What did you do?"

"I'm not sure what you mean."

"You're one of them, aren't you?" he demanded, the trembling of his jaw betraying his fear. Ah yes, fear—the form his gratitude took after she'd saved his wife from a sure death. Nhika remembered now why she'd stopped bothering with the others, why she'd left them with only placebos and tea oil. Wretched little heart, indeed.

"You'll have to be more specific," she seethed, drawing backward. "Do you mean Yarongese? Yes, my family is from the island. A sham? Certainly not, you'll find my methods tried and true. Before you hurt yourself, sir, I'd advise you to put down the knife." That last part was more for her sake; she didn't want to sour her act of healing with an act of violence, though she wouldn't hesitate to defend herself, if it came to that.

"No," he said, jabbing the knife through the air. "I know what you are. *Bloodcarver*."

"Bloodcarver?" She scowled at the word. "There's no such thing." Nhika was giving him a final out. A smarter man would've known that bloodcarvers didn't exist anymore, that they were a breed that fell with the island. But the man's ignorance was wide enough to come full circle and he was somehow, miraculously, correct.

"I saw it, what you did to her," he insisted, jerking the knife.

Well then, no point in keeping up the charade now. She eyed the knife testily, but his stance and grip were noncommittal. He'd probably never wielded a weapon in his life.

"I've been called many things," she said, stepping forward. He stumbled backward. "Witch. Liver eater. Necromancer."

His knife arm shook and he held the small hilt with both hands, as if her look alone could fling it from his grasp.

She glared at him, anger rising as a scowl. "But that might be the most accurate one. *Bloodcarver*." Now, she relished in the fear, because if he could not show his thanks, what else could he offer her but fear?

Nhika feinted forward, scaring him with a shout, and he fell backward. Taking the opportunity, she threw herself at him, hand clawing for his neck.

When they touched, she inlaid herself within his anatomy, his body secondary to her own. For a moment, she considered killing him instantly, burning all his fuel stores or stopping the impulse of his heart—maybe something poetic, sadistic, a blockage in the vessel just like the one she'd taken from his wife.

"What did you do to her?" he asked, voice hollow, and she hesitated. In his last moments, her hand around his neck, he was still thinking about *her*. His knife slacked in his hand, but not from her control—it must have been acceptance, then, that she would kill him. Yet the deep sadness in his eyes was not for himself. She could not source something as ephemeral as love with her gift, but now it poured from him like blood from an open wound, torrential and infectious. For a moment, she almost wondered what that must feel like, a love that weathered the threat of death.

Through the redness of her rage, she saw his longing, and it stopped her from carving death into him. With a visceral growl, she ripped the knife from his hand, drawing blood as the blade caught her palm.

"I healed her," she spat. "You *idiot*."

A muffled pounding on the door downstairs drew her attention, and she pushed herself off the man. Another second and she heard the front door slam open, followed by the sounds of footsteps and shoved furniture.

Nhika raced to the windows. With a grunt, she yanked down the curtains, pulling the rod from the ceiling. It crashed into the medical machine, denting the box's iron shell, but the woman wouldn't need that anymore. She threw a glance over her shoulder, finding the man trembling at the door, fingers massaging his neck. He didn't come for her.

Nhika kicked the door open and dragged the curtains to the balcony. They were heavier than she'd expected, heavier still from the fatigue that tugged at her muscles, but she hefted the weight over her shoulder as it trailed broken glass. With a heave, she tossed the bulk of the curtains over the railing, then tied the end to the baluster. Across the street, curtains parted behind windows, and she caught glimpses of the curious eyes that watched her behind locked shutters.

Nhika positioned herself onto the curtain just as the constabulary burst through the door.

Only, it wasn't the constabulary. No blue uniform, no silver trim. No service cap, no badges. Just bolas, wooden catchpoles, and gold-toothed smiles.

Her client had called in the Butchers.

— TWO —

NHIKA SCALED DOWN THE TOWN HOUSE'S FACADE, easing the silk curtain through her fingers. Her cut palm smeared blood on the fabric, red leaching into gold. This shouldn't have been so difficult, but her muscles shook with fatigue from healing that woman. *Never again.* But that's what she'd said the last time.

She hit the ground, feeling the rough landing in the rattle of her ankles. The Butchers didn't follow her from the balcony, but from inside the house she heard the crash of furniture and the clomp of boots on stairs; they'd be out soon. She turned down the street and ran.

The Butchers burst from the door like rats from a flooded gutter, finding her quickly against the pale limestone motif of the city. She flew into an alley, pushing past trash-collecting automatons and anyone who blocked her path. Aristocrats huffed with indignation as she shoved through them, but their complaints fell to shock when they saw the Butchers tearing after her.

She'd heard ghost stories about the Butchers, black-market bogeymen who dealt in rare goods—and what was rarer than a bloodcarver? For aristocrats, Butchers were a way to get children to eat their vegetables. For the Yarongese who the Butchers labeled and sold as bloodcarvers, the name "Butcher" was never more apt.

Her cut palm throbbed as she sprinted through the alleyways. She quelled those pain receptors. She'd heal the cut later when she had the time and energy to expend. But now, a heavy muddiness dragged at her spent muscles as she clambered through narrow streets and hurdled into private lawns. They bulled after her, uncaring of the mess they made of gardens and service automatons.

Her feet took her south, toward the parts of the city where she'd blend in: the tight roads of the Dog Borough or the bustling fora of the Pig. Throwing glances over her shoulder, she let her instinct guide her through familiar passageways and sharp turns.

Nhika followed the slope of the hill, dropping down onto tiled roofs where the neighborhood terraced itself on the incline. Soon, she'd left the suburbs of her client's house for the thicket of downtown, a girl adrift in a sea of peaked roofs and busy roads. Theumas was a landscape of dark blue facades, silk-black rooftops, and silver accents. Against it all, she and her brown garb looked painfully misplaced.

The Butchers were close behind, albeit clumsy on the roofs. Nhika caught sight of a trolley at the bottom of the street and hope flared in her chest. If she could make it, the Butchers wouldn't be able to drag her off without calling the attention of law enforcement. She slid off the rooftops and dropped down to the streets below. The distant clatter above her reminded her the Butchers were still in fervent pursuit, but all she had to do was reach the trolley and—

As she rounded the corner, Nhika collided into someone in a

flurry of paper. She stumbled to regain her balance, annoyance rising in her chest as she sized up the young man she'd crashed into. He was clearly a boy who belonged in this part of the city, well-fitted vest suit peeking out underneath the folds of his robe, shoes shined to a mirror finish, and black hair combed to frame a handsome face.

"Watch it!" he chided, his indignant expression mirroring her own as he collected his scattered papers and file folders. But his irritation melted away to surprise as he swept his eyes over her—her torn shirt, baggy pants, bare hands. Golden-brown skin, scattered freckles, dark eyes. He was her opposite in many ways, features sharp where hers were soft.

From down the alley, litter clattered with the Butchers' distant approach. The young man must've noticed it, too, because he grabbed her wrist to help her up. Only then did she realize that his hands were bare, and that he'd touched her without hesitation, skin on skin. She met his eyes, waiting for him to realize she was Yarongese, but the disgust never came.

"Are you all right?" he asked instead, drawing her onto the safety of the sidewalk.

"I . . ." Few had ever asked her that question in earnest, so she struggled to find her answer. Before she could, he threw a glance down the alleyway just as the Butchers rounded the corner.

His eyes flared with concern. "Are those——"

Nhika didn't let him finish his question before she fled.

When she turned at the bottom of the street, she found the trolley already pulling away, and panic thrummed in her throat as she heard the thunder of Butchers behind her. Cursing the

Mother, she dipped into the first alleyway she saw, stealing one last glance at the young man she'd crashed into. As the Butchers emerged onto the street, he spilled those papers again, delaying them as they attempted to round him.

"My bad," he said, kneeling to regather them. The Butchers scowled as they swerved around him, one of them tripping over an extended leg.

And then they spotted her. As they trampled across the young man's papers, Nhika dipped away into the alley.

She barreled down the narrowing street, following it as it angled, before staggering to a halt when the alley ended at an unyielding brick wall. Heart pounding, Nhika turned, only to see the Butchers blocking the other end.

Frantically, she searched for an exit, finding one in a low fire-escape ladder. With a running start, Nhika scaled the wall, fingers catching the bottommost rung and feet scrabbling against brick as she pulled herself up. She'd made it a few rungs up before the Butchers reached her, the tallest of the crew craning up to snag her shoe.

With a twist of her ankle, she kicked him off, losing her slipper in the process. Her bare foot slipped against the cold metal rungs, slick with blood from her still-bleeding palm, but she hauled herself higher and higher until—

A loop of wire caught her ankle and she felt a tug against her leg. She slipped as another catchpole snagged her other foot. Her fingers burned with the tightness of their grip as the Butchers yanked, until at last she lost her hold on the rungs, nails clawing metal, palm smearing blood.

Alarm spiked in her chest as she fell. Somewhere along her descent, her body slammed against the edge of a railing, but she couldn't reorient herself before she tumbled down onto the pavement. Something cracked in her ribs and she turned off the pain receptors as soon as the burning came.

Her first thought was not of any broken bones, but of something far more valuable: Her hand went to her sternum, feeling for the ring she wore around her neck on a string. For a moment she panicked, thinking it lost or broken, until she felt the coolness of it against her skin. Only then did she remember escape. Tasting blood, Nhika pulled herself forward. Her body was breaking down, but she'd heal it later. *With what energy?* That was also a problem for later.

With blood-caked fingernails, she yanked at the cords wrapping her ankles. Nhika silenced the pain receptors as they twinged to life, opened her airway as it filled with fluid, set the broken bones of her ribs—until she was doing too much at once, her attention so spread across her body and the catch-poles and the rooftops that it thinned to smoke.

The Butchers leaned over her, figures blotting out the sky. She crawled away with the pitifulness of an ant plucked clean of its legs, but one grabbed her by the hair to tilt her head back. She heard the grind of broken bones that she didn't feel—another problem for later. Nhika flailed against them, trying to catch skin but finding only thick gloves and long sleeves.

"Is it a real one?" one of them asked, and the man who'd grabbed her shook her hard.

"Course not, but she sure looks the part, huh? Probably full

Yarongese," another said. He tapped her with his boot. Though they didn't believe she was a bloodcarver, their superstition was evident in their layered garb. Their only mistake was in not concealing their faces.

Nhika darted out a hand, grabbing a Butcher by the face. They touched for only a moment before he reeled away, but it was enough. He staggered backward, coughing and gagging, with a bloodied nose and bloodshot eyes. He clutched his face and stared at her, eyes bulging.

She'd burst every blood vessel in the man's body she'd managed to grab.

"Shit, she's real!" he choked as a bruise bloomed in the shape of her handprint. Nhika took the opportunity to squirm away, but the plan was ill-conceived—another Butcher grabbed her with ease, pinning her arms behind her back with gloved hands.

"And to think, I almost sat out on this call," said the man who'd grabbed her. He pulled out a length of cloth to bind her hands, winding until it burned.

The pain receptors were turning back on, one by one. She'd expended too much energy. Nhika smelled blood with each breath as every ounce of pain returned, slowly at first and then all at once, until her vision pulsed. Her heartbeat pounded in her ears and she felt her consciousness ebb, though she clung to it with gritted teeth. The Butchers' dialogue muffled to a drone as she turned her attention inward, dousing fires across her anatomy. Already, she felt herself succumbing to the pain.

The edges of her vision darkened, breaths growing short. Through the foggy ringing in her ears she managed to discern the Butcher's words: "Would you look at that? A real, live blood-carver. How many of these do you reckon are even left?"

Then the tenuous cord of her consciousness snapped.

— ❧ —

Nhika blinked out of her heartsoothing stupor, slow to recall her surroundings: a warmly lit room, the windows flung open to let in fresh air, and her mother's bed beside her. It had been her mother to pull away, disconnecting Nhika's heartsoothing with the loss of their touch, but Nhika shook her head.

"I can do it," she said, grabbing her mother's hand again. Her heartsoothing enmeshed itself within thin skin, sank into frail muscle. It felt the frayed spindle of nerves, atrophied on her mother's right side. When her influence climbed the spinal cord, it fought against a buzzing, itching feeling—something viral, like claws against Nhika's own skin. Then, in her mother's skull, there was such a mess of her dura and brain tissue, but Nhika had no idea where to begin. Was it the swelling? Perhaps—she could take some pressure off the nerves, give back the function of her mother's limbs. Or perhaps it was all this dead tissue, but Nhika had no idea how to begin repairing it, not when her grandmother had passed the year before, not when she was barely a heartsooth, not when—

Again, her mother pulled her arm away. "Nhika, dear," she said, the words coming haggardly. She swallowed, but it looked painful.

"I can heal you," Nhika insisted, blinking back tears—they weren't helpful. She was only twelve, but she knew she had to be strong; she was the only one who could be. The two of them were all that was left of the family.

Her mother blinked, tilted her head. That was all the motion she was capable of. Even now, muscles thin and face gaunt, she was beautiful: the sun-loved skin, each freckle a kiss, and eyes a beautiful shade of black. Her cracked lips managed a smile. "You tried. It's okay."

Tears burned; Nhika bit them back. "I've been reading grandma's books—it must be a matter of dead nerve cells, if only I could heal them, then I—"

"No more, Nhika," her mom said, and the sternness of her voice was enough to still Nhika. Her limbs stirred beneath the sheets, each move a labor as she reached for something under her shirt.

It was their family bone ring, the only thing to survive the fire that took Nhika's grandmother. Even as her mother winced from the pain of removing it, Nhika didn't help—because that bone ring meant the end. It meant there was nothing else to be done.

Her mother extended it to her. Nhika didn't take it. Now the tears were falling.

"Please. Don't leave me," she said. What would she have left?

Tears welled in her mother's eyes, too. Her gaze fell to the ring, every band of white bone against the black onyx a promise of remembrance. Once it was her grandmother's, and once her great-grandmother's, and once her great-great-grandmother's, and . . .

And now it was hers.

Nhika swallowed. Stared. Sat frozen at the bedside, because what was she to do? If she could not save her own mother, then what was the point of heartsoothing?

With much effort, her mother swallowed, working up strength for her next words: "Just because I can't stay doesn't mean I'm leaving you."

Only then did Nhika place her palm in her mother's and accept the ring.

— ❧ —

Consciousness returned to her in the form of monkey chatter and birdsong, and then the chill of a cold floor beneath her. Pain came last, itching its way back under her skin despite her attempts to silence it. Every leak she plugged only caused another to spout.

Her cheek stung against the gritty concrete. With a groan, Nhika collected herself to a sitting position, eyes adjusting to the dark. Now she saw where the chatter came from—she was in a menagerie, turtles and colorful birds and monkeys stacked in cages, some dead. And she, a bloodcarver, was just another caged animal sitting in the midst of it. It was a small warehouse, and yet the Butchers had managed to stuff in as many black-market commodities as they could—ivory tusks spanning one table and powdered something or other caked into squares on another. Still more merchandise lay behind stapled wooden crates, labeled HAZARDOUS MATERIALS.

So, this was the Butchers' Row.

With a jolt, she remembered her ring. Nhika fumbled through her layered clothing with shackled wrists, ribs and shoulders wailing at every movement, until she found it still tangled around her neck; the Butchers must not have deemed it valuable enough to take. And truly, it wasn't—not to anyone but her. It was made of bone and onyx, with a fracture down the center from the fire. No one else could read the inscription on the inner band, three characters that formed her familial name: *Suonyasan*. No one else would find value in those insets of bone along the onyx, each fragment taken from a heartsooth in her lineage. No one else would notice that the band was incomplete, with space yet meant for her grandmother, for her, for those who were supposed to come after.

She tucked the ring back under her collar, then rose. Each breath came with a stabbing ache, but she knew her body intimately enough to understand what it was trying to tell her. Nhika staggered forward, fingers catching the chicken-wire mesh of her cage as she scanned for an escape.

Now she'd really done it. She'd played into many Yarongese stereotypes when she learned most Theumans wouldn't see her any other way—the blood-hungry bloodcarver, the sea-loving immigrant, the hapless charity case—but now she'd fallen into a new one: a ware in the Butchers' Row. Another item to cross off the list. Nhika felt no one could put her in a pigeonhole if she climbed in there herself, but this particular trope was deadlier than the rest. She tried not to think about how the Butchers' Row had commodified other bloodcarvers before her as exotic goods, and she didn't linger on the fate that awaited her if the wrong client purchased her. No, she was going to get the hell out of here.

A monkey perked up at her movement, then moved to the corner of its cage to watch her, head cocked.

"Hey, little guy," she cooed, dragging herself toward him. "We're stuck in this together, aren't we?" She extended a hand, three fingers pressed together as though she held a treat. It piqued his interest and he reached out, tiny fingers scrabbling at hers.

With newfound speed, she snatched his arm. From that touch, she flooded his anatomy with her own consciousness. She made it quick, shutting down his pain receptors before stopping his heart. That was easy to do with animals, much harder on humans; humans could feel her influence, so their own anatomies fought her for control. Animals were never so lucky; the monkey collapsed, and from his still-warm body she siphoned all his energy stores before they could dissipate in death.

With the newfound calories and nutrients, Nhika restored some of her wounds. She released the calcium from his bones to deposit into her own, reappropriated the components of his lustrous hair to seal the splits in her skin. Tissue generation was always an expensive process, and she sucked the monkey dry of his energy, watching as his body stiffened and seized with rigor mortis. It was a kinder fate than what awaited him on the Butchers' Row, if the table of severed monkey paws was any indication.

Some of her pain ebbed, the receptors satisfied with her soothing. Nhika stood, giving the monkey a grateful look. "Thank you. And, erm . . . sorry about that."

His corpse twitched in understanding.

Now, for her escape.

She yanked at the chicken wire, but it'd been fastened tightly. Then she jiggled the door, not surprised to find it locked. Nhika frowned. In Yarongese folklore, there were bloodcarvers who could give themselves superhuman abilities: a rhino's strength by maximizing the chemistry of their musculature, or unbreakable bones by perfecting their calcium matrices. Of course, she knew only of the legends. Her parents had fled Yarong long before she'd been born, and those abilities—if ever they truly existed—had been left on the island.

Nhika didn't dare try those tricks now for fear of wrecking her own anatomy in the process. A stone of calcium deposited in the wrong place, a muscle grafted to the wrong bone . . . She'd need more than monkeys to fix all of that. While Yarongese people with her gift had the ability to alter anatomy through touch and thought alone, it was as much a science as medicine, each procedure requiring practice and study like any surgery might. But desperation was a powerful motivator.

Before she could get desperate enough to experiment, the click of lights echoed around the warehouse and the rafters came alive with incandescent bulbs. Nhika's eyes adjusted again, blinking away the temporary blindness as the broad expanse of the warehouse came into full view. Creatures woke from slumber in the corners of the building, and she could see a metal door on one side, crowded with boxes, from which a group of people emerged.

They meandered their way between pillars of crates toward her, admiring wares on the way. A crocodile here, some snakes there—yes, yes, all fascinating, but Nhika knew she was the true marvel.

"And here we have her," said a woman at the front of the group. Her clothing was a mere imitation of refinement, with wraps of colored rayon and scarves to conceal a too-tight dress. Two of Nhika's captors were in her attendance, followed by a stately gentleman she assumed was the client. He had the posture of an aristocrat, back straight and neck angled, as though he was accustomed to looking down on people. A fine black robe, embroidered with silver herons, draped his shoulders to reveal a well-tailored dress shirt underneath.

He narrowed his eyes as he scrutinized her.

Good, there was a doubt there, and his lips pursed with the haughtiness of a man with something to prove. He looked her up and down, seeming unimpressed by what she had to offer, before passing the Butcher a trenchant look that held a silent question: *Is she real?*

"She fell down the side of a building just this morning," noted one of her captors, as though by way of explanation. "Now look at her. Back on her feet. She's healed herself."

"Oh? Was I meant to act injured?" Nhika quipped.

The client leaned forward, hands clasped behind his back and eyes narrowed. "I want proof before purchase. I'm not interested in consuming a regular human."

"Proof?" The Butchers looked uneasily between one another, but all Nhika heard was that he was planning on *eating* her. Panic spiked, slipping through her control, and she staggered backward in the cage. She'd heard of the superstition, something about how eating the heart of a bloodcarver could grant immortality, or good health, or libido—it changed with each iteration. All false, of course, but that had never stopped the Butchers' Row.

The woman cleared her throat. "Certainly. I, um . . ."

"A knife, if you would," the man said, holding out a gloved hand.

"What are you intending?" the woman asked, eyes narrowed.

"If she's a bloodcarver, she would heal a fatal wound," he

said. When they didn't give him a weapon, he scoffed and perused the tables, finding a knife near the animal cages still crusted in monkey blood.

The Butcher opened and closed her mouth with quiet protests, and at last she managed, "You would injure one of my wares?"

"Yeah, you would injure one of her wares?" Nhika echoed.

"It would not be an injury if she's truly a bloodcarver," the client reasoned. "Isn't that right?"

Nhika prayed the Butchers would keep insisting, but they only exchanged nervous glances before the woman dipped her head in resignation. Nhika threw up her hands. "Hold on a moment. Let's talk this through. You're a smart man—you caught the farce. I'll admit it: I'm a fake! No need to trouble yourself for proof," she babbled, her eyes trailing from his knife to his face. His impassive expression told her that murder was little more than an inconvenience to him.

Her gaze flicked to the monkey cages. Would she have enough energy to heal a fatal wound? And even if she did, her fate was determined—he'd buy her and chop her up for parts. Her bones would get powdered into tea and her liver eaten with shark fin soup, as though her gift of bloodcarving could survive beyond the grave.

Nhika swallowed. Perhaps, if she could feign death, bleed out in front of his eyes without dying, he'd pass her over. That'd give her more time for escape. But how? *How?* Her mind raced for ideas, recalling the old anatomy books she and her grandmother had stolen from medical colleges. How to die without dying? How to survive as a corpse?

The jangle of the padlock rattled her back to the present focus. The client was unlocking the door and she considered escape. But her legs and hands were chained—how far could she go? She searched the Butchers for a key ring.

"Careful, Mr. Zen, sir," the woman cautioned, her expression pained. Not for Nhika, but for her client. "One touch and she has access to all your vital organs. It's a certain death."

"I'm well aware," Mr. Zen said, but he opened the door anyway.

Nhika bolted, but he grabbed her wrists with a gloved hand and drove the blade straight into her gut.

The pain came before she could react. Nhika doubled forward, then fell to the floor as he withdrew the blade. She gasped on the concrete as her blood pooled beneath her. Her mind reeled with panic, so many emotions lighting up her attention at once, all her body's alarms flaring, every muscle clenched against the threat of death. Too much to parse through. Overwhelming. So much blood. She was dying.

No. Her focus returned to her, sharp above the muddle of her pain. *Breathe, Nhika, breathe.* She would not survive all these years alone only to die here, in the Butchers' Row—no, she'd make sure her death meant something.

Pain receptors off. Her skin fizzled to silence. There, now she had room to think. Next, she muted the buzz of adrenaline and stress hormones coursing through her—she'd take it manually from here.

First, stop the bleeding. She'd lost too much already in her floundering, but now she pulled every last ounce of energy out of her stores to mend tissue, starting from the inside out. Organs first, to stop the internal hemorrhaging. And then the peritoneum, to hold her viscera in place. As for her skin, she let that weep a little, just for show—convince him she wasn't a bloodcarver; give him nothing to bid for. She would not heal herself today just to get eaten tomorrow.

She'd have to fake shock. That wouldn't be hard; her body was already preparing for it. But she shunted her remaining blood inward, constricting superficial vessels, until she was sure she looked as pale and colorless as a Theuman. She felt the remainder of her fuel dwindling like a candle on its last inch of wick, and she bled it conservatively to feed her charade.

The client clicked his tongue. "Just Yarongese. Figured as much."

"No!" one of her captors protested. "She's faking it. I can assure you. She'll have a pulse."

Oh, Mother. If they checked her pulse, it'd be over. She couldn't risk shutting off her carotid, or else she'd truly be dead.

Keys jangled again. Nhika considered giving up her play and accepting her fate. Instead, she prepared to jump him, to suck him dry of his energy stores and escape the place. At the moment, with her body in torpor and her energy reserved, the very thought of moving sowed fatigue into her bones.

But when he stooped beside her, he didn't check her neck. Instead, he took her hand. Nhika resisted the smile. While she couldn't shut off blood to her brain, she didn't mind clamping off a radial artery.

The client placed gloved fingers at the edge of her wrist, but she'd already constricted the vessel. His fingers pressed deeper, trying to feel for a pulse through his silk gloves, and he waited a laboriously long time. Numbness needled its way into her thumb, tingles spiking across her palm, before he finally lifted his fingers.

Blood flooded back into her hand. The client clicked his tongue in annoyance. "Look what you've made me do. I've killed a girl for nothing."

"She's still breathing, I assure you," the woman protested. Nhika remembered to hold her breath.

"Enough of this," the client snapped. She heard the clatter of a knife. "The next time you call me, make sure it's not over a ghost story."

There was silence, and then footsteps, growing farther away from the cage. In the distance, the door opened and banged shut.

Someone slammed a fist against her cage, rattling the bars. "You insufferable witch," the Butcher growled, the malice in her voice lethal. "Wake up. I know you're alive."

Nhika opened an eye. Then another. Only the Butchers remained, and she rolled herself onto her back, too spent to sit up. Blood stained the floor, caking her hair to her face and wetting her clothes. She was alive, though she must've looked like a corpse.

"You won't be able to pull that trick every time," the woman spat.

"What trick?" Nhika rasped. "Your client wanted a demonstration. I thought I put on quite a show." She licked blood from her teeth, her stomach flipping with hunger at its sweetness. "If you don't mind, I need food."

"You think you can make demands here?"

"Healing expends a tremendous amount of calories. If you don't feed me, my death won't be an act."

"No more tricks, bloodcarver."

Nhika drew herself up against the back of her cage, feeling the mesh dig into her skin. Everything felt a little raw, the skin learning to feel again after she'd shunted away its blood. "Let's make a deal. If you can find a buyer who doesn't plan on killing or eating me, I'll be cooperative."

The woman gathered her things to leave, hesitating with an answer. Nhika wondered if she was actually considering it, making bargains with her merchandise. But she turned to leave with her lackeys and gave a huff as a final parting gift. "We'll sell you to the highest bidder. What they plan to do with you is not my concern."

— THREE —

AFTER ALL THAT, THEY DID BRING HER FOOD, IF IT could be called that. She figured it must've been the same stuff they gave to the animals: leftover meats, bones, and vegetables all ground into a slop. Nhika turned off her taste receptors to get it down but couldn't deny the nutrition it provided. Taking her time to avoid scarring, she expended the new energy to tend to her wounds.

If anything, perhaps there was a bright side to this. It'd been a long, long time since she'd had reliable meals. While she wanted to resent the client and his wife who had landed her here, she couldn't. Nhika had done this to herself, really. Once upon a time, her gift was meant for selfless purposes. It was intended to be shared, celebrated, known, but she didn't have that luxury anymore. Now, it was used solely for survival.

They kept her in the dark most of the day, turning on the lights only when they brought in new clients or wares. She wondered where this place might've been—probably near the Rat Borough, where no one cared if a few girls went missing, where the constabulary relaxed their supervision. The city couldn't eliminate the Butchers' Row even if it tried; it was not a place but a concept, a vast economy of purloined goods and poached animals. It was a stain on Theumas, where people worshipped the scientific method over the gods of old and ignorance followed faithfully in the shadow of achievement. They claimed that innovation conquered all, but Nhika knew best that fear and superstition were immortal.

Maybe the Butchers did heed her bargain, because the next bidder was an elusive and shadowed man who wanted her not for food, but as an assassin. He looked to be one of those underworld types, with gold rings marking his fingers and dragon tattoos lacing his skin where it wasn't covered. He made an ostentatious display of not being afraid of her, reaching into her cell with bare fingers and lingering near the bars with open robe. Nhika considered maiming him for it, but that would land her nowhere. Besides, all things considered, his was not the worst gig.

He placed his bid: five hundred thousand chem. More money than Nhika had considered in her entire life, enough to buy a house outside the Dog Borough and retire comfortably.

The next bidder went even higher. It was an aristocratic lady with a dead husband. Still in mourning silks, she must've been desperate, because even the Butchers seemed to know a bloodcarver couldn't bring back the dead, though they conveniently forgot to inform their client. Selfishly, Nhika hoped this client would win her auction anyway, because she looked too frail to put up a fight if Nhika wanted to run away. She bid seven hundred thousand.

Throughout the next couple days, bidders came and went through the warehouse doors. Whenever Nhika hoped for a high bid, she demonstrated her gifts. Other times, the Butchers had to threaten it out of her. She hadn't forgotten escape, but it became apparent that here, under cage, lock, and key, escape was a narrow prospect. Instead, her best chance was to be bought by a fool who underestimated her, someone she could intimidate or escape from with ease.

The last bidder of the day came later, when Nhika was already drowsing off in the corner of the cage. The lights forbade rest as they blared to life, and she blinked annoyedly at her moonlight bidder.

He came with the female Butcher, but they were otherwise alone at this hour. Nhika narrowed her eyes at his approach, trying to discern his attire, but everything about him was nondescript—black tunic, belted at the waist; ebony hair, peeking out beneath a hood. Everything, that was, except the mask he wore.

It was one of those old theater masks, plain bamboo with stark features painted in saturated color. A bit theatrical—literally—but she understood why an aristocrat might not want to show his face around these parts. The mask was some kind of animal.

A fox.

In Yarongese folklore, the Trickster Fox was a shape-shifting villain, beguiling and wicked. Nhika's grandmother had orated stories about how the Fox deceived the Mother's heartsooths to their deaths, how he defiled their gifts, and how the Mother punished him duly—carving his nine tails down to one and cursing his predecessors to forever walk the earth as shadows of their former selves. Whether or not this man's mask was an intentional allusion, it struck fear all the same.

"Why is she covered in blood?" the masked man asked, voice low in a strained kind of timbre, as though he were modulating it.

"A previous client requested a demonstration," the Butcher said. "And she proved to be a true bloodcarver."

The man looked at the Butcher, his expression concealed. "Heartsooth. In their culture, they call themselves heartsooths. Isn't that right?" Hearing that name—one she hadn't heard in a long, long time—shocked her. It was a name passed through her family, uttered between mother and grandmother. A name she called herself, when no one else would. A name that felt appropriated on a Theuman tongue.

In her surprise, it took her a moment to realize he was addressing her.

"Y-yes," she stammered. When had she lost her wits? Now she saw how tightly collared his robe was, how his black gloves ascended far up his sleeves, how the mask concealed the last bit of his skin. Her blood grew cold; this was no ordinary client. This was someone who had researched her and her kind.

And that terrified her.

"Would you like a demonstration?" the Butcher offered, drawing a knife from her sleeve.

The man held up a hand to dismiss her. "No. I'd like to place a bid."

Bid low, she prayed. If this man bought her, what might he do? Something warned her she would not be able to easily escape him.

"The current highest offer is eight hundred thousand chem,"

the Butcher said. Nhika wished she could see his face to gauge his expression. She could make do with a mourning woman, or even a man who wanted her to be his assassin, but this bidder was unreadable. Expressionless. And that made him dangerous.

"I'll offer a clean million," the man said after a pause.

Nhika's heart sank.

But the Butcher's expression sparked with enthusiasm. "You may as well consider her yours, sir," she said, sweeping a voracious look at Nhika. "The listing ends tomorrow. My associates will be in contact should we close with you."

The masked man nodded. It was simple, resolute, but terror lightninged through Nhika's chest. As he turned to leave, she found her voice to blurt, "Who are you?"

He hesitated, and their eyes caught. His were dark behind the mask, hardly discernible and shadowed in thought. When at last he spoke, he said, "Someone who has been looking for someone like you for a long time." As if that answered her question at all.

Only when he left did her breath return to her lungs, her wits slowly after.

A million chem. Who had that kind of money?

Or rather: What did he plan for her that made her worth that much?

— ❦ —

With morning came her reckoning. Nhika weighed her options in the corner of the cage. She could try to escape now, before the man returned to collect her. But that meant fighting her way out of the warehouse in chains. Or, she could take her chances with the bidder. In the clarity of the morning, she wondered why she'd been so afraid before—so, he knew what a heart-sooth was. Perhaps the knowledge was more common than she'd thought.

Still, she paced back and forth, smudging the bloodstain in her cell. The animals were garrulous today, birdcalls competing with anxious monkey hollers. It left little space for her to think.

In the chaos, her thoughts returned to Yarongese legends, those immortalized heartsooths who used their arts for more than just medicine. Her grandmother had raised Nhika on those stories, such that when her heartsoothing first manifested, she'd thought herself one of those heroes, able to shape her anatomy any way she wanted—until she'd knotted her muscle into a painful lump in her bicep and cried until her grandmother could soothe it out.

Then, her grandmother had taken Nhika's hands between hers, her skin a shade darker than Nhika's, and straightened out the strands of muscle one by one. "Do you know why the art of heartsoothing is dying, Nhika?" her grandmother had asked.

"Because Daltanny took over." As a youngling, she only understood that Theumas's neighbor, Daltanny, had invaded the island of Yarong and driven those like her family out. Only later would her mother harrow her with the details of genocide and colonization.

Her grandmother had accepted the answer, but her frown

was still dissatisfied. She'd always been a woman to wear her emotions plainly on her face, all her wrinkles and papery skin a ripe canvas. "Because there are no more people to remember it as it's meant to be remembered. We are losing teachers. Children who get the gift don't know how to use it properly. Now, I'll teach you how to soothe, but no more playing around like this, okay, *khun*?" The term of endearment held an edge of sternness.

"What's the point of heartsoothing if I can't play around with my own anatomy?"

Again, her grandma had looked crestfallen, but not disappointed in Nhika herself. "To heal" was her short answer. Her longer one: "That is the core of heartsoothing. Not to harm. To heal."

That had all been good and well until her grandmother died. Then Nhika had messed around with her anatomy by necessity, had bruised constables and carved Butchers, with nothing but a bad pinkie to show for it. For the last six years, her heartsoothing had been many things—hidden, forgotten, misused—but it had seldom been nourished, not without a teacher or anatomy books. Those were things she'd lost with her family.

The lights came on again, and Nhika readied herself. It was still so early, considering how late the masked bidder came the day before—she hadn't even had time for breakfast. But when the Butchers rounded the corner, it wasn't with the masked man.

It was with a girl.

She was dressed in the long white dress and silk pants of a socialite, face hidden behind a painted fan and heavy makeup.

It aged her, but Nhika discerned the youth beneath the veneer. She must've been a few years younger than Nhika—maybe fourteen or fifteen. Much too young for a place like this. She was the image of Theuman beauty: lips like lily petals against pale skin, straight black hair like a river of ink, and monolid eyes touched with blush. If Nhika had to guess, probably a bored debutante who'd caught word of a bloodcarver and wanted to see for herself.

The girl leaned close to the cage, fingers tracing the bars. The clean fabric of her gloves came away with rust, or perhaps dried blood, and she rubbed the sediment between her fingers with a look of distaste. "How much for her?" she asked as though inquiring about a new pet.

"Highest offer on the table is a million chem, flat," the Butcher replied. Nhika raised an eyebrow—why humor this girl? But this was someone Nhika could escape, a youth with a large wallet and a dangerous curiosity.

"Are you a true bloodcarver?" the girl asked, leaning close enough to whisper. Her perfume wafted off her, floral and sweet.

"Tried, true, and worth every coin," Nhika said, flashing a grin. "I can demonstrate if you'd like."

"Oh?" The girl turned up her nose, undoubtedly observing the ungodly amount of blood caking Nhika's clothing.

"Come closer." If the girl were keen, she'd see how Nhika's arm hairs twitched at her command, or how her pupils dilated and constricted as she wished. And if Nhika were a kinder person, she would've scared the girl home, would've saved her from the Butchers' Row and ushered her back to her jade palace and stone gardens. But, Nhika had already paid once for her sympathy.

When at last the girl noticed Nhika's small demonstration, her eyes flared with fascination. She leaned close, so close, that if Nhika swiped her hand past the bars she could grab a fistful of the girl's hair and carve her. But Nhika stayed her hand.

The Butcher cleared her throat. "So, what is it, girl? Here to spend Daddy's money or not?"

At the comment, the girl flinched. With a snap of her fan, she regained her composure and drew back from the cage. "One million chem, you say?" She tapped the fan against her lips.

"The bidder collects later today."

"What do they want with her?"

"Damned if I know."

The girl hummed with thought and Nhika wondered if she was actually considering this, or pretending for show. But then she smiled, and said, "I will not bid."

"Figured so," the Butcher said.

"Instead, I will make an offer. One and a half million chem, but I get her now. Take it or leave it."

Nhika's lips parted with disbelief. What purpose did an aristocratic teenager have for a bloodcarver? And how did every bidder have so much money to throw around? No one had cared about her value when she peddled snake oil to put food on the table, yet she was somehow so priceless when bought and sold. If Nhika was lucky, she'd be an expensive novelty, and the girl would quickly lose interest in her. She was hoping, praying, that the Butcher would take the offer.

"We have other bidders who may want to compete with that price," the Butcher began.

"If that's a no, then I'll take my leave." The girl turned—was it a bluff, or was that relief Nhika caught in her expression?

"Wait," the Butcher said, holding out a hand. She squeezed her chin, brow furrowed in consternation. Her thoughts were easy enough to discern: One and a half million chem was more than enough to retire her, but would the masked man increase his bid?

"When will I get the money?" the Butcher asked.

"Up front. I'll send it in paper, unless you prefer gold." The girl kept her poise. Behind the fan, it was hard to discern her true emotions, whether she closed the deal with ease or trepidation. For Nhika's purposes, it hardly mattered.

"Paper will do," the Butcher said.

"I'll return later with the chem. As for her, I'd appreciate it if you found her a new set of clothing. It won't do to pick her up like . . . that." The girl's eyes flicked over Nhika's bloodied garb. "I'll be back by autocarriage. Please, have her ready for me by noon."

The Butcher nodded, grin wide. "Certainly."

"Splendid. I'll see you both then." She lifted the fan over her face again, and then she was gone. The exchange had happened so quickly that Nhika had hardly gotten a witticism in. All she could do was stare, unsure how to feel about her future prospects, as the Butcher hurried to usher the girl out of the warehouse.

When the lights flicked off, she settled again in the corner, parsing through the events of the past couple days. A last-minute offer, too good to pass on. A mysterious man in a fox mask, outbid by a teenager. And here Nhika sat, sold to the girl in white.

A smile spread over her lips. This—this, she could work with.

— FOUR —

NHIKA LOOKED FORWARD TO THE AUTOCARRIAGE. She'd only been in one once before that she could remember, a long time ago, so she figured she'd escape after she got in it, just to have the experience. And at the very least, she'd be out of the Butchers' Row.

Breakfast was her final meal with the Butchers, but she picked through it with disinterest. Considering how much money her sale had made them, she felt they could have been more generous with the meal, but it didn't matter anymore. She'd gleaned all the calories she could.

Before noon, the Butchers and a couple attendants came to fulfill the client's wishes. They brought clean clothing—dark red to hide any stains that might arise—which they squeezed into her cage. The clothes were a couple sizes too large, and Nhika held the pants up to her waist with disdain.

"Turn around," she told the Butchers. "I'd like some modesty, please."

"Just put it on." The woman sighed, the exasperation thinning her voice. "I'll be glad to be rid of you."

"I hear that a lot," Nhika said, but she obliged, stripping to her undergarments and snaking into the new clothes. The drawstring at the hip made her pants fit, and she sashed her tunic at the waist to bring in the form. After that they gave her a basin of water and towelettes, instructing her to clean herself. When she was done, the water ran red with dried blood and the side of her face was raw from scrubbing. Nhika probably looked the cleanest she had in a long time, though they didn't offer her a mirror to check.

Shortly after, they took her from the warehouse. Many Butchers came for that, wrapped to Heavens in scarves and garments. They bound her hands again as they drew her from the cage, gloved fingers clamped onto every segment of her arm.

They took her out of the warehouse by an exit in the back that opened onto a loading dock, facing water. From the positioning of the harbor, she tried to discern which borough she was in, but they moved her quickly along until she stopped before a long black autocarriage in the shadow of the warehouse.

The buildings were close here, offering cover from curious eyes, but the driver, a young man who filled out his seat with his broad shoulders, still looked antsy as he fidgeted with the tinted windows. When his eyes met Nhika's, they narrowed with discontent, as though he'd been expecting something . . . more. The girl in white sat beside him.

Nhika examined the carriage. The back compartment was longer than most autocarriages she'd seen in the streets, with no doors nor windows. Instead, the metal body had been accented with gold filigree of flowers and cranes. With a drop of disappointment, she realized this wasn't a passenger carriage at all.

It was a hearse.

"In you go," said a Butcher, opening the back and lifting her in. Inside was a long, empty chamber with a loading apparatus for the coffin. She frowned as they closed the doors behind her with a click of the lock.

A sliding window at the front opened and the girl in white peered into the cabin, her wide eyes holding a smile. "I hope you find it comfortable back there."

"It's fine," Nhika grumbled, finding a corner to sulk in. The window slid shut and she heard the rumble of an engine before the hearse lurched forward. She spent a moment in the corner, miffed at being duped out of an autocarriage ride. And now, with her hands tied, she could hardly try to escape.

Instead, she knocked at the sliding window. There was a pause before it slid open again. "What is it?" the girl asked.

"Where are we going?"

"To my home."

"Who are you?"

"Congmi Mai Minlan," she said. So, she was from one of *those* families, with middle names passed down from member to member. More monikers, more esteem. Nhika was so caught on the length of it that she almost missed the familial name.

When realization surfaced, she widened her eyes. "Congmi, as in—"

"Yes." The girl smiled, bringing a finger to her lips as though they shared a secret. "Congmi Industries. You can call me Mimi. Everyone does."

Nhika recalled the papers, the headline news: The founder of Congmi Industries had just passed. So often, she'd seen that name on front pages—whenever a new automaton line released, whenever the family donated some ostentatious sum to charity—but there was something surreal about being *bought* by a Congmi herself.

Nhika narrowed her eyes. If this was a hearse, that meant there was an upcoming funeral, and . . . Mother, did this girl expect a feat of necromancy? "I can't bring him back," she said, leaning close to the window. "I'm afraid you've wasted your chem."

A part of her hoped that, with the revelation, Mimi would simply drop her off on the streets. The other part, which she tried to quash, pitied a girl who would spend so much on a lost cause.

But Mimi responded, "I know. I know he's gone. That's not what I bought you for."

"Are . . ." Nhika hesitated. "Are you going to eat me?"

Mimi laughed, a tinkling noise. "I'm not a cannibal."

"Some don't consider us humans. So they justify it in their heads."

"And what are you, exactly?" Mimi turned a curious eye on Nhika. "What exactly is it that lets you . . . carve?"

Once upon a time, Nhika had tried coming up with an explanation for it, but it was hard to describe how it felt, being so entwined in another, at once so intimate and removed. She didn't have the words to explain that kind of connection—how did one describe color to the sightless? So, in her daydreams where someone grew close enough to ask, she'd made something up that Theumans might be able to digest, and over time she'd internalized a bit of it as truth. "We have an empathy organ, a bit of tissue that you don't have. It's just like flexing a muscle to us. That's all."

"An empathy organ?"

"Like, how you can connect with another emotionally. We can connect with another *physically*."

"Interesting," Mimi hummed. "My father would've loved to understand that."

At that, Nhika felt the slightest nip of guilt, because the empathy organ was a lie. In truth, she didn't know how heartsooths were any different from Theumans, why it was an art only some Yarongese could learn. But she knew that every time she connected with someone, there was a pesky little voice in her heart that urged her to soothe their ailments. What could that voice be, other than an empathy organ? One that secreted hormones and desires into her wretched little heart? Yet, Nhika had spent her whole life exploring the intricacies of her own body, until she understood it as well as she understood the streets of the Dog Borough. No such organ existed at all, or she would've carved it out years ago.

"So, what is it that you want from me?" Nhika asked to change the subject.

Mimi tapped her fan against her chin. "Let me tell you in my brother's audience. It'll be easier to justify myself only once."

She left it at that and turned back to the driver. But she kept the window open, and through it Nhika watched as the auto-carriage turned into a fenced courtyard, with walls of white limestone and an entryway flanked by stone lions. From her perspective, the roofed gate framed a manor, though the place was too big to capture through the sliding window. Nhika stared at the building, so symmetrical and sprawling, curved eaves capped with statuettes and the black dragon-scale tiles lined in silver. She expected them to drive up to the central fountain, which featured statues of bowing cranes and spitting fish, but they turned past the gardens toward the back of the manor.

The gardens were a sight in and of themselves, long lawns and covered ponds, palisades and arched bridges. If she hadn't known there was no place for monarchy in Theumas, she might've thought this a palace. And perhaps it was, with aristocrats turned into royalty by industry.

A part of her hoped to be able to walk through the front doors, but they took her to an outbuilding in the back, with a door that lifted open on a system of cogs and pulleys. Once inside, the engine silenced and Mimi disembarked with their driver. The doors closed behind them.

There was a brief silence, and Nhika heard their muffled conversation outside the autocarriage. The driver's voice was urgent but Mimi's held that same unaffected whimsy, as though she hadn't just returned from the black market.

"Just get Andao, please," Mimi said, and the footsteps rounded the hearse.

A few moments passed in silent expectation. When nothing happened, Nhika peered through the window slot at the rest of the outbuilding, where tool racks lined the walls. This was not the only autocarriage here, and she felt a bit of chagrin when she saw a sports carriage, its top open. They couldn't have retrieved her in that one?

Once drunk on her fill of the opulence of this simple out-building, Nhika fell to scheming. Surely, if she made herself a problem, they'd let her go without much thought, price be damned. She'd never had to try very hard to play the part of a nuisance.

The lock clicked on the hearse and Nhika composed herself, posture relaxed against the back of the compartment. The doors opened, revealing three people: Mimi, the driver, and someone who Nhika presumed was the brother. He was tall and thin, perhaps a few years older than Nhika, and she couldn't tell if he looked haggard all the time or just now, looking at her.

His expression was frozen in the wide-eyed, *O*-mouthed look of shock. Mimi and the driver looked at him expectantly, Mimi with a cautious smile on her lips.

"Heir to the fortune, I presume," Nhika greeted, holding out her bound hands. "Pleasure to make your acquaintance."

He didn't take her hands. He was gloved, anyway. The brother only stared, as if she hadn't spoken at all.

"Andao, I know how this looks but—" Mimi began, but her brother cut her off.

"Mimi, you can't buy a human!"

"I didn't buy her like *that*. You should've seen her before, covered in blood. I'm *saving* her," Mimi objected, but Nhika didn't quite see the distinction. "Besides, didn't we talk about this?"

"As a joke!" His voice adopted a tinny ring, stretched with anxiety. But the driver placed a hand on his shoulder and the gesture seemed to quell him.

"Andao, it'll be all right," the driver said, voice tender. "I wouldn't have accompanied Mimi if I didn't think we could handle this."

"Is she even real, though?" Andao asked, then seemed to realize the stupidity of his question. He pinched the bridge of his nose. "For crying out loud, Mimi, I was drunk and joking. Where did you find her, anyway?"

"The details are unimportant," Mimi said in a rush, waving her closed fan. "What's done is done. Trin and I can manage her by ourselves. You don't have to worry about a thing." They passed their words over her, as if she were a dog they were debating keeping. It wasn't anything that surprised her.

Nhika cleared her throat, reminding them she was still there. Andao caught her eye and, seeming to remember she was, in fact, human, straightened and gave her a courteous bow. "My apologies, bloodcarver. My name is Congmi Quan Andao. This is my sister, Congmi Mai Minlan—"

"—Mimi," Mimi interrupted.

"—and my attendant, Dep Trin." He gestured to the driver. "And what should we call you?"

"Nhika," she said, shifting her jaw. When they blinked in expectation, she remembered to add, "Just Nhika." Her ring burned at her chest, as though in revolt that she could forego her familial name, Suonyasan, so easily. Here, among this lustrous company, that name held no meaning.

Nhika drew forward in the hearse, and though her onlookers retained their refined postures, she noticed how they stiffened. Nhika sat, chin raised, at the edge of the trunk, hoping that her small frame carried an aura of fierceness, aided by bloodcarver rumors. "I'll make this easy on you. Seems to me like you three are in over your heads, looking for something your money can't buy. Do you know what I am?"

Nhika waited for them to respond, but they didn't, so she continued, rising as her words came. "I'm a bloodcarver. Liver eater. Mother worshipper. Witch. Let me go, or else I'll carve out your heart and eat it. I'll tear you limb from limb with just a thought. I'll send so much—"

Trin drew a pistol from his hip and pointed it at her head.

"Or, we can talk this through," she petered out. Trin was all corded arms and bulky physique; she didn't doubt he knew how to pull a trigger. Only when Andao gave him a subduing look did he finally lower the gun.

Mimi shooed the threat away with a wave. "There won't be need for that here, Trin." Her next sentence was pointed at Nhika. "*Right?*"

Nhika smiled ingratiatingly. "Right." The scare tactic had been worth a shot, but now she gravitated toward a different strategy. "The curiosity is killing me. What business does a Congmi have for someone like me?"

Mimi and Andao shared a look, but Mimi gave him a resolute nod. Andao let out a breath. "I presume you know that our father was recently in an accident."

Nhika nodded, holding her tongue against careless remarks.

"He didn't survive. But the driver, a close family friend, did. He's currently comatose and the doctors don't see a chance of recovery for him, so we've brought him home to keep an eye on him."

"And you want me to heal this driver?" Nhika anticipated.

"Our father once told us stories about magical healers on Yarong. Perhaps it was stupid to consider a bloodcarver for the job, but . . ." Andao swallowed. "Yes."

They shared a long stare, and then Nhika erupted in laughter, which turned into a wheeze, because they'd paid 1.5 million chem for her to do the same thing that had landed her in the Butchers' Row to begin with. There was something so poetic about that, and if ever she worshipped the Mother it would be now, because this seemed too serendipitous to be the work of mortals and coincidence. No, some goddess above must've been toying with her.

They gave her wary looks, as though she wasn't a bloodcarver after all, just deranged. But her laughter trickled to an end, her chest light, and she raised an eyebrow at the three of them. "Is that all you want?" she asked. No miracles? No assassinations? None of her hair ground into their flour?

They hesitated, probably wondering how else they could milk her services. But Mimi said, "Yes."

"How much did you spend on her, Mimi?" Andao wondered aloud.

She gave him a placid smile. "No need to worry about it, Andao. And surely, Hendon's life is priceless. And, um . . ." Her eyes trailed to Nhika, and the rest of her sentence was lost to silence. Nhika narrowed her eyes, but Mimi turned away and pulled her brother aside.

They stepped out of the outbuilding, leaving Nhika alone with Trin. Though he didn't pull his pistol on her again, his hand remained steady on the grip, and she wondered if he'd try it again now that his employers had left the room.

"Relax," she said, eyeing him over, looking for skin. Despite his proletarian position, he wore similar refinery to Andao's: a smart, brocaded tunic, collared tightly around the neck with silk gloves to match. His hair was cut short and neat, its angularity matching the boxiness of his features, and his eyes were the shape of willow leaves. His stern expression discouraged nonsense.

"You're not going to have to use that," Nhika said. "If all you want is for me to heal your friend, I'll be good. Promise."

He snorted but didn't take his hand off the gun. "Sure."

Nhika frowned. "Out of curiosity, how much did they pay you to fetch me from the Butchers' Row? After all, you're now an accomplice to an illicit exchange." She remembered his nervousness at the warehouse. "Surely, you untie me, and we can forget that ever happened, *Dep Trin*." Nhika said his name as a threat, just to let him know she remembered it.

He scoffed. "Save your words, bloodcarver. I don't do it for money. They're friends."

Nhika searched his face for a lie. "Friends with deep wallets?"

"Forget it. I wouldn't expect you to understand."

She drew into herself at that. Though she shrugged it off, she felt a sting from the flippancy in his voice, followed by indignation. What did he know of her? She wanted to tell him that she wasn't spawned of boiled blood; she had a family, too. Once.

A retort died on her tongue as the siblings returned, with

Andao having smoothed out the stray strands of his hair and Mimi beaming—Nhika guessed she had won whatever they had been negotiating.

"Sorry to keep you waiting, Nhika. But we've sorted it out and Andao is *delighted* to have you join us for today." Mimi gave her brother a sidelong glance, eyes holding an imperative playfulness.

Nhika leaned back against the bay of the hearse. "And what's in it for me?"

Mimi almost looked offended. "Freedom from the Butchers' Row isn't enough?"

"Right, the freedom to now serve an entitled aristocratic family with chem coming out of their—"

"We'll compensate you, of course," Andao interrupted, handing his sister a stern look. "Will five hundred chem be suitable to cover the cost of your services?"

It was more than any client had ever paid her for snake oils, certainly, but piddling compared to how much Mimi had thrown away at the Butchers' Row. "I thought your patient's life was priceless."

"One thousand, then—what we might pay for a consult from a highly accredited physician," Andao decided in the conclusive tone of someone unaccustomed to haggling.

Nothing near 1.5 million chem, but Nhika relented. At the very least, it was preferable to being eaten. "Fine. Take me to your patient," she grumbled, then lifted her still-bound hands. "And untie me."

"Not yet," Mimi responded with an innocent smile. "You

must understand our caution. Just try to keep a low profile in the house and, please, don't take it personally."

Nhika waved a tired hand. "I'll be sure not to."

"Perfect. Come with me, then."

With a sweep of her hand, Mimi gestured for Nhika to follow her out of the outbuilding. Nhika obliged with a sigh, wondering how her life had come to this, being ordered around by her junior. Annoyance trawled up a variety of complaints to her tongue—they would pretend she was the criminal when they were the ones who *bought* her?—but Nhika saved her energy.

She had the feeling she'd need it soon.

— FIVE —

THEY TOOK HER THROUGH THE SMALLER HALLS of the manor, avoiding the galleries and dining rooms and kitchens. Still, through arched windows and square entryways, Nhika managed to catch sight of atrial gardens and open foyers and wide solariums, brimming with sunlight and foliage. Now she saw how Mimi could throw around so much chem with such ease.

Though they didn't show her the main sights of the manor, even the hallways were furnished to elegance, with a simple color scheme of dark blues and silvers, nowhere near the level of gaudiness she'd seen in the houses of her wealthier clients. Vases were simple painted porcelain, wall scrolls a brushwork landscape. The wealth here didn't need to call attention to itself; it was implicit in the modern construction, the rich wood, the subtle gilding.

With how immaculate the manor was, Nhika was sure there would be a wealth of servants busying themselves somewhere within the spacious halls, but the siblings took her through a route that avoided the staff. She thought she saw one, once, a musician sitting in the corner of a living room and drawing a weeping tune from an erhu.

But upon further inspection it was just an automaton, so

lifelike it didn't feel right to call it a simple machine. Metal hinges jointed its fingers as they glided over the two strings, its porcelain face painted in makeup and eyelids fluttering with the music. For a moment Nhika felt that engineering these automatons must not have been so different from heartsoothing, both a matter of studying the body long enough to reconstruct it from heart.

There were other automatons, too, the kind that Nhika was more accustomed to—ones that cleaned, or carted trays of tea on automated wheels, or folded laundry. The ones that were unmistakably cog and metal.

Finally, they reached a sparsely decorated room in the corner of the manor, with a sleeping area partitioned off from the rest of the living space by a thin wall of wooden latticework. A window inside revealed a low bed, atop which was a sleeping man. Tubes surrounded him, similar to the woman Nhika had soothed the other day. But this medical unit was a newer model, emblazoned with the cogwork seal of the Congmi name.

"You're going to have to untie my hands if you want my services," Nhika said, lifting her wrists toward Mimi. Now she wondered if they'd come this far just to back down at the sight of bare hands.

It was Trin who stepped forward. Despite his gloves, he took care not to touch her skin as he unbound the wrapping, and when he pulled the cloth free, she found her palms clammy and fingers aching. She stretched them, watching how the siblings stared with trepidation at her fingers. Their eyes followed her to the bedside, where she stood over the patient.

He had a variety of cuts and bruises, which marred the state of his otherwise peaceful slumber. Purple mottled the bags beneath his eyes and the wrinkles in his forehead stretched up into his bald scalp. They made him look older than he was, which must've only been around Nhika's father's age—had he still been alive.

Nhika extended a hand, but Mimi took a sharp breath, halting her. It was the first time Nhika had seen her doubt, her fist curled in its glove. But her shoulders eased and she said, "Just . . . please, don't hurt him."

Her expression was mournful, eyes beseeching. In that moment, Nhika envied this man, despite his injuries, that his deathbed solicited so much chem and so many tears. With that envy came a strange anger—at Mimi, at the Butchers, at her last client and his wife—because she'd passed through their hands and their homes, defying death to serve them. And yet, she was nothing more than a chance miracle to them, used and forgotten. Her deathbed would be surrounded only by ghosts, her coffin forgotten before she even passed. With her, the art of heartsoothing would die a much-prolonged death, one meant to have happened a generation before with the war on Yarong.

Nhika curled her fingers into a ball, calming the unwelcome surge of melancholy. She smiled at Mimi to dispel the pain. "Don't give me any ideas," she said, and when Mimi's eyes widened with horror, she snorted. "It's just a joke."

Only when Trin's hand eased from his pistol did Nhika extend hers again, making a show of taking her time. She reached for the pulse by instinct, though there was no need for the pretense with this company. When they touched, Hendon's body opened up under her control.

First, she felt the scars. His body had been through much recently, still raw from bruised organs and cracked bones. Although they tugged on her influence for satiation, Nhika avoided those regions lest the pain bridge to her own body. They weren't the reason for his coma.

Nhika climbed his spinal cord toward the brain, feeling a bit of a resistance at the jump. She detoured around it and her influence blossomed across his cortex as a wave of activity. He spasmed lightly, his muscles tightening, and Mimi sucked in a breath.

"Just me," Nhika apologized, her voice feeling disembodied as she continued exploring his cranium. When her mother had fallen sick, Nhika had never thought to study the brain—not until the paralysis set in, but by then it was too late, and she no longer had her grandmother to guide her. It was a fuzzy organ to her, and though she could leaf around with her influence, many of its intricacies remained clouded, like smudged pencil. Still, she was experienced enough to glean one thing: His brain activity had quieted. In all other people she'd soothed, even their basal levels were electric, like standing on a mountaintop before a lightning storm—a tingle in her hair, a buzz on her skin. Even while asleep, their rhythms were periodic, active. But Hendon's brain was a muted place; Nhika's senses were muffled in the bloat and silence.

Perhaps it was the swelling. She'd fixed that before—when her father came home overworked, when gnat bites riddled their legs in the summer. Now she stretched her soothing through the vasculature and lymph system, drawing in fluid and tightening vessels. His body aided her by itself, veins swelling elsewhere to accommodate the new volume. His heart rate slowed and she let it, allowing the water in his skull to be wicked away with the lazy flow. Those were all good signs; his body still understood how to compensate.

Through it all, she barely burned any of her own stores, though her abdomen twinged with warmth at the site of her liver. After this, she'd demand a lavish meal on top of her measly payment—it was only fair.

The bloat eased, but his brain remained stubbornly quiet. Nhika frowned, rooting around some more. The resistance still hindered her, something she could not discern, and frustration mounted in her chest. This was a brain beyond her control, a body she could not soothe.

She let out a noise of effort as her influence thinned with impatience. Even without the bloat, it felt a mess to wade around his brain, like trudging waist-deep in mud. The frustration plucked out a fleeting memory: the stubborn anatomy of her mother's brain, soundless and unyielding no matter how much she begged her heartsoothing for an answer.

Nhika pulled back, but her influence caught again, stuck in his cortex before she rerouted herself. There was some blockage there, one she couldn't visualize. It killed her that she couldn't see it, something hiding just beyond the limits of her understanding. It killed her more that she couldn't soothe it, teasing her with its near attainability.

This . . . *blockage*—it must have been the problem, if only she could better conceptualize it.

But how? She'd learned heartsoothing from her grandmother, who walked her through the body step-by-step. Almost everything she knew came from those nights spent in the bedroom, poring over stolen textbooks with her grandmother's finger tracing the words, learning to read at the same time she'd learned to soothe. How was she meant to cure the unseeable when she had no mentor? When she'd spent the last six years using heartsoothing selfishly, rather than how it was intended?

When . . . she hadn't even been able to save her mother from such a similar fate?

Grunting, Nhika snatched her hand away. The rest of the world returned in a flare of sensory overload. She blinked back to reality, meeting Mimi's wide eyes and Trin's hesitant frown.

"Wh . . . what did you do?" Andao asked cautiously.

Nhika let out a withered sigh, crossing her arms. "I . . ." She lingered on the next words, reluctant to admit them to herself. An image flashed in her mind, her mother's palm in hers. Finally, she finished, "I can't figure out how to heal him."

Defeat shattered Mimi's expression and Andao turned away, letting out a shaky sigh. In a second, Trin was at his side, a reassuring hand on his shoulder. Nhika kept her focus on Mimi, whose lower lip trembled with the promise of tears. She opened her fan across her face to hide it, her eyes deflecting to the floor.

Disappointed. They were disappointed in her. Nhika felt an unfamiliar tightness in her chest, followed by a familiar annoyance. Did they think her a miracle worker? Did they think she owed them anything just because they'd taken her out of the Butchers' Row?

When Mimi spoke again, her voice was fragile. "Is that it, then? You can't do it? Aren't you a *bloodcarver*?"

Anger, brought on by frustration, spiked in Nhika's throat. Her attention curdled around that word, *bloodcarver*, and though she'd heard it so many times before, it throbbed at the forefront of her mind anew. "You've heard only myths. That's no fault of mine."

Mimi snapped her fan shut, eyes etched with desperation. "So you can tear my limbs apart and crush my bones and . . . and squeeze the air from my lungs, but you can't wake him?"

Nhika slammed her palm down at the edge of the bed. Trin was quick to draw the pistol; this time, Andao didn't call him off. She wondered if he would shoot her. Even heartsooths died with a well-placed bullet. Pierce her heart or her skull, and she wouldn't have time to heal it.

To avoid drawing the ire of his trigger finger, she kept her voice measured as she said, "This is nothing new. Even with all this power, people die. They die because I'm not a miracle worker, and heartsoothing isn't a magic. It's a science, something learned through teachers I no longer have, and . . . and there are some things even I don't understand. Some things I can't heal." She choked out that last part, voice clawing up from the back of her throat.

Andao stepped in front of his sister, arm outstretched, as if to protect her and Trin. Would they dispose of her now to hide evidence of their illicit purchase? Trin could do it in an instant.

In the moment she didn't care much. This anger rose from this incessant echo of the past, the injustice of being used and discarded, the understanding that this had all spawned from a simple act of compassion. Cursed, wretched little heart.

But they didn't move to shoot her. Instead, Andao raised a hand to steady Trin's gun, and said to her, "We can't provide teachers, but would it help if you had the resources to understand what's ailing him?"

Nhika kept her eyes narrowed in suspicion, lips still scrawled into a scowl. But she let his words in, trying to parse the meaning behind them. "What are you offering, exactly?"

"Our father studied anatomy to design his automatons. His collection is still in the library. It's at your disposal, if it would help."

Some of the red edged away from the periphery of her vision, the pounding loosening in her skull. Nhika let out a warm breath through gritted teeth, feeling shame follow the dregs of her anger, as though she were a child caught in a tantrum quelled simply by candy. "Oh," she said, smoothing out her hair. "Yes. I suppose that'd help."

"Then it's yours to peruse," Andao offered, though he didn't ease his defensive stance. "But in private. Gossip spreads among servants and guests."

"No need," Mimi interjected, and with her hope returned her composure. "The funeral is soon. With a change of clothing, maybe a shower, she'll look just like a guest. We can say she's one of father's old acquaintances from out of town. That's a better excuse than any to justify her stay."

"My stay?" Nhika asked.

Mimi's eyes widened. "Oh, I just thought that, since you'd just come from the Butchers' Row, you would prefer to stay in some place . . . off the streets."

Nhika raised an eyebrow, about to argue that—unlike what her situation would suggest—she wasn't a vagrant. And then she paused, taking a moment to absorb the full extent of the offer. Mimi was giving her a chance to stay *here*, in the Congmi manor, to luxuriate in their wealth like a tick on the underbelly of a show dog and earn four months' rent at the end of it, all for healing one man.

They were offering her something else, too, unbeknownst to them. In the past, none of her clients had ever known she was a heartsooth, would never have hired her if they did. But with the Congmis, who knew exactly what she was yet were desperate enough to let her heal anyway, came a rare opportunity: to learn. Perhaps that's all she'd needed six years ago, a chance like this.

That, far more than aristocratic dinners and goose-down comforters, was a gift too rare to refuse.

"I find that acceptable," Nhika said. "But I'll need more than just literature. I'll need food, too. Energy. Time."

Trin raised a brow but deferred to Andao and Mimi.

"You'll have it," Mimi promised eagerly. "The library, a meal, a bed, and certainly a change of clothes. We can make it happen. Right, Andao?"

They all turned to Andao for a final verdict. The Congmi heir studied her, taking in her baggy clothes and raggedy hair and surely wondering how they'd make a socialite from such a shoddy template. But as his gaze fell to Mimi, who clasped her hands in hopeful supplication, he was resigned. "Yes." He sighed, addressing Nhika. "You may stay here as a guest. I suppose it's the least we can offer, if we're to ask this job from you."

"Just remember that it *is* a job," Trin added, not so mild-mannered. He shifted, just enough to draw attention to the gun at his hip. "If you can't do it, or if I catch you exploiting us, I'll return you to the Butchers myself."

Big words, but Nhika wasn't deterred. She was a business-woman, after all, and lies were her trade; even if she couldn't heal Hendon, she'd have the Congmis believe she could. "Don't worry. You focus on your funeral, and I'll focus on waking your friend."

Mimi's eyes fell to Hendon, brimming with victory. How lucky he was, to have a family beyond blood. Nhika wondered how anyone managed to win such love. But she knew that to be loved was to give love, and look what a wreck that had made the Congmis, such that they bought her to patch a hopeless problem.

But with their desperation came her good fortune. She'd sleep on their plush mattresses, eat from their kitchen, and learn from their library. If she managed to heal the poor sod, she'd earn the good graces of an aristocratic family. And if not, she'd escape one way or another.

She'd been called a mutt all her life. Now she had the chance to become a pampered little pooch.

— SIX —

THEY GAVE HER A ROOM ACROSS THE HALL FROM Hendon, citing ease of access. Really, Nhika guessed it was about keeping both of them sequestered away where only home nurses and cleaning staff would chance upon them.

But she couldn't complain about the room. The bedroom space alone was larger than Nhika's entire apartment. The room had a living space and bathroom beyond it. For all the places she'd moved through, she'd never been in one with hot, piped water. Here, the hardwood was so polished it somehow felt soft underfoot where it wasn't covered by a lush, embroidered rug. Though Nhika knew little of architecture, she had to appreciate the room's symmetry—not a haphazard arrangement of furniture as her rooms always were, but an aligned path of energy that drew the eye from the comfortable living space to the circular divider to the window, where a view of the gardens awaited below.

Mimi had brought her some amenities, more creams and toiletries than Nhika knew what to do with. A new change of clothing came with it all, the silk pants and split dress of aristocracy. It wasn't so sumptuous as some of the outfits Nhika had seen from other rich clients—no cinched-waist bodice nor puffed shoulders—but it still sported a high collar that hugged her neck and well-fitted sleeves that traced the full length of her arms. The pants were, by contrast, loosely fitted and crisply pleated, which Nhika imagined was the ever-changing fashion. She never kept up enough to know for sure, what with her usual wardrobe of ill-fitting tunics and torn trousers.

With the ensemble, Mimi had given her a pair of matching gloves, wrist length. These, Nhika ignored.

After she had showered and changed, she felt like an imposter looking in the mirror. Dark brown hair clean, skin glowing against white silk, near-black eyes rested—the Nhika she knew melded sloppily with a girl she'd never thought she could be. As she looked over Mimi's makeup she almost considered it, powdering her cheeks and pinning up her hair and lining her lips red.

But she left herself in this quasi-aristocratic state, afraid that doing anything more would cement the lie in her heart.

When she exited her bathroom, she saw Trin's silhouette on the other side of the sliding door, pacing back and forth. She knew he could see her, too, shadowed by the light of the tall windows. But she no longer planned on escaping.

She opened the door and Trin balked at her change of clothes, eyes lingering on her bare hands. "Mimi left you gloves," he said, edging away at her approach.

Nhika glanced at her bed, where she'd discarded the gift in a crumpled pile of silk. "I don't like covering my hands," she said.

"It would give Andao some much-needed peace of mind if you wore them, at least while romping around in his home."

She flashed a grin. "Is that all you care about? Andao?" And she relished in the way a blush crept up his cheek.

"I care about eliminating threats to the household, such as bloodcarvers who run about with their hands bare," was his stalwart response.

"Oh," she said, and opted for the gloves.

Nhika followed Trin out of the room, yanking the gloves up her wrists to straighten the fabric. She fidgeted with them the entire way down the stairs and through the halls.

Nhika looked up when they got to the library, and then she couldn't tear her eyes away. The doors opened into a spacious circular hall, like the atrium of a pagoda, the ceiling vast and the windows tall. And it wasn't so much a library as an antiquarian's eclectic collection: taxidermied specimens on plinths between shelves, precious minerals as bookends, fossils labeled by taxonomy, and Mother—was that a real whale skeleton, suspended from the rafters? As they drew close enough for Nhika to read the plaque, she saw that it was—killed by Mr. Congmi himself. Its bony figure arched into a dive above the stacks. By habit, she imagined how many calories could be gleaned from such a thing, if they'd been used in heartsoothing. Instead, they'd been wasted in ornamentation.

Books lined the shelves, which curved to contour the walls. There was a method to them, organized by subject and alphabet, and Nhika found a sudden reverence for this man she'd never known, one who could spare the time to read it all while building an industrial empire. Or perhaps the two came hand in hand, and now she could see how Congmi submarines drew from the anatomy of a whale, their dirigibles finned like carp, their automatons just man turned porcelain.

Mimi was already waiting for her by the biology section, taking the liberty of collecting books for Nhika's reference. She was short, needing to stretch onto the balls of her feet to grab the higher books, but she'd gathered a small stack on the table.

"You took your time showering, didn't you?" Mimi asked, not drawing her gaze from the shelf. She reached for a high tome and Trin wheeled over the ladder to aid her. But she refused it, finger catching the edge of the spine and easing the book out. At last, it toppled and she added it to her stack.

When she turned, Nhika saw she'd removed her heavy makeup, going for a simple powder and blush. She'd also pinned up the ribbons of her inky hair, which, along with the evenness of her bangs, showcased the delicate symmetry of her features—pale and rosy. Nhika could better discern her age: definitely no older than fifteen. She could hardly believe this same girl had dealt with Butchers just this morning.

"I took the liberty of collecting some starting material. Not everything in this library is anatomy, or even medicine. But my father was a biologist before he was an engineer, so hopefully you'll find his collection helpful."

Nhika picked up the first of the books and flipped through its contents. Medical diagrams, anatomical figures, physiological charts . . . These were just like the books her grandmother had raised her on—only, legally acquired.

"Will these help?" Mimi asked. Nhika thumbed through

the spines—anatomy book, anatomy book, research journal, anatomy book. "I'm looking for texts about the anatomy and function of the brain," she said. It was a tall order; she wasn't even sure if they taught that topic in the colleges. Most likely, it was still at the forefront of inquisition in the research hospitals, but she figured that a Congmi might be able to pull some strings.

Mimi frowned. "Then you might have to look for them yourself. I can't make heads or tails of all this terminology."

"I'll start with what you have," Nhika said, taking the stack and settling into one of the benches, feet up on the table. She'd bleed the Congmi library dry of its knowledge before she finished with the job. A man in a coma could wait, surely. Hendon had nothing if not time. And this opportunity—reading through the Congmi collection itself—deserved ample time.

As Nhika drew the first book into her lap, Mimi's inquisitive gaze followed her, relegating her to a tiger preening behind the glass of a zoological garden. Nhika dragged her focus down to the bold black lettering in the textbooks, but Mimi's stare nagged at her periphery, and now she realized that Trin was watching her as well, his broad figure looming behind a shelf. The shine of his pistol gleamed beneath the library lights.

Nhika scanned the text. This was a standard anatomy textbook, detailing basic knowledge, and in her disinterest her mind wandered back to Mimi and Trin, neither of whom had stopped staring. As a demonstration of her annoyance, she snapped the book shut and shifted her jaw. "Don't you have somewhere to be? Other guests to entertain?" Her gaze moved to Trin. "Am I under guard?"

"Nothing like that," Mimi dismissed quickly. "But we promised Andao we'd take care of you. He has enough to worry about, taking over the business and all. I hope you understand."

Nhika pursed her lips. "If I wanted to, I could rend that smile from your lips with a touch. I could split your face to scar so ugly that you'd never be able to show yourself in high society again. I could, but I won't. So there's no reason to guard me."

"I believe you," Mimi began in a tone to suggest otherwise, "but it's nothing personal. We just like to err on the side of caution, and I think this is for the best."

Nothing personal, and yet Nhika had heard words like those from so many clients before, murmured under their breaths as they put away their jewelry boxes and pulled up their gloves. For some reason, this instance especially tired her, being trusted enough to be bought and hired to heal a family friend but not enough to be respected. Still, she held her tongue, because she *had* considered swiping a geode or two. Miffed, she returned to her book.

She read through the day. Mimi and Trin took breaks to grab food, but Nhika was too enamored by the literature. The anatomy of the human body she knew well, but these texts filled in the gaps of her semantic knowledge, and she found herself putting names to structures she'd known only by touch and influence. They were fairly modern books, too, some from this year. Some terminology had changed since her grandmother had taught her.

Nhika finished perusing all the images and chapter headings of one book, prepared to move on to the next, when she faltered. At the top of the stack was a familiar cover, one with a human skull drawn in excruciating detail, simply titled *On the Human Body*. She'd seen this book before; her grandmother had purloined an earlier edition of the same book from a college library.

She'd sat Nhika in her lap with the book open before them, fishing a chunk of charcoal from the hearth to annotate. Atop the drawn diagrams of humans, their limbs spread wide in the anatomical position, she would chalk directional pathways through the body, marking out lines of influence.

"See, Nhika, Theumans don't heal others the way we do," she'd explained. "That's why they have to draw everything out in detail, because that's the only way they can recognize it. But we . . ." She smudged the charcoal with her fingers, darkening some parts with pigment and leaving others without, until she'd highlighted all the main pathways through the body. "We don't need every detail. We just need to know how everything connects, how it all works together."

Nhika had protested and squirmed, appalled that her grandmother had gone through such lengths to steal a book only to destroy it. "You covered up all the most important stuff," she'd whined, to which her grandmother had only laughed.

"Did I, *khun*? You know, back on Yarong, not all heartsooths learned from books. Your *gensaoi*, your great-grandmother, taught me with other people. But now that we live in Theumas, we have to learn from a book. I am trying to make do."

Nhika remembered her grandmother's face, then touched by a gentle sadness, one that drew back the corners of her mouth and dimmed the light in her eyes. Recollections of Yarong always brought on that look, and some of that same unspeakable grief had rubbed off on Nhika. But hers was for a different reason: not heartbreak for a culture forgotten, but the fear that, living in Theumas, she might never know that life at all. That if she didn't learn it exactly as her grandmother did, then she could not pass it down as her grandmother could. That with each band of bone added to her family's ring, the gift of heartsoothing would only grow weaker and weaker, until one day she'd lose it completely.

That had been the fear of a younger Nhika. Now she had come to accept that she would never get the chance to pass down her heartsoothing at all.

Nhika put the Congmis' copy of the book aside, knowing that she lacked the emotional fortitude to read it in Mimi and Trin's audience. There was nothing new to be learned from it, anyhow. She was just about to move on to the next book when a servant arrived, announcing dinner.

Dinner.

At its mention, she realized the late hour and her stomach growled with hunger. Nhika wondered if they would give her a meal or if, like the Butchers, they'd only bring her leftovers. Mimi and Trin both stood to depart and her eyebrows arched with interest—would they finally leave her alone?

But they turned, Mimi tapping her arm. "Aren't you coming?"

"To . . . dinner?"

"Yes. After all, you are a guest of this manor now. Remember?"

It took a moment for the words to soak in. Nhika stood, hands clammy from the gloves, and set the books aside. "Oh. Okay."

They turned to leave the library, their backs exposed to her. By instinct, she found the little sliver of exposed skin on their necks, right beneath Mimi's pinned curls and Trin's tapered shave. For a moment she froze, questioning this reality of dining with the heirs of the Congmi estate. She had anticipated eating their meals, but sitting at their table? That felt a world apart.

Then Mimi and Trin disappeared around the corner and her indecision was dashed as she started after them, afraid she'd lose her chance at dinner.

Her bewilderment soon sobered into hunger-driven excitement as they reached the second-floor dining room, with a view overlooking the garden. It felt private, not much glamour nor presentation, with simple chairs and a circular table. But the glass chandeliers and musical automatons reminded her she was still in the company of one of the richest families in Theumas.

Andao was already seated. If it was possible, he looked even more tired than before but kept a straight posture as they joined him. Mimi and Trin took seats on either side of him, but Nhika hesitated, until at last a servant pulled her a chair at Mimi's side.

She sat. There were a couple other seats at the table, unoccupied and without table settings. No one spoke as they waited for the food to arrive. Nhika couldn't remember the last time she'd had a meal around a table. With place settings. And a family. The last time her family had been complete had been ten years ago, when she was eight, and her memories of dinner glowed with warmth and raucous laughter.

"Did you find anything?" Andao asked, clearing his throat and breaking her thoughts. The formality of his tone reminded her that they weren't her family, and this manor wasn't her home, and this dinner was only a meal, calories for her soothing. If she wasn't able to heal Hendon, they'd discard her without a second thought.

"I'll need to understand more of the neuroanatomy," she said, matching the decorum of his tone.

"Oh, I see." Andao left it at that. He glanced at Trin, and then at Mimi, and their exchanged looks held unspoken words and secret meanings. Nhika tried deciphering them but only gleaned that they wanted to talk about something—something they couldn't discuss with her at the table.

A waitress and her automaton companion, a laden tray on wheels, emerged from the servery with platters of food. The table let out a collective sigh, all of them grateful for the distraction of food. The waitress unloaded the automaton, setting the plates on the center turntable to be eaten family style, more variety in one course than Nhika had seen in her entire life—sweet-fried fish, tapioca dumplings, rice-paper rolls.

Mimi gestured to the food. "Please, eat." But Nhika had already discarded etiquette in her rush to fill her plate. It was more food than she needed, but she piled it on by instinct, and a little bit of greed, taking a bite of every dish and ignoring how Trin wrinkled his nose at her.

She stuffed her mouth after a mumbled thanks, the flavor bursting across her tongue. If she knew how to enhance her own taste buds she would've, but the food was plenty savory by itself. So she just ate, and so did they, and the silence was dispelled by the sound of her slurping and chewing. She felt the nutrients flood her system, stocking her abdomen and even her blood, the buzz of energy awaiting expenditure.

But the meal couldn't last forever, and as the servants cleared empty dishes and dirtied plates, the silence precipitated again. Nhika licked the lingering flavor from her teeth, watching as the others exchanged their wide-eyed looks, at once ignoring her and treading lightly around her.

Mimi cleared her throat, wiping her mouth with a napkin. "I suppose we should address the upcoming funeral," she said, voice growing heavy. She drew a slow sip from her cup before continuing. "It's scheduled over three days—the rites, the wake, and then the procession. Nhika, since I've told the staff that you knew my father, you'll have to attend the wake and procession for the sake of appearances."

"Though if it's too much to ask, we can make other arrangements," Andao was quick to add, and she could read his thoughts: He figured she'd make a scene. His next words came as a caution. "There will be many important people in attendance."

"No worries. I'll behave," she said, leaning back in her chair. Death was a sacred thing. Perhaps Theumans didn't believe in afterlives and ghosts, but the Yarongese superstition of her upbringing was hard to shake, and she wouldn't mess with a funeral for her life.

"What year was it that Father traveled abroad? We could say he tutored her while he was a professor in college," Mimi thought aloud, but Andao shook his head.

"Yarong was already under Daltanny occupation when he was teaching, and Nhika would've been too young," he said, picking at the last of his food. "That'd be a complicated time line to justify. I'd prefer we keep it simple."

"My parents and grandmother were from Yarong. But not me," Nhika spoke up, and their attention turned to her. She'd never even been to the island and doubted she ever would. Ever since Daltanny had started its occupation of Yarong, the tiny island had acted as a naval base for that warmongering country, and her parents and others were lucky to get out when they did. Although Theumas remained neutral in the war against Daltanny—and still did today, even as Daltanny fought with the city's neighbors—it had tentatively opened its arms to Yarongese refugees. Sometimes, Nhika wondered if Theumas regretted that decision now.

"So maybe Father met you here. Before he went into the automaton business, he dabbled in medicine. We could say you're one of his students," Mimi suggested.

"I've never had any formal medical education."

"So? You definitely know more than the students there. I'm sure you can improvise something," Mimi said, and Nhika's chest bloomed with a strangely pleasant vindication—no one had ever recognized the depth of her knowledge before.

"Just say you spent a couple years at Zhalon College of Medicine. Father was a lecturer there, and they let almost anyone in."

"But just in case they see through your education, you can say you've since dropped out," Andao added. And there it went, precious validation. Although, he did have a point—she'd been improvising alternative medicine for the past six years, but she'd be among learned meritocrats at the funeral.

"What about your family?" Trin brought up. His look held expectation, and she realized he wasn't asking for the fictionalized background. He was asking her, genuinely.

"Gone," she said. Nhika figured that was something the siblings might sympathize with, having just lost their father, but in their uncomfortable frowns, their crinkled brows, she found only pity. She continued, "But I'll tell the guests something boring. Maybe my parents are bankers, or officials for the Commission."

"Bankers, then," Trin said. "The guests will know all the officials and delegates. If your parents worked for the Commission, they'd want to know a name."

Nhika shouldn't have been surprised, and yet she was amazed anew at how vastly different the Congmis' lives were from her own; she could barely name all five commissioners, even though the Commission was the elected head of Theumas's technocracy. Now the looming funeral felt like a test of how well she'd honed her ability to lie. This time, she wasn't selling a sham cure or fraudulent tonic. She was selling herself.

"They'll ask about occupation, too," Andao added.

She waved a flippant hand. "I'll make something up."

"It's important that—"

"Don't worry. I won't mention bloodcarving."

"Nhika," Andao stressed, voice so laden with urgency that she quieted. "This is crucial. Please, we can't have anyone discovering what you are."

Her first instinct was scorn, but his expression wasn't ashamed. None of theirs were, and she realized this wasn't just about their reputation or the legality of her acquisition. There were those glances between them again, and behind the furtiveness she caught a poignant apprehension. It reminded her that her bidders in the Butchers' Row had been elites like these. Perhaps the Congmis weren't planning on dismembering her, but Nhika wondered if the funeral attendees would be so generous if they discovered what she was.

"Okay," she said, voice sobering. "I won't stir trouble—promise."

Andao's shoulders fell at that, though tension still corded his body. "Thank you," he said, the words sounding obligatory. "It's for the best. Our safety depends on it. And maybe . . ." He shared a look with Trin and Mimi. "And maybe yours, too."

— ༄ —

Nhika spent her first night atop a silken comforter staring at the ceiling. She'd traded the dress for an equally exquisite nightgown, and now she relished in how soft it was on clean skin, how smooth the bed felt against bare feet.

Over dinner, they'd ironed out the details of her life, turning her as Theuman as they could: her truncated surname, her polished family history, her impressive education. She was Suon Ko Nhika, daughter of bankers and old mentee of the late Congmi Vun Quan, and who may or may not have flunked out of Zhalon College of Medicine. Now Suon Ko Nhika slept on beds like these every day and ate dessert with every meal. Suon Ko Nhika could trace her family back beyond her grandparents, as though her heritage hadn't been abandoned on the island, stifled by war and colonialism. And when people touched Suon Ko Nhika, they didn't fear death. So she'd been touched, and hugged, and kissed. Skin against skin.

And maybe Suon Ko Nhika could live just a little bit longer. Nhika still didn't grasp the root of Hendon's injury, but she was close. It was some blockage in the neuroanatomy, if only she could understand it. And then, one step further, she'd have to repair it where she never could before.

That was a problem for another day, though. Nhika rolled over in bed, staring out her windows into the gardens that rolled into the sprawl of Theumas's cityscape beyond. If her grandmother's beliefs were true, and the ghosts of her family were hovering over her now, would they think she looked happy? Would they think she looked at home?

Before coming here, she lived in a forgettable attic apartment hidden away in some corner of the Dog Borough that reeked of fish and prawn. But it wasn't really home; that implied attachment. Nhika never got so far as to have a future, and her past had gone up in smoke and ash. This was the first time she was expected to *be* somewhere tomorrow, and the next day, and the day after that.

A sigh tapered through her lips, equal parts exhaustion and comfort. *Another day.*

— SEVEN —

BY THE TIME SHE WOKE UP, IT WAS NEARING noon. She hadn't meant to oversleep, but in the Dog Borough, she'd always relied on the rabble outside her window to stir her, the clamor of dockworkers who woke with the dawn. With this estate in the Dragon Borough, its acres of land every which way, the mornings were eerily silent.

Except, there was a commotion coming from just outside her door, the creak of hardwood and a low collection of voices. Nhika roused, and when she heard the rumble of an unfamiliar voice, she remembered to change into something presentable, one of Mimi's long-sleeved dresses. The gloves were an afterthought, grabbed on the way out the door.

The voices emanated from Hendon's room and when Nhika drew closer, she heard low conversation between Mimi, Andao, and a third voice—not Trin but someone else. The door was ajar, and when she put her ear to it, she caught a bite of somberness: "I'm afraid there's been little change. And there aren't many medications I can offer. We just have to wait. And hope. But Hendon has always been strong."

Beneath his voice, she could also hear something whirring, clicking, scribbling.

Then Andao said, "Will he keep his memory when he wakes?"

"It's hard to say at this point," said the unknown voice.

A sigh from Andao. "This doesn't feel right, worrying about his memory when his life is on the line. But if he doesn't remember that night, then—"

"Eavesdropping, are we?" Trin reprimanded, his voice blotting out the rest of Andao's sentence as he appeared behind Nhika. She startled, then straightened her dress in a bid for dignity.

"Don't make it a habit, but I'll introduce you to Dr. Santo," Trin said. "Just don't mention your . . . occupation."

She wasn't planning on it, but now his contempt made her want to. "And why not?"

"Because he's a doctor, and you're, well . . ." He didn't finish his sentence, though the answer was obvious.

Nonetheless, she followed him into the room, finding Mimi and Andao sitting beside Hendon's bed with an older gentleman pulled up to the bedside, right where she had been a day earlier. He was a thin man, with a clean swatch of whitening hair across his forehead and a round face framed by trimmed facial hair. Reading spectacles sat at the bridge of his nose, and they nearly fell off as he looked at her. This was the doctor, then; yet he wore humble clothing, just a dress shirt tucked into his pants.

"Oh, hello, Nhika," Mimi said, and all conversation ceased as she entered. When Nhika rounded the panel divider, she found a new medical device—this one the size of a game board, with a mechanical apparatus affixed to the top and a drawer holding a coil of paper. A needle produced a series of scribbles atop the paper, and Nhika realized that the machine wired back to Hendon, who wore a strange headpiece.

"I don't think we've been properly introduced," Dr. Santo said, drawing her attention away from Hendon and the machine. He wore linen examination gloves rather than silk ones, which he extended toward her in greeting. Advancing a step, she took his hand and he gave her a firm, fatherly shake.

"Uncle Shon, this is Suon Ko Nhika. She's staying with us for the funeral," Andao said for her, as though he didn't trust her to remember her own false identity. His words came out scripted.

Nhika helped him along. "Just here to pay respects. Mr. Congmi was an old teacher of mine."

Dr. Santo's eyes glimmered with welcome. "I'm Santo Ki Shon, but you can call me Dr. Santo. I was Mr. Congmi's close friend," he said. He turned a solemn gaze toward the man on the bed. "And Hendon's. But he's not yet lost—and, we must hope, neither are his memories."

"Why's that?" she asked.

Dr. Santo gave her a curious look. "Because—"

"Because we wouldn't want to lose the Hendon we know and love, of course," Andao interrupted.

Nhika narrowed her eyes, scouring for more. The siblings exchanged glances with the same nervous energy they'd had during dinner, but she didn't pry. Not yet.

"What's this machine?" Nhika asked instead, sizing up the medical apparatus, which continued to scribble out peaks and troughs, like the sketch of a long mountain range.

"An EEG," Dr. Santo responded, an answer that meant nothing

to her. Yet, she felt a strange competition with it, with this doctor, because Hendon was *her* patient, after all. The siblings had told her the doctors had seen no hope for him, but Dr. Santo didn't seem like what she imagined a doctor to be. No loose-sleeved robe with embroidered pockets, just a man who looked like he belonged around a game board at the park with a group of other seniors.

"What does it do?" she asked. Trin gave her a testy look, as though to dissuade her from talking, but she pretended not to see him.

Dr. Santo, on the other hand, seemed eager to share. He reached over to point at the coil of paper, which ran underneath the inked needle and came out inscribed with close scribbles. "It measures electrical activity in the brain, see?"

While that made intuitive sense, she had no idea how he translated the waves to brain activity. When she was in the brain, soothing Hendon and others, she could *feel* the electricity, the way it raised the hairs on her arm and bit at her skin. It was interesting to see, then, what a Theuman had invented to replicate that feeling.

"This machine tells you that Hendon's in a coma, rather than asleep?" she guessed, because she could tell the same from her heartsoothing.

His eyes alighted with approval. "Yes, exactly! It's a very small, but crucial, difference. Most people don't see that."

Most people weren't heartsooths, she wanted to say.

Andao cleared his throat, stealing back Dr. Santo's attention. "Can the EEG tell you the cause of the injury?"

Nhika listened in; knowing the problem was half the trouble

of heartsoothing. But Dr. Santo shook his head, solemn. "Not without further research. This machine is still prototypical."

Nhika examined the scribbles, trying to make sense of them. There were patterns there, certainly—some rolling like the tides of the ocean, others fine and close, like spiked mountains. Not as visceral as heartsoothing was, but she knew the language of Theuman medicine placed a machine between the healer and the patient.

"It's okay, Uncle Shon," Mimi said, her tone cautiously optimistic. "It was worth a shot. At least you're still trying."

With a touch of shame, Nhika no longer felt slighted that the Congmis would employ both her and a doctor; let them throw every ounce of chem they had at this problem. And Dr. Santo had something over her: a personal connection with Hendon. Her grandmother had always told her that the connection with a patient was the most powerful concept in heartsoothing. But her mother's death had taught Nhika an equally memorable lesson—that sometimes, it wasn't enough.

"Dr. Santo," called a voice, drawing their attention to the door. "You have a meeting at the thirteenth hour you can't miss."

When she turned, she found someone new. From where she stood behind the panel divider, it was hard to discern his features, but she caught a glimpse of his stern eyes, his unabashedly bare hands, and found she knew exactly who he was.

That was the boy she'd run into in the Horse Borough, the one who'd dropped all his papers.

And most importantly, he was someone who might know she didn't belong here.

Nhika shrank back behind the divider—he hadn't seen her yet—as Dr. Santo disassembled and packed up his EEG, removing the headpiece from Hendon's scalp and stilling the needle.

"Don't give up hope," he reassured the Congmis before moving to leave. "This isn't the end."

As Dr. Santo exited the room, the man lingered just a moment longer at the door, and Nhika worried that he'd seen her. She only released her breath when he turned to leave, the last of his tailored outfit trailing out of view.

"Who was that man?" she asked Mimi and Andao.

"Mr. Ven? He works with Uncle Shon," Mimi replied.

"Do they know why I'm here?"

"No," Mimi admitted. "If Uncle Shon learned I made a Butchers' Row transaction, he'd never let me leave the house again. Best to keep that to ourselves."

Nhika wasn't sure about the value of discretion if the boy from the Horse Borough might recognize her anyway, but that was for the Congmis to handle—it wasn't her who'd made an illegal purchase. She had other problems. "If Dr. Santo wakes Hendon first, do I still get paid?"

"We'll make sure to duly compensate you for your time," Andao answered noncommittally.

Nhika shifted her jaw in thought. It wasn't a race, and yet she felt a strange urge to beat Dr. Santo to the answer, to heal Hendon with her hands where Dr. Santo needed his gloves and his machines. Now, which would it take to heal a man in an unwakeable coma: Theuman medicine or Yarongese heartsoothing?

And, would she even make it that far if the mysterious boy from the Horse Borough recognized her first?

The funeral rites began the next day with a family-only ceremony. Nhika and Trin watched from the gallery as the Congmi siblings departed for the funeral home by carriage, dressed in solemn white. The manor fell to mourning, too, with the automatons rested in respect and most of the servants retiring early for the day. With little else to do, Nhika took herself back to the library to finish the stack of books she'd started on.

Trin followed her, ever loyal to the siblings, and settled across from her as she read. She gave him furtive looks out of the corner of her eye, gaze occasionally flicking to his pistol. But she didn't think he would use it—not now, at least.

Nhika thumbed through an anatomy reference book until her finger snagged on diagrams of the brain, cut in various orientations. The images here were drawn, rather than photographed, and the artist had colored the different parts accordingly. They almost looked like dried slices of pomelo. Nhika whispered the names of the structures to herself to commit them to memory.

The cortex she knew. That was the part that lit up in activity when she soothed, an electrical storm of light and color. Sometimes, steeping herself in another's cortex brought on nausea.

Then the cerebellum, drawn as a fernlike burgeon of growth.

That was a solid chunk of tissue, something she could ground herself in when she synapsed.

The brain stem next. She rode that up from the spinal cord; it was how she'd learned to move her influence toward the brain. It felt like a rush of speed, faster than lightning.

Now, she recalled the sensation of influencing Hendon, of that blockage, the resistance while jumping from brain stem to cortex. There was only one structure in these diagrams she didn't quite recognize from her explorations in the brain. The artist had depicted it as a pink, pinched structure, sitting above the brain stem, but there was no label for what it was, other than DEEP BRAIN. She checked the print year of the textbook on its spine—1010. A few years outdated.

Nhika snapped the book shut, drawing Trin's attention. He blinked the haze from his eyes and straightened in his seat, eyebrows raised.

"Did you find the answer?" he asked. He made it sound easy, as if these science textbooks could translate so easily to heart-soothing. As if these words were written for people like her.

"No," she said curtly. Nhika caught the sleepiness in his expression, and when he stretched, her eyes drifted down to the pistol that revealed itself beneath his jacket. "How long have you worked for the siblings?"

"Since I graduated college." His response was terse, but his voice held nostalgia. She tried to gauge his age—older than her by some years.

"So, what is that, just a couple of years?" she estimated. "You've become quite close to this family in such little time."

When she realized she'd let curiosity slip into her voice, she drew a new book into her lap to feign apathy.

"I've known them for much longer than that," he said, but didn't elaborate.

"But you knew they were one of the richest families in Theumas."

His angular eyes grew especially critical and he folded his arms. "Are you trying to suggest that I only work for them for the money?"

"Took the words right out of my mouth."

"The Congmis are family to me."

"And yet, you weren't invited to the rites, a ceremony meant for the family."

At that, his expression sharpened with annoyance. "Why do you do that?"

"Do what?"

"Try to get under my skin. Seed doubt and conflict."

She shrugged, avoiding the heat of his gaze by cracking the spine of a new book. "Just seeing what it'll take for you to use that pistol, I suppose."

"It's infuriating. And it's certainly not making you any friends."

"I'm not in the market for any," she snapped, then smoothed the anger out of her voice. She wanted to call him presumptuous, thinking he could read her so easily. But the words failed her, and she remembered she didn't need to justify herself to a stranger like him. She never had before.

"Even bloodcarvers must get lonely," Trin continued.

"And what would you know of bloodcarvers?"

"That you're just human, aren't you? That's what their father believed."

The annoyance simmered down into quiet regard as she looked Trin over a second time. Maybe he wasn't the brute she'd first imagined, but she wasn't going to take life advice from a hired hand.

Without deigning to answer, Nhika turned back to the book, searching for the section on neuroanatomy to distract herself. This book was published just this year, and when she found the sagittal drawing, she discovered they'd given that deep brain space a name: thalamus. She tried the word on her tongue. It sounded a tad fictional where the other structures—cortex, brain stem—sounded more intuitive. But maybe it was the answer. If anything, at least a start. She narrowed her eyes with renewed interest.

"If you're going to linger, you might as well make yourself useful," she said, holding the book open before him and tapping the anatomical drawing. "You see this word? Thalamus? Find me papers and books with any mention of it. And keep it recent, this year or the last. I want to know what it does and what it's made of."

With a begrudging grunt he lurched to his feet, giving her a beleaguered look. "A 'please' would be appreciated."

"Aren't you used to being ordered around?"

"Mimi and Andao don't order me around," he reproached. "They ask kindly, and I oblige. How long have you been without a guardian, again?"

"Since I was twelve."

The corner of his lip quirked with a knowing smile. "Yes, that sounds about right."

"What are you trying to say by that?" she grumbled, but he only shrugged with infuriating evasiveness.

When he reached the shelves, he turned, arms crossed, and waited. It took her a moment to understand that he actually expected her to beg, and from the bottom of her diaphragm she drew out a withered, loathful, "*Please*."

"Thank you." He plastered on a smile and got to work on the shelves.

Now that she had some idea of what she was looking for, she could pick up her reading pace, sorting books by year and skimming through them for that structure. With Trin's help, as much as it begrudged her to admit it, things went faster. She told herself she'd take her time in this library, but this was an exhilarating feeling, being so close to the answer. Now she raced to find it.

He brought her text after text, and a new stack collected at her feet. Despite it all, she'd reached another dead end. All these anatomy texts had images and labels, but none would tell her what the thalamus actually was. None would tell her how to fix it.

Maybe nobody knew. The mystery of it was murderous. But she kept reading anyway, breaking only to eat or relieve herself. The sun set incrementally, the room darkening every time she looked up from the pages until the library swam in golden light.

A break in her attention came that evening, when a servant poked her head into the library and announced, "The masters are back!"

Trin drew himself up. His attention left her, and Nhika followed him out of the library, through the halls, toward the central foyer.

They reached the mezzanine just as the Congmis returned, still garbed in white. Nhika lingered on the upper floor as Trin descended the stairs to meet them. Even from her vantage point, she could see the redness of their eyes, the solemnity of their expressions. Mimi met her gaze, eyes full with tears, but she turned away before Nhika could say anything. Trin was at Andao's side, hand on his back as the three of them fled to their own corner of the manor.

Nhika trailed behind like a misplaced ghost. Her feet moved of their own volition, creeping down the stairs and following the siblings at a distance to their room. They escaped to a private parlor, leaving Nhika to linger outside the door.

Her heartsoothing could not quell this depth of sadness in anyone, or else she would've done it for herself long ago. Besides, it wasn't her comfort those three longed for. It was Hendon's, or their father's, or one another's. Bloodcarvers like Nhika formed only one kind of connection, and that was at the junction of skin on skin.

She turned to leave when a hiccuping sob paused her. Mimi's crying then turned to wails, the angered pain of a young girl betrayed, and the sound took her back in time, to an apartment in the Dog Borough. To the moment her mother's paralysis had finally seized her lungs, leaving Nhika truly, irrevocably alone.

She'd wished for anyone in that moment, her grandmother or her father, someone who knew her grief more intimately than she did. Someone who could tell her it would be okay and know it to be true. But her father had been lost at sea, and her grandmother had passed in the house fire that took her childhood home, and Nhika had never felt more like the last bloodcarver, not even able to save her mother.

Nhika understood Mimi's pain now, maybe even better than Trin or Andao could. For a moment, she wondered if she should open the door, be the person she'd wished she'd had when her mother died.

But it was not her place.

As she was about to exit, a shadow traced the entrance of the foyer. Startled, Nhika slipped into the cover of an armoire just as Dr. Santo entered the room, carrying a covered baking dish. He strode straight to the door and knocked without the hesitance that had frozen her.

"Mimi, Andao, it's Uncle Shon. I brought your favorite," he said. Even from across the room, she could smell the waft of butter and pastry.

Trin let him in, and after the door closed behind him, Nhika drew out of hiding to listen to the muted conversation inside.

"I don't want to go, Uncle Shon," Mimi pouted through a full mouth.

Dr. Santo let out a sympathetic breath. "I know it's hard, Mimi."

"I don't know if I can bear to see his body again." This time, her words were accompanied by sniffles, the suggestion of tears.

"It's not for us, the ones who loved him privately. It's for his friends, coworkers, acquaintances—the ones who loved him in public. They deserve a chance to say goodbye to him, too," he said, adopting a tone that almost reminded Nhika of her grandmother's: gentle, stern, and instructional all at once.

"But how are we supposed to act?" Despite Dr. Santo's mollifying tone, Mimi's voice crescendoed. "Are we supposed to pretend this is just a funeral, that all the attendees loved him?"

"We have to put our best face forward, chin up. Remember, we're there to honor your father."

"I don't see how, when . . ." Mimi's voice cracked with tears, and Nhika held her breath for her next words. ". . . when Father's murderer may well be a guest."

— EIGHT —

MURDERER.

Nhika had never felt so much like an outsider, not even when she was bound in the back of a hearse, than now—because the Congmis had forgotten to mention a tiny little detail about their agreement: They were asking her to heal the witness to a murder.

Well—her stay with the Congmis had been luxurious, but it was over. She'd leave now while Trin was occupied. Nhika backed away from the door and bolted out of the room. This was the part of every client–sham doctor interaction where she ran away. This time, she'd take something as a souvenir, just to make this mess worthwhile. Her new clothes, or Mimi's makeup, and definitely a bauble from the library.

Nhika hurried up the stairs toward her room. There, she stuffed a bag with pillowcases, pants, paperweights. She was just leaving her room when her feet ground to a stop of their own volition, and Nhika stood frozen in front of Hendon's door. For a moment she couldn't move, and the door pulsed with its own heartbeat.

In her mind, it shifted—no longer a stately door of the Congmi manor, but a timeworn entrance to a Dog Borough apartment. Half immersed in memory, Nhika pushed it open.

Inside was her old apartment, pulled out of the past, and her mother asleep in bed. Dropping her bag of stolen items, Nhika approached her and saw the extent of her illness—the thinness of her arms beneath the sheets, little more than bone, and the wrinkles smoothed out by sleep. One last time, Nhika soothed her.

She fell into the past. Such a familiar anatomy, the calluses on her mother's palms and the deepness of her smile lines. And such a familiar problem: a ruin of tissue somewhere inside the brain, something Nhika could sense but couldn't soothe. Even now, this wound remained unyielding, like it was taunting her. A reminder that, even after six years on the streets, using heartsoothing to heal scrapes and scam clients, she'd learned nothing.

The memory shocked away when Nhika withdrew her hand, finding herself not at her mother's bedside but at Hendon's. The room was silent—the first time she'd been here without someone to guard her—and she let herself steep in Hendon's quiet company, in this waking memory before her.

"Why did you have to go and injure yourself this way?" she asked through her teeth. Was the Mother still teasing her, sending her a haunt of her mother's condition, the one thing Nhika'd never been able to heal?

Or . . . was this a second chance?

Nhika touched the ring around her neck. She could've run, then, put this mess of the Butchers' Row and Congmis behind her. If their conspiracies were true, perhaps this job brought more trouble than it was worth, and a smarter Nhika would've taken the chance to leave. To return to her forgettable corner of Theumas and bid farewell to endless dinners and gilded libraries.

But that also meant spurning the chance to use her heart-soothing as it was meant to be used. To learn from an endless library of resources, funded by Congmi wealth.

To heal the one injury she'd failed to heal before.

"You bastard," Nhika said to Hendon, knowing her heart wouldn't let her leave. "I hope you're worth it."

Even as she cursed him out, Nhika picked up the bag of goods and returned to her room. She restored the items to her closet, her desk, knowing that each was another anchor to her decision until it finally sank in: She was staying. Even if healing this man came with funerals and murderers, she had to at least try.

"Nhika," came a voice at the door, and she turned to find Trin. He looked breathless, like he'd just rushed up the stairs. "I thought you'd run away."

She shrugged, trying to conceal how much she'd considered it. "Why? Is there some reason I would run?" Nhika goaded him toward the truth. Didn't she deserve it, considering what they asked of her?

But all he said was, "Call it reasonable suspicion."

With a scowl, she waved him off. "I'm not going anywhere. I've a funeral to prepare for and a false identity to rehearse."

Only then did she remember what Mimi had said . . . *when Father's murderer may well be a guest.*

Their suspects lay within the attendees of the wake.

— ༄ —

The Congmis had mostly composed themselves by morning, though bags pulled at their eyes. Even Mimi looked haggard at breakfast, strands of hair breaking free of her coiled bun and makeup remaining from the night before. And Andao, well, he always looked sleep-deprived. Breakfast was a solemn affair, and afterward they all went to ready themselves for the wake. Even Nhika. Thoughts of last night's revelation kept her quiet more so than the somber environment did.

Now, Nhika didn't complain about the gloves—one less thing for the family to reprimand her about—but the funeral outfit was constricting, a plain black dress with silk pants to match and a white headband wrapped around her forehead.

They departed in a caravan before noon, with Nhika in an autocarriage—a real one, this time—alongside Trin while the siblings rode on ahead. On the road, she reminded herself that she was Suon Ko Nhika now, and that she was meant to stay quiet and out of the way. At least that was something she was accustomed to, and she could feign grief just fine.

When they pulled into a gated courtyard, Nhika realized that they hadn't been keeping the body at a funeral home as most folks would. Rather, this seemed a private estate, much smaller than the manor but matching it in elegance. A line of carriages circled the central driveway, dropping off guests at the door-step, a swarm of black and white. When her carriage rounded the steps, the driver opened the door and they streamed out, finding the siblings in the crowd by their distinguished white garments.

The estate's doors had been propped open, welcoming the

guests to the wake. Inside, friends and relatives had begun to gather—friends in black, relatives in white—with heads bowed and silent in mourning. She found the casket by following their gazes past the foyer and into the central living room, toward the back. Solemnity and silence hung in the air like a blanket, and Nhika took the opportunity to find a lone corner in the back of the room to watch.

It was the largest wake she'd ever seen, with an abundance of guests. And yet, few cried, so she didn't stand out, dry-eyed as she was. Nhika took the opportunity to watch the people.

Even though they all dressed simply for the occasion, everyone in the room exuded wealth with their careful makeup, glittering jewelry, and manicured hairstyles. It was a beautiful room full of beautiful people whose grieving didn't steal from their elegance. The constabulary was here, too, and though they'd swapped their uniform for funerary colors, they still sported pistols and batons on their belts. It took her a moment to realize that they weren't here to protect the funerary services; they were here to protect the guests, because if the Congmis were to be believed, this funeral would be a congregation of the technocratic leaders of Theumas: commissioners, industrial executives, doctors, and engineers. Powerful people who no doubt each had ample motive for murder.

More than suspicion or dread, she felt pity for the late Congmi, that his funeral might invite enemies along with friends, one indiscernible from the other.

As she traipsed toward the back of the parlor, Nhika impressed herself with how well she managed to blend into this crowd. All it took was a shower and clothes that covered every inch of her exposed skin, her faded scars and blotchy arms and cracked nails.

But still, she worried her etiquette might betray her origins, so she stood rooted in the corner, mimicking those around her and bowing her head to any who acknowledged her. The crowd eddied with shuffling gaits, guests taking their turns at the casket, but she only observed.

As her eyes swept the crowd, they caught on the few people she recognized: Andao and Trin, standing shoulder to shoulder; Mimi at her father's casket, head bowed; and Dr. Santo talking with a guest.

Her eyes narrowed—no, not just any guest, but the boy from the Horse District. Mr. Ven. It had taken her a moment to recognize him in the black funeral attire, but now she saw him in full: the styled wave of his hair, the darkness of his eyes, the tailored neatness of his suit. It was undeniably him.

Before she could avert her eyes, he glanced in her direction, and their gazes caught. She tried to divert her attention, but he didn't look away, even as his conversation with Dr. Santo continued.

Did he recognize her? Or did he just notice she looked misplaced?

His gaze held hers with intrigue. Knowing she'd been found out, Nhika decided to approach him. Gathering every ounce of boldness and social etiquette, she crossed the room and inserted herself into Mr. Ven and Dr. Santo's conversation.

"Dr. Santo," she greeted, keeping Ven in the corner of her vision. "I'm glad to find a familiar face here."

"Ah, right—you're from out of the city. Well, I hope you don't find yourself too isolated here. You'll learn names soon enough." Dr. Santo gestured to the young man. "Let me introduce you to Ven Kochin."

Ven Kochin—it satisfied her to know his full name. She gave him a short bow. Their eyes locked; she measured his for recognition, finding only scrutiny. "Suon Ko Nhika."

"Pleasure." The word came out disinterested. He cocked an eyebrow. "Waitstaff, I presume?"

"Kochin!" Dr. Santo reprimanded just as indignation spiked in Nhika's chest. So, he did remember her in rags and matted hair, even though she so clearly wore the funeral attire of an aristocrat now. Curiosity and shock she could've anticipated, but she hadn't expected . . . contempt.

"Guest," she ground out. Briefly, she wondered if she'd misremembered their encounter in the Horse Borough—was he truly thwarting the Butchers then, or was he simply gathering his papers?

"Hmm. You don't exactly seem like you belong here," he said, and both she and Dr. Santo opened their mouths to respond when Andao cleared his throat at the front of the room.

As the siblings gathered behind the podium, everyone took their seats and Nhika was jostled into a chair in the back, rehearsing a dozen retorts in her head. Kochin, sitting near Dr. Santo at the front, didn't give her another glance, but Nhika stared at the thin line of skin beneath his high collar and imagined what she might do with it.

Her attention only drew away from him when the eulogies

began, family first and then friends. She shouldn't have been surprised, but some were luminaries whose names and faces she recognized from newspapers.

One was Mr. Nem, who dealt in the arms industry—military technology like artillery, bombers, and ammunition. Nhika figured that must've been a rough industry to be in, considering Theumas's staunch neutrality in the war, but he didn't seem too taxed about it as he took the stand. "The city has lost a flame," he began, his voice stentorian. "Quan was taken from us before his time, and Theumas will always be left to wonder what could've been. He was an arrow nocked for greater things—philanthropy, grandfatherhood, maybe even the Commission. Those of us here today will not be alone in mourning his loss—the entire city will be mourning with us, such was the spread of his influence."

The Commission? Though Nhika never kept up with politics, she knew of the open chair for commissioner. It was big enough that even she had heard of the coming election, but she hadn't known Mr. Congmi was running.

Mr. Nem's eulogy ended with a slow collection of applause, and another took the stand behind him. Nhika didn't recognize him at first, not until he introduced himself as Ngut Lien Buon, from Ngut Inventions—the other big name in the automaton industry, although none could come close to the renown of Congmi Industries.

"This week, we mourn the loss of a great man, father, and friend," he said. "Theumas has no kings, but if ever there was a man to have been our vanguard, his name was Congmi Vun Quan. While many would've looked upon our industries' relationship as competition, I knew him only as a great role model and greater friend." His voice took on a theatrical timbre, his eulogy just a soliloquy for this tired audience. Nhika fidgeted with boredom as Mr. Ngut continued.

As aristocrat after aristocrat stepped up to prove their posthumous love for the late Congmi, Nhika looked for the faces of her bidders. None of them seemed to be in attendance today, but she saw how this crowd, with its endless wealth, could find interest in the limits of what money could buy: illicit drugs, exotic animals, odorless poisons. Bloodcarvers.

Her first funeral was her father's when Nhika was eight; it was her first reckoning with death. Her grandmother had always told her that death was meant to be a celebrated thing, a reunion with the Mother and a return to the cycle, but that had always been hard to believe. Things died, she knew—animals, people, even heartsooths—but nothing had felt so final as adding her father's portrait to the family shrine. It had been surrounded by other relics of their family history: photographs her grandmother had salvaged from Yarong, a box of prayer items from her time in the priesthood, a ring made of onyx and bone. Because they had no body to remember him by, her dwindling family of three used his portrait for the wake and memorial. Today, the service was so full that everyone sat elbow to elbow, and yet she'd never been in a room that felt so empty.

Around her, guests stood. Nhika blinked back to reality, realizing the eulogies had ended. She was slow to move, following the languid crowd as they crawled to the parlor. Small groups split apart into quiet conversation over finger foods and Nhika grew wary of eye contact, lest she be drawn into one. Instead, she winded back toward the casket, daring to come close now that others had cleared.

It was a simple coffin, all things considered, the dark mahogany polished to a shine and inlaid with lush velvet. The man inside did not fill up its space, but flower bouquets buffered the emptiness. Despite the traumatic cause of death, his body didn't look too worse for wear. The embalmer had given him an imitation of life, and Nhika could imagine this man as he was: tall, features rounded, and expression sagacious. Of course, there were details that betrayed the illusion, like the pallor of his cheeks and the sunkenness of his eyes. Nhika glanced between Congmi Vun Quan's body and his framed photograph just behind the coffin. Somehow, he looked younger in death than he did in the photograph, the lines of his face smoothed away by funeral preparation and his complexion made spry by waxlike makeup. She could see his resemblance in his children: The elegant nose had gone to Mimi, the stern brow to Andao, and his diamond face to the both of them.

"I'm sorry about my aide," Dr. Santo interrupted, materializing behind her. "He's normally more respectful than that."

"It's no trouble. I get it a lot," she said. So, Ven Kochin was merely a physician's aide. Nonetheless, working under Dr. Santo must've been a prestigious and lucrative position if he'd been invited among this company.

"But you shouldn't. And especially not from someone who works under me." He stepped up to stand beside her, the both of them drawn toward Mr. Congmi's body in its coffin. For a moment, silence settled, until Dr. Santo said, "He almost looks as though he's sleeping, doesn't he?"

Nhika thought of Hendon in his coma, of how similar those two bodies looked. And yet, if she could soothe them, their anatomies would be worlds apart. "You see death enough and it looks indistinguishable from slumber." She hadn't meant to sound so dark, but Dr. Santo nodded thoughtfully.

"Not your first funeral, is it?"

She resisted a laugh. "No."

He looked sympathetic. "I'm sorry to hear about your loss. It's not mine, either."

"Because you're a doctor?"

A rueful smile played at his lips. "Yes, patient funerals, but also my son's. But it's . . ." A muscle moved in his jaw. "It's different, losing someone slowly and losing someone all at once."

"What do you mean by that?" she asked, because his words hinted at feelings she'd parsed through, too.

"My son was born with a hole in his heart. From the moment I found out how bad it was, I knew he was dying. It was a race against time, trying to find any way to give him one more day—surgeries, medications, therapies. But, that's the thing about losing someone slowly. Every day, you have to watch them slip away from you, no matter how hard you hold on to them. Some days, it feels like things might improve, but then comes a fresh cycle of grief. At least with Quan, I lost him all at once."

"I'm sorry about your son," Nhika offered, the most genuine thing she'd said the entire funeral. In that moment, she saw a glimpse of herself in him, losing her mother the way he'd lost his son. Had he been chasing that failure ever since, each patient a new mirror of his loss?

"It's nothing you have to be sorry about," he said, and straightened his jacket with a huff of self-conscious laughter. "Look at me, just an old man babbling to anyone willing to lend me their ear."

"You're in luck—I've no one else to talk to."

He gave her a curious look. "Well, I can introduce you to some of the bigger names here, if you'd like."

"Like who?"

He gestured for her to follow to a private corner of the room, a more fitting place for conversation than in front of a casket. "Mr. Nem and Mr. Ngut, for two—they're both candidates for commissioner. Leading candidates, I suppose, now that Mr. Congmi is . . ." His sentence tapered into a sigh.

"Right, Mr. Congmi was running," Nhika said, knowing that only from Nem's eulogy. In the Dog Borough, the tides of politics were not so important as the tides of the ocean, and most things got lost in the waves. The leaders of Theumas always claimed every person had a voice, but Nhika learned chem could buy ten, twenty, a hundred voices. Better to keep her head down and her voice to herself, especially when it never made any difference.

"It's a tragedy," Dr. Santo continued. "He aced his Candidate Placement Exams—I don't know anyone who would've made a better commissioner."

"A tragedy indeed," she echoed, finding Mr. Nem and Mr. Ngut in the crowd. She recognized them both from the eulogies.

Behind them, someone cleared their throat and they both turned. It was Ven Kochin, who gave them a curt bow, hands clasped behind his back. "Dr. Santo, Ms. Mieu is about to leave, in case you had hoped to catch her," he said, and Dr. Santo straightened.

"Right." He patted the pockets of his chest until he found something in the inner jacket. When he pulled it out, she realized it was a business card, which he held out to her between two gloved fingers.

"For me?" she asked, hesitant to grab it. Nhika made a quick scan for Andao or Mimi, someone who might think she were taking advantage of the funeral to network, but found them absent from the room.

"I'm the research director at Theumas Medical Center," Dr. Santo clarified. "If you find yourself wanting to stay in the city, give me a call. I'm sure we can find somewhere for you to fit in."

The business card lingered in the air between them, clean white against leather black, an invitation into this world. But as with her name, her education, her occupation, it would all be contingent on a lie, because she couldn't possibly *belong* in a place like this.

Could she?

"I'm not sure what to say," Nhika stammered by way of thanks, because she truly didn't. Nonetheless, she accepted the card, finding it embossed with his name, seal, and office line.

"You don't have to say anything—it's the least I can do for a student of Quan's," Dr. Santo said, bowing as he exited.

Ven Kochin remained, even as his employer disappeared into the other room, his hands clasped behind his back and his shoulders squared against her. "That sets you apart, you know," he said, moving to take Dr. Santo's spot.

"What?" Nhika scowled, stuffing the card into the sleeve of her glove.

"*That.*" He jerked his chin toward her sleeve. "Hiding business cards like you're afraid of them."

"I'm just surprised by his offer. It is, after all, a funeral."

"You must be new," he said, and she didn't love the surety with which he said it. "This is a gathering of the greatest minds in industry and technology, a rarity in this city. It would be remiss to hold sanctity over opportunity."

Nhika scanned the huddled pods of conversation. Now that he'd pointed it out, she noticed how business cards passed between gloved hands, how conversations were scheming, not a tear in sight. Nhika realized a fate worse than death: a funeral that bred not remembrance, but nepotism.

"Since it's making you so uncomfortable, I'd be glad to take that card off your hands," he continued, holding out an expectant hand.

She turned away from him, crossing her arms to hide the spot in her glove where the card lodged. "I think I'll keep it. After all, Dr. Santo did invite me to join his research initiative."

Kochin's eyes narrowed, almost imperceptibly. "And why was he interested in you?"

She heard the note of suspicion in his voice and felt the rise of indignation in her throat. "Why wouldn't he be?"

"Dr. Santo only takes interest in . . . certain kinds of people." Kochin was careful with his tone, but she read his condescension from his words alone: He didn't believe Dr. Santo should've solicited someone like *her*. Nhika only wondered which part of her he was disdaining: the Yarongese part, the girl in rags part, or all of that together.

"What kind of person does he take interest in, then? Someone like you?" she snarked. She sized him up, wondering what he had to even be arrogant about, and was disappointed to discover that he wasn't too hard on the eyes. He had that lighter Theuman skin, but his features still stood out in a crowd. Something about the elegant part of his hair, the intelligence in his black eyes, the way it felt as though he'd been born to wear that tailored vest suit—among this crowd, she wouldn't have been surprised if he'd come out of the womb in it.

"Yes, like me," he returned, as though she'd complimented rather than impugned him. "I'm just surprised, considering the conditions of how we met."

"I was in a rush," she said defensively. Her pride forbade her from apologizing to him.

"That much was clear."

Nhika imagined what kind of debacle a girl of this society might find themselves in. "I was running from suitors."

Amusement quirked in the corner of his lip, the first smile to reach his dark eyes. "I'm sure you get a lot of them." His sarcasm did not go unmissed. "Suitors with nets and catchpoles."

A small stone of dread deposited near her heart—if he recognized those men as Butchers, and if he knew the reasons

Butchers caught Yarongese people . . . could he figure out what she was?

"Don't worry. I won't tell anyone." Kochin smiled, but it felt like a false offer of peace. "But, girls in rags don't walk into silk overnight. You're in over your head, Ms. Suon."

Nhika let out a quiet breath; as long as he considered her *only* a girl in rags, and not a bloodcarver underneath them, she was safe. With newfound audacity, she said, "Sounds like you're afraid I might replace you."

The discreet flare of his eyes told her that she'd guessed correctly, but he said, "Of course not. I just imagine your talents would be better suited elsewhere."

Outside of medicine, he meant. That insinuation was nothing new to her—that any Yarongese who held an affinity for medicine must've been a bloodcarver, or why else would they have taken such interest?

Well, he happened to be right. But Nhika would never give him the satisfaction of knowing that.

"And what are *your* talents, exactly?" she pressed.

"I take care of matters for Dr. Santo's research initiative."

"Ah, so you're a secretary."

Kochin tweaked his cheek. "I prefer physician's aide."

"Doesn't seem so difficult."

"Looks can be deceiving."

"You know, Dr. Santo was just telling me about all the important people in this room, and he failed to mention you."

"Oh? Then who did he name?"

"Mr. Nem and Mr. Ngut." Nhika realized, then, that she

hadn't had the opportunity to finish her conversation with Dr. Santo due to a certain physician's aide.

Kochin must've realized it too, because he grinned. "A short list."

"Who else is of any importance here, then?"

"Everyone" was his brief answer, but he elaborated. "Pick anything that interests you, and I'll give you a name. Interested in the forefront of deep-sea exploration? Mr. Aom's submarines can take you six hundred feet under the surface. Want to see a film in color? Ms. Lienva is changing theater. Want to see a man's bones through his skin? Dr. Vhit is inventing imaging film that'll allow it." He rattled out the names with a sense of flippancy, as though he weren't listing revolutionary inventions. As if this crowd had long since bored him with their whims and miracles.

Momentarily, she wondered what had jaded him. Perhaps it was regularity that bred boredom; this society produced marvels as the night sky produced stars, and even the sun might lose its luster if placed within the Star Belt. Somewhere, behind all the aristocratic arrogance, Nhika thought she caught a glimpse of something real in his eyes: resignation.

Then his gaze met hers, and all that haughty charm returned. "You better not be hoping to fit your name on that list."

"I'm just here for a funeral, Mr. Ven," she said. "Not to be accosted by a secretary."

Kochin blinked in surprise, as if he'd been nothing but cordial. "Take my words not as harassment, Ms. Suon. Take them as a warning."

"A warning about what?"

"That you don't belong here."

Before she could counter, someone called her name. It was Trin, appearing from the other room and bowing to them both. "Excuse my intrusion. But our autocarriage has arrived to take us back to the manor." He extended his arm for her to take, but it wasn't so much an invitation as a demand.

Nhika withheld a sigh, wondering if Trin had only called the autocarriage once he'd seen her talking with Kochin. But, anything for the Congmis, she supposed—even if that meant he had to leave the wake early, too.

She gave Kochin a bow, at once happy to be saved from conversation and disappointed to be chaperoned. "Pleasure to meet you," she said, the words a formality.

"Likewise," he said. Before she could turn away, he'd taken her hand in his, silk against bare palm, and lifted it to his lips. His eyes watched her as he planted a kiss against the fabric, at once firm and gentle.

It must've been a simple act of etiquette, over in a second, but Nhika stiffened as though he'd nipped her. Her hand lingered in his for a breath too long, and she cursed the gloves, wishing she could feel this touch the way Theumans did, skin on skin with nothing else behind it. Not *his* touch—he was a boy who wanted to push her out of this world—but *someone's* touch. A parting kiss on bare knuckles rather than gloved hands around chafed wrists.

Remembering his insults, Nhika snatched her hand away. Only seconds had transpired, yet she reeled her mind back to earth. Momentarily, she wondered why Kochin—who was so convinced she wasn't an aristocrat—would recognize her with the gesture of one. To save face before Trin when they both knew it was a mockery? Without another word, she took Trin's arm and let him guide her out of the estate. Though she didn't look back, she knew Kochin's gaze followed her.

"Why were you talking to Dr. Santo's aide?" Trin asked, voice edging suspicion.

"He approached me. It would've been stranger if I hadn't," she grumbled, flexing her hand. "I obeyed all your rules; don't worry. You say sit, stand, beg—and I do all that. What did I rehearse my story for, if not to talk?"

His expression flashed an apology, and he cast his eyes to the ground. "You're right," he managed to say, as though the words pained him. "I shouldn't be so harsh."

Nhika watched him out of the corner of her eye and saw the extent of the fatigue behind his words. It was a reminder that he was grieving where she was not, so she remained quiet as their autocarriage rounded toward them. As she stepped inside, she removed her glove to free her hand, still burning where Kochin had kissed her.

— NINE —

FOR THE REST OF THE EVENING, THERE WAS NO more Suon Ko Nhika, just Nhika in a library, trying to read but instead occupied by thoughts of the wake. Of Ven Kochin. And of those who might eulogize Mr. Congmi in one breath and kill him in another.

But, she had no one to share her thoughts with: The siblings and Trin were busy preparing for the final day of the funeral, and not even Dr. Santo came by to visit.

The last funerary custom, the procession, came the next day with the same guests in attendance. Unlike the wake, it was a stiff, orchestrated affair, which meant that Nhika didn't have to worry about making conversation.

For this, even onlookers joined in the ceremony, congregating as the procession rolled through the streets of the Dragon Borough by hearse and marching band. It seemed everyone in these parts understood whose body lay in that coffin, and everyone stopped for a moment in bereavement or curiosity. That never would've happened in the Dog Borough, not only because full processions were so rare, but also because the thick, sluggish crowds there never parted for anything. There was no sympathy for the dead when, on some days, death felt like a blessing.

Their procession took them to a private cemetery, a gated lawn scattered with tombs and headstones bound by one similarity: the Congmi name. Nhika frowned at that, this little patch of grass in a metal city reserved solely so that a few dead might be remembered for nothing more than their name. But she felt a twinge of envy for the Congmi siblings, whose long lineage was apparent in the sprawling tombstones, and she morbidly realized they'd end up here, too. Laid to rest, eternally surrounded by family. There were certainly worse ways to go.

Flowers were left, speeches were given. Journalists and photographers crowded outside the locked gates, cameras clicking and flashing with blatant disregard for the mourners. The pallbearers lifted the coffin into the mausoleum, disappearing behind its stony walls and emerging again bereft of burden and casket. Now Nhika watched the siblings. Mimi was a sorry sight, makeup running with her tears, and Andao must've sprouted a dozen more white hairs overnight. It seemed masochistic to draw the funeral out over so many days; one had been enough for her, and now Nhika itched to return to the library.

She got her wish soon, in a way. The procession retired to the Congmi manor for a feast, and Nhika got to witness the grandeur of the banquet hall, which made the Congmis' private dining room look like a puddle beside an ocean. Here, curtained windows spanned the walls, overlooking the front lawn and lifting the viewer's eyes toward the wooden caisson ceiling. The servants had prepared the tables, which were draped and dressed like dancers circling one another in a ballroom. Gold accented the white across the room, yellow chrysanthemums blooming in bouquets of white lotus atop every table.

The guests settled as they filed in, and Nhika found herself seated between two chatting men and an older woman, none of whom seemed to notice her as they made themselves comfortable. She recognized the men as Mr. Nem and Mr. Ngut, remembering their faces from the eulogies and their names from Dr. Santo's introduction—they were both candidates for commissioner. Up close, there was nothing to set either of them apart from the average Theuman other than trim suits and brocaded gloves, yet Nhika knew she was a mortal at a table of deities, of commissioners and multimillionaires and geniuses. It made her feel smaller than her eighteen years, like a child sitting with adults for the first time.

Food came before long, the dishes separate rather than shared. Though her stomach flipped, she obeyed etiquette for the sake of the Congmis and waited for all the plates to arrive before digging into hers. She appreciated how the room fell to relative silence as people ate; at least she was not alone without conversation.

But the quiet didn't last before guests resumed their discussions, now over food. The older woman at Nhika's right was talking to her partner about the meal, while the candidates had rounded toward respectful conversation about the late Congmi.

"It harrows me to think I might've been one of the last people to speak to him while he lived," said Mr. Ngut, wiping his lips with a napkin. "If I could go back to that phone call, I would just tell him not to make the drive."

"No one could've known," replied Mr. Nem. "I have plenty of regrets with the late Congmi that I'll take to the grave myself."

"You two always were at odds, weren't you?" Mr. Ngut reminisced.

"I wouldn't say that we were at odds," Mr. Nem corrected promptly. "But, knowing each other as long as we did, we were sure to run into disagreements. Though, never something that a night at the bar couldn't smooth over." Nhika slowed her chewing as unsolicited thoughts came to her—were these motives, perhaps, for murder? The events of the funeral had distracted her from such thoughts, but now her interest renewed. Her eyes explored the room in an attempt to hide her eavesdropping.

They met Ven Kochin's.

He snapped his gaze away, returning his attention to his table and tenting his bare hands in an idle gesture. Despite the innocuous act, she realized he'd been watching her, and Nhika felt the hairs on her neck rise.

"—Yarong anymore, right?" Mr. Nem was saying, and the word dragged Nhika's attention back.

"Maybe so," Mr. Ngut responded. "But Mr. Congmi loved the island. Shame Daltanny never reopened the country in his lifetime. He would've had a lot of things to say."

"Like what?" Nhika spoke up, and they turned to her. Blanching, she cleared her throat and adopted the speech she'd observed at the wake: "Excuse me, I couldn't help but overhear your conversation. My name is Suon Ko Nhika." She dipped her head in a short bow.

"Nem Boch Kenyi," Mr. Nem introduced himself. He was a

large, broad-shouldered man with the same demeanor as a bear standing on its hind legs. Gesturing to Mr. Ngut, he said, "And this is Ngut Lien Buon."

"You're Yarongese, aren't you?" Mr. Ngut asked crudely, eyes gliding over her coarsely. What gave it away—the golden brown of her skin, the darkness of her eyes, the freckles on her nose?

She nodded, already regretting the conversation. "I just never knew Mr. Congmi was interested in Yarong." When most people talked about Yarong, it was usually in the context of the tragedy, the wastefulness of Daltanny. Nhika couldn't blame them; that was the only piece of Yarongese history relevant to Theumans. But she would not have been surprised if Mr. Congmi, worldly as he was, was actually interested in the culture of the island.

"Oh, he *loved* the place. Are you from the island?" Mr. Ngut enunciated the last part, as though she might not understand him if he spoke too quickly.

"Theuman born and raised."

"Great misfortune, what happened there," he continued, though his performative tone betrayed his aloofness. "It's such a shame, really. I'm sure the place is crawling with Daltans now—warmongers, all of them." Well, at least that was something Nhika could agree with.

"Yes," she said. "A true tragedy."

"The bigger tragedy is that we've let Daltanny keep spreading their influence across the island," Mr. Nem interjected, and she gleaned that there was more he wanted to say that he withheld for propriety's sake. She was doing the same.

"Yes, absolutely," she agreed, nodding along. Sarcasm came to her by instinct, and she bit it back from her voice, because the truest tragedy of Yarong's fall was that, in a circuitous fashion, it had landed her here in this stiff conversation with these two bland men.

The next entrée arrived then, and Nhika took that as an opportunity to remove herself from their conversation. The food was plentiful, with a variety of courses, overflowing cups, and desserts to follow. Nhika ate far past a respectful threshold, hoarding calories as a miser hoarded chem.

As dinner ended, guests dissolved from the tables and banquet hall, disseminating around the mansion and chatting over goblets of wine. Nhika left with them, escaping conversation and candidates for the respite of a quiet library. Still in black mourning attire, she returned to the shelves, finding her stack of books untouched. A few guests came and went, admiring the shelves and the whale skeleton, and Nhika felt oddly territorial, as though this was her space they were invading.

She headed for her books, turning the corner around a glass case of primate skeletons—

And found Ven Kochin.

One leg draped over the other, he sat at the bench she'd used to study, her stack of books before him and one open in his lap. Only when she halted before him did he look up.

"These are yours?" he asked, scrutinizing the stack.

"And what of it?"

"Never took you for a reader."

Nhika scowled. "Never took you for a stalker."

Unaffected, he exchanged the book in his lap for the next one on the stack. "Studying for something?"

"Call it a personal interest." She narrowed her eyes at him, knowing he could understand these textbooks just as well as she could. But would he be observant enough to connect all the dots—the anatomy books, her Yarongese origins, and their run-in on the streets? Would those clues so obviously spell *bloodcarver*?

"Is that why Dr. Santo solicited you?" he murmured, as though talking to himself. "You've expressed interest in medicine?"

More than he could ever know. "Aren't you his aide?" Nhika tilted her head innocently, though the words were a challenge. "I thought he told you everything."

Kochin examined her, too carefully for her taste, and his next words were deliberate. "Your name doesn't come up in conversation. I'm just curious why you've caught his attention at all." Before she could shoot back—*Why not?*—he asked, "So, you're staying with the Congmis?"

"How did you know that?"

He gestured to the table. "The books, obviously." When she didn't deign to respond, he tilted his head toward the open seat beside him. "Come. Sit. I won't bite."

She had her reservations, but Nhika joined him on the bench. "You sure enjoy monopolizing my time. What if I planned to network?"

He made a quick scan around the room. "There's no one else here worth talking to," he determined.

"And you are?"

"I'll let you decide. Trust me. I've heard the stories of everyone in this room." His eyes wandered again, dancing between the laden shelves, the taxidermied birds, and the whale skeleton. At last, they landed on her. "Everyone, that is, except you."

Nhika caught the irony in that—Kochin was so quick to disdain her background, yet he found such interest in it. "What's there to know?"

"How do you know the Congmis?"

This again? Nhika tamped down her annoyance. "I studied beneath their father. I'm only staying for the funeral."

"And then, back out of town?" He lifted his brow.

"Maybe. Maybe not. I'll have to see." She remembered the card from Dr. Santo, a ticket into this society on a false identity.

"What would keep you here?"

Nhika mulled the answer. "What would drive me away?"

He flashed her a look and, without honoring her with an answer, stood. Dropping the book back onto the table, he said, "You're interested in Hendon's condition, aren't you?"

Nhika straightened all too quickly, eyes narrowing as she watched him with renewed interest. "You know about Hendon?" Trin and the siblings had given her the impression that Hendon's condition had been a secret.

Kochin's smile was cold. "I'm Dr. Santo's aide. He tells me everything." At that, he straightened, brushing the dust off his pants. "Anyway, I won't keep you any longer. Wouldn't want to *monopolize your time*."

He turned to leave, but she stopped him. "You keep asking me about my story, yet you haven't told me yours." He must've been around her age, but with the wealth and splendor of Theumas behind him. She didn't want to believe he had worked for it. Better to deplore him if he'd been born into it, but then, where was his family at these functions?

Kochin halted midstep. When he met her eye, his look held something between apathy and sadness, but he was quick to regain his composure. "Nothing to tell" was all he said before walking away.

Nhika watched him leave, but he didn't return to the dining room, where most of the guests socialized.

He headed deeper into the manor.

Nhika's brow furrowed, eyes locked on the smooth black of Kochin's funeral suit disappearing down an unlit corridor. There was something about Kochin—the way every word seemed to hold a double meaning, the way he sought her out only to disdain her. Despite it all, he drew her interest as much as she did his.

Nhika started after him, turning down the corridor only to find a long, empty hallway, with all the doors on either side closed. There were no guests here—the siblings had left the lights dimmed—but she heard the rumble of voices down the hallway nonetheless. She followed it, ears trained for Kochin's voice but finding three others instead: Andao's, Mr. Nem's, and Dr. Santo's.

"Mr. Nem, give the boy some time. This is a *funeral*," Dr. Santo scolded, his voice emanating from the last door on the left.

Nhika crept up to the door, finding it cracked open. She placed her eye up to the opening, knowing that the darkness of the hallway kept her safe, and peered inside. Andao, Dr. Santo, and Mr. Nem were inside, each standing over an armchair as though they'd just risen from their seats.

"I understand your grief, I truly do," Mr. Nem drawled, voice teetering on the edge of sobriety. "But the world does not wait on your grief, Andao. Your father may not have considered war his arena, but your father isn't here to make that decision anymore. Since you now stand in his place, it's your decision whether you'll turn a blind eye while Daltanny oppresses our neighbors, or whether you'll use all that influence to stand up for something. To *fight* for something."

"But . . . my father was a pacifist, Mr. Nem," Andao said. His words were strained, unsure; in the moment, he sounded like just a boy, thrust too soon into a robe three sizes too large.

"But you are not your father."

"That's enough," Dr. Santo said, wagging a stern finger at the glass in Mr. Nem's hand, empty. "You're drunk, Kenyi. Walk it off and book a formal appointment with Andao if you wish to discuss this further."

Andao deflated, either from relief or defeat, but Mr. Nem complied. With a shake of his head, he started toward the door; Nhika took that as her cue to leave. She scampered around the corner just as Mr. Nem emerged, muttering to himself and stomping down the hall with a half-drunken gait.

It wasn't until he was gone and the hallway returned to silence that Nhika realized Ven Kochin had disappeared.

Having lost Kochin, Nhika returned to her corner of the library to finish reading, now with a half-empty wine bottle she'd swiped from the closing bar. She abhorred the taste, but wine had been one thing passed around at family dinners that she'd never gotten to try before, so she drank it now to make up for lost opportunities. Around her, funeral guests retired home, and before the sun even set the house had returned to its usual state of quiet. She caught no sign of Mr. Nem or Kochin the rest of the night.

When the wine had heated her cheeks, she closed the book and looked up, finding the library newly dark and empty. Even Trin had forgotten to check in on her, but Nhika had no reason to stray. Not when they kept her full on dessert and alcohol. Not when she was so, *so* close.

Bottle in hand, she staggered to her feet and traced the walls toward Hendon's room. Even with the door closed, she could hear the mechanical click and whir of the medical machine inside. And something else behind that noise: a quiet, murmured voice.

Nhika opened the door to find Mimi inside, having pulled up a chair to Hendon's bedside. Mimi startled at her arrival, but when she found only Nhika, she put on a languid smile. Her puffy eyes and pink nostrils betrayed the smile, though, and Nhika was slow to enter the room.

"Am I intruding?" she asked.

"Not at all," Mimi responded, her voice a tired drawl.

"Is Trin here?" Nhika glanced around the room as she approached the bedside.

"No. Should I be worried?" Mimi gave her a look under half-lidded eyes.

"If you keep feeding and clothing me, then no." As Nhika passed, she caught a whiff of alcohol—and not from herself. Mimi eyed the bottle and held out her hand. Nhika passed it over, thinking Mimi might confiscate it, but instead the girl downed a generous swig.

Heavens, was Mimi drunk? Nhika hid her surprise behind narrowed eyes.

"Maybe I'll take that back," she said, reaching for the bottle, but Mimi shouldered it away like a child with a stolen toy.

"I'm a bad sister," she said, moping at the bedside. Nhika took a seat across from her, surveying Hendon's sleeping form.

"How so?"

"Leaving all the funeral planning to Andao. But I hate funerals. And this one especially."

"Don't blame yourself," Nhika said, unable to think of anything else more comforting. She'd seldom had to comfort another before. Not with words, anyway.

"But I am to blame. I'm sorry we've been so secretive with you even though we've asked so much," Mimi continued. "And I'm sorry if we've made you feel unwelcome, despite your services. And I'm sorry—"

"Mimi," Nhika interrupted before the girl could pour any more of her heart out on her drunken tongue. "Stop."

Mimi gave her a fuzzy smile. "I'm sorr—Er, okay." Her gaze lowered to Hendon. "Have you made any progress with the books?"

Nhika pulled off a glove, keeping her hand at the bedside to show she was not a threat. "Maybe. That's what I came here to see." She found Hendon's slack hand beneath the bedsheets and curled her fingers around it.

Her influence crossed into his body again, and she found its faculties even more muted than before, as though his systems had entered torpor. She recalled the images of the thalamus in the books, and now climbed to his, pushing through fog and haze. She ascended the spinal column, clawing her way up vertebra by vertebra, until she sat at the base of the skull.

Nhika let out a breath, face pinched with concentration as she inched her influence forward. That invisible block met her again somewhere in the brain and when she tried to balance on that fine point between brain stem and cortex, she found that she couldn't. This was the problem; she was certain of it now. The same way dead tissue in her mother's brain had paralyzed her, there was cell death in Hendon's thalamus that kept him from waking. Nhika's soothing drew back into herself, toward her own thalamus, and she mirrored that feeling in Hendon.

It wrapped around the blank space of Hendon's brain, drawing a shape out of emptiness, painting in the details of his anatomy as she explored her own, one a template and the other a fractured copy. When she managed to overlay the two, it was like static crystallizing into music, and she smiled as a new, uncharted structure opened up to her influence. But everything fuzzed as she tried to explore them both, influence drawn too thin between two poles.

Hendon's anatomy was still damaged, somehow, warped

compared to her own. There was a mess of electricity and vasculature there, and though she tried to make sense of it, she was quick to lose her grip on his anatomy.

She'd never understood the cells of the brain meticulously enough to know what they were meant to look like. They weren't the same cells she found elsewhere in the body, compartmentalized and structured. These were directional, and she knew if she hitched her influence onto them, she could travel a great distance across the body. But she was merely the rider on an untamed stallion, gripping its mane just to avoid getting bucked. Here, now, while she saw his anatomy mirrored in herself, she had little idea how she might begin fixing it.

With a sigh, Nhika drew away, her mind settling back into the right body after exploring Hendon's for so long. When her senses returned to her, she found Mimi looking at her hopefully.

"I understand the problem," Nhika offered, anticipating her question. "But to draw a man out of a comatose state, that . . . That may have been something the old heartsooths knew how to do, but not me."

"Are you saying you can't do it?" Mimi asked. Her voice trembled dangerously near tears.

"I'm saying that you and Andao should prepare for a reality where I can't," Nhika said, and she knew what her words meant: prepare for another funeral, just like this one Mimi hated so much.

For a moment, Mimi only stared at her, and Nhika feared that, in admitting failure, she would lose all the Congmi hospitality and find herself back in the Dog Borough. Then Mimi's lip quivered, brows knit with uninhibited grief. The tears came shortly after, and the girl buried her face in Hendon's chest before letting out a muffled wail. Her shoulders shook with sobs and every muscle in Nhika tightened.

She was too stunned to move. She was the only other person in the room; was it her place to comfort Mimi? Or was she meant to give Mimi her privacy?

"He can't be gone!" Mimi cried. "How is it that his heart can beat, and his lungs can breathe, and he's alive, but not awake? If he survived where Father hadn't, only to die two weeks later, after all that hope, all that grief, I . . ."

The rest of her words were lost to stuttering hiccups and Nhika grimaced, extending a tentative hand toward Mimi's shoulder. She knew that physical comfort was meant for a situation like this, but she wondered if Mimi would welcome the touch of a bloodcarver in the place of another, or if that could only bring revolt.

When she had sat by her mother's deathbed, her touch had been just a touch. At the end, no soothing nor medicine could cure that extent of sickness, so Nhika's hands weren't those of a heartsooth. When she laced their fingers, her mother's clammy and hers dry, it had just been the touch of a daughter too afraid to let go.

Remembering that, Nhika dared to extend her hand and squeeze Mimi's shoulder. Mimi didn't stiffen or shudder away. She leaned into the touch, and her sobs calmed, slowly, to shallow gasps. Sitting at the bed, accompanied only by the soft whir of the medical machine and Hendon's quiet breaths, Mimi reminded Nhika so much of herself, years ago—still grappling with the new concept of death, feeling so betrayed by it because she'd always thought herself immune.

She recalled their suspicions of murder. Nhika had been in that position, too, inventing conspiracy out of death because she'd lost so many—how was it fair, when she was a heartsooth? But finally, when she'd had no one left, she'd come to accept that Death didn't conspire to beguile. Death only took, and took, and sometimes there was no justice in it at all. Sometimes, Death was content to steal the last of a dying lineage by accident and ash, pruning away a family that no longer needed to exist.

Surely, that was the same injustice Mimi felt now—the city's most industrial man, felled by a carriage accident? Heartsoothing had never made a difference for Nhika, and it seemed that, for all his influence, Mr. Congmi had still met a mortal fate.

When Mimi's whimpers fell to silence, Nhika pulled her hand away, eyes exploring the tear-streaked makeup and red-rimmed eyes. Mimi's nose twitched, but she managed to draw back the sobs enough to say, "Does it ever get better?"

Nhika cocked her head.

"You said your family was gone, too," Mimi explained. "Does the pain ever get better?"

"Yes," Nhika said, only because it's what Mimi needed to hear. In truth, it got better and it didn't. Most days, Nhika could forget that she'd ever lost anyone, so occupied with pressing tinctures and scamming clients.

But there were days, moments, little things to remind her all over again—an anatomical textbook, a family dinner, a fractured ring—and it would be as though she'd never healed at all. The grief would come with all its claws and teeth, and the scars her heartsoothing could not touch would rupture back into wounds.

Instead of all that, she just said, "It will get better."

Something crumpled in Mimi's expression. "There's something I have to tell you. We love Hendon, but it's not the only reason we need him to wake up. It's also because—"

"You believe your father was murdered, and Hendon would know the truth."

Mimi blinked in surprise, slow to understand through the wine. "You . . . know?"

"I overheard it," Nhika said. "You should've told me up front."

With a look of shame, Mimi lowered her gaze, and Nhika watched something mature and sober flicker behind her eyes. "I just . . . You're right. Please don't think me selfish. Just desperate. If it's too much for you, we can renege on the terms of our agreement. Consider your liberation from the Butchers' Row an act of Congmi philanthropy. Especially if . . . especially if there's nothing to be done for Hendon."

"I didn't say there was *nothing* to be done," Nhika amended. She wasn't sure why she was so quick to correct Mimi, why she continued to entangle herself in these aristocrats' lives for a simple sum of chem. Giving up felt like more than just forsaking a dying man; it felt like admitting that, even after being given all these resources, she still couldn't learn to heal an injury like her mother's. Like she wasn't even a heartsooth.

"What are you saying?" Mimi asked, and that youthful hope flickered like a tea light in her soft voice.

Nhika was saying that she wanted to stay, because the heartache of loss was not something she could soothe away, but a brain injury was. It was too late for her own mother, but there was still hope for the Congmis. And that's what her grandmother had always told her, right? That the role of a heartsooth was to heal. If she could perform this one act of healing and be true to her family's memory just once in her life, to her mother's fate and her grandmother's teachings, then perhaps she could earn an indelible spot on her bone ring even if no one would exist to remember it.

"I'm saying you shouldn't give up yet," Nhika said, and knew her lips would betray her with a promise. "I can heal him."

— TEN —

THE ESTATE WAS SLOW TO RECOVER FROM THE funeral. Servants tidied up the dining hall and reawakened automatons, but the somber aura that lingered in the air was not reachable by mop or feather duster. Nhika let them work, hiding away in her corner of the manor.

Lying atop her bed, she stared at Dr. Santo's business card in her hand. Perhaps she wouldn't be able to join his research initiative, but his invitation had spawned another idea: asking him for literature. The only problem was that talking to Dr. Santo at his workplace incurred the risk of running into his secretary. Not to mention, contacting anyone outside the manor would mean bringing Suon Ko Nhika back to life, and she was a charade meant only to last a funeral.

Well, a telephone call couldn't hurt.

Nhika stood, drawing her gloves on before she left her room to find Trin and a telephone. The Congmis had dropped their guard, perhaps realizing how much food and shelter had placated her, but she didn't want to test their generosity.

By now, she knew this manor and its occupants well enough to understand that finding Trin meant asking the staff for Andao. Her inquiry led her to Mr. Congmi's study—or rather, Andao's, now—and she found the door ajar with a sliver of light.

"I can't keep going like this." That was Andao's voice, thinned by the usual fatigue. She heard the scratch of a pen, the crumple of paper.

"It'll be okay." Trin's voice, softer than she'd ever heard it before.

Nhika approached the door and peered through the crack. Mr. Congmi's private study strayed away from the modernity of the rest of the manor—a collection of laden shelves, bulky desks, and sagging furniture beset by a dark, monochromatic setting. Trin and Andao sat across the desk from each other, Trin leaning over with Andao's hand in his. Scrapped paper littered the counter and Andao hung his head, limp strands of hair falling over his eyes.

"What am I supposed to say to him? Nem wants a response. I feel like I've made enemies before I've even had a chance to sit down at Father's desk. How long can I keep stalling before I end up like . . ." He didn't finish his sentence, but Nhika understood the context. *Like my father*, he was going to say.

"You won't," Trin said, the words definitive. "I won't ever, *ever* let that happen."

Their hands melted together. No gloves, just skin on skin. She saw their tender looks, the way their eyes spoke more than their mouths. She caught how their gazes swept over the intimacy of their touch, the closeness of their bodies. And when Trin leaned forward to kiss Andao, she imagined the warmth of it on her own lips.

Nhika snatched a breath. That was the thing about being a heartsooth—her body understood how it all felt because it'd seen it all. Sometimes, if she let her empathy organ have its way, she could trick herself into believing she'd experienced those things for herself.

Trin pulled back, but the softness lingered. "Has Nhika made any progress?" Andao asked, voice unrestrained.

"We're feeding her, housing her," Trin said. "I wouldn't be surprised if she's taking her time. I hardly understand what she's been up to, but . . ." He deliberated on his next words. "Not even Dr. Santo has hope for Hendon anymore. She may be our only option."

"Or we accept that, maybe, we shouldn't bet on miracles where medicine has failed." Andao sighed. "I'm just afraid that Mimi will be crushed."

"I'll take care of Mimi. And Nhika. You don't need to worry, Andao." There it was, that gentleness again.

Nhika took the opportunity to shoulder her way in, relishing in their flustered expressions. Trin gave her a weary look, his hand still wrapped in Andao's. Their eyes followed her as she took a seat, but she gestured to the rotary dial. "I need to make a phone call, if that's okay."

Andao straightened. "Heaven and earth, Nhika—I'm so sorry. We've been so busy that I didn't consider that you might have someone worried about you. Please excuse our—"

She cleared her throat to interrupt him. "I don't. It's for the job."

At that, he blinked at her, then re-collected himself. "Oh, of course."

"For what?" Trin interjected, pulling back from Andao only

to cross his arms. Nhika gave him a nasty look, beleaguered that she still had to justify herself.

"I've read your library dry, so I was going to ask Dr. Santo if he had anything to offer."

Trin and Andao shared a look of interest. "Not a bad idea," Andao said. "Uncle Shon probably has access to the latest research."

Trin crossed his arms, ever skeptical. "Just be on your best behavior."

"When aren't I?" Nhika dismissed.

"I hope you understand the gravity of the situation," Trin insisted.

Nhika thinned her lips in challenge. "Because you suspect someone at the wake murdered Mr. Congmi?"

The room stilled and Trin's stare turned especially frosty. "What did we say about eavesdropping?"

"Mimi told me," Nhika said, not a full lie.

Andao pinched the bridge of his nose in consternation. "And what is it that she told you, exactly?"

"That you believe your father was murdered, and you want me to wake Hendon for answers," she said.

"Not just for answers," Andao responded quickly. "He means a lot to our family. But . . ." His words were lost to another sigh, as though he'd lost the energy to explain.

"But Hendon would be able to tell us for sure if there was foul play involved," Trin finished. They were coordinated, the two of them, finishing sentences as though they were tethered by the brain.

Nhika shook her head. "If you're unsure, why speculate at all?"

"I know it sounds unlikely, but we have our reasons," Andao said.

"Like . . . ?"

"The night before the accident, Mimi overheard him arguing with someone on the phone. Threats were exchanged. We don't know who the caller was."

She wasn't wholly convinced. "So what *do* you know?"

"We know Father was meant to make a public appearance to announce his new automaton line, but none of the autocarriages would start," Andao added, growing adamant. "We know he went by horse carriage, along a path the horses have traveled a dozen times before. We know they were spooked around a curve—what's more, they were dead on-site. The only thing we don't know was what happened the day of the accident."

And that's where Hendon came in, Nhika supposed—where *she* came in. "You suspect someone from Mr. Congmi's inner circle because of the phone call," she guessed.

Andao shook his head. "Not only because of a phone call. My father was a well-loved man, but one doesn't get to where he was without making enemies. And for people like him—like *us*—our greatest rivals stand within our friends, our colleagues."

"Where was all this information when we were rehearsing my backstory?" Nhika grumbled.

Andao gave her a meek smile. "We . . . didn't think it mattered."

"Why wouldn't it matter?"

"Because you're here for a job," Trin said, not so apologetic.

"You should consider yourself lucky—home nurses don't get the room and board you do."

There was something more to be said—that heartsoothing was so much more intimate than medicine, so she was more entwined than a home nurse could be. That she was sleeping under their roof, listening in on their conversations, at once privy to their secrets and excluded from them. That this was such a half welcome, allowing her to dine with the semblance of a family for the first time in six years, yet keeping her in the same corner of the manor as a comatose body.

But Trin was right. This was just a job with a generous payment and the added perk of their amenities. Perhaps she'd mistaken proximity for trust.

"You think your father may have been killed for political reasons? The candidacy?" she asked instead.

Andao gave her an uncertain nod. "It's certainly a motive. My father tried to keep his candidacy plans quiet. But when he aced the Candidate Placement Exams, word got out. With the candidacy, his enemies no longer cared about wealth. They wanted power."

"Same thing, no?"

Andao tweaked the corner of his lip. "Nuance. Especially with war talks."

Nhika had seldom considered the war—that was a far-off prospect, teased too often and with too little action to be taken seriously. She knew war raged around Theumas, and Daltanny's naval base on Yarong loomed like a threat to the south, but she was too absorbed in her own life to consider fighting for another's.

"So that's what you and Mr. Nem were talking about last night?" she murmured to herself, and watched Trin's eyes twitch with annoyance.

"Really? Eavesdropping *again*?" he said, sounding exasperated.

She waved an indifferent hand. "I was just passing by. What exactly is it that he wanted from you?"

Again, Andao and Trin traded their uncertain looks, speaking full sentences with their eyes alone, until Andao said, "He wants me to endorse the war with the Congmi name. And, if war comes, he wants me to divert my factories to the war effort."

Nhika barked out a laugh. "Well, there's your murderer. Kill the pacifist father, influence the impressionable son—he gets his war, his artillery industry booms, and he becomes a leading candidate as a bonus."

Andao winced, Trin's expression flattened with distaste, and Nhika realized she'd pricked a vein too deep. Sobering, she added, "What is it that *you* want?"

Andao shook his head. "If I knew, Nem would already have his answer." He waved a hand, dashing the topic. "Anyway, you wanted me to dial Uncle Shon?"

Nhika drew out the business card and offered it to him. She would've dialed it herself, but she'd never used a telephone before. Never had anyone to call. "He gave me this office line."

"I have it memorized," Andao said, rejecting the card and swiveling the dial. Nhika watched him enter the number, the frontal circular apparatus clicking as it rotated, until at last he held the telephone out to her. Trin leaned closer.

"Oh, we're all going to listen in?" she asked pointedly, but accepted it nonetheless. She held it as she'd seen it held before, but Andao silently gestured for her to flip it around.

A mechanical buzzing noise greeted her ear when she did. She looked at Andao in question, but he merely mouthed, *Wait*.

After a moment, something clicked on the other side. "Dr. Santo's office." It was Kochin's voice on the line.

Caught by surprise, Nhika floundered for words, though she should've expected the aide to manage the phone line. At last, she managed, "It's Suon Ko Nhika."

"Ah, Ms. Suon." She could hear the disappointment in his voice. "I wasn't expecting a call from you."

"Well, I won't be in town for too long." She said this to appease Trin and looked deliberately at him to make sure he understood that. "So, I thought I might use my resources while I have them."

"Do you mean Dr. Santo's research initiative?" The hesitance was palpable in his tone.

"I was actually interested in what kind of literature he might have access to."

"Well, I have some things that might interest you, if you'd like to plan a time to meet in private," he offered. Trin shook his head with stern disapproval, but it wasn't as though she were planning to meet with Kochin alone, anyway.

"I was hoping to just set up a meeting with Dr. Santo. Is that within your ability as his aide?"

"Of course," he said, but instead of annoyance, she heard amusement in his voice. "I can make an appointment."

"Perhaps sometime soon? My schedule is quite *strict*." She said that last word as another jab toward Trin.

The line went silent for a pause, and Nhika wished she had a number to bypass Kochin and speak directly to Dr. Santo, because she didn't fully trust him not to end the call right then. Thankfully, he said, "He seems to be free at noon. The address is on the card—I assume you kept that."

"I'll stop by then," she said, and it was Trin who ended the call before Kochin could, finger pressing down a button on the stand.

She handed the receiver back to Andao. "All right. I'll be off now." Nhika pushed herself off the desk toward the door, but Trin stepped before her.

"I'll go with you," he said, and it wasn't so much an offer as it was a statement.

She gave Trin a tired look and glanced to Andao for reason. "Surely, it would raise questions if I showed up with your six-foot bodyguard."

"I'd feel a lot better if you didn't go alone," Andao said, and she realized he wouldn't take her side on this one. "Please, Nhika. Trin knows Dr. Santo and his people. It's just to ensure that we don't have any . . . social mishaps."

She looked between Andao and Trin, wishing Mimi was here to defend her. As she'd observed, that was the hierarchy within this family—the household deferred to Trin, Trin deferred to Andao, and they both deferred to the whims of the little sister. But she let out a defeated sigh, knowing it was futile.

"Fine. But, if I'm to jump through all your hoops just to heal Hendon, I need you to tell me things. I want to be in the know," she said, using the moment to leverage what she could. "You can't ask me to practice discretion when I don't know what to be discreet about."

Andao sighed behind a thin smile. "I . . . You're right. You deserve to know."

Even Trin looked agreeable, confirming with a terse nod. "Very well."

"Good," she grumbled, but her chest bloomed with warmth at their consideration, like she'd just earned her first real foothold in this home. "Let's go, Trin."

Trin shifted his jaw.

"Please."

"There we go," he said, sounding satisfied with himself, and stepped out of the office.

Nhika gave Andao an incredulous look. "You two are involved? I wasn't aware he was capable of emotion."

A soft look came over Andao's eyes. "It's not about what he says, but what he does."

"Isn't that what you hire him for? To do things?"

That elicited a laugh from him. "He's hired only to keep me alive. Yet, I wouldn't want to live without him."

With no argument for that, Nhika turned from the room and followed after Trin.

— ELEVEN —

THE MEDICAL CENTER, A MODERN CONSTRUCTION, hardly looked like it belonged in this city. It was all arches and windows, straying from the traditional pagoda architecture but for its tiered, curved roofing. In a way, it more resembled a university, from whose libraries Nhika had stolen books before, than a hospital. But then again, Nhika had rarely frequented hospitals—not even when her mother was sick on her death-bed, because hers had been an illness neither heartsoothing nor modern medicine could solve. She checked the address on the card out of habit, as if this grand building would be anything but the Theumas Medical Center.

Trin held open the doors for her. She felt out of place entering through the front doors, despite her clean dress and scrubbed skin. Thankfully, the bustle of people in the lobby seemed too busy to notice her.

Trin studied the directory at the stairs. "Fourth floor," he said. "Let's go."

"Does it hurt you to smile?" she asked, watching his stony expression as they ascended the stairs. "If it's a musculature problem, I could probably soothe that out."

He flinched, eyes wide. "Don't mention that here, Nhika."

An impish giggle bubbled out from her. "Relax. No one's

listening." The stairwell and halls were empty, and no one would understand what it meant to soothe rather than carve, anyway.

"Still, do you know what physicians might do with a—" He caught himself. "With you?"

Of course she knew. When Daltanny took over Yarong, many of its residents went to labor camps to build the new naval base. Only the heartsooths were exempt from labor—at first a blessing, until the researchers attempted to determine what, exactly, made a heartsooth tick. And if they ever found an answer before they cut through all the native Yarongese heartsooths, they hadn't shared it with the rest of the world. Theumas had its own problems, but at least she didn't have to worry about getting vivisected here.

When she looked at Trin, his frown was etched with genuine concern, and her retort stuck in her throat like a hiccup. "I appreciate the concern, but I'm not worried," she said, hoping to lighten his anxiety.

Trin let out a strained breath. "We—well, Mimi, but now all of us—brought you into this mess. I'm not sure the siblings could forgive themselves if something happened to you because of it."

"It's nothing new to me. My life was already a mess before I entered this one." She remembered her tinctures, the little attic room she'd rented out. Nhika wondered what had become of it with her absence, with her rent due at the end of the month. Back then, she lived day by day, never trying too hard to sort out her future because she figured, with her family's track record, she'd never make it particularly far. And so, the troubles had piled, her clients inevitably saw her for the sham she was, and she never stayed in any corner of the city for long.

"Because of your magic?" he asked, the last part a whisper.

Nhika measured his expression—small talk, or genuine interest? For once, it was hard to tell. "Yes, in part, because of my *gift*."

"Why don't you just . . . not use it?"

That was a genuine—but foolish—question. She opened her mouth to answer him—would he not fly if he had wings?—but she didn't know how to express the answer in a way he would understand. Surely, he didn't see heartsoothing the same way she did, because how could he? How could he understand that it was her connection to her lost family, a culture she'd never had the privilege of truly knowing? How could he know how it felt to soothe, to connect to someone so intimately, not a mere substitute for empathy but a step above it? How could he see that it was not some magic she could switch on and off at whim, but a permanent fixture of her identity?

These thoughts simmered under her tongue, but all she said was, "Because it's fun."

He snorted, but from his smirk alone it was hard to tell if he was ridiculing her or if he saw through her. He left it at that, and they reached the fourth floor.

Dr. Santo's office was at the end of the hall, the door marked by a frosted window and a plaque with his name: SANTO KI SHON. Nhika rapped a knuckle against the door, to no response. She gave it another second, then tried the handle.

It opened into a barren waiting room, with a curved desk

and its empty chair. The place was austere despite its windows, lounge chairs lined meticulously.

She and Trin took their seats, him sitting across from her even though there was perfectly enough space to sit beside her. Nhika frowned at his apprehension, his stiff-backed posture and hands folded in his lap. "Afraid I'm going to try something?" she asked.

"No. Just . . . never liked hospitals," he admitted, flicking quick glances at the door as though a corpse might walk through. "So cold, aseptic."

She understood that. The sweet smell of carbolic acid had followed them into the office, and the office was a few degrees removed from warmth. But hospitals had always held her fascination; Nhika was intrigued about the tools they invented, the procedures they used to mimic what a heartsooth could do in a breath. Still, there were things medicine could fix that she could not—systemic things, microme infections and diseases so dispersed through the body that her influence could not handle it all at once. From her history lessons, she recalled how Daltanny had utilized those limitations to conquer Yarong, defeating them with weapons to circumvent heartsooth mending: diseases that spread readily through touch and firearms that rained death from a distance.

"Never been in one before?" she asked, a part of her hoping she wasn't alone in that.

"I've been too many times, actually," he said. "This one, at least. I used to go with Mr. Congmi. But he preferred to deal with the bodies after they'd been discharged—that is to say, dead. He and Dr. Santo took me to the mortuaries and ana-tomical theaters."

She raised an eyebrow in interest. "Back during their med-ical studies?" Mr. Congmi's life confused Nhika—she didn't understand how one man did so much in so few years. At points, it seemed he was a medical lecturer, a biologist, and an engineer all at once.

"More recently than that—when he was perfecting his lifelike automatons, just a few months ago. He was always reverse engi-neering the human body to build it back up again with metal and glass." There was reverence in his voice, and Nhika felt a distant connection with a man she'd never known—she under-stood what it felt like to break the body down into parts, to reshape it in her mind's eye. If she had met Mr. Congmi in life, she imagined they'd have a lot of ideas to exchange.

"Is that how he made all his automatons so ingeniously, then?"

Trin gave an affirmative nod. "The way he explained it to me was that the human body was nature's greatest feat of engineer-ing. And it's true—if you look at the joint of the shoulder, the elbow, or study the physics of muscle."

She gave him an impressed look, lips twisted into an amused grin. "You know, I always thought you were just some hired muscle who worked for the smartest man in Theumas. But you're pretty sharp yourself, aren't you?"

He gave her a dubious look. "Is that a compliment?"

"A question."

"Well, you spend enough time around Andao, and you start to pick up a little genius, too, I suppose."

"And how, exactly, does one woo the heir of Theumas's largest industry?" Nhika asked. "You know, in case I run into any other eligible billionaires."

He gave her a sardonic smile. "Wouldn't you like to know?"

"He didn't buy you from the Butchers' Row, by any chance?"

"Not quite."

A click of the door ended her line of questioning. She turned to find Dr. Santo stepping into the waiting room.

Trin stood to bow and Nhika remembered to imitate him. "Morning, Dr. Santo. I know we're a little early for our appointment, but—"

"I didn't know I had any appointment at this hour," Dr. Santo interrupted, regarding them with a moment's surprise.

"Oh," Trin said, giving her a curious look. Nhika shared his confusion until she remembered that it'd been Kochin who booked them—he must never have scheduled any appointment at all.

"Is it urgent?" Dr. Santo asked.

"No, we're just . . ." Trin glanced to Nhika, deferring to her.

"We're looking to access some reference literature. I figured that, since you were the research director, you might have access to more recent publications."

Dr. Santo's expression lit with curiosity. "Oh, well you figured correctly. What's the subject?"

"The neuroanatomy of consciousness."

"I see," he said. "I was just about to head out for lunch, but I'm sure I can find you something to help."

Nhika glanced at the empty desk and the phone behind

it—where Kochin should've been, perhaps. Briefly, she wondered where he found the audacity to schedule her an appointment with Dr. Santo when he'd planned to be out for lunch. The annoyance was fleeting as Dr. Santo opened the door.

"Right this way," he said, his smile jovial, and ushered them out.

They followed him down the stairs, across the gallery that connected the offices with the rest of the medical center, and into some clinic spaces. Here, the medical center was abuzz. Nurses shoved past them, carting trays of equipment to be sanitized. Others ran with soiled linens and full bedpans, screaming bloody murder at those who stumbled into their way. The clicking of cogs filled the gaps between the chatter, and in every room, at every bedside, were assortments of medical machinery with a variety of different command rolls. Few were without the Congmi insignia.

Dr. Santo spoke to them above the clamor. "I hope you don't mind me taking a detour to see one of my patients. And Nhika, if you're looking to stay, remember I have a few open positions."

Her chest warmed, and she nodded before he slipped into one of the clinical bays, cordoned off by a curtain. She could still see him through the crack and admired the extensive machinery in just this room, an automaton to push fluids and another that inflated cuffs to massage the patient's ankles, machines in place of a human. Nhika watched as he pulled a chair up to the patient's bedside. His manner was soft as he took the patient's hands into his. It would've almost looked like heartsoothing if not for the examination gloves—protocol, she was sure, but there was dissonance there, touching without warmth, comforting without feeling.

This medical center, these patients . . . they called to her the same way her heartsoothing did, with an intense desire for connection. So many people to be healed, and so many ways to use her gift. Nhika wondered if someone like her could ever belong here, with curtains drawn between patient and provider and a machine to rule them all. If she could win the favor of a man like Dr. Santo, could she fit in without forsaking her heartsoothing in the process?

"Getting along with Dr. Santo, are you?" Trin asked, pulling her attention away from the patient.

Nhika shrugged. "He's kind. And . . ." And the kind of person she might've been, in a different lifetime. Someone healing others because they couldn't heal themselves. "And he helped me learn names at the funeral."

"We'll be sure to give him a good excuse for when you leave."

"When I leave?" Nhika echoed. She knew it was an inevitability but didn't appreciate how Trin treated it like one, too. "He did just offer me a position."

"But he doesn't know that you're . . ."

"A lie?" Nhika couldn't conceal the chagrin in her voice. She scowled. "You really think I would hurt patients just because I could?" It was always the same rhetoric: Never let a bloodcarver touch you, because then they'd do who knows what with your anatomy. The same Theumans would place themselves unconscious under the sharp end of a surgeon's scalpel, and pay *money* for it.

"I don't think that. I was thinking more about the danger to you," he said, and, due to the levelness of his voice, Nhika took a moment to register it as concern.

"I've never had any trouble managing myself before," she said, but there came comfort in his consideration. "How hard could it be to fit in? His research can't be that difficult if he asked me to join without even knowing my credentials."

Trin quirked a skeptical eyebrow. "You haven't heard about his research projects?"

"You act as if I have time to read the journal every morning."

He let out a low chuckle. "I thought it was common knowledge. Dr. Santo was the first and only man to succeed with live organ transplant."

"Like . . ." She grappled with the thought of it. "He put a new heart in someone?"

"I think he did the kidney first. But yes." His smile was victorious, as though he'd finally found something he knew that she didn't.

Live organ transplant. That was another thing that heart-soothing couldn't do. "And the patient lived?"

"More or less, from what I understand. Since then, he's been working on a few other projects. It's a pity you can't stay in his lab—that's a rare opportunity, indeed."

"Yes," she said, her lips pressed thin. She thought of Dr. Santo's son, born with a hole in his heart. Had that been what drove Dr. Santo into the transplant business, finding a new heart for his son? Trying to stave off death, if even just for a day? He must not have had the breakthrough in time to save his own child. "A pity."

Dr. Santo emerged again, exchanging examination gloves as he did. "Apologies for that. Generally, I leave these post-operative checkups to my aide, but it seems he's stepped out for a moment."

He gestured them down the hallway. They snaked through the clinical ward, past locked medical record rooms and operating suites, and into a secluded wing of the hospital.

"This is my lab," Dr. Santo introduced. "As part of the grant for the Santo Research Initiative, the hospital provided a ward of the building under my sole supervision. If you can't find what you're looking for in its library, then it hasn't been discovered or invented yet." He beamed, the confident smile suggesting his statement wasn't an exaggeration.

As they stepped through the double doors, Nhika felt as though she were stepping into the future. Here, rather than grimy curtains and cramped clinical bays, there were spacious rooms walled in newly painted brick and tall windows overlooking the downtown streets of the Cat Borough. And, where outdated machines cluttered the hallways of the other ward, Nhika found only modern technology here, things she never saw on the streets of Theumas or in any of her clients' houses. In one room, a metal cylinder the size of a cot sat in the corner, the window in its side revealing a dummy automaton within. In another, a row of machines with many-pronged hands assisted a surgeon while she operated on a chunk of imitation flesh, passing rags and tools as she sutured up a cut in the rubber. Nhika blinked in surprise when the surgeon looked up from her work, revealing dusky skin—she was Yarongese.

They passed a few more rooms—offices, operating rooms, even a mortuary—before Dr. Santo stopped before a door around the corner. He withdrew a busy key ring, fumbling a moment to source the right key, and let them in. Just as with the rest of the lab, the library was clean and contemporary, with none of the extravagance of the Congmis' library but all its dignity. Tidy shelves aligned themselves in rows, sections marked by alphabet and books matched cleanly in height. Even a preliminary look at the spines revealed recent dates, some coming from this very year. Perhaps Dr. Santo was right: If this library couldn't save Hendon, nothing could.

"There you are," Dr. Santo said, sticking his hands into his coat pockets. "Just try to be mindful of the employees who come in and out. I hope you find what you're looking for and, if you have any questions, don't hesitate to ask." His wink was an invitational one, and her pride swelled at the thought of having friends in high places, no matter how undeserved.

Trin bowed again, and Nhika followed suit. "Thank you, Dr. Santo," Trin said. "Please, let us know if we can repay the favor."

"It's my pleasure." Dr. Santo smiled as he bowed, then turned to leave.

Nhika hit the shelves, tempted by habit to pocket some books. And she might've, if Trin wasn't watching her every movement. First, she took herself to the anatomy section, but a few minutes spent here revealed nothing too new about these structures in the past couple years.

Then she rounded toward more recent research journals and

papers. It was all organized by authors' familial names, so she and Trin took to the laborious task of skimming abstracts and perusing titles. Nhika ran across a section of publications authored by Dr. Santo himself: a few papers from his organ transplant years to more recent inventions, machines that inherited the functions of the organs, pushing blood and ventilating the lungs when the brain no longer could. Machines that came so, so close to heartsoothing. She wondered if she'd seen any of those in the hall outside.

Now she was the slightest bit grateful for Trin's company, because doing this alone could easily consume a week. They'd collected enough papers to sprawl across the low table before she started reading. Many of the papers were unusable—too specific about a certain macromolecule, or she'd misread the title and it was irrelevant to Hendon. For the first time in a while, she labored through viscous jargon, brain befuddled by the new, made-up terminology—neuro signalers, myelin sheaths, electroencephalography? By virtue of her grandmother's teachings and those stolen medical textbooks, some of the new words came intuitively to her. But others . . . Mother, it was as if they'd been invented to confuse on purpose.

Nhika struggled to conflate the words on the page with the things she felt while soothing. Large anatomical structures were easy enough—there was some kinesthetic feedback to them. But these papers were talking about minute, unseeable things, twisted little proteins and structures on the scale of micromes. Things her influence skimmed over, or maybe controlled without her conscious doing.

The papers focused on a particular frontier of recent research:

neuro signalers. Tiny little chemicals with confusing names that Nhika wasn't sure what to do with. But presumably, the right balance of the right chemicals at the right times controlled consciousness, controlled the movements of muscles and the beat of the heart. As she read, her frustration only mounted, because these chemicals meant nothing to her, but it was all these wordy scientists seemed to care about. She just wanted to heal a thalamus, whatever that was, Mother damn it all.

"Anything of use?" Trin asked when they'd dwindled their accumulated resources down to a couple of papers.

Nhika shook her head, too tired for words. That's all these papers were—just words—and if she wanted to heal Hendon the way heartsooths did, the way her grandmother did, she was all but sure the answer wouldn't come from these books.

Dr. Santo was right. Maybe the answer hadn't been discovered or invented yet. And maybe it never would be, because the heartsooths who could teach her had been lost to the machinations of time.

For a moment, Nhika grappled with the thought of failure, and having to tell Mimi to plan another funeral because she couldn't wake Hendon. Of returning to her unchanged apartment, as though she'd never even taken the time away. To eating alone again and sleeping on that noisy mattress.

Nhika closed the book before her, its words and images swimming in her vision even after she pushed it back at Trin. Was this it, then? Was she giving up? The act of resignation came with all the resistance of taut muscle—it was admitting that heartsoothing hadn't been enough, yet again.

Something squeezed in her chest, right where her heart was. No, she would try once more. With all she'd learned, with all she had left to try, she would give Hendon one more chance. Her heartsoothing *had* to be enough.

Just then, the door to the library opened. Trin hurried to clear space on the table for a physician, but it was only Kochin who rounded the shelves. He looked a little unkempt, his collar unbuttoned and hair windswept. A bag hung from his shoulder, and he smiled, though his gaze grew wary when he turned the shelf to see Trin sitting there beside her.

Nhika narrowed her eyes. "You booked us over Dr. Santo's lunch," she grumbled, though there was a great deal more she would've said if Trin hadn't been here.

"Did I? Ah, no wonder he had no appointments at that hour." Kochin feigned innocence with an ingratiating grin. "Seems like you had no trouble."

She shifted her jaw.

"Anyway," he continued, "I heeded your request for literature."

Kochin shrugged off the bag, unbuckled it on the table, and slid it over to her. Nhika eyed it warily, trying to discern whether he was being genuine or deceptive. A nod encouraged her to accept it, and when she opened the bag, she found three books within—their titles revealed they were introductory books in biology, not even anatomy. The kind meant to teach children.

He smiled scathingly. "I figured you might need to start with the basics."

His insults had never broken skin before, but this—atop

her growing defeat, the futility of her heartsoothing—pricked something fragile. Tears welled in her eyes, and she bit them back as her fingers curled around the bag.

"Thank you," she said through gritted teeth, glaring up at him.

Nhika turned, not wanting to give him the satisfaction of having wounded her. Before he could get another word in, she pushed past him toward the door.

As they left the medical center, Trin sidled up to her. "What did he give you?"

"Nothing."

"Are you . . . okay?" He gave her a wary look, like he was afraid of prodding a tiger.

"Fine."

Trin swallowed. "Do you want to . . . talk about it?"

"No."

Respecting her request for silence, Trin ceased conversation for the rest of their journey back to the Congmi manor. Nhika tossed the books in her trash can as soon as she reached her room.

— TWELVE —

NHIKA WOKE THE NEXT MORNING TO A COMMO-
tion outside her window, a rattling from the gardens. Groggily,
she smoothed her unkempt hair back and went to investigate,
finding a truck parked up the path, full of guests.

She squinted, blinking the sleepiness from her eyes. Those
weren't guests; they were automatons, rows of them, propped in
sitting positions in the back of the truck. The doors opened, and
where Nhika expected workers to disembark from the truck, it
was Kochin who slid out of the driver's seat.

Nhika frowned, eyes narrowing. After their meeting at the
medical center, she could've gone a lifetime without seeing him
again. She watched him round the vehicle and enter the solarium, wondering if he knew she was still here with the Congmis.
As if to answer her question, Kochin's gaze swept across the
upper stories of the manor, and Nhika retreated from the windows, wondering if he'd seen her.

The creak of hardwood from outside her room drew her attention away from the garden. Slipping into an easy outfit, Nhika
exited the room to find Hendon's door wide open. She crept across
the hallway and, as with the first time she met him, found Dr.
Santo sitting beside Hendon's bed. This time, he was alone, placing a stethoscope beneath the unbuttoned collar of Hendon's shirt.

Dr. Santo gave her an inviting smile when he noticed her. "Morning, Ms. Suon."

"Dr. Santo," she greeted, feeling at ease when there was no Trin around to dissect her every word. Now comfortable within the space of Hendon's room, she pulled up a chair across from him and observed Dr. Santo as he worked.

"I'm glad to see you're still in town," he said, moving the drum of the stethoscope around Hendon's chest. "Did you find what you needed in my library?"

"Yes," she lied, her mood souring at thoughts of Kochin's books. "You have a very informative collection."

"What did you say your medical background was, again?"

"I studied briefly at Zhalon," she said, omitting the part of her false backstory where she'd dropped out. It shouldn't have mattered, but she didn't want Dr. Santo thinking any less of her. "You're not in the office today?"

"Home visits," Dr. Santo clarified. "Gives me an excuse to stop by. The siblings like to think they're all grown now, but they're never too old for their Uncle Shon."

"Do they pay you?" Nhika cocked a brow, wondering whose time they considered more valuable—his, or hers. She had a feeling as to the answer.

He waved a hand. "They've tried, but I couldn't charge them for this. Not when I can't actually *do* anything for Hendon. Besides, those closest to Quan always did serve him for love, not money."

Nhika watched him, waiting for him to realize the contradiction there—that not *everyone* had been loyal to him. Not at the end, anyway. When he didn't, she said, "You know about the siblings' suspicions, don't you?"

He regarded her with new interest. "About their father?"

Nhika nodded. "Do you believe them?"

After a pause, he drew away from Hendon and removed his stethoscope bud from his ear. His words were slow, but thoughtful when they came. "I'm a man of science. I try to wait for evidence before I make any conclusion, and I have to say there hasn't been much evidence," he said, echoing some of her thoughts. "*But*, I believe in the strength of the siblings' conviction. If I could heal Hendon for them, give them their peace of mind either way, then it's what I'll do."

Nhika watched Dr. Santo thoughtfully as he returned to his examination: taking a pulse, measuring the blood pressure, pinching Hendon's fingernail beds to check for blood flow. Though she'd learned many of medicine's basic procedures from stolen textbooks, she'd never considered the ways they matched and strayed from heartsoothing. It was all the same healing, just with a different set of tools.

In the moment, he reminded Nhika so much of her own grandmother, healing with the same balance of meticulousness and empathy. An ache bloomed in her chest, followed by jealousy, because the siblings had something that she'd lost and they didn't even know it. "You must love them."

"Mimi and Andao, like my own children. And Trin, I've known him since the night he tried robbing the place."

"Trin did *what*?"

Dr. Santo laughed heartily at her surprise. "You didn't know?

Quan all but adopted Trin from the streets. The boy attempted robbery and Quan financed his education. But I suppose it would be hard not to, considering how Trin and Andao had grown on each other."

Trin? Robbing the house? She couldn't imagine him stealing a thing, not even a kiss. But, if that were true, and Mr. Congmi had found Trin from off the streets just as the siblings had found her, then maybe it wasn't such a stretch to imagine herself here, too. Her honest, true self.

"Dr. Santo," she began, feeling a touch of hesitance where she never had before—because he'd offered her roots here, but he didn't know who she truly was. Still, he turned his full attention to her, again taking the stethoscope bud out of his ear.

"Did you really mean what you said, that someone like me could belong in your lab?"

"Why not?" he answered easily, and she reminded herself that her background was falsified. He elaborated, "Of course, we could start you in a learning position until you get comfortable. Then, we can explore the limits of what medicine can truly do."

The limits of medicine . . . Nhika wondered if Dr. Santo would consider heartsoothing within that caliber. "It's all in memory of your son, isn't it?"

He nodded, hanging the stethoscope around his neck and turning toward her, expression somber. "Yes. His name is— *was*—Leitun. I'm working toward the day where conditions like his aren't the end."

"And you're not just asking me as a formality?" Nhika realized her insecurity was showing and pulled it back with a dismissive laugh.

"Definitely not," Dr. Santo assured her, maybe a little too quickly. "I handpick all my employees."

"Did you handpick your aide?" Some of her snideness slipped through as she forgot her audience, but Dr. Santo only chuckled.

"Yes, I did. He already stood out as the youngest in his class, but I'd never met anyone with so much ambition. Took one look at him and thought, 'There's a boy who would do anything to achieve his goals,' and knew I had to get him on my staff."

As if the mere mention of his name summoned him, Kochin materialized at the door and cleared his throat. Nhika straightened promptly, wondering if he'd listened in.

"Dr. Santo, Ms. Suon," he greeted. "All automatons are accounted for and undamaged from the commute. Actually, Ms. Suon, Mr. Dep and I could use an extra pair of hands unloading them, if you wouldn't mind?"

His eyebrows lifted in question and she gave him a steely glare, her jaw gritted against further insults—she had ripe things to say about his audacity, his scorn, and his "gift," but not in front of Dr. Santo.

"Very well," she ground out, only because etiquette would expect her to agree. She stood, stiffly, and bowed a farewell to Dr. Santo. "Until next time, Doctor."

Annoyance simmering just beneath her skin, she followed Kochin out of the room. She didn't speak to him—he didn't deserve her words, not even her insults, despite how she longed to spew them.

"Not going to talk to me?" he asked, frustratingly observant.

"I don't see what there is to talk about." His introductory textbooks were meant to solicit a reaction, so her anger would be his victory.

He watched her out of the corner of his eye, as though cautious to the full extent of her coldness. "And here I thought we were getting along."

"You have slighted me at every opportunity, failed to book my appointment with Dr. Santo, and given me beginner textbooks when I asked for literature," she reminded him. They descended toward the garden entrance, strides matched. "But sure, we're getting along."

An infuriating smile teased at his lips, as though the list of his offenses invoked fond memories. "There. Now you're talking to me."

Annoyance prickled at her throat—that he'd outplayed her again when she wanted to be removed from his game entirely. They'd entered the solarium by now and she turned to fully face him. Nhika balled her fist, yearning to hurt him—not a skin-on-skin act of heartsoothing, but more a knuckles-against-cheek act of human rage. "You want to talk? Let's talk. I don't understand you. When I first ran into you, I almost thought you were trying to help me."

"You never thanked me for that, by the way."

"You've been hostile ever since."

"You've been equally so."

"What's your play, Ven Kochin? Are you trying to edge me out because I ruined your papers? Are you really so vindictive?"

"It's as I told you at the wake. You don't belong here."

She narrowed her eyes. "That's a lie. I know Dr. Santo has people like me in his employment. So what is it, then? You feel threatened, for some reason, that I might—"

"Nhika," he interrupted, his tone shaped with imperative, "have you considered that I'm only trying to help y—"

Kochin caught his words, dragged them back, clenched his jaw. The stone in his throat bobbed as his contempt returned, but Nhika had caught the crack in his mask. Behind it, she saw something vulnerable and honest: desperation.

"Help me?" she asked. "Help me what?"

Before he could respond, the door to the solarium clicked open and Trin stepped inside, clipboard in hand. At the sight of her, his expression settled into its usual wariness, as though waiting for her to do something brazen.

Nhika wanted more time to demand answers from Kochin, but he continued his business with Trin as though she weren't in the room. "Mr. Dep. Is everything in order?"

Trin straightened the clipboard. "Seems so—only four of twelve automatons ever used, no damages."

Kochin nodded, looking satisfied. "Great. I hope you don't mind, but I wrangled Ms. Suon to help us."

Trin flashed her a punitive grin. "No, I don't mind one bit," he said before exiting the solarium.

Nhika followed begrudgingly, sending a glare to the back of Trin's neck as he led the way toward the garden, where a truck bed full of human-size automatons awaited them. They were smaller up close, each only about her height and the metal carapace thin. They'd been strapped down in gangly positions, jointed limbs askew and heads lolling. In parts, the metal had been padded with rubber, and their mouths were agape in wide *O*'s, lending them the eerie look of ghosts.

Trin unstrapped one, hefted it down from the truck, and deposited it into her arms. Nhika staggered underneath the weight, shifting the metal carcass in her grip until it flopped like a hollow bride in her arms. Though it was unwieldy, the automaton was lighter than it should've been for metal and rubber, a testament to Mr. Congmi's craft.

By the time she'd adjusted her grip, Trin had already hoisted another automaton over his shoulder, and smirked at her struggle as he turned toward the garage.

"Need a hand?" Kochin asked, loading an automaton onto his own shoulder. She wasn't sure if it was a taunt or a genuine offer.

"I'll manage," she muttered as they continued after Trin. She gave Kochin a sidelong glance, suddenly aware of how he tread in step with her. The urge to continue their earlier conversation pricked at her patience, but she hadn't missed how Trin stayed only a few steps ahead, deliberately within earshot.

"What are these automatons for?" she asked instead, her tone docile.

"Medical training dummies, a collaboration between Dr. Santo and the late Mr. Congmi," Kochin responded. He was playing nice in Trin's audience just as much as she was. "They've got tracheas and esophagi and pharynxes for intubating. And their chests are meant for practicing resuscitation. Just something for the students to beat and bruise, rather than live patients or cadavers."

Though Nhika could appreciate the genius in that, there was no replacement for a live patient in heartsoothing. The metal and rubber of a mannequin, no matter who the artisan, would never be able to mimic an anatomical system in action, the way blood pulsed with life, the muscles with electricity, the lungs with volume. If any of them could soothe, they would understand how nonsensical a goal this project was, trying to make an automaton anything more than metal and cogwork.

But, for the sake of Suon Ko Nhika, she said, "Their ingenuity never ceases to amaze me."

When they reached the outbuilding, Kochin withdrew a key ring from his pocket, which held a lone key. Wrestling the automaton across one shoulder, he fumbled with the lock until it clicked open, and all three of them hoisted up the weight of the outbuilding door. It opened to reveal the late Congmi's autocarriages, as well as the hearse yet to be returned. The corner of the outbuilding near the workbench had been cleared, and Trin laid down the automatons across the floor. Nhika and Kochin followed suit, lining up automatons on a dirtied white tarp like bodies from an epidemic.

The light of the sun caught the key in Kochin's hand as he palmed it to Trin. "Here. I won't be needing this anymore, so I figured I'll return it now before I forget."

Trin made a noise of agreement, pocketing the key. Even after it had disappeared from her view, the key retained Nhika's attention, and her brow creased with focus as she fielded a haphazard thought: Hadn't Andao mentioned something about tampered autocarriages the day of Mr. Congmi's death? What was Kochin doing with a key to the outbuilding?

Before the thought could blossom into something dangerous, Trin gestured them toward the garden to ferry more automatons. Kochin followed.

"Wait," she said, pausing Kochin midstep. She waited a beat for Trin to continue out of earshot before saying, "What did you mean by what you said earlier? Help me what?"

Kochin turned, his expression unreadable. "I'm not sure what you mean."

"Kochin."

His gaze flicked far down the path, where Trin disappeared around the corner. Something warred behind his eyes, the muscle in his jaw twitching in the long pause. At last, he said, "Help you make the right decision."

"About what?"

"Something gilded is only gold on the surface."

She cocked a weary brow. "I'm not a poet, Kochin."

The look he gave her was a poignant one and he thinned his lips, as though debating his next words. At last, he chose, "I know you're not from this part of Theumas."

Nhika readied an excuse. "Well, I—"

"You wanted honesty. The least you can do is not lie to me." His eyes held candor, gaze so sharp that she knew he'd long since dissected the shell of her false identity. "If you're smart, you'll heed my advice: Run back to wherever I found you in the

Horse Borough. Spend too much time in this part of the city, with these people, and you'll only get hurt."

Were his last words a threat, or a warning? She wasn't sure how to parse out his honesty; she'd all but asked for it, but now she preferred the condescension, because at least that was something she was accustomed to.

Without any more elaboration, Kochin continued back to the truck. Nhika let him fall out of step with her, lagging behind as he walked just so that she could observe him: the self-assurance in his stride, the sharp line of his jaw, the exposed lengths of skin where Nhika's fingers could reach, if the need arose. With so many secrets in the air, she had to wonder who Ven Kochin, with all his cryptic words, truly was. Just a physician's aide, or something more, something sinister?

They didn't speak much further as they carted the rest of the automatons to the garage. When they did, it was just niceties for show, Kochin holding the door for her or helping her handle the dummies. In a coincidence of timing, Dr. Santo emerged from the garden entrance just as they finished up, carrying a briefcase of his instruments. He gave Nhika a considerate nod before dipping into the passenger's side of the autocarriage.

Kochin circled the bed of the truck, coiling up wires and buckling straps. Before he embarked, he paused to address her. "Ms. Suon," he began, his expression cryptic, "you didn't actually read the books, did you?"

"I found them beneath me," she responded.

Something shifted in his eyes. "It's better that way," he said, and hopped into the driver's seat without another word. In the next moment the engine was on and the truck was pulling down the road.

"What did he mean by that?" Trin asked, crossing his arms and giving her a sidelong glance.

"Your guess is as good as mine." Her brow knit, mind returning to the day before. She hadn't even opened the books before she'd thrown them in the trash.

"You seem to be getting close with Mr. Ven," Trin said.

"One could misread it as closeness, sure," she returned, her thoughts elsewhere. Already, her feet were taking her past Trin and back into the manor, up the stairs, into her room. She dropped to her knees before the trash can and fished out the limp bag of books.

Nhika poured them out onto her bed, three in total, wondering if she'd misread their titles. But no, they were still the same introductory books, teaching biology at a grade schooler's level, until . . .

She thumbed the dust jacket of one of the books; it came off easily, too loose. Beneath it was a leather cover softened with age and splitting in corners, a ratty thing that belonged in no library. The other three were the same. She was almost afraid to open them, fearing they would crumble beneath her touch.

But she did, and her heart stuttered as she saw the text, the language, the diagrams: passages written in character, bodies drawn along lines of influence, pictures colored by synesthetic sensation.

They were heartsooth books.

— THIRTEEN —

HE KNEW. VEN KOCHIN KNEW.

What else could the heartsooth books mean? She only had to wonder *how* he knew. Was it a lucky guess, compiled from all the circumstantial evidence: their run-in at the Horse Borough, her Yarongese roots, her interest in medicine?

Or, was it something more ominous? Nhika thought of all the ones who knew she was a heartsooth, how the information could get out. Andao, Mimi, and Trin knew, but they wouldn't have let it slip. The only others were those who'd attempted to buy her on the Butchers' Row.

Like the man in the fox mask.

A man who knew what she was, who'd used that word, *heartsooth*, with an incongruous familiarity. Had he learned that word from books like these? She had assumed the Butchers' Row hadn't followed her here, but perhaps she'd been wrong.

She'd run into Kochin during her escape from the Butchers. He must've learned, then, what she was. He must've realized she would end up in the Butchers' Row. He must've donned the black hood and fox mask the very next day, prepared to buy her.

The question still lingered: *Why?*

It didn't matter. He'd made his warning quite clear. Nhika should've left then—taken the books and fled the Congmi manor—but she'd made a promise to give Hendon one more chance. After that, she'd take the money and run far, far from this entire mess.

Just leave it all now.

But she'd promised.

Promised whom?

Hendon, of course.

Hendon's in a coma; he'd never know. Try again.

The Congmis?

That was for a price, but if you can part with the chem, you can leave it all behind.

Herself, then. Nhika had made a promise to herself.

As the quaver of her heart trembled near stillness, as the pounding in her ears quieted to a whisper, Nhika realized that her motives were selfish, they always had been. She was doing this for herself because she had something to prove, because she needed to know if she could.

Because the role of a heartsooth was to *heal*, and if she had not been able to heal her mother, then damn it—she would heal Hendon.

Gathering the books close, Nhika drew out of her room and slipped into Hendon's, finding him alone in his bed by the window. There, as she had many times before, she settled beside him and curled her fingers around his hand.

Nhika soothed.

Her hearing was muffled as she reimmersed herself, as though she'd dipped her head beneath the surface of water. The bloat returned, his body as lethargic as a fly caught in molasses.

Nhika pushed her way back up to the thalamus, trying to imagine those tiny little chemicals from Dr. Santo's literary journals. She swept her influence through the cerebrospinal fluid, but it was a net meant to catch fish, not prawns, and though she could push and pull at the fluid, salt or embitter it with latent instinct, she could not grasp at those neuro signalers that the modern journals had praised. She could rake her influence through the blood, the thalamus, through every last inch of his cranium, and still never see the microscopic processes that Theuman doctors exalted. Because that wasn't what heartsoothing was meant to do.

Frustrated, she snapped her hand away, feeling the rise of annoyance—and a little bit of panic, incurred by the fear of having to leave the Congmi manor with nothing to show for it. Deflating, Nhika watched the entrance, waiting for her grandmother to emerge from the door and give her an answer. She'd never learned how to heal something so foreign before, not without another heartsooth to guide her. But her grandmother wasn't here, and neither were her ancestors, and the ring that hung around her neck was just a cold band of onyx and bone.

Hesitantly, her eyes flicked to the books, stacked beside the bed. They entranced her as whale songs did, lyrical and dangerous, a call to the deep unknown. From Kochin, they served as a threat. But, what if he wasn't the masked man? What if these books hadn't come as a warning, but as a peace offering?

Nhika drew the first book off the stack and let it fall open. Hand-drawn images, colored in by pastels, reimagined anatomy using the paths of influence, the networks that a heartsooth took to navigate the body. Many of the sentences were in Theuman, but the images were all labeled in Yarongese characters she didn't recognize. She longed to understand those most of all, to learn the true name of the brain, the liver, the lungs. To know that word, *heartsooth*, as it sounded on the Yarongese tongue.

Once Nhika started reading, she couldn't stop. As she continued, it felt as though the words had been written to her, a love letter to whatever heartsooths remained in this city, an author fervently journaling the last of their art. Did this author know their words would reach her, perhaps the last person who could understand them?

And it was as if they understood her in return. The books taught in the School of the Sixfold, the traditional style of heartsoothing that her grandmother had practiced. That was back when heartsoothing had structure and tutelage, before Daltanny. While her grandmother had always insisted on the Sixfold and its six "rights," those were a privilege Nhika hadn't had on the streets. So, she'd always skipped the traditional steps, the permission and intimacy. She'd just carved, and carved, and carved.

Inexplicably, Nhika found herself crying. She set the book away as the tears came, afraid they'd run the ink. It'd been so long since she'd cried that she'd thought her tears spent, withered on the day of her mother's death. But here they came again, unbidden but not unwelcome, and she wasn't sure if they came from happiness or longing or sadness—or from the overwhelming sensation of being seen, for the first time in years. It all came from this author chronicling the technicalities of their art, a heartsooth from a life before hers who may never have foreseen the descent of their shared culture.

Did they know what their words meant to her? Did they know how she pored over every misspelled word, every aberrant stroke? Some of it was in a language she couldn't fully read, the language passed only between her mother and grandmother. But as she patched together recognizable characters and radicals, a clumsy mimic of the language returned to her, and Nhika felt closer to her family than she ever had before.

Just earlier, she'd prayed that her grandmother would arrive with answers; well, here she was now, a hand pressed over Nhika's shoulder, a breath near her ear, a finger tracing the words over her shoulder as Nhika read.

"It's okay, *khun*," she whispered. "I know you couldn't practice heartsoothing the way I did, the way our family did. I know that this city gave you no choice. It's not your fault."

Lip trembling, Nhika glanced up to meet her grandmother's eyes. "Have I lost touch with our family legacy, Grandma?"

Her grandmother's eyes were kind, warm the way embers were. "Never, Nhika. Legacy is not about us. It's about the things we leave behind. I passed heartsoothing on to you. One day, you will pass it on to another. It doesn't matter if it's not the same kind that I practiced, or that my mother practiced. Heartsoothing is ever changing. To remember it at all . . . That would be enough."

Then, it wasn't just her grandmother filling the room, but her mother. Her father. The faceless matriarchs before them, each sliver of bone in her ring coming alive at the bedside before her.

"See, Nhika?" her mother said, expression aglow, body untouched by disease. "We never left you."

"How do I heal him?" Nhika asked to all of them and none of them.

"Nhika, my love, it's like I always said." Her grandmother smiled, fingers grazing Nhika's cheek with a lifelike warmth. "Heartsoothing was never meant to be learned out of a book."

That's where she'd been wrong all this time; healing—the way her grandmother had learned it, the way the heartsooths before had taught it—was an intimate act of connection, the bridge from one to another. All that science was only secondary. As soon as she'd had that epiphany, the rest of the answers fell into place like tumblers aligning in a picked lock.

Within seconds she was on her feet, racing toward the door. She faltered as she neared it, taking one last look at her family—not memories, but spirits. Somehow, Nhika knew that this was not the end, that she would see them again soon. For now, her task at hand weighed on her, and she had to leave them.

With that knowledge heavy against her heart, she went to Andao's study. Behind the door, she heard the muffled conversation of both the siblings and Trin, their tone grave despite the dim hour.

"It was Mr. Ngut who talked with him on the phone that night," came Mimi's voice. "I'm sure of it. They were arguing about the engine patent."

"Killing Father doesn't retract the patent." Andao's voice was tired.

Trin cleared his throat. "But it could prevent it from being renewed."

"What about Mr. Nem?" Mimi suggested.

Again, Andao offered skepticism. "Why murder a man you've always been so vocal about contending?"

If there was one thing Nhika looked forward to, it was putting their conspiracies to rest. She stepped into the study, the creak of the floorboard heralding her arrival. Even before she pushed open the doors, all three of them were already looking her way.

"I'm ready," she announced with all the gravitas such a statement deserved. "I'm going to heal Hendon tonight."

— ❧ —

Where the ghosts of her family had stood just before, now sat the siblings and Trin around the bedside. Hendon lay between them all, unresponsive, and neither of the Congmis nor Trin looked particularly hopeful. But they didn't understand what the heartsooth books had given her.

"I've had a breakthrough," she said, reluctant to admit the true nature of her revelation. "The heartsooths before me, they didn't learn from textbooks or publications. They learned off other people."

They returned blank stares until Mimi spoke up. "So, what does that mean?"

"It means . . ." This was the part that Nhika was begrudging. "It means that if you want me to heal him, I need access to a healthy template."

"As in . . . ?" Mimi's expression was imploring.

"As in, one of us?" Trin said.

Nhika set her brow. "Yes. One of you."

She waited, but no one volunteered. They only stared, muted, as if she weren't the same person they'd shared their roof with for weeks. As if she asked them to lay themselves bare on an operating table, awaiting her knife. Annoyance rose in her throat and she opened her mouth to say as much, but Mimi interrupted her.

"I'll do it," she offered, lifting her chin as though paying tribute.

"No," Andao interjected. "I'm the eldest. I'll do it."

"I was the one who brought her here from the Butchers' Row," Mimi countered. "It should be me."

Nhika watched them throw themselves before the knife, at once amused and irked that they treated it like some valiant sacrifice, as if they expected their anatomies to be irrevocably altered by her touch. But, through the siblings' bickering, Trin met her eye and drew off his gloves.

She raised a tentative brow.

He extended his hand. "If you're looking for a template, I resemble Hendon most, physically. That should help, right?"

Nhika wasn't sure, but she didn't argue with his logic. As Mimi and Andao watched, eyes bugged, Nhika reached out and slipped her hand into Trin's. The instinctive twitch of his fingers did not go unnoticed, but his expression remained stalwart.

"I'm not going to hurt you, you know," she said.

It took him a moment to respond, but when he did, his tone

was reassured. "I know." Trin took a breath, his shoulders falling and fingers slacking on the exhale, and she recognized the look in his eyes: trust. Only once he nodded permissively did she begin to soothe.

Nhika pictured the drawings in the books, overlaying them with what she felt in Hendon's mind. She didn't imagine the thalamus as that nebulous region like the anatomists had drawn it. Instead, it was a bridge that her own influence crossed, the wind it caught into a lightning storm. She saw it not as a physical space, but as a current at her ankles, compelling her forward into the cortex. And when she did, it opened to her in color—a relay station of signals like a skein unspooled, with her standing at the center of it, drawn in every direction but allowed to linger. For Hendon, some threads had been snipped with reckless disregard while others were pulled too taut. Signals flared to silence at the end of their journeys, while few circled backward in futile loops. Inlaid in her synesthesia came the anatomy, and now it made itself apparent to her, too: truncated nerves, swollen vessels, bloated tissue.

She hadn't had a moment so beautiful, so colorful, since she'd first started soothing. Just when she'd thought she'd learned all there was to know about the body, another system introduced itself to her, filled in first with color and then with blood, tissue, lymph. Now she was beginning to understand why her grandmother had been so adamant that it was an art, unlike the sciences that Theumans touted around as scripture. Hendon's thalamus was a meticulous knot come undone and tangled, and now that she saw it so tangibly before her, Nhika knew she could fix it.

With an exhale to refocus, Nhika diffused her influence through both Hendon and Trin, at once split and conjoined.

Trin's brain was alight with electricity. She felt it uptick as she nestled herself into his thalamus, but he didn't move. Hendon's, in comparison, was a ghost town, the impulses few and languid when they came, tangling themselves in the snarled structure of his broken anatomy.

The contrast in their bodies was apparent. She'd never soothed two people at once before—Nhika had barely ever soothed anyone awake, other than her family. Who would let her? Now she saw why the heartsooths of the past had chosen this method of learning, why words and drawings could never compare. Trin's body was a blueprint unfurled, and she saw the gaps in Hendon's anatomy plainly when she compared the two. Tissue here, an axon there, blood filled in elsewhere—she perceived the damage from the accident more clearly than she ever had before, felt it throb beneath her influence.

Nhika drew stores from her liver. Her sugar burned, entering her veins and migrating to her fingers where they rested on Hendon's hand. Heat bloomed at the site of transfer, the energy crossing between their bodies as surely as her influence did. She snaked that energy up to the brain, following the spinal arteries, until it flooded Hendon's brain stem.

Then she got to work fixing it, regrowing tissue and mending axons, extending vessels and generating synapses. Trin had relaxed completely under her influence, and soon their structures looked mirrored and almost identical. The only difference was her touch; she'd rebuilt along the skeleton of Hendon's torn structures, stitching together what was already there and grafting on what wasn't. All the while, she fed him a continuous stream of her own sugar until her liver petered toward empty and her stomach flipped, a visceral reminder of her growing hunger.

Her patchwork wasn't perfect. Maybe this was an injury nothing could truly heal, not even heartsoothing, but when she was done, her energy spent, she felt that blockage clear from Hendon's brain, the threads rewired and the center alive. Slow, at first, but she stimulated them with an exhale of electricity. Once she'd started it, his brain no longer needed her help, the electrical storm buzzing back to life before she even pulled her hand away.

Nhika peeled back, arms shaking from the fatigue—that had been too much, taking more than anyone she'd healed before. The tissue growth hadn't been voluminous, but it had been a meticulous and energy-heavy process, and her influence had been split between two bodies. Now she sagged back in her chair, letting out a deflated breath as the world returned to her. Lights, the crinkled silk of her outfit, the quiet snore of Hendon before her.

He was sleeping. This time, it was truly sleep.

Andao was tending to Trin, who blinked wearily as though waking from slumber. Nhika watched him carefully, anxiety rising with her nausea—that she had unknowingly hurt him, that it hadn't been enough to save Hendon, that something had gone wrong in her experimentation.

Then Hendon shifted, the first movement he'd made on his own since she'd been here, and Nhika released a long breath.

"Is he . . . ?" Mimi's voice grew wary with optimism.

"Yes," Nhika said. None but those in the room would know what had transpired tonight—no one could ever learn—but Nhika felt like the world had stopped to watch her. Not Theumas, no, but *her* world: her family above. *See, Ma,* she wanted to say. *I healed him. After long last, I healed him.* Now Nhika could truly claim that title she'd used for herself, heartsooth, and if she were to die tomorrow, a slice of her bone might even belong on her onyx ring, accompanying the heartsooths of the past.

Curtailing her triumph came a wave of nausea, washing over her gut. It deepened as she tried to stand unsuccessfully. "I'm hungry," she said, the simplest way to say that her stores felt bone-dry, her liver puckered, her blood thirsting for sugar.

Andao jumped to his feet. "Of course!" he said, then hesitated a moment, as though remembering he didn't know how to prepare a meal without servants. "Rice crackers. And tea. I'll be back."

Trin and Mimi stayed rooted, both eyeing Hendon. "What did you do?" Trin asked.

"That thalamus we researched, I patched it back. His own brain was struggling to communicate with itself after it was injured in the accident," she said. "As for you, I removed your happiness centers. So, I changed nothing, really."

He blinked a moment before it registered to him as a joke. And Trin laughed. He *laughed*, just a quiet rumble behind closed lips, but a laugh nonetheless. Even Mimi stared at him in surprise, her smile cautious but genuine. She took Hendon's hand in her small, long fingers and held it up to her lips in a kiss that belied a smile. From that kiss, from Trin's laugh, radiated hope, warmth renewed in this cold bedroom. Then came the familiar feeling that Nhika didn't belong here, enveloped by their growing happiness. She'd done her job; she'd get her pay in the morning when Hendon woke. Maybe she'd even milk a parting meal from the Congmis. But she'd healed Hendon, and anything more would be overstaying her welcome.

Her success tonight came tinged with disappointment, and when Andao returned with her crackers and tea she took them, standing too quickly. Nausea roiled across her again, her stomach churning on empty and black swarming her eyes. She'd done it again, spending too much and forgetting herself in her soothing.

Her vision vignetted, the plate slipping from her hand as her feet fell from underneath her. "Somebody catch me," she said, just before she fainted.

— FOURTEEN —

NHIKA DREAMED OF DYING. NOT THE WAY HER family had, nor the way she'd imagined it for herself, but peacefully. Happily. Willingly. Stepping into death as one stepped into an embrace, because there would be her mother on the other side, not yet emaciated by fever; and her father, two feet on firm ground and unclaimed by saltwater.

Her grandmother would be there, too, more than ash, arms wide open.

Nhika stepped forward, but she moved nowhere. Something yanked her back, as firmly as a cord around her waist, but she dragged her feet forward, an arm outstretched.

"Not yet," her grandmother said. "You've life yet to live." She held the expression Nhika remembered most from her, stern but doting, at once a display of love and caution.

Then Nhika flew backward into sudden wakefulness, heart drumming against her ribs and lights blearing her vision. Languidly, her surroundings came to her: the tucked covers she'd just pulled out, a clunky medical device assembled on one side of her bed, and a hazy figure pulled up on the other.

Nhika blinked away her fogginess, and the figure's features sharpened to form Dr. Santo, sleeping in a chair beside her bed with his arms crossed, collar unbuttoned, and spectacles sliding down his nose.

"Dr. Santo," she said, her voice haggard. She cleared her throat and tried again. "*Dr. Santo*."

He startled awake, fumbling to push up his glasses, and blinked at her in surprise, looking almost as dazed as she was.

"Oh, what a relief," he sighed. "You're awake."

"Is Kochin here?" Nhika asked groggily. Wherever Dr. Santo was, Ven Kochin was sure to follow, and Nhika wasn't sure she had the wits to confront Kochin at the moment.

Thankfully, Dr. Santo shook his head. "The siblings called me—said you fainted."

Only then did she realize it was completely dark outside and the catheter dangling from the medical machine traced back into her arm. Nhika shuddered, now sensing the extraneous fluid mingling with her blood. Her body bucked at the thought, and she moved to yank the cords from her skin, but Dr. Santo leaped up to stop her.

"Careful, now," he admonished. "Let me take care of that."

Nhika stiffened, hand still wrapped around the catheter. She hadn't been in the care of another in years, and never in a true physician's. But she relented, watching him round her bedside and take her IV.

"Where are the siblings?" Nhika asked, remembering Hendon. She hadn't stayed conscious long enough to see him wake and worried what he'd be like when he did.

"They're across the hall." Dr. Santo removed the catheter with experienced hands—she barely felt a thing—and pressed a wad of gauze against her skin. She could've healed it herself, but she let herself be cared for by him, because that was such a rare feeling, to be healed by another.

"Nhika," he began, drawing her thoughts back. "While you were asleep, there was a miracle."

Her eyes lit up in hopeful expectation. In her silence, he elaborated, "Hendon woke out of his coma."

"He did? He's okay?" Nhika asked, her breath shuddering, and realized that all the muscles of her shoulder had been tensed in anticipation.

"He's . . . better than we could have hoped for." Dr. Santo's word choice was noncommittal, and her brow furrowed with concern. In a rush, he added, "It'll just take time."

"A miracle," she murmured, repeating his words from earlier. As Dr. Santo bandaged her arm, a part of her rejoiced that he would consider it such, that she had beaten him to the cure, and a part of her was disappointed that that's all he'd ever consider it. Just a miracle, not an act of heartsoothing.

"Can I see him?" she asked, lifting herself out of bed as soon as Dr. Santo had patched her up. Without waiting for an answer, she tipped herself forward onto wobbling legs, searching for balance against the bedside. Dr. Santo quickly lent a hand, but she waved off his assistance, already feeling her strength return.

An unfamiliar laugh came from the room across the hall. Nhika staggered toward the door, still dressed in a nightgown. She sourced the laughter to Hendon's room—then came more of it: Mimi's tinkling laugh, Andao's breathy one, Trin's quiet chuckle. Still there was another's, deep and honeyed, one she knew—hoped, *prayed*—was Hendon's, but didn't confirm until she pushed open the door.

There he was, dressed and sitting up in bed, face flushed pink with life. There were still things she saw to heal; his hands tremored as he held a teacup. He looked thinner now that he was out of blankets, cheeks sallow and skin waxy. But he was upright, talking, *laughing*.

The room silenced as all eyes turned to her. Nhika held Hendon's stare with the wariness of a street cat, but after a tense pause, Mimi broke the silence.

"Nhika!" she cried, and before Nhika could greet her, she'd bounded across the room and wrapped her arms around her in a tight hug. Nhika's chest collapsed, either from the strength of Mimi's embrace or the surprise of being touched or from the relief that it had *worked*, and she'd healed a man, not through Theuman techniques but through heartsoothing.

Mimi pulled away, as though suddenly remembering decorum, and brushed smooth the wrinkles from her blouse. She cleared her throat, eyes suddenly bashful. "Thank you, Uncle Shon. We were all so worried."

Dr. Santo bowed his head in welcome. "It was just a fainting spell, it seems. A few days of rest should be all she needs."

Or a big breakfast, Nhika thought. Everyone was still looking at her as though she were the miraculous recovery, but she stared directly at Hendon. She opened her mouth, trying to find the words to ask if he felt the impression of her touch, or if it was nothing more than medicine to him.

"Suon Ko Nhika, I presume," he said instead, and she

nodded. "And Shon." His words were lucid, at least, and his memory seemingly intact.

"That's right, Hendon," Mimi said, beaming.

"But, Quan, he's . . ."

Andao shook his head. "Gone."

Hendon thinned his lips into a frown. "I keep asking, hoping the answer will change, that I've remembered incorrectly."

"And what do you remember, Hendon?" Dr. Santo pulled a chair up to Hendon's bedside, taking a doctorly position as he had with Nhika earlier.

With a long sigh, Hendon shook his head, as if the act of recollecting pained him. With an ounce of panic, Nhika worried she'd erased something in using Trin as a template, had left something unrepaired. But he responded, "Only bits and pieces, here and there."

"Can you recall the year?"

"1016."

"And the month?"

"The Third."

"And . . . the events leading up to the accident?"

Hendon winced, a distant look coming over his eyes. "I . . . I don't remember every detail. In fact, it's all a bit hazy. But I know Quan and I were headed to the Cat Borough for his exhibition. The cars wouldn't start, so I had the staff tack up the horses." He paused, brow scrunched and bald head beaded with sweat. "I remember starting on the journey, but no more after that."

"Do you remember going around the bend?" Mimi pressed. "That's where the carriage rolled."

Hendon's wrinkles deepened. "I . . . maybe. Yes, you're right, I lost control of the horses. They sped."

"Why? What spooked them?"

He crushed his eyes shut. "A . . . a wolf, maybe? Or . . . I might've heard a gunshot, a stray bullet. Hunters, somewhere?" Nhika frowned—in all her time living here, she'd never seen a wolf in the city.

"Was it a stray bullet, or an intentional one?" Mimi persisted.

"Mimi," Dr. Santo chided. "It's all right, Hendon. It'll come in time."

Hendon's fatigue returned suddenly, overtaking his earlier liveliness, but Nhika knew that none of his ailments could be soothed away—not the deep wrinkles in his forehead, nor the hollowness of his cheeks, nor the thinness of his wrists.

"Mimi, is there something I don't understand?" Hendon asked, and she gave him a crestfallen look.

"Well, I . . . We . . . We thought that . . ." Her voice trembled, nearing tears.

Nhika opened her mouth to finish the thought for her, but Dr. Santo was faster. "They suspect that Quan was murdered."

"Murdered?" Shock inflected Hendon's expression, weak considering his condition. "I'm sorry, Mimi. I . . . If you were hoping I would wake with any answers, I've disappointed you."

Nhika watched Mimi's face, finding a combination of defeat and understanding. It should've been a good thing, hearing that their father hadn't been murdered, but there was sadness that came with the alternative: that it was just an accident. That, for all his wealth and ingenuity, their father could still be stolen from them by fate's whim. Death was, after all, the ultimate equalizer.

Andao clapped his hands together, dispelling the solemnity that had settled with Hendon's words. "Perhaps we should go to sleep," he suggested, trying in vain to put on an optimistic smile. "It's been an exciting night. I think we all deserve some rest."

With varying degrees of agreeability, they all nodded. After exchanging their good nights, the group dispersed: the siblings to their rooms, Nhika to hers, and Dr. Santo to his home.

Nhika didn't realize how tired her bones were until she was back under her comforter, her muscles weak. Now that Hendon was healed, and the conspiracies had amounted to nothing substantial . . .

That was the end of her involvement, wasn't it? Tomorrow, she would get her pay and prepare to leave this manor. That saddened her more than it should've.

She let the heaviness in her chest drag her to sleep.

— ⚬↭⚬ —

When Nhika went down to the breakfast table the next morning, it felt as though the happenings of the manor had resumed after the funeral: Andao signed checks at the table and Trin sifted through a stack of contracts, both ignoring their rice porridge. There was also the addition of Hendon, sitting in the seat that Nhika normally took. Cautiously, she found a new space at the table, across from the rest of the family.

"Nhika," Hendon said, straightening. "I wanted to thank you. The siblings told me what you did and . . . what you are."

Nhika frowned. "Oh, we're telling everyone, now?"

Mimi gave her an apologetic look. "I just thought he should know who healed him."

"When they told me it was a bloodcarver, I almost didn't believe it. I always thought that bloodcarvers didn't exist in Theumas, so it's been . . . an honor."

An honor? That was new, and Nhika realized this was the first time any of her clients had ever thanked her. "Heartsooth," she said, because she felt they deserved to know its true name. "In my culture, we call ourselves heartsooths."

They all looked at her appreciatively and she could almost imagine herself here, sitting at this table, for many dinners to come—until Andao tapped his pen against the checkbook.

"Speaking of which, we should figure out the cost of your services," he said.

Her spirits fell at his formality. "Right."

"The original agreement was one thousand chem, but considering how long you've spent with us, I think it's only appropriate to match it in price. Three weeks, at an average physician's salary . . . What is that, roughly twenty thousand chem?"

At that, her mouth hung open. Twenty thousand chem, an amount that she'd once only dreamed about, an amount that could keep her stomach full and blood fed for an entire year. She should've jumped at the sum, should've taken all that chem and sprinted from a manor that brought only funerals and speculations of murder, but instead, she felt her heart drop at its suggestion. The Congmis had fed and welcomed her best they could—the Butchers' Row had been a rough start, but she realized she'd never wanted for anything more while she stayed here. As soon as she reintroduced the language of chem, this relationship would mirror the one she'd shared with all her previous clients: a transaction, and nothing more.

Mimi tugged at her brother's cuff. "Wait a minute, Andao. Have some consideration. Dr. Santo suggested she rest—let's have her stay until at least the dinner party."

"Stay?" Nhika echoed, ashamed at how her hopes leaped at the suggestion. And then, "Dinner party?"

Andao nodded thoughtfully. "An event to celebrate Hendon's recovery."

Nhika gave him a skeptical look. "Are you sure that's the smartest idea? What with . . ."

She wasn't sure why she was entertaining their conspiracies anymore, but Andao said, "We live very public-facing lives. Such an event is expected."

"Besides, Hendon doesn't recall anything worrisome," Trin added.

"And if our suspicions still hold merit, perhaps the dinner will be enough to scare our perpetrator into showing themselves," Mimi finished. So, they'd already discussed this together.

"Sounds dangerous," Nhika thought aloud.

"Well, if anything happens, we do know a blood—I mean, a *heartsooth*—we can employ."

Nhika wanted to warn them that there were some afflictions she couldn't heal, death being one of them. The siblings seemed to be getting a little too comfortable using her ability as a cure-all.

But all the more reason for her to stay, right? "I'd be happy to stick around," she said, flashing an eager grin. She glanced at Trin, expecting him to make some skeptical comment, but he only smiled.

Andao closed his checkbook. "If that's the case: Mimi, can you send for the tailor for her dress?"

"I'll take care of it."

"Out of curiosity," Nhika interjected, "who might be in attendance?"

"Those who know Hendon," Andao said. "Father's business associates and family friends."

And certain physician's aides? Nhika wanted to ask, but she didn't, thinking instead of the heartsooth books on her nightstand. She had unresolved business among this company.

And his name was Ven Kochin.

— FIFTEEN —

IN THE WEEK LEADING UP TO THE DINNER, THE manor saw unending activity: business associates walking in and out of Andao's office, tailors coming to take measurements and test color swatches against Nhika's golden-brown skin, and staff scrambling to ready meals and tea for guests. Suon Ko Nhika returned to life, and now she was glad she had cemented her backstory for how often she made small talk with visitors. Only then did she understand why the siblings valued discretion so much; this manor hardly felt like it belonged to them now that it had resumed full business.

Today, the staff polished the halls and cleared the office space in preparation for a scheduled appointment with Nem. Nhika caught snippets of gossip in the air; the man had a reputation of abrasiveness, so Andao's office quarters were void of staff when he finally did come, carrying with him an aura of authority.

Not even Trin accompanied Andao and Nem in the office, and Nhika found him lingering just down the hall, pacing back and forth, brow creased with anxiety. He only ceased when he caught sight of her.

"Here to eavesdrop again, are you?" he asked.

"No," she lied. "Why aren't you with him?"

"I should be," he said quickly, then sucked in a breath as though those words had slipped past him. More deliberately, he added, "I support Andao in everything I can, but there are some things he needs to do alone."

"What is he going to say to Nem?"

Trin let out a slow sigh, shaking his head. "I'm not sure if even he knows that yet." He let his shoulders fall, the tension loosening from the sharp ridge of his jaw, and said, "I've actually been meaning to talk to you."

From his flat tone, Nhika wasn't sure what to prepare for—a lecture or a request. Trin continued, "I wanted to say . . ." He cleared his throat, as though the rest of his sentence had lodged there. "I wanted to say thank you. I hadn't gotten much of a chance earlier, but it's been long overdue."

A thank-you from Trin? Nhika cocked her brow, waiting for the other shoe to drop.

"And . . ." These words seemed to pain him even more than the last. "I'm sorry. For the way I treated you when you first arrived at the manor. I should never have treated you with anything but civility."

A thank-you *and* an apology? Perhaps her soothing had broken him after all.

"Thank you," she returned, "for letting me use you as a template to heal Hendon. It was . . . brave."

"No, it wasn't." He shook his head, lips thin. "Or, I mean, it shouldn't have been. Because I think, deep down, I knew you wouldn't do me harm."

Nhika had to smile at his honesty. She also had to wonder

where it was all coming from—Trin, of everyone in the manor, had always been the most reserved around her.

"You know, Dr. Santo mentioned something funny to me," she began, recalling a conversation from long ago. "He said that you'd once tried to steal from Mr. Congmi." She watched his expression, waiting for any reaction.

As expected, his expression yielded little, other than the hint of a smirk. "Did he?"

"He said that Mr. Congmi caught you, and instead of sending you to a juvenile cell where your law-breaking self belonged, he made the questionable decision of putting you through college."

"Those were Dr. Santo's exact words?"

"I'm paraphrasing."

"Well . . ." Trin shifted, sticking gloved hands into his pockets. "It's true."

Nhika always knew it had to be, but her mouth still fell open with surprise.

"Nhika, I can tell that you want to stay here. And I understand where you're coming from because I was there, too, once upon a time. Walking in on all this luxury and comfort, watching this unbroken family from afar, and never thinking it could be mine. But Mr. Congmi was kind, and so are his children. If you want to stay, we can make it happen."

Nhika watched him with new regard; he'd read her like an open book when she'd thought she'd been so closed, and hope rose at his words. Until he added, "But it has to be honest work, of course—no more secret gifts and sneaking around."

With that, her spirits fell. Trin was right that he was just like her, but there was one thing he'd never be able to understand—the need to use a gift like heartsoothing. He could clean himself up, throw on a suit and dress pants, get a university education, and be a perfect addition to the Congmi family.

Nhika, on the other hand . . . No matter how much makeup and silk she put on, how far up her arms she pulled these gloves, Nhika would never be able to change the fact that she was a heartsooth. Despite that, she had the favor of the most influential family in Theumas, and a position in Dr. Santo's lab awaited her after all this. Was that enough to find a place here, heartsoothing and all?

Because he'd given her his honesty, she gave him some in return. "I appreciate it, Trin. I really do. These past few weeks have been the first time I haven't felt alone in a long time. That has been worth more to me than the chem—though, you're still going to pay me."

"Of course."

"After the dinner party is sorted out, maybe I could—"

Before she could finish her sentence, the door to Andao's study burst open. This time, Nem had no alcohol on which to blame his rage, but it rolled off him in waves. "War is coming, Andao," he said, the threat in his voice loud enough to carry down the hall. "We'll see if you change your tune when you have something to lose."

Nhika figured Andao must've refused to endorse his war. Nem stalked down the hall toward them, and Nhika—never so afraid of anyone—drew behind Trin by instinct.

"I'll escort you to your autocarriage," Trin offered in a

palliative tone, and led Mr. Nem down the hall. As they turned the corner, Nhika caught Nem's eyes, finding a tumult of displeasure pounding behind them.

Then he rounded the corner and disappeared from view.

Nhika glanced back at the door of the study, which remained as open as an invitation. Maybe Andao meant for Trin to come in; instead, she took it upon herself in Trin's absence.

Just inside, Andao sat with his chair swiveled toward the window. She knocked and he promptly turned around, looking like he expected someone else.

"Nem sounded angry," she said, if only to shatter the heavy silence between them.

Andao waved a hand like he was trying to force indifference. The tightness of his shoulders betrayed him. "Mr. Nem has a hot temper, but he never sits on his grudges for long."

"I take it you turned down his offer?"

He nodded, then gestured for her to have a seat. She made herself comfortable in one of his armchairs. "I told him that I could not, in good conscience, use my pacifist father's capital to fund a war campaign."

"Ah," she said, and the silence settled again. He seemed deflated in that chair, trying to fill a seat too large for him.

For a moment, neither of them said anything, and Nhika wondered why her feet had taken her in here—to console? To gather more secrets? Then Andao asked, "Does your culture believe in an afterlife?"

She glanced up at him. He'd never paid much interest to her personal life before, even when they invented her background;

it had always been business between the two of them. "Yes," she replied. But Nhika wasn't sure if *she* believed in one.

"I'm glad I don't," he admitted. "I don't know if I could live with the idea of Father seeing me now."

"Why's that?"

He took a moment to find his words. "I lost him so quickly, and so unexpectedly, that I never had a chance to ask him how I was meant to carry on his memory."

His words touched on a depth of sadness Nhika understood so intimately, because hadn't she lost her grandma the same way? All she had left was a cobbled-together form of heart-soothing, one her grandma might never have approved of. Nhika was almost surprised to find those feelings mirrored in Andao, who was so Theuman where she was so Yarongese. "I would imagine your father didn't create his empire just so you could carry on his memory. Maybe he gave you all of this so you had the freedom to live for yourself."

He gave her a thoughtful look, as though surprised to find such words coming out of a bloodcarver's mouth. "Maybe so. Sometimes, it's just that his legacy feels so much larger than me, than my wants and whims." He sighed, a tacit request to table the conversation.

Trin returned at that moment, knocking on the door to draw their attention. "Are you all right, Andao?" he asked, brows laced with concern.

Andao's apprehension melted. "I am now."

It seemed she was forgotten; Nhika took that as her prompt to leave, passing Trin on her way out of the office. She caught a snippet of their conversation just before she drew out of earshot:

"You did the right thing, love."

"It was an easy choice with you beside me—but Mr. Nem is right. I don't know how I'd act in a world where you were endangered."

A breathy laugh. "Hey, aren't I the one meant to protect you?"

So that was love, then? Nhika thought. *The things we protect and the people we can't live without?*

She pondered it as she walked away.

Hendon's celebratory dinner loomed on the horizon. Between the bustle of cooks preparing the banquet and the clamor of servants tidying the house, the week came to a quick end, and the Congmis opened their foyer and dining rooms to a moderate company of aristocrats. Where guests had once dressed in black-and-white funeral attire, now they came in dazzling gowns and prim suits, and Nhika saw, for the first time since she'd arrived in the back of the hearse, the highest echelon of fashion their money could afford. Women wore headdresses like crowns, as though the very sun were setting upon their hair, and their dresses were threaded in gold and silver. Those in suits wore them with taste, the buttons and cuffs emblazoned with seals of their family name, their company, or whatever piece of their industry they particularly wanted to show off tonight. Everyone took liberties with their gloves, too: some patterned like snakes or dragons, coiling up the arm; others sheer and laced, having forgotten the original intention of gloves; and a few of them feathered and bejeweled, as much a part of a cohesive outfit as jewelry or shoes might've been.

She'd thought she'd fit in tonight, wearing the dress Mimi had gotten tailored for her—dark red, high collared, and slit tastefully at the hip to reveal the lustrous purple of her pants—but her gown still looked humble compared to others. With no need to imitate mourning on this occasion, no one had held back an ounce of extravagance.

As she descended the stairs into the midst of the company, Nhika's eyes scanned the crowd, looking for that familiar sweep of hair, the midnight eyes, the smile that was half charm, half wit. Ven Kochin.

She didn't find him before she reached the main foyer, slipping into the crowd. Instead, she found many guests who had attended the funeral, hardly recognizable behind their new makeup and finery. There was Mr. Ngut, speaking with Andao over finger foods. And then Dr. Santo, entertaining some of the Congmis' younger cousins as their parents stole away for a glass of rice wine. Even Mr. Nem was in attendance, and Andao must've been right about the capriciousness of his grudges—he seemed placated here, taking advantage of the open bar.

But no Kochin.

Just then, the hum of conversation and laughter quieted, and Nhika followed everyone's gazes up to the mezzanine. Hendon stood at the top, gloved hand curled aggressively around the banister as he struggled down the stairs. Trin was beside him, shouldering his weight with each step, and as they reached the bottom of the stairs, the crowd swelled to greet them. There were a series of *Congratulations!* and *You look well*'s, but as everyone was watching Hendon, Nhika was watching the guests.

"I suppose I was wrong," came a familiar voice beside her, and Nhika whirled to find Kochin standing there, as though he'd materialized out of thin air. In place of his usual vest suit, he wore a midnight-blue tunic, beautifully embroidered in silver—nothing so flashy as other guests, but simply elegant. She imagined, then, a fox mask fitted over his sharp jaw, a black robe thrown over those shoulders. The image aligned all too well.

Nhika steeled herself; she'd tried so hard to look for him, but it would seem he found her first. "To which instance are you referring? There are too many to count."

"Girls in rags *can* walk into silk overnight." He smiled, falsely charming. "And they can wear it as though it suits them."

"It does suit me," she said.

Kochin's eyes narrowed as they glided over her dress. "Yes, it does."

Somehow, even his compliments felt like hidden jabs. "I expected to find you here," she said, trying to be every ounce as ominous as he always was. "I've been meaning to talk to you."

Looking more eager than put off, he tilted his head toward a quiet corner for conversation, a hallway offshoot from the foyer.

She let him guide her there, but no farther; Nhika would not let him get her alone on his pretense.

"The books," Nhika said, folding her arms. "They were in Yarongese. This may come as a surprise, but I can't read Yarongese."

"You can read pictures, can't you?"

"Couldn't make heads or tails of them."

"I thought you might find them interesting anyway."

"What gave you that impression?"

"A hunch." They were both playing games now—they both knew what those books were, but neither would say it aloud.

"I can't very well understand them, so they're worthless to me," she lied, though it pained her to spurn the very objects that had made her feel found. "Where did you find them, anyway?"

"I collect things," he said, shrugging innocently. *Things like heartsooths?* she wondered. "Consider them a gift."

Kochin was layered in discrepancy: flirting with heartsooth accusations but foregoing gloves as if Nhika weren't one; pushing her out of high society through cryptic words and concealed warnings but seeking her out at every opportunity; giving her heartsooth books, as damning as any accusation, and acting as if they were nothing more than a gift.

"*Why?*" she pressed. Her eyes drilled into him. "Why did you give me those books, Kochin?" She was past the games, her desperation showing in the strain of her voice.

Like a mask dropped, his expression hardened; the softness of his charm melted away from her eyes, his smile. Nhika might've

204 —

been afraid if not for the reassuring proximity of the party, but there came a verity in his eyes that was almost . . . relieving. It was a promise that no matter how he played with his words, his next ones were truthful: "Because you needed them."

Her heart stalled. Was that an indictment? The fox mask had never looked more fitting over his face, because how else could he know what she was with such certainty? "Needed them? For what?" She put on her best guise of innocence but wondered if it was futile.

Instead of any heartsooth allegations, he said, "To remind you that you don't belong here. That beneath this dress, no matter how ornate or expensive, there's some unchangeable part of you that this society will never accept. Whatever you may think of me, I don't mean it as an insult."

It was the most she'd ever gotten from him, and he said it with such surety, as if he'd seen the rise and fall of those like her before. As if her estrangement from the world of manors and banquets was already a foregone conclusion.

Nhika wanted to ask how he could be so confident that he knew her when he was Theuman aristocracy and she was a Yarongese heartsooth. When he could be Dr. Santo's aide, healing the way Theumas accepted healers, while she had to hide her art behind homeopathy. When he might be tired of this city, these glittering people and their shining inventions, but she still yearned to break in.

"I'll try not to take it as one," she said, and she must not have sounded all too convincing, because his brows knit with a subtle disappointment.

Kochin shook his head, the candor in his expression drawing back. "If you truly don't want those books, I'll take them back." He borrowed a napkin and a pen from a passing waitress. Using his palm as a writing surface, he scrawled something down on the napkin. "But, not during work hours. Tomorrow, sixteenth hour. This address."

He held out the napkin and she hesitated to take it when she saw the address: 223 Gento St. Pig Borough. A city away from the pearlescent Dragon Borough, sitting next to her very own Dog Borough. A place where she would not expect a boy who could afford suits like his.

At last, she took it and his thumb slipped over her fingers, keeping her gloved hand for a moment in his bare one. "Nhika," he said, his voice lowering, "if there is anything you have left that you don't want to lose, you'll take my words to heart."

Her breath hitched in her throat as he drew back his hand. She clutched the napkin in her palm, finding the ink already bleeding near illegibility.

"I—" A shout from the party interrupted her; it was a half-drunk Dr. Santo, his audience of children growing as he waved Kochin over.

"Duty calls," Kochin said, giving her a deep bow. As he straightened, his eyes held hers for a fraction too long, drawing her in with the same gravity of nebulae. Then Ven Kochin dipped back into the crowd and disappeared.

Long after guests had gone, after the servants had swept and polished the foyer and dining room, Nhika sat awake on her bed in night silks, turning Kochin's napkin over in her palm. By now, she had Kochin's loopy scrawl memorized: 223 Gento St. Pig Borough. A borough in southeast Theumas popular for its outdoor markets and street food carts, but certainly not for its luxury. So why did Kochin want to meet there?

Finding no new answers in the napkin, Nhika tucked it away on the nightstand and herself under the covers.

She hadn't gotten far into drowsiness when a pained scream pierced the air. In seconds she was on her feet, following the cry to Hendon's room. The door was unlocked, and she burst inside, only to find Hendon still in bed, the covers thrown to the floor.

Rushing to his side, she looked for any sign of forced entry. When she found none, she looked for any injury on him. Nothing but a glean of sweat across his skin, the intense furrow of his brow. He let out another cry and she realized it was not an intruder, but a night terror.

"Hendon," she said, rattling his shoulder. "Wake up."

He didn't rouse, and she placed a hand on both shoulders to give him a solid shake. "*Wake up*."

His eyes flew open and his limbs flailed, a limp fist catching her across the jaw. She stumbled backward against his wooden room divider. He panicked against phantom assailants, arms thrashing with surprising strength.

"Hendon, it's me, Nhika!" she said, but that seemed only to

inflame his frenzy. He cowered from her on his bed, breath hiking up in speed.

"No . . . please . . . *don't touch me!*" he managed between gasps, and Nhika was hurt until she saw his delirium. He was addressing something beyond her, apparitions in the night.

"You're in the Congmi manor. You're *safe*," she said, and only then did lucidity creep into his eyes.

Everything about him settled but for his chest, still heaving with breaths, and he drew himself upright through wooden motions. With growing alertness, he assessed the room—the blanket on the floor, his abused pillows, and Nhika standing pressed against the wall.

"Nhika?" he said, as though he didn't recognize the name. Then, more surely: "Nhika . . ."

"Are you okay, Hendon?" Again, she feared a mistake in her own heartsoothing, feared the consequences of experimentation her grandmother had always warned her about.

But Hendon seemed to be coming slowly into clarity, blinking away his nightmares. She still kept her distance, wary of another stray fist.

"I . . . What happened?" he asked.

"It was just a dream."

He shook his head vehemently, his brow knit with labor. "No, not a dream. Blood, a wound in my chest, and . . . you, standing there."

Her lips thin, Nhika shook her head, feeling almost mournful—were these scattered memories her doing? "I wasn't there, Hendon."

He pressed his eyes shut. "But I thought I saw . . ." His words came out nearly delirious, on the edge of mania. "A wolf."

"A wolf?"

When Hendon opened his eyes, they held dread. "Someone was there, the night Quan died. Someone in a mask—but not a wolf. It was . . . a fox."

— SIXTEEN —

ALL IN NIGHT LINENS AND VARYING STATES OF drowsiness, the Congmis, Trin, and Nhika collected around Hendon's bed. They brought him tea and warm towels, listening intently as he began again with growing clarity.

"We started around the bend when a gunshot spooked the horses off-trail," he said, each word laborious. "I was flung from the seat. The carriage continued. Rolled down the hill. Everything started going black, and . . ."

"And you saw a man in a fox mask," Nhika said.

He narrowed his eyes at his cup, as though trying to find answers in his tea leaves. "I never said it was a man."

She swallowed—that was her own conjecture, because she knew exactly who had been at the scene. But she hesitated to reveal to the Congmis just what she knew and who she suspected. That meant detailing all of Kochin's hidden threats and snide remarks, and she worried they might not find anything wrong with a Theuman trying to push her out of high society. She needed proof first; accusations came later.

"I knew it," Mimi said. "I *knew* it. There was someone else at the scene, someone who wanted Father dead. It was more than an accident."

"But why go to the lengths of a mask if they were going to frame it as an accident?" Trin wondered aloud.

"Maybe it's as we thought—someone we know. Perhaps someone recognizable. Someone who didn't want to take the chance of being found out," Andao speculated.

"Then why leave a survivor?"

"Does it matter?" Mimi interrupted. "Hendon has just confirmed what we've all been fearing. Father was murdered."

Everything in the room settled for a moment, even dust, as her declaration sank into the hardwood. For the Congmis, surely the revelation brought more questions than answers.

But Nhika had never been so sure of anything: Ven Kochin was the man behind the fox mask. And now he was also Mr. Congmi's murderer.

It was too perfect. How else would he know what she was? Why else would he give her those books and seek her out, at every opportunity, despite her antagonism? Why else would he mock her, warn her, threaten her? She thought back on all their conversations, the words she'd once misconstrued as weapons of an arrogant aide. Now she saw them for the message they were: Leave the Congmis, this society, this city. Leave the murder alone, Hendon comatose. Leave, before she healed the last witness of his crime.

Well, now she had, and Kochin knew full well that Hendon was awake. At the party, he'd warned her to escape if she had anything left that she didn't want to lose. Nhika wondered if he was referring to her life.

Suddenly, her meeting with him tomorrow made sense. The Pig Borough was not a place for aristocratic boys in vest suits, but it was a place where a heartsooth might go missing and no one would bat an eye.

"Do you know who it was, Hendon?" Andao asked, breaking the silence.

Hendon squeezed his eyes shut, wincing as though reliving the memory "I . . . I don't know. Maybe. There was this feeling, something so familiar. The person behind the mask, I know her, I think."

"Her?" Mimi asked.

Something sure set into Hendon's features as he opened his eyes. "Yes, I remember now. The person behind the fox mask, it was . . ." His gaze met Nhika's, filled with new apprehension. "It was you."

Nhika's throat dried as everyone whipped their attention around. "He's . . . confused," she stammered. "Hendon, I told you I wasn't there." Under the heat of their stares, she staggered backward, once again excised from the family.

"You're right," Hendon said, looking pained. "I must be misremembering."

Some of the scrutiny lifted from Andao and Trin, but Mimi's stare was unyielding. "How . . . curious," the girl said, narrowing her eyes as though mulling something new.

"Mimi," Nhika said, her tone cautionary. "I promise, I had nothing to do with the accident. Maybe it was my heartsoothing—implanted false memories, or . . . something. I don't know."

"You knew our father was murdered before we ever told you."

"I overheard your conversation."

"Now that I think about it, what landed you in the Butchers' Row to begin with?"

"Listen to yourself," Nhika snapped, bitterness rising in her throat. "I healed him. Why would I wake him if I'd killed your father?"

That seemed to quiet Mimi. Though she didn't raise any more arguments, Nhika saw a flicker of doubt in her eyes, in the slightest furrow of her brow, and it was enough to spark indignation. Nhika had spent weeks toiling to wake Hendon, only to be repaid with an accusation of murder. She looked to Hendon, to Trin, to Andao, but none of them came to her defense, and she was reminded of how contractual their relationship, how flimsy the trust between them. Trin had offered her a stay, but there was no place for her here.

Perhaps Kochin had been right—no matter what she did, this society, this family, would never truly accept her.

Trin stepped forward, shattering some of the ice between her and Mimi. "It was a nightmare, nothing more," he said, his tone definitive. "We'll all sleep on it and see if the memory still sticks in the morning."

The tension remained in the room, even as they shuffled around; Mimi eyed Nhika, and Nhika eyed Hendon. Beneath her frustration at him—he'd returned her kindness with doubt—there was fear: that she'd done something erroneous in healing him, miswiring his anatomy or leaving his memory shattered.

Her head swarmed with worries as she returned to her room. Nhika stopped in front of her bed, where a napkin lay atop the nightstand.

223 Gento St.

Earlier, she'd debated going. Now she had to, because the

only way to convince Mimi of her innocence was to find Mr. Congmi's true killer, and she knew exactly who it was. Tomorrow, she would see who awaited her at 223 Gento Street: Ven Kochin, physician's aide, or the man behind the fox mask.

— ❦ —

Nhika woke with a sense of finality. Already, it was noon, and she collected herself in the hours that remained. All the while, she avoided the Congmis and Trin, not a difficult task in such a large manor—the next time she faced them, it'd be with their masked man. Still, Mimi's accusation had sank in its teeth, and it clung to her like a leech.

When the time neared, she threw on a quick robe, sashed around the waist; in the Pig Borough, she would stand out in silks. Afterward, she made her way to the Congmis' kitchens, overturning drawers and cabinets until she found a paring knife, just a few inches long, that she fit into her boot. Just in case.

When she returned to her room, she lingered by the door, looking over the space she'd called home for the last few weeks. It was a well-loved place, the bed in a constant unmade state and her clothes piled over the back of an armchair. The realization came bitterly that, depending on who it was she found in the Pig Borough, she might not come back to this place. Nhika paused at the desk. For a moment, her fingers twitched toward the pen and notepad, wondering if it was wise to leave a message. If Kochin was who she believed, and if he could best even her heartsoothing, did she want the siblings to know where she'd gone off and died? Or did she want to follow her family, disappearing from the city like the crest of a wave, there one moment and gone the next?

She decided against it—she was not dying today.

With little ceremony, Nhika left, carrying the bag of heart-sooth books over her shoulder. The knife rubbed against her ankle with every step, a comfort despite her chafing skin.

She took the trolley, slotting a coin into the fare-collecting automaton, which lifted its gate to grant her access. By street-car, no borough was too far from another, not even the Dragon from the Pig Borough. As was everything in Theumas, there was a method to the boroughs, and Nhika observed their strata as she passed through each in turn: the modern buildings of the Cat and Tiger Boroughs, in a process of northern expansion; the industrial brick of the Ox, drawing the line between upper and lower city; the stained facades of the Rat, its tight-packed homes showing the first signs of saltwater damage.

And finally, the Pig Borough. Wide roads and stone-walled lawns had turned into narrow streets, where homes were stacked atop storefronts and broken automatons sat abandoned on doorsteps, their hulls repurposed as cigarette receptacles. Despite their dinginess, these parts came with a sense of comfort—crowds she could disappear in and buildings that looked as weathered as she did, so Nhika didn't fear standing out. But a physician's aide, and certainly one as pretty as Kochin, had no place here.

She hopped off at a stop in front of a pawnshop, checking

the address. The streets were intuitive, and she found herself at the right intersection with ease. From there, she followed the numbers in ascending order.

As she continued, the low, squat bars around her gave rise to towering, cantankerous shophouses, crammed together with little regard for architectural congruity. Broken shutters and cracked colonnades faced the street, bleached by the sun, while languid markets sat at the base of the shophouses, their patrons few and far between. This was where the address led, to a particularly downtrodden pink house wedged between two others.

Nhika checked the number on the shophouse. This was a familiar scene, standing before a stranger's house, not knowing what to expect. The only thing missing was her bag of tinctures and high spirits, replaced by heartsooth books and aching dread.

Nhika lifted her boot, grabbing the knife and shifting it against her wrist, where she concealed it in her sleeve.

She eyed the street clock again; it was a couple minutes past the sixteenth hour. Hitching her breath, she strode forward and knocked on the door.

A moment passed. Then two. After being eyed by some of the neighbors, Nhika considered turning around and leaving, but a lock clicked and the door opened to reveal Kochin.

He was in business attire. She narrowed her eyes, fingers wrapping around the knife. Today, he wore gloves.

"You came," he said, and she found her own trepidation mirrored in his voice. His eyes glimpsed her hands, but the knife was hidden in her sleeve.

"Were you hoping I wouldn't?" she asked, glancing about the

shophouse. Over his shoulder, she could see the emptiness of the shop, whose peeling counters stood empty.

At that, he managed the slightest smile. "No. But you'll have to excuse the location. Sometimes, I find the Dragon Borough . . . suffocating."

Her fingers twitched with anticipation at how he curdled that last word with displeasure. He turned to welcome her inside.

She stepped into the shop, following him as he took her to a door at the back that opened to stairs. These, compared to the rest of the house, were well maintained, but the lonesome door at the top promised tragedy. He walked ahead of her while she stared at the nape of his neck, where skin showed between his collar and his hair. Her thumb rubbed circles against the hilt of the knife in her sleeve, prepared to use it, if need be. All she needed was a sign, any confirmation of malevolence.

Kochin opened the door for her at the top. His expression was grim; she knew her own mirrored it. Was there still a charade between them, or did they both understand what this meeting was intended to be, a confrontation between a murderer and his loose end?

As she stepped inside, the noxious smell of too many animals in too small a space disarmed her senses. Birds came alive at their arrival, and now she saw the room was a stark miniature of the Butchers' Row. Caged animals lined the walls, a variety of mice in glass terrariums and birds in aviaries and guinea pigs circling their pens. But none of these animals were rare or illicit. They were the variety found in a common corner pet shop; she was the strangest thing here.

Then she spotted it, hanging from the coat hook. A mask, painted in the style of traditional theater.

A fox.

Nhika heard the door close behind her, but she stayed deathly still, even as the sound of the lock slid into place. Her heart hammered in her chest, her knuckles white around the hilt of the knife.

"You know, don't you," he said, his voice eerily calm. Nhika dropped the bag of books where she stood. Though she didn't turn to look, she could feel his heat just a couple bounds away, and she flipped her knife out of her sleeve.

"You killed Mr. Congmi," she said, giving words to his insinuation. *Deny it*, she begged. Some part of her, despite the dangling fox mask and the meeting and the heartsooth books, hoped to find a different tune in these notes, a melody that spelled innocence for Kochin and her both. Let those heartsooth books be a gift, and nothing more. Let his words be taken at face value, a physician's aide who'd grown tired of his gilded life and warned her about the same. Let him be innocent, because he'd known what she was all this time, and still planted the kiss on her hand when they'd first met.

She waited for what felt an eternity, the silence stretching the distance between them, but he didn't deny a thing.

That was all she needed. Her fingers clenched around her knife as she whirled around to face him, eyes homing in on the space between his ribs.

He was faster. From his robe he drew a pistol, halting her as he aimed at her chest. She froze with her hand outstretched, the knife a plaything when contesting his pistol. The evening light ringed around the barrel and she saw his dark eyes behind it.

"Nhika, I don't want to hurt you," he warned, thumb fingering the hammer as a threat. But he hadn't cocked it yet, and that gave her time. "Put the knife down."

"Put the *gun* down." Nhika leveled a glare at him, drawing up anger to conceal the fear needling through her skin.

He returned her stare with steeliness, a muscle twinging in his jaw. "I tried to push you away from this."

"But you couldn't." Her voice was tremulous, but it was anger, not fear, that rasped at her throat. Somehow, this felt inevitable, an early and violent death, hidden between the walls of the Pig Borough. But by his hand? Spittle on the grave.

"I can't let you return to the Congmis," he said.

"Are you going to kill me, then?"

Kochin sucked in a breath.

It was all the opening she needed. Nhika lunged toward him, ducking beneath the aim of the gun and redirecting his arm. He stumbled in a moment's surprise as she drove the knife forward. His gloved hand caught her wrist, but not firmly enough; her knife slipped further, where it sank into his abdomen.

Letting out a pained gasp, Kochin staggered backward until she'd slammed him against the wall, the knife plunging deeper. His fingers wrapped around her knife hand, warring for a grip on the hilt, but she held fast. They were a mess of elbows and limbs, her fingers vying for the gun until at last she swatted it from his grip. It skittered across the floor, just out of their reach.

Nhika eyed the sliver of his neck. She snapped out a hand,

but he caught her wrist, grunting as her knife slipped deeper into his gut.

"I will not die by you, Ven Kochin," she seethed. Even as the knife drew deeper, she feared he'd overtake her at the first opportunity. With gritted teeth, he tightened his grip, one hand around her wrist and the other fighting her blade.

For all the bloodcarver rumors and for all Nhika's threats, she'd never taken a human life before. Despite everyone she'd injured and endangered, killing Kochin with the same art she'd used to heal Hendon felt like a violation. Like a revocation of her title, heartsooth. Like an indictment of a different one, *bloodcarver*.

But she would not let Ven Kochin kill her here.

She twisted the knife. Kochin's eyes flared in agony and he sucked in another breath, grip slackening for only a moment. Nhika overpowered him then, fingers latching around his neck, her victorious smile a reminder of what she could do with a touch, of what she was.

Bloodcarver.

Her influence seeped into him, dropped down his throat, curled around his chest. As she tightened her fingers, so too did her influence tighten around his heart, eliciting a stutter there, a threat backed by blood.

"Give me one reason not to kill you here," she demanded, a scowl carved in her lips.

His expression was laced in pain, but there was no fear there. Instead, his eyes were almost . . . calm. "I can't let you end up like me."

A murderer? No, this was not an act of murder; this was

self-defense. She could kill him in an instant: a halted heart-beat, the organ squeezed to burst, or his lungs shriveled clean of air. But her influence stalled with the cadence of his pulse, and Nhika hesitated with her grip around his heart. A question remained unanswered, keeping her fingers from crushing down on his neck: *Why?*

Why keep Hendon alive at the crime scene, but kill her? Why lend her those books when he knew she might use them? Why wait until now to kill her, when Hendon was already awake?

Curiosity be damned; she would not take the risk and die here. Nhika closed her influence around his heart—

And found that she couldn't.

She drew a sharp breath of surprise, feeling the presence of something new: a second influence, contesting her own. Before she could act, a visceral sensation flooded her finger-tips where they curled around his throat, her hands steeped in warmth. It spread up her arm, coursing through her bones and climbing into her muscle. It advanced across tendon and sinew, leaching up her shoulder and washing through her chest. There, it quelled the drumming of her heart and eased the tightness of her shoulders. Nhika felt the instinct to fight it, but it was all the comfort of being held, all the relief of letting her aching muscles rest. It was a familiar feeling, a memory pulled from a childhood she'd forgotten: her heart-soothing lessons, where her grandmother had soothed her muscle by muscle, bone by bone, until Nhika had learned to do it herself.

Kochin was soothing her.

With a jerk, Nhika yanked herself away, his influence snatched back with their sudden disconnect. It took her a moment to blink out of her stupor, but by the time she did, Kochin had retrieved his pistol.

Again, he aimed it at her chest, but his expression was anything but murderous. It was a fragile, devastated thing, lips scrawled in a grimace and eyebrows knit. His hand was clamped around the wound in his abdomen, but he didn't move to heal it.

"You're . . ." Nhika let out a breath. The sentence didn't finish itself. That flaming anger from earlier had eaten itself to embers now, leaving only the ashes of heartache. Because at long last, here he was, a heartsooth like herself, but he stood on the other side of the gun.

"You must hate me," he said. Torment carved itself into his haggard expression and now she saw the pain to be genuine. "I didn't bring you out here to kill you, but I can't have you exposing me to the Congmis. Do you see my predicament?"

He would kill her to hide his secret; she would turn him in to absolve herself. A predicament, indeed.

"Does it mean nothing to you what we are?" Her voice came out small, surprising even herself. She wanted him to lower the gun, not because she was afraid of dying, but because she didn't want *him* to be her killer. Because at long last, she wasn't alone.

His arm faltered, his lips pressed together with a withheld thought. She watched his eyes for her verdict, finding a tempest behind his clouded irises.

"I . . ." His lips remained parted with a half-formed word for just a moment before they closed again.

No words? Here she was, at the end of her rope, and he had nothing more to offer her? "Shoot me, then, but don't aim for the chest. Aim between my eyes. Make it quick, and I won't try to soothe myself." She spat the words out like bitter medicine, and she saw the fracture in his expression.

She lowered her arms, dropping her knife to the floor. A new fatigue dragged its way through her muscles, which still tingled with the longing for his influence again. Now she no longer wanted to fight him. No longer needed to know why he'd done it. Nhika only wanted him to stop looking at her like that, as though pulling that trigger might kill him as much as it would her.

Nhika awaited the pain, not bothering to numb herself because she trusted Kochin would make it quick. If these were her final moments, she wanted to feel something.

But Kochin didn't shoot her. She saw the indecision behind his eyes, and if she could soothe him now, she would not kill him. Instead, she yearned only to understand the thoughts that agonized him. And more than that, she wanted to know why he hesitated.

Did he feel it, too, the loneliness lifted off his chest? They were eclipsing planets, lining up in orbit for just a breath before the death of their star, two whales crossing paths in the desolate vastness of the ocean.

She saw that longing etched in his expression, in the tremble of his arm. So even before his finger withdrew from the trigger, even before he lowered the gun, she knew he would not shoot her. He couldn't.

Kochin set down the gun; Nhika let a withheld breath escape between her lips.

He exhaled, and pinched the bridge of his nose as he collapsed in a chair. "I've spent so long looking for someone like you."

Someone like you. "Yet you would kill me to hide your crime?"

Kochin winced. He was growing paler, and blood trailed him on the ground. "No." He flicked his hand toward the discarded gun. "I don't think I could live with myself if I did." If ever he had been honest with her, it was then, because his tone was touched with a vulnerability that crystallized him in glass, as though a hateful look from her might break him. More questions rose to her tongue, but another wince drew her attention to his wound. The bloodstain still expanded—why didn't he heal himself?

"You're losing blood," she said, if only to take his eyes off her. She couldn't stand how much she saw herself in them.

As though just remembering, Kochin lifted his hand to reveal a bloom of blood across his white dress shirt. He crossed the room toward the birdcage, opened the door, and drew out a canary in his fist. Discarding his gloves, Kochin enclosed it in his palm, and when he opened his fingers, the bird was limp, and the cut in his skin was gone but for a red mark. Though she'd done the same for herself so many times before, seeing another soothe felt like witnessing a miracle.

Now the pieces fell into place, the books and the Butchers' Row, the knowing looks and furtive glances. Her mind reeled as she replayed their encounters, but it caught on a single revelation like a broken clock: She wasn't alone. For the first time since she'd lost her family, Nhika wasn't alone.

"Why didn't you tell me what you were?" she said.

Kochin tossed the dead bird into a trash can. "I didn't want to give you any reason to stay," he said. "The heartsooth books . . . I shouldn't have given them to you." Nhika read between the lines—no matter how he'd tried to scare her away, he couldn't ignore the one thing that connected them.

Kochin closed the remainder of the space between them. He was close enough for her to smell the blood on his clothing. Maybe she should've been afraid, given his propensity for murder, but in the moment, she only wanted him to soothe her again. He swallowed, and she could see the bob in his throat. "Nhika, I'm sorry to have involved you. But now that I have, you can't go back to the Congmis."

"Why not?" she asked, and her thoughts spun back to her original question. "Why did you kill him, Kochin?"

He retreated a step, placing that cold distance between them again. A muscle flickered in his jaw, betraying his indecision. Kochin opened his mouth to speak, but a shout from outside drew their attention.

"Nhika!" That was Trin's voice, hollering from below the window. With a jolt of terror, Nhika crossed the room and glanced down at the streets. There he was, slamming a fist against the door, looking out of place in this borough with his tailored shirt.

"Shit," she murmured.

"What?"

"It's Trin. He must have followed me," she said, realizing she'd left the napkin on her nightstand.

Trin rapped his fist against the door. "Nhika, I just want to talk. I believe you."

He *believed* her. Would his faith still hold if he found her with the masked man? With a hiccup of guilt, Nhika felt herself tearing in two: bring the Congmis their murderer and clear her name, or help a heartsooth escape until she could hear his story?

"What does he want with you?" Kochin asked. Already, he was tying off his ripped shirt and donning a robe over it all.

"They hired me to heal Hendon." But he already knew that.

"Right—the driver I saved."

Her thoughts stumbled on his phrasing: *saved*. "You. It was *you* he remembered that day in the fox mask, but when he woke up, he thought it was me."

"Come with me, then." The urgency of his voice unsteadied her. "You're not safe with them. But I can take you somewhere safe, somewhere away from this mess."

Not safe with the Congmis? "But I'm not the one who killed their father," she said, the words catching him like a net. "You are."

Kochin halted in the middle of straightening his robe, watching her. "Are you going to turn me in?" he asked. Their stares contested each other, daring the other to speak. Nhika eyed the pistol on the desk, wondering if he'd move to grab it. Instead, he spread his arms, as though laid bare on her operating table. Downstairs, Trin continued banging, until she heard the lock break free of the door.

She wouldn't have to turn him in. She would just have to stand here, unyielding, until Trin came up to the door; somehow, she knew Kochin would not leave her. Still, she hesitated, even as she heard the hardwood creaking a floor below them. "Why did you do it?" she demanded, her lips pressed thin.

His eyes grew guarded. "Because I had to."

"Because he discovered what you were? Because he threatened you?" Nhika wasn't so sure why she needed to know, why she hoped the reasoning would absolve him. "Please, Kochin."

Indecision warred behind his expression. "I've made many choices to get where I am," he started, words measured. "Now a demon has come for its due. But it doesn't have to come for you, too. I don't want you to end up like me."

He'd made a similar comment before, with her knife in his stomach; she'd thought he'd meant a murderer. Now she wasn't so sure. "And what is that, exactly?"

He paused, as though the question surprised him, before saying, "A bloodcarver." The word passed between them like an omen, and he extended a hand to her, his outstretched fingers an invitation. "Come with me, Nhika. I'm asking you to trust me."

He'd kept secrets from her. He'd murdered a man. He'd pointed a gun at her.

Yet, Kochin hadn't pulled the trigger. Kochin had lent her heartsooth books. And Kochin was just like her, a heartsooth, and for the same reason he couldn't shoot her, she felt herself step toward his hand. Because she'd gone so long in a drought that even if this was a well laced in poison, she would drink.

Nhika started into action, hooking a chair beneath the handle of the door and passing him his fox mask, lest Trin break through.

They slipped out by the fire escape, hopping down the ladder and landing behind the cover of trash receptacles, where Kochin heaved aside wooden crates to reveal a sewer hole.

"A hand?" he requested, crouching by the cover. Together, they hefted the metal hatch open, revealing a tunnel into darkness.

A crash came from above, followed by a voice. "*Nhika!*" It was Trin, standing at the top of the fire escape. His eyes widened when he saw Kochin, masked. "What are you doing?"

She knew how this must've looked, her here with the Congmis' masked murderer. Nhika looked away from the intensity of his gaze, knowing that any suspicions he had had just been confirmed. She wanted to tell him that she would return with all their answers—but she couldn't blindly give Kochin up.

"You . . ." His expression, always so staunch, now shattered with disbelief. Trin's hands wrapped around the railing as though he were prepared to jump down three stories. "Mimi was right."

"Let's go, Nhika," Kochin said, offering her a hand down the sewer tunnel. His eyes coaxed her behind the mask.

Nhika hesitated, caught in indecision, frozen between Kochin's outstretched hand and Trin's steely glare. A breath of silence settled, reined only by the tinny screech of canaries. Now it wasn't about any paltry sum of chem; it was about promises made and broken, lives saved and lost, friends found and abandoned. She stood before a choice: help the first family to trust her or follow the last person in the city who might ever truly understand her. Between the two, the choice was simple.

"If you know what's good for you," she said, "you won't follow us."

Trin slammed a fist against the railing, rattling old metal. "They trusted you!" The crack in his voice sent a shard of ice through her heart. His voice held unbarred malice, and she knew he'd been anticipating this moment since the beginning, a reason to distrust her. Well, here it was.

Nhika turned away, staring instead into the sewer hole. She bit back thoughts of Mimi, or Andao, or Hendon, who'd extended their grace and their home. No, instead, she thought only of Kochin, of a loneliness dispelled by carving touch. "That was their mistake," she muttered.

Then she took Kochin's hand.

— SEVENTEEN —

NHIKA AND KOCHIN FLED BY THE SEWERS. IN A
city like Theumas, even the sewer systems had order. Still, she
stumbled behind him, almost clumsy in the dark, relying more
on his hand around hers than on her eyes. In the blackness, she
saw Trin, silhouetted by the shophouse, eyes frozen in betrayal.
She blinked the image away.

Kochin seemed to have the path memorized, turn by turn.
Sewer grates and storm drains lit their path with slits of dying
light, sunset subsiding into dusk as they continued along. By
the time they came to a wide coastal sewer grate, the moon
was rising, bathing the rocky shores of the dockyards in silver.
This was a sight she was accustomed to, the stark construction of the docks silhouetted against an ocean of glassy crests
and shattered moonlight. With the details washed away in the
darkness, the city seemed almost an extension of the cliffs,
with a contour made ridgelike by pagodic crests and swooping
roofs.

But Kochin didn't take her back into the city. Instead, they
continued where the dockyards jutted out into the water, har-
boring leviathan cruise ships and their fanlike junk sails rising
between flat barges. This was a landmark of the Dog Borough,
the southernmost tip of the city, a place she'd frequented while

her father still lived. Back then, he'd carried her on his shoulders, showing her the massive storybook ships and claiming he owned them.

Despite the growing dusk, languid activity still hummed on the dockyards, boat workers tethering ships for the night and engineers welding panels onto skeletal frames. They passed cruise ships suspended from cable cradles and submarine vessels that resembled beached whales in the darkness, metal carrion picked dry by shipbuilders. Now free from the sewers, Kochin removed his mask and fell to a slower pace at her side. She hadn't noticed when her hand had slipped out of his, but her skin still buzzed at the duration of their touch.

"I think it's safe to say we've escaped," she said, but he didn't stop walking.

"I know better than to underestimate the Congmis by now," was all he said. He watched her out of the corner of his eye but Nhika kept her gaze fixed forward, almost afraid to invite him into further conversation. Looking at him wrenched guilt in her stomach, a feeling she tried to quell. So what if she had broken her agreement with the Congmis? She'd never owed them anything. As with all her clients, she'd offered them a placebo of trust, and they'd been fools to take it. So why did it feel so terrible this time?

Trin's pained expression flashed in her mind again, and Nhika swallowed the lump in her throat.

"Thank you, by the way," Kochin said, as if an afterthought. "For trusting me. I know it's a lot to ask."

"Trust comes with answers," she countered. Some part of

her, still clinging to the Congmi household, needed to find the true reason behind their father's murder.

"I'll answer your questions, Nhika, but I won't drag you into my mistakes."

She set her jaw with annoyance. Wasn't this how the Congmis had acted, keeping her out of their conspiracies? Nhika had hoped Kochin would be different. Still, she let the topic slide, for now. "How is it you soothe, then? I didn't know Theumans could have the gift."

"They can't. But I'm not just Theuman. I'm Yarongese on my mother's side. Got all the looks of my father, though, didn't I?" He smiled at her, dark eyes alight as that familiar charm returned.

"Did you learn from those books you lent me?"

"No, I learned from my mother. I have family in the countryside."

"She's another heartsooth?" Nhika asked, her eyes widening.

"Yes, though she hides it, too."

"Do you . . ." Nhika recalled him at the Butchers' Row and the chem he was prepared to spend on her. "Do you know any others?"

His lips thinned into a frown. "No. And I've spent all my years in Theumas looking."

"So it's just us."

"Just *you*," he amended. "I'm not as gifted as you are—you healed an injury I couldn't. And I can't expend my own calories to soothe."

"That doesn't make you any less of a heartsooth." Nhika had

doubted her own connection with the gift for too long to let him discredit himself. No matter how big or small his gift, he was a heartsooth, just like her.

Kochin blinked, looking disarmed, as if no one had ever told him that before. Maybe no one had. "Then I'm the only heart-sooth who has to use animals to fuel my soothing."

"Perhaps something's just missing," she mused aloud. "Like the empathy organ." As soon as she'd said it, she realized how foolish she sounded.

He only gave her a curious look. "Empathy organ?"

"Nothing real," she said dismissively. "Just, something I've used to rationalize the source of heartsoothing. My grand-mother used to tell me that soothing was all about the connec-tion, but I could only see it as an organ."

Kochin smiled wryly. "You mean . . . a heart? Pretty sure I have one of those."

They reached a small jut of the dockyards, where a cluster of rowboats huddled behind a wave breaker, shielded from the violent rocking of the ocean. There, Kochin untethered a wide dinghy, its colorful paint peeling to bare wood.

"Be my guest," he said, sweeping an arm toward the back seat. She stepped inside, catching her balance as it teetered, and he took a spot at the bow. Kochin looked incongruous here on the water, garbed in well-fitted black attire with sleeves pushed up to his elbows.

"Feels an awful lot like you're taking me somewhere they'll never find my body," Nhika remarked as they pushed off into black waters.

"Let's not forget who stabbed who," he returned.

"You pulled the gun on me."

"You pulled the knife first."

"I think I was justified."

"It still hurt. But I suppose you know that." He grinned, a wan thing, and she realized she'd never had anyone else explain the nuances of heartsoothing to *her* before. His eyes fell to the waters, and he added, "I'm sorry for putting you in that position. I only wanted you to leave the Congmis and escape this city while you still could. But I wouldn't have pulled the trigger. I'm no . . ."

Murderer, he might've said, but he didn't finish the sentence. Nhika felt now wasn't the time to press for answers, so she asked instead, "Where are we going?"

"Somewhere no one knows about. Somewhere safe." Where once those words might've sounded cryptic, that sinister edge was now rubbing off. Though she didn't fully trust him, she owed it to the Mother, who had brought together the last heartsooths in Theumas, to at least hear him out.

The dinghy sailed forward in time to his rowing, water sloshing against its sides. At this time of spring, dusk was a welcome reprieve from the heat, and the journey was a placid one. They followed the coastline, then slipped up the delta into the rivulets, where Kochin nosed their dinghy into an inlet of water cupped in the cliffside. There, sitting atop the mirror surface of the river, was a lone houseboat.

From a distance it seemed a small thing, but as they grew closer, she saw how wide and long it was, its curved hull large enough for a miniature solarium at the stern and a living compartment toward the bow. Thatched awnings curved over windows and a veranda sat at the top with a view overlooking the black water.

"You can stay here while I sort things out," Kochin said.

As they approached the porch at the back of the houseboat, Kochin oriented their dinghy parallel and Nhika caught the ladder. He pulled himself up and found the rope in the darkness. Together, they tethered the dinghy in place as the night dipped into full blackness, the last of the sunlight dissipating under the horizon. Kochin replaced it with generator-powered incandescence—she heard the slosh and smelled the odor of gas before a strip of light bulbs blinked to life, illuminating the rest of the vessel.

It was a homey space, larger on the inside than it looked. They passed through the solarium, which housed a small garden of potted plants, and entered into the main cabin. There was a kitchen space on one end and a large bed on the other, hidden behind a sheer curtain. In the space between was a plush lounging area, warmed by a woodstove and softened by a colorful collection of pillows. A stairwell flanked by bookshelves led up to the roof, letting out into what Nhika assumed to be the veranda. She'd never been on such a luxurious vessel before and was impressed by the construction until she saw the emblazoned seal on the railing: Congmi Industries. Of course. The sight of it deposited a new pit of guilt in her stomach.

"Make yourself at home," Kochin said, tossing items from his pockets onto the table. Then he looked at her, as though awaiting her appraisal. It was a comfortable space, but she noticed there were only furnishings for one: one bed, a table, and a single dining chair beside it.

"You've made yourself a nice place here," she remarked. "If you'd taken me here instead of that pet shop, maybe I wouldn't have stabbed you." Nhika kicked her shoes off and collapsed into an armchair. "Now that we have a bit more privacy, is there something you'd like to tell me?"

Kochin gave her a thin smile, propping open the awnings and preparing the woodstove. "Not particularly."

"I've abandoned the Congmis, you've taken me far from the city—surely by now, I deserve answers."

"Why does it matter so much to you?"

"Because Hendon wakes up accusing *me*, so I need to know the truth."

"So you can tell the Congmis? Do you really care about them?"

She shrugged to cover up the guilt lodged in her chest. "They fed and housed me. I'm grateful. But I don't owe them anything. You said he didn't discover or threaten you. Then why? Simply because you could?"

His eyes flared at that. "I didn't enjoy it, if that's what you're saying," he said, a withheld force behind his words. His expression darkened. "It wasn't my choice. But in the world of the Congmis, in my world, anything can be exploited, even something like heartsoothing. That's a lesson I learned too late."

She opened her mouth to tell him that she'd already learned that lesson, years ago, but realized that she hadn't—not in the way he had. Now she saw that heartsoothing was not the same thing for the two of them. For him, it sounded sacred, newly defiled; for her, heartsoothing had always been a practical thing, so integral to who she was that it could not be divine, for she was so haplessly mortal.

Instead she said, "I'm sorry. I'll be out of your hair by morning."

He gave her an unconvinced look. "You have nowhere to go."

"I have an apartment in the Dog Borough," she said, though she wasn't even sure of that anymore, with the rent overdue.

"As long as it's not the Congmis'."

"Because you're afraid I'll turn you in."

"No, not that."

"Because you still think I don't belong?"

"No, no—"

"Then *why*?"

"Because I'm trying to protect you!" he said, stilling the room. For a moment, Nhika could've sworn that even the houseboat stopped rocking. If that was the truth, and it was an act of concern rather than contempt, she wasn't sure how to respond.

At last, she managed, "Protect me from what?"

"From *whom*," he corrected, and something clicked in her mind. Kochin had never wanted to kill Mr. Congmi; he'd said it was a demon coming for its due. He'd been *coerced*.

"Someone used you to kill Mr. Congmi," she realized aloud.

Though he didn't answer, the set of his jaw confirmed her suspicion.

"Who?"

His eyes revealed nothing. "Surely, you know by now."

Her first instinct was the Butchers, but Nhika parsed through his words, his actions. Everything he'd done, forgetting her appointment, interrupting her conversations, driving her from this city—Kochin would have her believe it was all meant to protect her. If that was the case, then there was a single man at the heart of it all, someone she'd considered the sun to Kochin's shadow, who had hooked and reeled her only for Kochin to cut the line. It could've only been—

"Dr. Santo," she said, her throat growing dry. The realization settled in like rigor mortis—Dr. Santo, who loved the siblings, who shared in all their conspiracies, the murderer? Something about it felt so wrong, but the pieces fit no other way.

Kochin nodded, wordless, and leaned against the windowsill. "So now you know why you should stay."

"Why did he do it?"

"Why do you care?"

"You tell me, and I'll stay."

Kochin let out a ragged breath. "I won't lie to you. But I'm not involving you."

"So, what's your next move? Stay under his employ, live a lie, *murder* again if he asks for it?"

Something fragile fractured across his expression. "Nhika, I'm offering you safety and freedom. Isn't that enough for you?"

"Maybe once," she said. "But it gets tiring, being thrown away and kicked out after I'm done being useful. Any time I finally feel like I might belong somewhere, it's based on conditions and pity. And now . . . Now I find someone just like me—learn that

I'm not alone in this city anymore—and he's so eager to send me off, as if we're not the last heartsooths in Theumas. As if . . . as if that doesn't mean anything to him."

The words felt messy as they escaped her. Maybe, she'd misjudged him. Maybe, she'd invented this longing, the loneliness of two flytraps in a garden of orchids. Maybe, growing up with a family, within the upper city, Kochin had never wanted for more. Now she only awaited his judgment, wondering if he knew his next words had the power to break her.

At last, he said, his tone distant, "I've been stabbed today. I'm tired. We can talk about it tomorrow."

Nhika stood speechless. That was it, then? She could wax her sadness, pour the contents of her chest out onto the wooden floor, and that's all he had to say?

"I'll spend one night," she said. *And leave in the morning.* To where, she wasn't yet sure—not the Congmis, because they'd sooner confine her than believe it was Dr. Santo behind everything. But anywhere other than here.

When Kochin still offered her nothing, she scoffed and pushed past him toward the top of the houseboat, some privacy on this small vessel.

The view over the water, framed by the slopes around the inlet, unfurled like a scroll. Nhika seldom had time to appreciate the city's beauty, but she breathed it in now, climbing atop the wooden veranda. Unbridled nature was a scarcity in Theumas, and she took the moment to appreciate it, legs dangling over the side of the boat and body caught between two oceans: one of stars and one of salt.

The brightest star in the sky was called Majora. Her father had taught her that; he'd told her it would always guide her home as it did him. Except, it hadn't guided him home, not at the end, and she no longer knew what home meant.

She had almost thought she'd find one with the Congmis—in Dr. Santo's lab, with Trin's offer—but that had never been an option. Not when they would accuse her over a misremembered dream, not when she'd thrown the opportunity away. She'd spent weeks with them and healed their driver, but all that had been reneged by one act of betrayal.

And for what? For a heartsooth who had, from the beginning, only pushed her away?

Suddenly, the injustice of it reared its indignant head. It wasn't fair—that choosing a heartsooth meant betraying the Congmis; that she'd taken off Kochin's fox mask only to find another one underneath.

Before she could help it, a tear welled in the corner of her eye and rolled down the contour of her cheek. She lifted a hand to her chest, rubbing the lump where her bone ring dangled beneath her shirt. The ring was an act of remembrance, but it felt hollow when she'd spurned the only family who might begin to welcome her.

"Hey," came Kochin's voice behind her, and Nhika hurriedly swiped at her eyes. When she turned, she found him emerging from the stairwell with a blanket and a plate of seared rice cakes.

"You mind?" he asked.

Nhika didn't respond, looking instead over the dark water. With a shaky exhale, he approached her, draping the blanket over her shoulders and sliding the plate toward her—a peace offering, she supposed. Even as he sat beside her, she didn't meet his eyes.

For a long pause, neither of them spoke, both watching the sway of the water. She heard the draw of his breath, as reliable as the rhythm of the ocean.

"I'm sorry, Nhika. I've been a shoddy host, haven't I?" he said at last.

"The worst," she agreed, not deigning to meet his gaze.

"It means everything to me what we are," he confided, and only then did she look at him. "I know I've been distant, but I don't mean to hurt you. That's the last thing I want."

"Then why scare me away?"

"Because I wish someone had done the same for me. If I had the chance to escape this, I'd take it in a heartbeat."

Nhika watched him, wary of their new proximity. "You told me to leave before I lost whatever I had left. What did you lose?"

He let out a long breath, vulnerability softening his expression. "Everything," he breathed. "My freedom, my peace."

Something about him deflated, and suddenly he didn't look at all cold or menacing, just . . . tired. Lonely. Like he'd spent years trying to hold his world together, only for her to pry it apart. For a moment, she forgot about the Congmis—their murder and accusations. It was just about Kochin, and her sitting beside him, two heartsooths snared by the same city.

After a stretch of silence, Kochin spoke again, his voice unguarded. "Dr. Santo had taken so much from me that I'd run out of things to give. And I'd always resigned myself to lose those things because they were only ever mine to lose. Then you show up—a heartsooth, the only thing in this cursed city that matters—and he's trying to take you, too. I can't . . . I can't let him destroy you. Not like he's destroyed me, my life, my heartsoothing."

His admission left her breathless, a quiet truth when she'd heard so many lies. Something shifted in her chest, a tugging feeling, and Nhika found herself wanting more than just answers—she wanted to help him.

"I'm sorry, Kochin," Nhika said, and she truly was.

"Stay," he said again. "I'll tell you everything, but there's somewhere I want to take you first. Can we agree on that?"

His eyes beseeched her. If she knew what was best for her, she would take his dinghy in the night and row herself back to some forgettable part of the city, somewhere they'd never find her. She would forget the existence of another heartsooth, because what difference did it make when he pushed her away? She would silence the new, unwelcome warmth in her chest when she thought of Kochin, who'd killed one of the most influential men in Theumas.

But Nhika did none of those things, rationality be damned. She might've wondered why she'd helped him, why she'd abandoned the Congmis for him, why she stayed even now, but she already knew.

It was because he was a heartsooth. In this city, that was reason enough.

"Deal," she said. Then, "Where are we going?"

"Somewhere removed. And safe," he said. "My home."

— EIGHTEEN —

NHIKA WOKE IN A BED, SUNKEN INTO A PLUSH OF blankets and pillows. Something sizzled beyond the draped divider and aromatic smoke wafted from the kitchen. The night before returned to her: She'd been on the veranda, falling asleep to stars and rice cakes.

With a swallowed yawn, she sat up and pulled aside the curtain to find Kochin in the kitchen, frying a pair of eggs. His eyes flicked to her as he worked. "Good morning."

"You carried me to your bed?" Nhika noticed the blanket and pillow nested in the armchair; he must've spent the night there instead.

"You fell asleep on the roof. The boat tends to rock at night, and I didn't want you to drown."

"How considerate," she said, though her muscles tensed at the thought of him carrying her down here. "Look, Kochin, about last night—"

"Breakfast first," he insisted, plating the eggs beside neat domes of rice and pork before setting the dishes on the low table. "Here, I'll hazard you my cooking."

Nhika bit her tongue, surveying the room. In the daylight it was a different atmosphere, lacquered wood glowing gold and houseplants nestled into every possible corner. Shelves lined the curve of the hull, laden with books and journals, and the idyllic reflection of the water danced across the ceiling.

She slipped out of the bed, aware of how dirty she was inside this well-kept houseboat. Compared to what she'd experienced, his cooking didn't look bad at all, though it was a far cry from the Congmis' chefs.

It felt unfamiliar to share a meal with him, and if Kochin had given her this dish a week ago, she would've thought it poisoned. But Kochin dug in as though they did this every day, and some part of her thawed at the sight of his own comfort. Now, in the warm glow of the houseboat, she noticed his Yarongese features where she never had before: the darkness of his eyes, the slope of his nose, the wave in his hair—all concealed behind that pale Theuman skin.

"We'll leave after breakfast," he said.

"You promised me answers."

"Answers once we get there."

"Answers *first*."

A bout of laughter escaped him. "You're incorrigible. One answer now, take it or leave it."

Nhika thought hard. While there was so much she needed to know, she remembered the Congmis, and her first question was on their behalf. "What motive would Dr. Santo possibly have to kill Mr. Congmi? He loves that family."

"He loves his research more."

"But Mr. Congmi? They were partners, *friends*." That couldn't have been the only reason, a life ended over scientific prestige.

She wasn't sure if it was unbelievable or if she simply didn't want to believe it.

"Mr. Congmi's only sin was his righteousness. He discovered Dr. Santo's scientific methods were illegitimate. Falsified. Unreproducible," he responded, giving her a dark look. "He told Dr. Santo to come clean, or he would, and Dr. Santo doesn't take ultimatums lightly."

Nhika's heart dropped. "And that's where you come in."

Kochin nodded, crossing the room to a chest beneath his bed, from which he pulled out an envelope. When he returned, he placed it in front of her, beside her abandoned breakfast. "A couple months ago, I received this letter under the door of the shophouse."

Nhika took the envelope between her fingers, looking for his permission to open it. He gave her a slow nod.

She read the brief letter within:

I HAVE NEED OF YOUR PARTICULAR TALENTS. CONGMI VUN QUAN HAS AGGRIEVED ME FOR FAR TOO LONG; HE IS AN OBSTACLE THAT MUST BE ELIMINATED. I WILL LEAVE IT UP TO YOUR DISCRETION AS TO HOW THAT MAY BE ACCOMPLISHED. LEAVE NO WITNESSES.

AND REMEMBER, I KNOW.

A dozen more questions sprung to mind—know what? And how did Dr. Santo learn about Kochin's heartsoothing? But one in particular vexed her: "You said earlier that Dr. Santo's research was illegitimate. Illegitimate how?"

Smiling, Kochin clicked his tongue. "Ms. Suon, I believe I only agreed to one question," he said, and left it at that.

— ❧ —

They took the houseboat upriver. For how homey it was, Nhika hadn't realized it was also a functional boat. Sitting at a wheel and lever at the bow, Kochin guided them toward the inner parts of Theumas, using civilian waterways and avoiding commercial barges.

For the hours-long journey, she sat next to Kochin at the bow, her feet dangling over the side and bare toes almost skimming the water. Mostly, they sat in silence, but she was content just to watch the city from an angle she never seen before: the fishing boats and yachts, the bottoms of bridges she'd only known from a trolley rail, the small parts of people's lives she captured at the edge of the water. The boroughs were harder to distinguish by boat travel; rivulets carved circuitous paths around the city, not deigning to obey the strict order of the roads. There was comfort in feeling that the water belonged to her, even if the rest of the city didn't.

Soon, they escaped the urban heart of the city to its rural outskirts. Out here, terraced farmlands replaced the industrial cityscape, and the dark-roofed houses hid between trees, rather than the other way around. For how small Theumas was compared to its neighboring countries—the city-state was comprised of just Central Theumas and its surrounding territories—Nhika had never been this far into the country. Her entire life had been contained within the twelve boroughs of Central Theumas.

It was only when their houseboat puttered off the main water-ways and toward inland ones that Nhika drew back from the water and looked at Kochin.

"How much longer?" she asked.

"An hour or so. It's . . . it's been a while."

"When was the last time you came home?"

He pressed his lips together, eyes steady on the horizon. "Three years."

Family within a day's travel, and he hadn't seen them in three years. From the solemnity in his eyes, she knew it was not simply out of neglect. "What happened?"

"I . . . I'll tell you when we get there," he said. "What about your family?"

He was avoiding answers again, but she read the apprehension in his expression and let this one pass. Few had asked about her family in earnest. Some clients had tried, an attempt to ease the mood of the room while she played with tinctures and ton-ics. Those, she usually shut down with a grim answer—*My parents died when I was young and I lost my grandmother to a house fire*. But she didn't want to shut Kochin down.

"I don't know much about who they were on Yarong. I just know my grandmother on my mother's side was a heartsooth matriarch, so when Daltanny invaded, the village banded together to help her escape to Theumas. They knew she would be interned other-wise. She met my father's family in Theumas, and my parents fell in love as children. As I've been told, my father was at sea when I was born, but he saw three cormorants flying low over open water, and somehow knew I'd arrived, so he begged his captain to turn back to shore." Her mother had recited this story as they both counted down the days before her father would return from sea, but Nhika had never told anyone else before. Her parents had had a fated love, one she couldn't imagine for herself—mostly because her grandmother advised her so often to hide her gift, and who could love her if they didn't even know her?

"My mother's side was not too different, escaping Yarong like that," Kochin said. "Only, instead of finding anyone of Yarongese descent, my mother fell for a Theuman scholar. I'm not sure what he was more infatuated with, her or her heartsoothing, but they do love each other, in a way."

"In a way?"

"Their love was give-and-take. He opened doors for her; she opened his mind." He draped an arm over the wheel in a pensive pose. "But I suppose that's what love is, isn't it? An unspoken contract?"

"Is that how you feel?" She leaned toward him, part curious and part amused. This was a language she understood, conceptualizing romance with logic.

"No, I guess not. I find it a little absurd," Kochin said instead. "In all the history of heartsoothing, there have arisen many taboos: taking lives, bringing back the dead, breaching consent. But you know what isn't taboo? Planting love."

"Because it's not possible."

"Exactly." He smiled, and she realized he'd anticipated her answer. "So, if we can't possibly soothe or source love, who are we to define it? Being honest, I'm not sure it's even biological. Otherwise, wouldn't we have felt it in patients before?"

Nhika turned her eyes toward the river, where vegetation brushed against the side of the boat. Her last client from the Horse Borough came to her, that man with a sick wife. Though his love radiated from him like heat from a young sun, she hadn't felt it from her soothing. It had come from the tender look in his eyes, the softness in his words when he spoke to her, the lightness of his touch.

"Maybe." Nhika met Kochin's eye. "I never would've thought you a romantic."

"Oh? What did you think of me?"

"When I first met you? An asshole," she said plainly, drawing a laugh from him.

"Well, forgive me for trying to save the only other heartsooth in Theumas."

Nhika watched him, reading the loneliness behind his humored words. She placed herself into his shoes, finding another heartsooth like himself after so long but choosing solitude over the chance that she might know any of his suffering. "Truthfully," she began again, "when I first met you, I thought you had it all. A position in high society, respect, money."

"A mask, Nhika," he said gently. "I wore a mask to pretend I belonged there. It takes something from you each day, denying a vital part of yourself. I didn't want you to have to go through that, too."

She almost had, hiding her gift behind gloves and butchering her familial name to fit in. "I appreciate that. But were the insults necessary?"

"They would've worked on me. Though if I'd known how prideful you are, I might've tried flattery instead."

"How very thoughtful, Ven Kochin."

"You're welcome, Ms. Suon."

The false name dislodged something fragile in her throat, her ring feeling especially heavy. "It's Suonyasan," she said. If anyone deserved to know, it was another heartsooth. "My real name is Suonyasan Nhika."

"Suonyasan Nhika," he said in a tone near reverence. "What a beautiful name."

To hear her familial name from the lips of another pricked something deep in her chest, an organ she'd thought dormant. She returned her gaze to the water, to the pink lilies that bloomed between aquatic weeds. "Yes," she said. "I've always liked it."

When she looked back at him, she found his attention on her. He regarded her as she'd regarded the ocean: with equal parts awe and fascination. Like she was both the tempest that sank junks and the gentle lap of water at the side of his houseboat.

"I wish I'd met you in another life," he sighed over the steering wheel, so quiet that it might not have been meant for her ears. "The Mother is never fair, is She?"

Nhika didn't know how to answer that. So their conversation fell to silence.

— ༄ —

At last, they reached the slow, calm waters of Kochin's hometown, where they docked between similar skiffs and fishing vessels. There, they dropped their dinghy and headed toward shore.

Rural Theumas was a world apart from its industrial counterpart: hilly, disorganized, and run-down, its streets paved with dirt rather than stone. At a glance, it might've just looked like a forested mountainside, but she saw the rice farms that sculpted the hills and the gloss of shingled roofs peeking out between gaps in the flora. The technology must've been a decade behind, clothes hanging from lines rather than tumble dried by automatons, but she noticed the Congmi name even here, though in automaton models that looked stiff and thick compared to the sleek ones in Central.

"Welcome to Chengton," Kochin said, sweeping his hand down the dirt road, which she then realized was the entirety of the town. She had to wonder how a little place like this spawned a socialite like Kochin.

"Quaint," she remarked.

"I thought you were used to quaint?"

"I've gotten used to ostentatious."

"Better get used to quaint again." He pointed to the hillside, where the white facade of houses dotted the landscape between forested thickets and winding dirt roads. There, at the top of the terrain, where the forest gapped for the evening sun, was a house flying a variety of fishing flags, flapping red and blue and yellow in the wind. "That's my home," he said.

"Kochin, why did you ever leave?"

He gave her a rueful look. "For the same reason you would want to stay with the Congmis. I saw something golden in the city and had to have it." With a sigh to dispel his sentimentality, he tipped his head toward the hill and they both started down the path.

Their route zigzagged up the hill, and Nhika found herself having fantasies about the house at the top. It was a house her family would've loved, near the water and out of the city. A house where she might've been able to wave to her father in his ships as they passed. A house that she could imagine calling home.

Just as they were about to crest the hill and see the house in full, Kochin stopped. Nhika nearly stumbled into him for how abrupt it was. She glanced up, awaiting an explanation, but he only stared at the top of the hill, his feet planted in the dirt as though something forbade him from taking another step.

At last, he drew an envelope out of his jacket pocket and passed it to her. "Please give this to them. It's the stipend I send home every month. Tell them the note is from me."

Nhika cocked her head. "You're not coming?"

"I . . ." For a moment, he seemed to consider it, the tip of his foot inching forward. In the end, he drew back. "I can't."

"Why?"

"I'm not the same boy they sent off to Central Theumas three years ago."

"But, Kochin, you—"

"Please, Nhika." He gave her an imploring look and she relinquished, knowing better than to argue anymore. "I'll wait for you at the beach."

With a nod, she started toward the house, clutching the letter in her hands. It was a house that teemed with character, floors stacked lopsidedly atop one another and a wild garden over-growing its picket fence. Now she saw the flagpole up close, its many flags dancing in the wind. As she drew nearer, the barking of a dog started up from inside.

Nhika reached the door. Raised her fist. Knocked.

The dog began another ruckus, and she could hear a woman's voice shushing it. Footsteps creaked closer before the door opened.

The woman was Yarongese. It was written there in her flat nose, tanned skin, black eyes. She had the complexion Nhika's mother had had, sun spots and freckles speckling her cheeks and hands weathered, but Nhika saw the features that she'd given Kochin—the intelligent eyes, soft lips, dark brow.

Nhika remembered to speak. "Mrs. Ven?" she asked. She thrust the envelope forward as though it could speak for her. "I brought a letter from Kochin."

At once, Mrs. Ven's eyes widened. "Kochin?"

"My name is Suonyasan Nhika," she said, surprising herself with how naturally her real name came off her tongue. "I'm a friend of your son's."

"Where is he?"

Nhika shook her head, apologetic. "He's not here, but I came to deliver this." She thought of Kochin, likely just a few steps away now, hiding from his home, his mother.

"Come inside. I'll start some tea. Stay the night. And you can call me Auntie Yetunla. Or Auntie Ye."

Nhika blinked at the trisyllabic Yarongese name, at the way Auntie Ye rounded it out with an accent, how *all* of her speech was filtered through that familiar, warming accent despite her perfect Theuman vocabulary.

She sat Nhika down in a chair and placed a kettle on the stovetop. As the dog inspected her shoes, Nhika's eyes wandered the house. Now, she saw the houseboat had been fashioned in its image, with houseplants stuffed in every corner and an abundance of natural sunlight filtering through cracked shutters and dusty windows. Her gaze landed on a wall of family portraits: a young Kochin with his mother, his father, two other boys, and a puppy. She could pick Kochin out from the three boys easily—the younger had a mane of curly hair, and the older had a stoic look that reminded her a bit of Trin. Even as a child, Kochin possessed the same charming smile and witty eyes. Both the puppy and the children grew through each portrait, with Kochin absent from the very last.

"I'm sorry," Auntie Ye said. "His father and the boys aren't home right now, but they'll be in tonight."

"It's okay, Auntie. I don't think I can stay that long." She placed the letter on the table. "Kochin wanted me to give you this. He said it's the monthly stipend. And a letter."

Auntie Ye brought over the tea and poured them each a cup before seating herself. She examined the letter, as though afraid to open it. Instead, her fingers played at the seal with hesitance.

"He's here now, isn't he?" she asked, her lively voice from earlier dropping into something subdued. "In Chengton?"

Nhika, not prepared to lie to a new auntie, nodded.

"Why didn't he come?"

"He's . . . not ready."

Auntie Ye's brows knit knowingly. "Well, tell him that we're ready for him." She took a draw of her tea, her eyes traveling up to Nhika. Examining her. "And who are you to him?"

"A . . ." Nhika searched for the right title. A coconspirator? A friend? "Another heartsooth."

That admission came with no ceremony here, and instead of surprise or fear, Auntie Ye's eyes only softened. "Ah, so you know about him. And me."

Nhika nodded.

"Did he do it, then?" she asked. "Kochin always told us he would show Theumas what it truly meant to be a heartsooth. That he would change the way they viewed it."

Nhika's chest fell. He'd entered a city hoping he could change it; the city changed him, instead. "Central Theumas is stubborn," she answered vaguely. "I don't think even Kochin could change its mind by himself."

"Seems like you know him well if he told you about his heartsoothing." Auntie Ye raised an inquisitive eyebrow, but Nhika couldn't offer her anything more substantive. "Tell me then, is Kochin doing well? He sends us money, but I would like to know the truth, please."

Nhika searched for an answer. When she'd first met him, she'd thought he'd been doing more than well for a boy his age. But the true Ven Kochin, the one behind all the masks, just wanted to go home. "He carries a lot by himself. But . . . he's not alone." Not anymore. "Beyond that, I don't know. I'm sorry."

"Let me see what this letter is all about, then." At last, Auntie Ye found the courage to open the letter, careful not to rip the paper. She pulled it out, a brief note and a tall stack of bills. As she read, her expression remained indecipherable as her lips shaped out the words. Poignant emotions passed through her eyes, but Nhika recognized one above them all: yearning. Auntie Ye simply missed her son.

At last, she set the letter down, shaking her head. "We cannot just move," Auntie Ye said, and Nhika cocked a brow.

"Move?"

"The chem is generous, but it is not an issue of money. Kochin is asking us to uproot our entire livelihoods," she elaborated, and Nhika caught on to the contents of the letter.

"I . . . I'll be sure to tell him that," she said, and Auntie Ye gave her a curious look.

"You will?" Auntie Ye gestured to the letter. "But he is asking us to take you with us."

Nhika's throat tightened as her brain processed those words. He'd lied to her. He'd *lied* to her. Kochin never had any intention of telling her the truth; he was planning on leaving here without her.

She stood, her chair scraping across the floor. "Thank you, Auntie Ye," she said in a rush, bowing. "Thank you for the tea. Thank you for the kindness. I need to go."

Auntie Ye opened her mouth to protest, but Nhika was already at the door. Before she left, she turned to say, "Auntie Ye, Kochin loves you."

Then she was gone.

— NINETEEN —

NHIKA RACED TO THE EDGE OF THE CLIFF, WOR-
ried that she'd see his houseboat on the horizon, drifting back
toward Central without her. The sun was setting on the water,
and she squinted against its quavering light, looking for the tell-
tale silhouette.

Instead, she found Kochin standing on the beach, his back
toward her as he watched the surf. Relief released through her
exhale, and she started down the cliffside, opting not for the zig-
zagging path but for a straight one, stumbling directly through
bramble and thicket.

"Kochin!" she called, and he turned just in time to catch her
as the cliffside spat her out.

"Nhika, you're—"

"Ven Kochin, how *dare* you," she seethed, with half a mind
to push him into the water and let the current take him. "You
strung me along with a promise of answers just to leave me
here?"

His expression grew apologetic. "I . . . was planning on it.
But not anymore. I remembered how relentless you are, and
you're right—that's not fair. I owe you answers. This time, I
won't evade them, I swear."

Now he offered answers, but Nhika was already beginning

to understand. "The letter Dr. Santo wrote, it said 'I know.' He was talking about your family, wasn't he?" That was why Kochin had sent them money to leave.

Kochin swallowed, the stone in his throat bobbing. "He knows what I am, what my mother is, where I live. He's threatened their peace, their *lives*. It destroyed me to take Mr. Congmi's life, but if I hadn't, I could have lost my family."

"So, you thought you could send me off with them, solve two problems at once?"

Kochin winced at her tone. "You're not a problem, Nhika. I just . . ." He turned back toward the cliff, where the roof of his childhood home peeked over the foliage. "I know my family would love you. And I think you could really love them, too—a family where heartsoothing is valued. A place you could belong. Don't you want that?"

Yes, that's what she'd always wanted, wasn't it? "But what about you?"

"It's too late for me. But not for you."

"You're giving up before you've even tried?"

"I *have* tried. And it cost me." The force of his words quieted her and, as though noticing her reserve, his expression softened.

With a long sigh, Kochin gestured her toward a secluded copse of foliage near the cliffside, a quiet recess that promised a story. Obliging, Nhika followed him. With their backs against the hill and their eyes turned to the water, they sat.

Kochin's lips parted. It took a moment longer for the words to come. "Three years ago, when I was sixteen, I came to Central Theumas for university. I'd won a scholarship to attend and in my acceptance speech, I thanked my mother. That's when Dr. Santo first approached me, much like he did you: with a business card."

He paused, as though these words were foreign to him when spoken aloud. As though he'd never had to confess the truth to another before. She almost wanted to coax more out of him, but she let his thoughts collect in their own time.

Eventually, he went on. "At the time, his research initiative was just beginning. It felt exhilarating, to be coming in on the ground floor of something that big. Dr. Santo took me under his wing and placed me on his personal project: organ transplantation."

Kochin said those final words with such foreboding that Nhika felt instinctive dread curdle in her stomach. Trin had told her a different angle to this story—the first doctor to perform an organ transplant. The medical miracle suddenly seemed much more sinister.

"What do you know of organ transplantation?" he asked.

"Very little."

"Well, organs don't like being outside their original owners. They rebel against new bodies; either they kill the body or the body kills them. You can surgically transplant a new organ without too much trouble—keeping it alive is a different problem. Dr. Santo discovered how to keep them alive, but for that, he needed—"

"A heartsooth," Nhika finished, catching on.

Kochin's expression set, a muscle clenched in his jaw. "I'd read his papers like scripture. I understood what would happen to those patients if I didn't use my gift. I think he must've guessed what I was from the very beginning. He took me to the postoperative ward and showed me all his declining transplant patients."

"And you told him you're a heartsooth?"

Kochin scoffed. "Idiot I was, I healed a man right in front of him. Quieted those signals that assailed the new organ, just long enough for it to recover. I hoped he'd see how medicine and heartsoothing could work together for the better. At first, he made me feel like his equal for it, like my heartsoothing was every bit as legitimate as his medicine."

"What changed?"

"Nothing changed. The mask just came off. I realized he was never intending to legitimize heartsoothing—he just wanted to use it for himself. At first, that was how he kept me—if I left, patients would die, because their transplant organs could not survive without heartsoothing. It never ended because there was always another patient to soothe, another organ to transplant—and somehow, he'd convinced me that if I had a gift like heartsoothing and refused to use it, the deaths of his patients would be on my hands. He told me he was giving me an opportunity; looking back, I see now he was only trying to use me.

"There came a point, maybe a year ago, when I couldn't stand it anymore. I tried to escape the city. He'd developed a new line of drugs to perform the job of my heartsoothing, and I thought he'd done it to replace me. So I left, figuring he'd let me go. Instead, he found something to drag me back."

"Your mother," she said quietly.

"My mother," Kochin echoed. "See, with Dr. Santo, it's not about the project. The innovation. The miracles of medicine. He wants the heartsoothing itself. He wants to control it. And he *has*. However Dr. Santo wanted me to use it, I did. He asks me to soothe transplant patients. I do. He asks me to preserve dead bodies for their organs. I do. He asks me to kill a man and . . ." He turned to her now, and she saw the torment in the trench of his brow. "And I do."

"I'm sorry, Kochin." Words felt futile, so she edged closer to him instead.

"I used to be so proud of my gift, being the only one of three sons to inherit it," he said. "Now? It just makes me sick."

The vehemency with which he spat out that last sentence sank teeth into her heart, and Nhika felt tears burn at her eyes. She couldn't imagine a worse fate, to hate her own heartsoothing, to have it stolen and misused and tarnished. Even if she had never been able to use it as her grandmother had, at least she'd always used it on her own terms. Now, more than ever, she understood why he'd tried to push her away. If their positions had been reversed, she might've done the same.

In the silence, she searched for the right words to say, but they'd all been spent. It didn't matter; her words had never been able to comfort—but perhaps, soothing could. If she taught him to see heartsoothing the way she did, could he remember to love it again?

Tentatively, she inched her fingers closer. He didn't pull away, not even as her hand slipped atop his. Further still, she took his palm against her own, laced their fingers. His hands, bare, were warm and soft where hers were dry and papery, but he still let their fingers entwine. Fear, grief, anger—those were not things that could be soothed away, but between two heartsooths, the last of their kind, perhaps it would be enough just to soothe.

"What school of heartsoothing did your family practice?" she asked softly.

Kochin regarded her with curiosity, wary of her new line of questioning. He responded anyway. "The School of Tenets."

That was a newer school, developed to accommodate the modern heartsooth and contingent on a series of tenets. Her grandmother had always snubbed Tenet practices, its newfangled shortcuts and clinical preferences, but Nhika didn't mention that to Kochin.

"I learned in the School of Sixfold," she said.

"Like the heartsooth books I lent you," he remembered aloud, and a genuine smile touched his lips for the first time that night. It warmed her far more than it should've.

"Yes, exactly." The School of Sixfold was the oldest, developed by spiritual leaders who saw heartsoothing as proof of the divine, a gift from the Mother.

"Remind me again, what are the six rights?"

"Right trust, right body, right mind, right spirit, right intent, right care," she listed, echoes from a memory of her grandmother, who had her count the six rights on her fingers until she babbled them in her sleep. To say them aloud to Kochin was such a peculiar feeling, because she never imagined herself placed in a position of the teacher when she still felt like a student herself.

"Seems a lot easier to memorize three tenets," he teased.

"Is it?" Nhika cleared her throat in preparation to recite what she knew of the School of Tenets, the long and circuitous preamble to their doctrine: "'I swear, as the Mother is my witness, that I will uphold, to the highest ability of my gift and giving, these three tenets bequeathed unto me by—'"

"All right, all right, I get it," Kochin said, but he was laughing behind his words. "No more—you've butchered the entire thing."

"Can you blame me? It's too convoluted," she joked, keeping her palm flat against his. "The rights are far simpler, and they guide you through the art. The first one—right trust. The agreement that initiates every soothing."

"Like the tenet of consent," he thought aloud, palm warm against her skin.

"In the Sixfold, it's more than just a contract. It's saying that you trust the heartsooth with your volition, your body, your mind." These were words borrowed directly from her grandmother, during Nhika's own first lessons in soothing.

"And I do." He said it so easily, as if she were merely asking him if he cared for a walk, that the rest of her words escaped her. She glanced up at him, disarmed by the way his eyes explored her hands, and swallowed the rising stone in her throat.

"I, um . . . The next step is right body, whose body you'll be entering with your influence," she said quickly.

He gave her a self-satisfied look, his smile charming.

Her tongue was beginning to tie itself; Nhika wanted to hurry toward soothing, because at least then there would be fewer words to stumble over. "May I soothe you, Kochin?"

"Yes."

With a breath to ready herself, she dropped her influence to her palm and pushed her way across the interface of skin against skin, finding his own influence there awaiting her. This was how her grandmother had done it, walking through the body together with influences intertwined.

Then came right mind. He had to orient his awareness with hers, align himself with the right perspective. For that, she wrapped her influence around his, feeling something tangible and warm just beyond his palm, and tugged it until it had matched hers. His palm twitched as she did, their influences skimming along nerves and tendons.

This was a new feeling for her, guiding another through the body. Her grandmother had always been the one to do it for her, walking Nhika through every channel up her veins, every branch in her nerves, and every node along her lymph system until she'd become a seasoned local in her own body. Now, Nhika enticed Kochin to travel the body as she did, at once a city and an artwork and a nebulous amalgamation of energy, sparking matter. He resisted, as though fighting his own habits, but at last she felt his influence give to hers. "That's it," she exhaled. "Right mind."

His palm pressed firmer against her hand, and then his fingers curled in the spaces between hers, as though afraid of losing the synapse.

"Now, right spirit," she continued, her voice delocalized. "Tenet heartsooths called them calories. In either school, it's the same energy—sugars, fats, proteins. The 'right' is about choosing whose to spend, theirs or yours. It can be a tricky thing, deciding. When in doubt, use your own."

"I don't think I can," he admitted, and she felt his influence recede. She gave resistance, not letting him give up until they'd at least tried.

She deposited his influence at the base of his liver, a marketplace teeming with produce. Where energy had to be squeezed and milked from muscle, it came in ready supply at the liver. She could feel its abundance, the ease at which she could draw from it if she wanted, but she waited for him to act first.

When he didn't, Nhika pulled his influence forward. Still, he resisted, until Kochin sucked in a breath and drew his hand away, the loss of his presence leaving her flinchingly cold. Nhika regrounded herself, the humidity of the beach returning as soon as her skin remembered how to feel again. When she met his eyes, he was recovering from the stupor just as much as she was.

"I can't, I'm sorry," he said, but she didn't need any apology. They hadn't been able to make it through all six rights, but neither had Nhika when she'd first learned with her grandmother.

"Maybe one day, I could teach you," she thought aloud.

"Maybe." His smile was wistful. "The School of Sixfold is very different from the Tenets."

She cocked her head. "How so?"

At that, he offered his hand, his smile ready. "I can show you."

This she took eagerly, lacing her fingers with his.

"Three tenets—consent, beneficence, nonmaleficence. As straightforward as it gets," he quipped, and left her no time for retorts before he pulled her in.

Her first instinct was to enmesh herself in his sinew and bone, but his influence caught her, dragged her back. They danced a moment together, a tug-of-war as she fought her usual habits, as he'd done before. This time, she relinquished herself to him, and when she did, it felt as though his influence were drawing her out of the body altogether.

The array of his anatomy opened into view before her, a diagram of muscle grafted onto bone and stitched together with nerves and blood vessels, all bound by skin. It wasn't the interlaced, close-up view that she had when she soothed. Rather, it was as if she'd stepped apart from him altogether and viewed his body from a distance—at once physically removed and achingly close.

She understood how this was a more modern technique given how clinical it felt, developed for practicality rather than spirituality. But, at the core of it, it was the same art; she'd dipped herself into his blood and bone-work just the same. Beneath it all, they were both heartsooths.

Here, she observed him as though his skin had grown translucent, his bones hollow. Nhika even found the point of her influence, watching it from afar as it rose up his arm and danced its way around his beating heart, like a mote of light lost in a sea of sliding fibers and squeezing vessels.

There was his heart, too, as though a window had been carved into his chest, as though she could reach out her hand and grab it, feel it. For a moment, he looked almost like one of the Congmis' automatons, his construction incomplete and parts laid bare. Like if she just played with his pieces, she could finally unlock those inner parts of him, hidden from all but her.

Before she realized, Nhika had placed a palm against his chest, meeting the resistance of fabric and sternum. Only then did she realize how close she was, one hand laced in his and the other pressed against his chest, such that a passerby on this beach might think they were nothing but clandestine lovers. His influence released her and they were no longer soothing, yet they stayed connected for a second longer, their breaths mingling and his eyes locked on hers.

With him so close, Nhika was no longer sure what she thought of him. She knew he'd killed a man, one she knew only from papers and never in person. She knew he was a heartsooth, and that alone bound them. But what if he was just Ven Kochin, not a physician's aide nor the man in the fox mask—nor even a heartsooth. Just a boy she'd met in the Horse Borough over a stack of flying papers, who'd since helped her escape a city that might swallow her.

Nhika didn't have the words to know what he might mean to her then.

She found that same conflict mirrored in his half-lidded eyes as Kochin raised a cautious hand to her face, catching a loose strand of hair and tucking it behind her ear. His fingers grazed her cheek as he did. For a precious moment, his hand hovered over her cheek. At last, with a regretful look, Kochin drew his hand away and Nhika read the same yearning in his eyes: *in another life.*

"You're right," he said, solemn. "There's beauty left in

heartsoothing, isn't there?" Even as he said it, his eyes lingered on her.

"You can be free of him, Kochin," she urged. And, in knowing who the true murderer was, she could help the Congmis, too. Perhaps even explain to them that Kochin's hand was forced.

He shook his head. "I can't risk his wrath. I can't be the one to bring another danger down upon my family—not after my mother has fought so hard to find peace."

"You don't think they'd want you to find peace, too?"

"I already told you. It's too late for me."

Her eyes bore into him. "You don't believe that. I know you don't. It's why you killed Mr. Congmi by carriage accident when you could've used heartsoothing and saved yourself the trouble. It's why you chose to save Hendon at the scene, even though you weren't meant to leave a witness. You still *care* about your heartsoothing, Kochin. And I'm not going to let Dr. Santo take it from you."

"Nhika," he said, sounding baffled, "why do you care so much what happens to me?"

No one had ever accused her of *caring* too much before, but now Nhika realized that she did. He was right; she should've been content to run away with a heartsooth family. But if Kochin had to lose his love for heartsoothing in the process, if he had to become the bloodcarver he hated, then she would not have it. With Kochin, it wasn't just about saving him—it was also about saving his gift—and only then did she understand there was something more important to her than chem or calories: heartsoothing, and the few who would remember it.

"It's in my nature to care," she said. "I can help you, Kochin, if only you let me."

Kochin sucked in a sharp breath. In the stillness that followed, she could see the war behind his eyes—to invite her into danger or keep her safe? She knew he wanted it as much as she did; loneliness lined the chambers of their hearts. All either of them wanted was to find a pulse that beat like their own.

At last, he relented, his shoulders falling with his exhale. "How?" he asked, and the simple question held fragile hope, buried beneath layers of hesitance.

She thought of Dr. Santo, the man who had to fall for Kochin's freedom, then of the Congmis, who were hell-bent on finding their murderer—their *real* murderer—with the wealth and resources of royalty behind them. Dr. Santo was a clever man, but his power lay in his connections, his deceit. Now that the mask had been stripped, Nhika wondered if they could out-play him, especially if they employed the siblings to their side.

"I have an idea," she started, "but it'll require something I've never done before."

"And what's that?"

She gave him a pained grimace. "Apologizing."

— TWENTY —

NHIKA HAD BEEN AT THE BOTTOM OF THE Congmis' gates many times before, flanked by its stone lions and dwarfed by the palatial manor. Now she felt as much a stranger as when she'd first arrived by hearse—no, not a stranger, but an intruder.

She'd brought Dr. Santo's letter with her, hoping it would act as ample evidence. Though it was unaddressed and unsigned, she gambled on the siblings recognizing their Uncle Shon's handwriting. Hate her or suspect her, but the Congmis would have to believe her.

With a breath to ready herself, she stepped onto the property.

Nhika almost expected the gardens to fold up and consume her, traitorous as she'd been, but the estate welcomed her back as though she'd never left. Nhika hiked up the long driveway, considered the front doors, then decided to enter through the garden. Sneaking past gardeners, their shoulders laden with bags of compost and potting soil, she slipped back into the manor with ease and found herself in recognizable hallways again.

To free Kochin, she would need the Congmis to believe her and, even less likely, she'd need them to help her. Nhika had to trust that their interests would align, that they'd want Dr. Santo behind bars as much as she did. The details of how they would prosecute him were for another time. Today, all Nhika needed was for them to trust her over a man they considered family.

Each step farther into the estate hiked anxiety up her throat. Nhika had little practice in facing her mistakes, much preferring the timeless method of running away from her problems, but she couldn't run from this. Not when Kochin still hated his heart-soothing and the Congmis invited a murderer into their home every other day.

As she had so many times before, Nhika found herself in a familiar spot: standing outside the office doors while voices were exchanged within. She recognized Mimi's and Andao's, then waited a beat more for Trin's, but his was absent.

Gathering all her willpower, Nhika rapped her knuckles against the door.

"Come in," Andao's voice called from within. Nhika stepped inside.

The siblings froze when they saw her, realization dawning upon them with varying degrees of quickness. Mimi first, eyes widening, with Andao slow to understand before he reached for the telephone—to do what, call the constabulary? Undeterred, she strolled to one of the armchairs across from Mimi and Andao; it must've been Trin's spot, judging by the recent imprint.

She made herself comfortable. "I hope you don't mind that I let myself in," she said when none of them spoke.

"What are you doing here?" Mimi's eyes narrowed with uncharacteristic steeliness.

"Clearing my name. I'm not the one Hendon remembers in the fox mask."

"Oh, we know. But you're in *league* with him."

There was no lie there, but Mimi's tone suggested Nhika was some mastermind, having planned it all from the start. "Trin doesn't understand what he saw."

"Then, what did he see?" Andao challenged.

"I found your masked man. But he's not the man you want. He's not the one who really wanted your father dead."

"Who, then?" Mimi demanded. It came out as cold and brittle as fractured ice.

At that moment, Trin entered.

They shared a stunned look, until Trin whipped the pistol from his belt. Nhika dove behind the cover of the desk, surfacing at Andao's side. A reckless idea formed, and in the heat of the moment she made the decision to grab Andao, one bare hand wrapped around his neck and the other wrenching his wrists behind his back.

He didn't resist, and when the dust had settled Nhika was breathless, staring down the length of Trin's barrel while Andao stilled in her grasp.

"Let him go," Trin said, his aim sure. His voice was patched up since she'd last heard it, a mortar of apathy over its cracks. "I won't miss."

"You wouldn't dare," Nhika growled. She understood their distrust, and yet she'd come with peaceful intention; Trin had elevated that to violence. Now here she was, in such a despicable position, the very bloodcarver they thought her to be.

"Nhika, why?" It was Mimi, her voice desperate, and when Nhika took her gaze from the gun she saw a broken reflection of the daring girl she'd come to know. Still, she didn't move.

"Put the gun down, Trin," Nhika commanded. He must've seen, by now, how she quailed before the gun. He must've known that it could bury a hole in her, too quick for heartsoothing to mend.

"Let him go," he said through gritted teeth. She saw something new behind the anger in his eyes: desperation.

"I didn't come back to hurt anyone." Frustration mounted in her chest. Andao must've felt it, too, because sweat beaded on the back of his neck. The letter in her shirt beckoned her—they'd believe her, if only she could grab it without being shot.

"And yet, here you are," Trin growled.

Nhika contested his gun with a glare of her own, and if heartsoothing could extend through sight rather than touch, she would've wrested that pistol from his grasp through pain and paralysis. Instead, all she could do was glare, eyes filled with anger, because she'd come to apologize only to be met with the cold end of a gun.

But the pounding in her heart settled when she saw their expressions: not fear or hate, but the pain of betrayal. Tears had welled in Mimi's eyes, wringing remorse into Nhika's chest—that she could cause that grief when Mimi had gone through so much already. This entire family had.

Nhika slackened her fingers around Andao's wrists. Betrayal spawned only from trust, so there must've been a time when they had trusted her. Not as a bloodcarver, and not as an asset to their mystery, but as Nhika.

She released Andao, who gasped as though she'd choked him, before stepping back. As soon as he was free of her, Andao rushed to the opposite end of the room, behind the safety of the gun, where his shaking hand found Trin's. The pistol still trailed her.

Now Nhika found herself diametrically opposed to this family who had once housed her. If they wanted to call the constabulary on her, she would have nowhere to go. If Trin wanted to shoot her now, there was nothing to stop him.

Yet, Nhika didn't draw up anger or cynicism to hide her vulnerability. Not this time. "I'm sorry," she said, the two words falling out like stones. "I understand you are all upset with me. I disappeared without warning, but I left to find the *real* murderer."

"Seems like you found him," Trin muttered.

"I know who you should truly be pointing your gun at. It's not me, and it's not the masked man. He was just a contracted killer. Don't you care about the man who really wanted your father dead?"

At that, Trin's aim wavered.

"Who really wanted our father dead?" Mimi demanded, voice edged with fierceness. It had been Mimi to first suspect her, and now, of all the eyes that bored into her, Mimi's held the most vehemence.

"You won't take my word for it, so I brought something to convince you." She made a show of moving slowly, reaching into the pocket of her shirt and drawing out the letter. She tossed it on the table between them, neutral territory, and Mimi snatched it up.

Nhika gave them a moment to digest its brief message before giving context. "Your masked man received that letter, asking him to commit murder. Do you recognize the handwriting?"

Mimi's eyes snapped to Nhika's—she had. And yet, she remained silent. Nhika only hoped it was because she was in shock rather than denial, because the letter had been Nhika's final play.

"Who wrote this, Nhika?" Andao asked, slower to connect the handwriting.

It was Mimi who spoke before Nhika could. "You'd have us believe that Uncle Shon would want my father, his closest friend, dead?"

"It's all there in the letter, isn't it?" Desperation slipped into Nhika's voice before she could bite it back; they still doubted her.

Mimi frowned, looking disinterested, and passed the letter to Andao. "Uncle Shon has done nothing but help us and Hendon since the very beginning, since before you ever even entered the picture. What reason could he possibly have to commit murder?"

"Your father got close to discovering the truth: that Dr. Santo's research was illegitimate, that he was using a heartsooth at the crux of his achievements."

That revelation made Mimi falter, but the girl recovered with a bat of her lashes. "That's certainly an interesting story, sure."

"Why would I lie?"

"What would we know of your collusion with the masked man? The motives could be many."

"I understand how close you are to Dr. Santo, but you need to believe me. Not just for my sake. For yours." This time, Nhika's words came out bruised, cracked with desperation. Trin's gun still traced her, and her pent-up anger burned the back of her throat; she would've released it if not for the fear of a bullet. "Why is that so hard?"

"We saved you from the Butchers' Row, Nhika, and you repay us by leaving with the masked man."

"You *bought* me from the Butchers' Row, Mimi," she hissed, no longer able to withhold her frustration. "You invited me onto a crime scene, asked me to heal the last witness of a murder, without ever considering the peril that put me in. You paid me a fraction of the amount you'd bought me with, chem I never even saw. You kept me on the other side of locked doors, at the far end of a dinner table, while expecting me to perform a miracle. How hard did I work to earn your trust, only for it to all disappear over a single night terror, one misunderstood act? I was never colluding with the masked man, and I'm not deceiving you now.

"Who was it that persevered when the physicians had written Hendon off as a lost cause, me or Dr. Santo? In the end, who was it that healed him?"

Her words had shaken the room; she felt as though the books might fall from the shelves and the chandelier from the ceiling. Trin lowered his gun, but Nhika still felt the heat of their judgment as surely as she had the barrel of their pistol, aimed between her eyes. Her muscles still trembled, buzzing with the release of adrenaline and anger, her lungs heaving for air despite the abundance of it. She could've soothed back the flush of her cheeks, the water in her eyes, the shake in her arms, but she let those all show, because she'd already laid out all her anger. Now all she had left was honesty.

At last, Mimi stepped forward, her expression that of a wounded animal. When she held up her chin, Nhika worried she'd persist with her usual stubbornness, but her next words held only humility: "You're right. We were wrong for that, Nhika."

"But do you believe me?"

"I . . ." Mimi ran a tongue over her teeth, looking to Andao for help.

It was Trin who responded. "Nhika, you're asking us to believe that Dr. Santo, someone who's been nothing but kind to us, who was Mr. Congmi's confidant, who we've all grown up with, would commit the most unspeakable act." His voice was gentle, and he'd holstered the pistol—he no longer considered her a threat, but what about an ally?

"I am."

"And you know this, because the man in the fox mask told you?"

"Yes."

"Have you considered that he lied to you?"

"Yes, but I believe him."

"Why?"

"Because . . ." Silence settled between them while Nhika searched for an answer, one she didn't quite know herself. Because he'd showed her his family, and she'd found that more compelling than Dr. Santo's lies. Because they all wore masks, but he'd taken his off for her. "Because he's a heartsooth."

Silence reigned at her declaration. A sequence of emotions passed through their expressions in turn: first shock, then realization, then understanding. Did they see now why she had left them?

Nhika continued, "Just when I thought I might be alone in this city, I found another. I don't expect any of you to understand how that feels, having one another the way you do. If only I could soothe it into you, then you might understand the loneliness. All I'm asking is that you accept why I left—it wasn't a chance I could turn down. But I've returned to ask your help in exposing Dr. Santo—justice for you, safety for me. If that's not enough for you, then there's nothing more I can offer."

Words had never been her gift; that was heartsoothing, and her fingers itched, wishing she could lace their bones with her longing. Her heart beat as though her chest cavity had been opened, as though they could peer between her ribs and through her sternum at the naked muscle. She wanted them to answer; more than that, she wanted them to understand.

Nhika had never asked for much before. She'd never wanted much, but she wanted *this*. For them to believe her over Dr. Santo, despite those years he'd accrued their trust. For any sign that she'd made an impression on them, that they could learn to care for someone like her. For her to be chosen, *for once*, not for a service or job, but as a friend.

"I want to believe you," Mimi began at last, her shaking tone breaking the silence. "But if it's not you, then who is the man in the fox mask?"

It was then that a knock came at the study door. They all turned as a butler leaned his head into the office. "You have a guest," he said.

The door swung open fully, and Kochin stepped inside. Nhika widened her eyes—she had not asked him to expose himself—but he gave her a sure look.

"Good morning," he said, and bowed.

— TWENTY-ONE —

THE ROOM STILLED, THE AIR SO BRITTLE THAT Nhika felt it might shatter with the strength of her heartbeat alone. It had never been the plan for Kochin to reveal himself—she'd feared what the Congmis might do with that information—but here he was, no doubt compelled by his guilt. She watched him out of the corner of her eye, how he kept his shoulders square and expression composed despite the lethality of Mimi's glare.

"Mr. Ven," Mimi growled. "What are you doing here?"

Nhika tried to interject, but Kochin beat her to it. "I think you may have already guessed."

"You're the one Hendon remembers that day?" Mimi's eyes were feral.

"Yes."

"You killed my father?"

Kochin sucked in a breath through his teeth. "I did."

Mimi fell silent, her fists balled at her sides. Nhika watched them all—Mimi's vitriol, Andao's and Trin's disbelief—and wished she could soothe understanding into them. But that wouldn't be fair; they were entitled to their grief.

With a sudden explosion of ferocity, Mimi grabbed a letter opener from the desk and leaped forward, wielding it as a knife.

Andao lunged up to hold her back, but Kochin didn't flinch, not even as the tip of the letter opener angled toward his eyes. Mimi fought in her brother's arms, small hands clawing at his sleeves, and let out a frustrated cry.

"Why?" she demanded, jerking the blade in the air. "Why would you do that? How could you do that? I'll *kill* you."

"Mimi, *please*," Nhika said. She moved to place herself between the two, but Kochin held up an arm to still her.

"I will," Mimi declared, the words guttural. "Apprehend him. Chain him. Lock him away. He's standing right there, the man who killed Father!" She struggled more but Andao, with strength Nhika didn't know he had, pulled her close to his chest and held her fast. There, in his arms, her shaking anger turned to sobs.

Only then did Kochin lower his gaze. Though his cool affect didn't break, a shadow of remorse came over his eyes. Nhika's heart ached for him, for all of them, try as she might to distance herself. This was not her feud, yet she felt directly responsible.

"I'm sorry," Kochin said, spurring Mimi into another fury. Her eyes bulged with tears and disbelief, lips curled dangerously.

"Sorry? You're *sorry*?" she cried, the tears flowing with the fervency of her rage.

"Nhika was telling the truth," Kochin said. "Dr. Santo was the one who asked me to kill your father. That letter serves as proof. I know it might not mean much to you, but he threatened my mother's life. My family's lives. I felt I had no choice."

"Why would I ever believe you?" Mimi spat. She'd slacked in Andao's arms, but her makeup ran with tears.

"Mimi." Trin's voice was firm, commanding her attention. "Look at the letter. Nhika didn't have to come back, but she did—to warn us."

Nhika nodded, appreciative of Trin's levelness. "We want the same thing, for Dr. Santo to face justice."

"I understand that, but I don't see why his accomplice shouldn't have to go to jail with him." Mimi narrowed her eyes, looking old beyond her years. "'Research Director and *Bloodcarver* Implicated in Murder.' That's a more accurate headline, isn't it?"

Nhika slammed her palm against an end table. "He's *not* a bloodcarver," she hissed, drawing Mimi's expression out of hate and into shock. "That's a name others use, not a name we made for ourselves. Dr. Santo sought him out for what he is, a *heartsooth*, and used him for it. If not him, then someone else like him. Like me, or his mother. Kochin is not a bloodcarver. I understand your pain, I really do—if I had someone I could blame for my family's death, I might want to carve them down to bone shards, too. But your father died trying to expose Dr. Santo for his crimes. If you let Kochin take any measure of the fall, then you'll have let Dr. Santo win."

The room returned to silence as Mimi studied her, eyes weighing the strength of her argument. Nhika had never known Mimi's anger for long enough to measure the readiness of her mercy, but something yielded behind her scrutiny.

"You care about this man, Nhika?" Mimi asked in a defeated tone.

Nhika met Kochin's gaze and found something wistful

there—beneath the guilt and apprehension, there was something else. "I do," she said, and watched the tension melt from his brow. She cared about his heartsoothing, his freedom, *him*.

Mimi opened her mouth to respond when a knock came at the door, followed by a voice: "It's Uncle Shon."

Before Nhika even registered the name, Kochin had flown across the room and grabbed her by the wrist. He pulled her behind the cover of the desk just as the door cracked open. There they huddled, foreheads nearly pressed together to both fit into the leg compartment of the desk.

"Oh good, you're all here," came Dr. Santo's voice as the door opened, holding that joviality Nhika now knew was an act. "Just stopping by to say that—oh, Mimi, have you been crying?"

"No," Mimi sniffled unconvincingly, her voice coming with the dregs of her temper. "Maybe."

Dr. Santo made a sympathetic noise in the back of his throat. "What's wrong, darling?"

For a moment, Mimi didn't deign to answer. Tension worked its way around the office in the ensuing pause and Kochin tightened every muscle of his shoulder. If Dr. Santo saw their shadows beneath the desk, if he rounded the office, Nhika wondered what they would do then—with no other weapon on hand, would they use their heartsoothing to commit a blasphemous act? If Mimi sold them out, would they even have the chance?

In the continuing silence, Nhika wondered if Mimi would be so punitive as to give them up here, while they were at her mercy.

"I was just afraid," Mimi continued, and ice hardened around Nhika's lungs.

"Afraid of what?"

It was hard to hear much over the pounding of her heart, but her ears strained for Mimi's response.

At last, she said, "Afraid that the man in the fox mask might be someone closer than we think."

If Dr. Santo's face revealed anything, Nhika couldn't tell from behind the desk. His tone was composed as he said, "Hendon's recovery is incomplete—his memory has not been as reliable as we may have hoped. This entire fox mask scare might simply be a delusion." He drew closer; the floorboards creaked with his weight. "Save your tears, Mimi. I won't let anything happen to you three."

Even now, knowing the truth, his assurance felt so genuine that Nhika warmed by instinct until she remembered it was just a mask.

"We know, Uncle Shon. We'll be all right," Andao said in a conciliatory tone, though his voice shook; he wasn't good at lying. "What was it you came for?"

Dr. Santo clapped his hands. "Just to say I'm done with Hendon's physical therapy. His health is still very weak and volatile. He retired to bed for the evening—best not to disturb him."

"All right, Uncle Shon." There was strain in Mimi's voice, but she found the strength to say thank you.

The shuffle of footsteps indicated Dr. Santo's exit. Only once Nhika heard the door of the study click close did she allow herself her first full breath. She shared a look with Kochin, finding her relief mirrored in the thaw of his shoulders.

"He's gone," Andao said, and he seemed just as shaken as she was. When Nhika emerged from the desk, she found Mimi with fresh tears in her eyes.

"Was he lying to me?" she asked in a small voice—the question wasn't meant to be answered by anyone in the room. "He wouldn't do that, would he?"

Kochin had other concerns, a hand pinching his chin. "He wasn't meant to make a home visit at this hour. It wasn't in his schedule."

Reading the insinuation between his words, Nhika's eyes flared at Trin and the siblings. "Did he know I left?"

"He'd asked. We told him you'd returned to the country," Andao replied, looking uncertain. "Why?"

A visit that wouldn't show up in documentation, just after Nhika had left . . . *Leave no witnesses*—but Kochin had. "Hendon . . ."

The siblings and Trin exchanged dubious looks, none of them conjuring a response. She didn't wait for one. Nhika pushed past them, giving the hallway a brief scan for Dr. Santo before rushing toward Hendon's bedroom.

This room plucked the strings of Nhika's memory; today, a curtain had been drawn over the windows and all the lights had been dimmed, as though to dissuade staff. As Dr. Santo had said, Hendon lay beneath the comforter, which strapped in all but his head and neck.

By the time the others reached the room, she was already at his bedside with two fingers at his neck.

A pulse. He was alive. She released a breath of relief, realizing that her suspicions might've been unfounded after all—

—until she looked at his chest, trapped under the tight fold of the comforter. There was no movement there, no rise and fall.

Hendon wasn't breathing.

— TWENTY-TWO —

"THE COMFORTER. TAKE IT OFF," SHE ORDERED Mimi, Andao, anyone. Trin and the siblings stood stunned, as though still grasping the reason for her rising alarm. It was Kochin who leaped into action, yanking back the tight comforter and exposing Hendon's chest.

Still, he didn't breathe. Without waiting for permission from the siblings, Nhika placed a palm over his bare forehead and soothed.

Nausea was the primary sensation, washing over all else. She'd felt something similar before in patients who took drug regimens, but never so potent. Distantly, she felt a tightness in his chest and a numbness in his limbs. When she tried to sow electricity through his motionless diaphragm, she found that she couldn't—the muscle sat lifeless as stone. Nhika drew her hand away as the malaise overwhelmed her.

"What's wrong?" Mimi asked, her voice frantic.

"He's not breathing," Kochin answered as Nhika regained her bearings.

She swallowed the acid in her throat. "There's some kind of drug there. I don't know how to soothe through it." Her words came out fast with panic.

"Let me help," Kochin offered, extending a hand toward Hendon in a gesture to soothe.

"*No!*" Mimi cried, coming alive with sudden fierceness. "Don't touch him."

"Mimi—" Andao began, but she shushed him with a pointed look.

"We don't have time," Nhika persisted, speaking through Mimi's venomous stare. "*Hendon* doesn't have time. He's not breathing, and Dr. Santo was the last to be seen with him. If ever you've trusted me, please, let it be now."

"I . . ." For all her earlier boldness, Mimi stood stunned. In the end, her mouth closed without an answer, and she looked so young and uncertain, again confronted with the fresh prospect of death.

"Please save him, Nhika," Trin said in her stead, and Mimi made no further attempt to stop them.

Nhika gave Kochin a beseeching look. "I can't do it alone," she said. Not without wasting time Hendon didn't have.

Kochin set his jaw in understanding, looking toward the Congmis a final time before he approached Hendon—not seeking forgiveness nor permission, but simply cooperation. Together, they soothed.

The nausea returned, but it wasn't so debilitating now that she anticipated it. She waded toward his lungs, dragging Kochin's influence with her. There she dropped him with desperate abruptness, showing him the unyielding diaphragm with the hope that he could do something, anything.

His touch was not so scattered nor distressed. As if he'd taken her hand, Nhika felt his influence guide her through the diaphragm. She saw the drug within, a languid sea of toxin. She watched it dispel under his influence, the queasiness abating and the electrical strength returning to the dormant muscle.

Testing her influence, she shocked electricity through his diaphragm. To her relief, the restored muscle spasmed, drawing a hiccup of breath, and she reworked the rhythm of her stimuli until she'd established a steady rise and fall. Nhika let out a tight breath just as Hendon drew one—they'd come just in time to save him.

Kochin tipped Hendon's mouth open, aiding the flow of air. He'd laid two fingers on Hendon's wrist to soothe, a physician's gesture.

"It's a neuromusculature-blocking drug," Kochin confirmed, his eyes glazed over. "It's caused paralysis, which reached his lungs. I can filter it out of his blood and into his urine. Until then, Nhika, you'll have to breathe for him."

"Whatever you need to do, please," Andao said. His knuckles were white with how tightly he held on to Trin.

Nhika was well acquainted with this position, wasn't she? Sitting at Hendon's bedside, being asked to heal him. This time, she didn't do it for chem or freedom, but because she cared for the Congmis, even if they thought her a traitor. Helping the Congmis, saving Kochin—Nhika did it all because she cared.

She stoked Hendon's lungs like a fire. Beneath her own work, she felt Kochin's influence sift through the blood. Perhaps this was how the art had always meant to be practiced, each heartsooth working together, demonstrating their own strengths. Kochin could not give his calories to Hendon's diaphragm, so Nhika did. She didn't know how heartsoothing might wring a drug from muscle into blood, blood into urine—yet, somehow, his could.

As Kochin worked, Hendon made a strained noise. Nhika might've thought it choking, but her stimulated breaths remained even. As the drug diminished further, his fingers began to twitch, eyes rolling behind closed lids.

Nhika drew in a sharp breath—he was awake. He *had* been awake this entire time, and now he was trying to move.

Cautiously, she drew her hand back. Hendon's gurgles turned to gasps; gasps turned to labored breaths. Soon, he was inhaling and exhaling in full measure, his eyes flying open with panic and muscle spasms working up his limbs.

Kochin stepped back, his work concluded. All of them watched as Hendon recovered from his paralysis, making arduous efforts to speak. Half words formed out of his labor, but they either died in his throat or came out incomprehensible.

Soon, the paralysis seemed to release his limbs. With great effort, Hendon pulled himself up in bed. His eyes, once fraught with fear, now subsided to the slow understanding that he was alive and safe.

Seeing him recovered, Mimi came to his bedside; Kochin stepped back to give her space. "Hendon, please, talk to us— what happened?"

Movement was returning to Hendon's facial muscles. He tried them in turn, lifting his brow and scrunching his nose. At last, he found mobility in his lips, just enough to say, "Shon."

Fingers wrapped around a cup of honeyed tea and peripheral muscles regaining fortitude, Hendon told them about his physical therapy session with Dr. Santo. As always, they'd worked on the muscle strength of his hands, something to alleviate the tremors. This session, Dr. Santo had also given him an intravenous solution of drugs for the remnant pain.

"He told me to rest in bed and when I did, I found that I couldn't move anything. Like I was trapped in my own body. I tried calling to Shon, but he just left . . . like he never even heard me. Then I couldn't even breathe—until Nhika showed up," Hendon finished.

Mimi's gaze lifted then, finding Nhika. "Thank you," she said, and though her eyes roamed over Kochin, she withheld her appreciation.

Kochin cleared his throat to gain their attention. He stood behind Nhika, arms crossed and two steps removed from the rest of them. "Dr. Santo meant to asphyxiate you. When they found you dead in the morning, most physicians would blame the irregular breathing on your recent brain injury, especially if his documentation noted a correlating decline in health."

"I don't understand—why?" Hendon's brow tightened with disbelief and Nhika remembered he wasn't there when she'd revealed everything. She pitied him—fighting out of a drugged paralysis was a jarring way to learn of Dr. Santo's betrayal.

"Because he wanted Mr. Congmi dead and asked me to do it," Kochin said, and the revelation shocked across Hendon's paralysis-weak muscles. "He was getting rid of his last witness."

"You, Mr. Ven . . ."

"Yes." Kochin drew back another half step, as though the family might turn on him again.

"It was you that day," Hendon continued. "Not Nhika. But it felt the same—because you both healed me. You saved me then, didn't you?"

Kochin's brow lifted with surprise, as though he hadn't expected his heartsoothing to leave such a mark. He opened his mouth to respond, but the words didn't come.

In his silence, Nhika said, "Yes, he did." She turned to the siblings, to Trin. "Please, I'm asking you to believe me now. Dr. Santo killed your father. He's now tried to kill Hendon, too."

Glances passed between the three of them. Mimi, ever persistent, said, "Could it have been a mistake? The paralysis drug might have been meant to help with the tremors."

Hendon shook his head, the quaver in his hands returning as he gripped his teacup. "He never told me there would be anything but pain meds. And a physician like him, administering a fatal dose by mistake . . ." His eyes drew darker than Nhika had ever seen them. "I believe them, Mimi. I believe Mr. Ven saved me the day of the accident, no matter his other crimes, and I believe he saved me again. I . . . I even believe Shon had intended to kill me just now, and if that's true, then I believe he wanted to kill your father, too."

It wasn't the answer Mimi wanted to hear; her expression collapsed with turmoil. "I need time. Maybe, we hide your recovery from Uncle Shon until we figure everything out. Maybe, we—"

Andao touched her shoulder and she quieted, as though already resigning to the truth. "Mimi," he whispered. "If this happens again and Nhika isn't around, we'll lose someone. I can't stand to lose you, or Trin, or Hendon. We have to do something, now."

Nhika hummed in agreement. "If Dr. Santo learns Hendon survived, he'll come back with a stronger dose. Either that, or . . ." Her eyes wandered to Kochin, whose countenance was grim, and she knew they shared the same thought. "Or he'll learn that a heartsooth aided you."

She wondered if they understood the gravity of that alternative—they didn't know the binds that held Kochin, only of the crimes committed against their father.

"Please, help us," Nhika continued when none of them spoke. "Everything is at stake. If Dr. Santo is placed behind bars, it's justice for your father, safety for you, freedom for Kochin, and . . ." And for Nhika? For once in her life, Nhika felt like she was doing something that might begin to honor her family's legacy. She was using her heartsoothing to heal. ". . . All I need is your help."

She could see all the strife that assailed Trin and the siblings: the shock of Dr. Santo's betrayal, the dread of losing someone else, the apprehension of having their masked man in the room. Trin and Andao were practical; she saw their uncertainty turn to quiet resolve, Trin's fingers tapping a silent message into Andao's hand.

Mimi was slower. Her gaze wavered between Nhika and Kochin, the look in her eyes the needlepoint between anger and grief, like a sharp breath might tip her either way. Nhika feared Mimi's anger, but her grief was somehow worse, and Nhika was asking her to salt a fresh wound by aiding her father's murderer.

At last, Mimi answered, "What can we possibly do?"

Relief melted the tension in Nhika's muscles, and she gave the Congmis an appreciative look. "The letter," she began. "Though Dr. Santo never signed it, it's in his handwriting. It details his intent and motive. You can come forward with that."

"But it's not enough," Trin told her. "Especially if everyone believes it was an accident. Threats are one thing—there's no proof that he actually went through with it."

Nhika frowned. "What about Hendon? He can make a statement about how Dr. Santo tried to kill him."

"And we've still no proof of it," Trin said again. "With Dr. Santo's social standing, they'd just blame it on delirium from Hendon's brain injury."

"What proof do we need, then?"

"A murder weapon, perhaps, unique to Dr. Santo," Andao suggested, but it would be near impossible to tie any weapon to Dr. Santo—not without implicating Kochin, too.

From his place in the back of the room, Kochin spoke up. "We have one. Not the one that killed your father, but the one that almost killed Hendon. The drug."

Andao's expression furrowed. "How will it help?"

"I recognized the feel of that drug. Dr. Santo developed it recently, a muscle relaxant called sancuronium—I've felt it in one of his transplant patients before, during surgery. As we've seen, a large enough dose can cause asphyxiation. Since it's still in a preliminary phase, the only bottle is in his home, but we can steal it and administer it to . . ." His sentence tapered off as though his next words would offend.

Nhika caught his gist. "We could administer it to your father's body," she said. "Put the separate pieces of Dr. Santo's crimes together for investigators to find."

"What does that mean?" Mimi asked, narrowing her eyes with scrutiny. "Are you saying you want my father . . . exhumed?"

Nhika set her lips in an answer.

"With heartsoothing, we can disperse the drug throughout his body," Kochin elaborated in an even tone. "We can make it look like the cause of death. To have your father exhumed for investigation, we'd just need Hendon to make a statement to the constabulary—that he had swerved not for the horses, but because he noticed your father choking in the back. That would be enough for them to suspect a medical death rather than a traumatic one. Enough, even, for a toxicology report that could detect the sancuronium. If we plant the drug in his office at the medical center afterward, somewhere only he has access, his culpability would be undeniable."

"That would be easy enough," Hendon said, but he deferred to the siblings for a final decision.

"No." Mimi crossed her arms. "Absolutely not."

"Mimi, let's think it through," Andao said, and Nhika could see the cogs working in his head. He believed in no afterlife; would he consider it so sacrilegious? "A murder weapon and a cause of death to pin on Uncle Shon. A letter in his handwriting to trace back his intent. Hendon as a witness on the scene. It would be enough. This is how we get him: with the very drug he tried to use against us."

Mimi's brow crinkled with despondence. In a small voice, she said, "But it feels like we just buried him. And we'd also have to . . . *tamper* with him."

"Father had always intended to donate his body to research when he passed. He just never had the chance to commit it to writing," Andao reasoned. "And I think that . . . I think that if he had been willing to go as far as confront someone as close as Uncle Shon, he would've wanted to see it through. He didn't leave us any instructions, Mimi, so we have to find some other way to carry on his memory."

Where Andao had always relented to his younger sister, now he stood firm in his opinion, and even Trin nodded in agreement. Mimi clenched her jaw, considering the suggestion more from her brother's lips than Kochin's.

"You're right," she said at last, words holding both resignation and resolve. She turned her attention back to Nhika. "So, you want us to exhume Father while you procure this drug?"

Nhika nodded, relieved to have finally won Mimi's cooperation. "But it must be discreet. If Dr. Santo learns what we're doing, it'll all be over."

Mimi turned to Kochin. "And you. If we're going to do this, I want your word that, after this, you'll disappear from our lives."

"I'll leave the city," Kochin responded. Nhika knew it was what he'd always wanted, but his declaration made her strangely melancholic. "You'll never see me again."

"Good," Mimi declared. "This isn't forgiveness, Mr. Ven. But for Nhika, for my father, we'll help. Now, let's get started."

— TWENTY-THREE —

AT THE END OF THE WEEK, THE CONGMIS INVITED Dr. Santo over for dinner, giving Nhika and Kochin a brief window to steal the sancuronium. They gathered their things—lockpicks, bags, gloves—and garbed themselves in black. Before they left, Kochin lifted his seat cushion to reveal a compartment in the bench. From it, he drew two masks.

She stared at them. Where Kochin's fox mask smiled emphatically, hers was a fish, comically sad with a lone tear falling from its bulging eyes. "Is this necessary?"

"Oh, absolutely."

"So, you're a fox, and I'm a . . . fish?"

"They're characters from Yarongese fables," Kochin said. Nhika had suspected his mask was a nod to the Trickster Fox when she'd first met him. With both intrigue and sadness, she wondered why, of all the creatures he could've chosen, Kochin had picked a villain.

She remembered the story of the Dismal Carp, too. "Isn't this the fish that cries so much he creates all the rivers on Yarong?"

"Yes," Kochin said, flashing her a grin. "He does nothing but complain all the time." Before she could reply, he'd hopped out the door.

They left in the evening, setting off across the water. This time, instead of returning to the dockyards, they pulled ashore in the Dragon Borough. There, they disembarked on a private beach of gray pebbly sand and dragged their boat toward the shelter of the cliff.

Up the cliffside, the spacious gardens and well lit streets of the Dragon Borough welcomed them. Dr. Santo's mansion was atop a hill, not with the acreage of the Congmis' manor but with a garden and a sloping driveway all the same. He had an eye for extravagance: finials atop every roof and limestone walls carved with intricate scenes. The home even had an outdoor water system, with waterfalls trickling through porous rocks and into koi ponds. Nhika whistled at the sight of it as she and Kochin found a place to observe, far from the house and out of lamplight.

"Does Dr. Santo have much of a family?" she asked, arms crossed as she watched shadows move inside the house.

"Not anymore," Kochin replied. "His wife left him after the death of their son."

Nhika recalled her conversations with Dr. Santo about his son—Leitun, was it? Looking back in hindsight, she was surprised it was the truth, rather than another part of his elaborate lies. "The boy with the hole in his heart."

Kochin nodded. "You can't help but feel bad for him, can you? Even after everything he's done. I can't even imagine that, losing someone you love when you feel you could've saved them."

Nhika made a noise of agreement, but she knew exactly how that felt.

The house brightened with lights. The hum of an engine announced Dr. Santo's autocarriage, which pulled down the driveway. She and Kochin ducked into the cover of the alley, watching him until he traveled down the road and turned the corner.

Before they entered, they waited for the house to settle, lights flickering back to darkness and quiet befalling the street. Then they meandered toward his home, acting as though they belonged there, their pace casual and inconspicuous. The temperate weather afforded them the leisure of a stroll, and when they slipped into Dr. Santo's garden, Nhika cast a glance over her shoulder to ensure that no one had spied them from an open window.

The garden offered a rock path that wound up the side of the property, a convenient avenue into the house. The entrance was through a garden portico, the wall lined with shuttered windows that Nhika shied from.

She walked past Kochin toward the door, leaning close in the dying light.

The mask constricted her view, as did the growing darkness, but Nhika had prepared for this. She slipped her lockpick set out of her bag and set to work on the lock, going by sound and feel more than anything else. Just like heartsoothing, lock picking was another skill her grandmother had left her, though sired more by necessity than tradition. And as with heartsoothing, Nhika had perfected it during her time on the streets, whenever she needed a warm place to sleep when she was between apartments.

Her lockpick ticked against the tumblers, ever light. She tapped them into place, feeling the resistance of the cogwork as she placed tension on the wrench. It turned in full when the last tumbler fell into place, and the lock clicked open.

"You make it look easy," Kochin said as she opened the door into a dark foyer.

"It is," she said, jerking her head toward the shadowed room. He stepped past her and she closed the door.

They crept forward in the darkness. Nhika fought the urge to remove her shoes when they reached the polished hardwood of the tearoom, with its low tables and chairs oriented toward the garden. Around the corner, from somewhere farther down the hallway, a light flickered and moved—a gas lamp.

Kochin took her arm, ushering her into the cover of the pantry. The whiff of pungent herbs and roots tickled her nose under the mask, a sneeze threatening to let loose. She bit it down.

The gas lamp passed. Nhika peered out of the pantry in time to see the back of a maid retreating down the hall.

"Going home for the day, let's hope," Kochin said. "Dr. Santo keeps his secrets close. I can't imagine he'd keep staff around after hours."

"I suppose we'll see. Where's his office?"

"Around the corner."

Nhika let Kochin take the lead as they slunk forward, the hardwood creaking underfoot. This house used more of an open concept than the Congmis' manor, rooms widening up into one another, walled by paper-screen paneling with few hallways in between. Sure enough, the office was down the hall, an inviting room. It was plainer than Nhika had expected, but that meant fewer places where the sancuronium could hide.

Careful not to displace anything, she and Kochin set about searching, pulling drawers and examining cabinets. Kochin had said it would be a brown-glass bottle, but she found nothing of the sort in his desk or shelves, just bound literary anthologies and medical journals. On the wall he displayed plaques of his credentials, gleaming gold in the light. Beside them hung framed publications; Dr. Santo had true achievements. But the most prominent paper, that of his groundbreaking transplant, left a bitter taste in her mouth. Kochin hadn't been credited at all.

"Any luck?" Kochin asked, drawing her attention.

"None."

"Me neither." She could hear the disappointment in his voice, though his mask concealed it. "Upstairs, then. He has a private study where he may keep research materials."

Private study it was. Clicking off the lights, Nhika followed him down the hall, where a cubic stairwell took them to the second floor. She glanced out the window as they passed, watching as a throng of women departed down his driveway.

"We might be alone now," she said, grin spreading. "Maybe before we go, we should take a quick peek at his pantry."

"What are you in the mood for?"

"I'm sure he has something expensive." Nhika thought back to the illicit goods she'd seen at the Butchers' Row. "Shark fin? Black chicken meat?"

"Shark fin? Black chicken?" He flashed her a look. "Aren't those aphrodisiacs? Now, why would you want those?" His teasing tone brought heat to her cheeks and Nhika was suddenly thankful for the mask.

"That's not what I meant. Surely, a medical professional such as yourself doesn't believe in such properties."

"Maybe I do. I *have* been in business with the Butchers' Row."

Nhika quieted, measuring his sincerity. He only gave her an impish look, eyes smiling through the mask, and she laughed. "And you must also believe that eating a bloodcarver grants you their gifts, don't you?"

"I believe the original myth was having the *heart* of a bloodcarver, which I already have."

His heart or hers? Nhika didn't want to ask.

They reached the top of the stairs and he turned the corner, stopping abruptly before a closed door. He tried the handle—locked.

"This is promising," he said, deferring to her. She retrieved her lockpicks again and crouched before the door.

This lock came undone with ease, and she swung the door open to reveal a dark study, smelling of ink and paper. No windows here, but she saw the shadowy outline of a desk. Kochin stepped inside and turned on the light.

Holy Mother, it was as though a library had swept through this room by monsoon. Where his office had been orderly, his private study was a mess of loose papers, opened books, torn pamphlets. Corkboards lined the walls, pinned with an assortment of scraps. The shelves were only half full, the remaining books occupying the floor in varying degrees of abuse. A typewriter sat on a desk in the middle of all the mess, a half-finished document in its platen.

Nhika navigated between the papers and books and open ink-wells to stand before the typewriter. It seemed to be a write-up of some research paper. She recognized terminology pulled from the literature she'd spent so long studying, something about life-sustaining technology. A quick scan of the surrounding documents showed that they'd been excerpted from past research, torn from journals, scribbled with notes.

"The man is undeniably dedicated," Nhika said, the gravel in her voice a symptom of her wariness.

"No," Kochin said, his tone hollow. He'd stopped in front of one of the corkboards. "He's . . . deranged."

Nhika drew closer to him, eyes exploring the corkboard. It took her a moment to comprehend what she saw, but then her lungs stopped working.

There was a photograph of a human chest splayed open, skin held back by pins to reveal the thoracic anatomy underneath, membrane encasing the heart and lungs open to the air. A scalpel hovered just in frame, blurred in the photograph. With the cold echo of horror in her own chest, she realized the patient was staring at the camera, still awake, not in surgery but in vivisection. And he was Yarongese.

Surrounding the photo were anatomical diagrams, meticulous and detailed, of humans sliced open, their craniums drilled, their brains exposed. Headlines and excerpts of articles joined them, written in Daltan—Reincarner ve Morts, Bludsculver os zen Vivex. Things she couldn't understand but recognized as horrific. With a shuddering breath she stepped backward, feeling pain bloom across her body as though it were her in those drawings and photographs.

"Did . . . Did he do this?" she asked, voice stricken.

Kochin peered closer. "No. These are Daltan photos." He shared a glance with her, and the room dropped a couple degrees in warmth. She'd heard about the Daltan experiments, the persecution of heartsooths when the island first fell under attack. She'd just never had an image to put to it.

"Let's find what we need and leave," he said, a hand on her arm to swivel her away. It was too late; the image was already burned onto her retinas.

They moved to the shelves, upending books in search of a drug bottle. What she found instead were Daltan journals, filled with studies on heartsooths. Volume after volume, some with detailed images and others with photographs. These were texts that Theumas had decried, not on grounds of immorality but invalidity—Daltanny had sliced through heartsooths with little method nor hypothesis, like children before a new toy. Yet, Dr. Santo had collected them all here in his twisted library, had used them as gospel. In those images she saw her mother, her father, grandmothers and great-grandfathers, and a long, broken lineage that had been lost to time.

No, not lost. Stamped out. Persecuted.

"Don't look, Nhika," Kochin said, the shake in his voice mirroring the tremble in her breath. "Let's just . . . focus on the sancuronium."

She nodded wordlessly, moving to the next shelf. They tore

through the study, searching beneath papers and behind columns of stacked books, but to no avail. Dread gripped her fingers as she examined Dr. Santo's desk, as though the drawers would hide more graphic images.

When she opened the uppermost drawer of his desk, her eyes caught on the silver frame of a portrait. She winced, fearing something gruesome, but it wasn't any Daltan vivisection. Instead, it was a photo of a younger Dr. Santo with a boy in his lap—wide eyes and chubby cheeks, looking flushed in tight and formal clothing. Dr. Santo, who'd locked a grip on his shoulder, smiled placidly at the camera, but the boy stuck out a playful tongue at the photographer. His face blurred with mischief.

"They're not here," Kochin muttered, appearing at her side.

Nhika surveyed the Daltan papers strewn across the room one more time. Her eyes ended on the photograph of Dr. Santo's son, so out of place in this room. "Let's lock this room back up. We weren't meant to see this." She almost wished she hadn't.

Without needing any more prompting, Kochin took her from the room, locking the door behind them. Keeping quiet, they scoured the other rooms that might hold medication—the kitchen, the bedrooms, the basement. Kochin upturned every cabinet; Nhika sorted through every drawer. Time pressed on, and Nhika feared she'd hear the rumble of Dr. Santo's autocarriage returning before they found the sancuronium. At last, with few other rooms left in the house, their search led them to the conjoined carriage house where Dr. Santo kept his vehicles.

As soon as Nhika stepped inside, her gut told her they'd found the right place; the room was chilled compared to the rest of the house. This was smaller than the Congmis' carriage house, but it had space enough for autocarriages and horse tack, with one vehicle absent from Dr. Santo's earlier departure.

Kochin moved toward a row of steel cabinets in the back, then threw a glance over his shoulder. "A medicine cabinet." He removed his mask and drew close to the glass. "It's too dark to read."

Nhika searched for a light switch. There was a chain dangling from the ceiling, and she yanked down on it. Dim, yellowed light flooded the carriage house, and she joined Kochin's side at the cabinet to find its shelves full of glass bottles, stout and tall, with a variety of different clinical labels. They reminded her of her tinctures, leaf juices pressed in rubbing alcohol and corked in glass. These, however, sported their name, dose, and usages on the front, printed in a clear font. Nhika scanned the labels—a variety of household medications she recognized, a cough syrup or two, and a few medications with names long enough to wrap all the way around their bottles.

Then, on the bottommost shelf, she found their drug: sancuronium.

With gloved hands, Kochin slipped open the cabinet door and grabbed the bottle, rearranged the others to conceal its absence, and held the drug up to the light. It was as he'd said: brown, labeled as a muscle relaxant, and missing a dose's worth of liquid.

She and Kochin shared a look, and Nhika let out a breathless gasp. "This is it?"

"This is it."

"Then let's get out of here." But she'd spoken too soon. They heard the creak of a floorboard, and lights turned on in the hallway.

"Shit," Kochin hissed, and pulled her flat against the wall. A singsongy hum emanated from the house. Fear prickled through her, but all Nhika could think about was how Kochin had spread his arm across her chest, how he leaned in so close she could hear his breath.

They'd left the door to the carriage house open with the lights on. Here, pressed up against the wall, there were few places to hide without passing in front of the door. Nhika wished for the cover of an autocarriage, but already, a shadow swayed on the other side. The sound of approaching footsteps halted just before the door, and the maid's humming stopped on a questioning lilt.

Nhika sucked in a breath.

The footsteps drew closer. Nhika tugged off her glove, preparing for the worst. Putting someone to sleep—that would be easy enough, just a matter of quieting the electricity in their brain. But if the maid saw them, it would all be over. Nhika stepped forward as the shadow grew closer, but Kochin placed a hand on her arm.

Nhika looked at him, perplexed, as he passed her his mask and the bottle of sancuronium. He brought his finger up to his lips, then stepped toward the door.

The maid screamed. Nhika's heart spiked in her throat, fearing he'd hurt her, until she said, "Mr. Ven! Oh, you gave me such a fright. I thought I was alone in the house."

"Sorry, Tinai. I was finishing up some work for Dr. Santo and thought I'd take the liberty of dropping it off myself."

"Well . . ." Nhika heard the maid dusting off her clothing. "I'll tell Dr. Santo you stopped by."

"No need," Kochin said quickly. "It's nothing important. Feel free to go home for the night—I can lock up after you're gone."

There was a tense pause, where Kochin blocked the door and Tinai didn't respond. Nhika wondered if she would step past him, into the carriage house. If she did, even with how dim these bulbs were, she would see a girl garbed in all black who certainly didn't belong.

At last, Tinai let out an assentive sigh. "All right, Mr. Ven. Have a good night."

"Good night, Tinai."

A moment passed with some shuffling, and Nhika watched Tinai's shadow shrink from the door. Only once she heard the footsteps recede and another door close in the distance did she let herself breathe again.

Kochin wrung out a long exhale, then glanced at her. "Are you all right?"

"Yes." Nhika drew her glove back on, still feeling her pulse in her arm. Her fingertips tightened around the glass bottle. "You?"

"I'm fine." He leaned against the door, flexing his hand as though it ached.

"I probably could've put her to sleep," Nhika thought aloud.

"I know. But I don't want either of us to have to use our

heartsoothing that way anymore. Not when we don't have to."
His eyes, when they met hers, were somber.

"It's all right. We should just go before we get caught."

A solid breath escaped him. "I couldn't agree more."

Nhika followed him out the back of the carriage house, ears trained for any more surprises. The night air brought a breath of relief and she felt lighter to be rid of the house, of those shadowed walls and Daltan texts. She held on to the bottle of sancuronium like it was a buoy and these Dragon Borough streets were the roiling waves of a tsunami.

As they started down the path toward the dinghy, Nhika cast a final glance back at the mansion, the carriage house, and its dark windows. For a moment, an inkling of concern crawled up her throat as her mind lingered on the maid, on the consequences if she alerted Dr. Santo to their presence tonight. But those thoughts were quick to flee as Kochin rowed them back.

— TWENTY-FOUR —

WHEN THE EXHUMATION DATE ARRIVED, NHIKA and Kochin set out toward the Congmi graveyard by dinghy, changed into somber attire and taking the sancuronium with them. Everything hinged on this exhumation—and the subsequent planting of the sancuronium in Dr. Santo's office.

With each stroke of the oars, Kochin drew them closer to the cemetery where Mimi, Andao, and Trin awaited them.

Nhika had lied and trespassed and stolen before, but never had she felt this nervous. In the past, the worst she could lose was a handful of chem or her dignity, but today the livelihoods of those few she cared about had been thrown into the gambling pot.

While he rowed, Kochin's eyes scanned her face. Somehow, he could read her easily, and he asked, "Worried?"

"A little," she admitted. She'd prepared for the exhumation mentally, but that did little to help the nervousness now.

"What for? Won't I be the one doing the soothing?" he teased. It was best that way; Kochin had experience soothing through drugs.

"I'm worried on your behalf, then," she returned. "Aren't you?"

His answer took a moment to come. "I'm terrified," he admitted. "This is the first time I've defied Dr. Santo since I tried to leave the city. I keep fearing there'll be the same consequences as before, that he'll find something new to take from me. But, more than worried, I'm . . . hopeful."

"Hopeful?" Nhika realized she was smiling.

"Yes. This isn't the first time I've tried to escape him, but it's the first time I'm not doing it alone." His eyes glided over her and a delicate smile tugged at his lips. "I feel like everything I've learned under Dr. Santo has been preparing me for this. It's almost poetic."

"You knew how to soothe the sancuronium from Hendon's body because of Dr. Santo?"

"Yes. I've read enough of his papers to know what I was looking for. Heartsoothing and medicine can be combined to amazing effect, but the world might never know that." His expression turned solemn. "He taught me to soothe dead bodies, too."

"He made you soothe dead bodies?" The thought was instinctively revolting to her, feeling death while soothing as intimately as she felt sickness.

"Donor corpses. He wanted me to restore dead organs for transplantation."

"I didn't know heartsoothing could do that."

"I'm still not sure it can, really. I could return their function, sometimes. But not in any way that satisfied him." The memory must've been a distasteful one because Kochin's eyes darkened. "He always treated my gift like it was some kind of science."

Nhika wanted to interject that it *was* science, something to be learned and taught, but his reverential tone told her he felt otherwise. "What is it, if not a science?"

"I don't know," he said, "magic?" Nhika fought her instinct to refute that. Coming from most, delegitimizing heartsoothing as *magic*—the same kind of paltry parlor tricks and sleight of hand performed before a half-enthused audience—had always been an attempt to disenfranchise people who possessed a gift that Theumans could never have. But from Kochin, the word held only wonderment.

"Magic?"

"As in . . . something that could never be explained, no matter how hard we dissect it. Something where rules exist not as limits, but only to help us understand the next boundary. Where rules exist to be broken." His sentences came out as a collection of scattered thoughts, as though they'd only ever existed in his head, never aloud. It was a beautiful thing, the way he viewed heartsoothing. Such a perspective was rare within the industrialized confines of Theumas, but it must've been how the first heartsooths viewed their abilities, labeled as a gift from the divine.

The dreamy look in his eyes reminded Nhika of her grandmother, who spoke of heartsoothing only ever as a blessing and a duty. Nhika, however, could not accept it as magic, because this city had shown itself adverse to the inexplicable, and she didn't need another reason to feel as though she didn't belong. Strange, she thought, how two heartsooths could know the art so differently yet cling on to it with that same desperate, unending tenacity.

They rounded the bend of the cliffside, and the dockyards came into view. Her anxiety lurched at the sight, knowing that a grim exhumation awaited them there. As long as she was here, on this dinghy, she could almost pretend that this moment would last forever.

"What are you going to do when this is all over?" she asked. "You have a lot of money to spend."

He snorted. "Maybe once I would've liked such an auspicious life, but I'm trying to settle for different ambitions now."

"Like what?"

He took a moment to think. "Peace. Freedom." He shrugged. "Love." She felt her heart stutter at the way he wrapped his breath around that last word.

Peace, freedom . . . love. Words she understood but couldn't conceptualize. "But just as lofty, aren't they?"

He let out a humored breath. "Well, I think I might've stumbled into a couple already."

Nhika clenched her jaw when he turned his charming gaze on her, wondering if that had been a declaration, or if he hadn't meant it in that way. They'd both hidden behind so many second meanings and half-truths when they'd met at the funeral, when he was just a physician's aide to her, but Nhika wanted nothing but openness with this Kochin.

"Freedom first, then peace, right?" she said.

His eye twinkled, but he didn't respond directly. "After I'm free of Dr. Santo, I'm going to return to my family. It's long overdue, and with him behind bars, I can go home without the fear of bringing the city with me."

Nhika smiled. "Your mother misses you, Kochin. She'll be so happy to see you."

"I know." Kochin gave their dinghy another solid stroke

before he rested the oars. The boat slowed to an idle glide atop calm waters, bobbing up and down in time with the waves. He gave her an intent look, something shifting behind his eyes: a vulnerability that didn't come from heartache, or fear, but from something new.

She gave him a quizzical look. "Why are we stopped?"

For a moment he didn't answer, instead lacing his fingers together. "I've been meaning to ask you something," he began. His hesitance bled onto her; she'd never seen such a nervous side of him.

After a pause, he continued, "Nhika, I'm sorry I tried to push you away when we first met. I was afraid because I saw so much of myself in you, the person I was before Theumas. Now I see you're not like me at all—you're braver, smarter, fiercer. After this is all over, I'm going to go home, but there's something I need to know first."

His confession touched on naked sincerity and she nodded, almost afraid of his next words.

"Will you come with me?"

The question settled into the bare wood of their dinghy, sank beneath the uneven waves. Nhika only stared at him. He'd asked her before to go stay with his family—he'd nearly left her there. So, what was so different this time?

When she didn't immediately respond, he added, "Only if you'd want to, of course. You would have the company of a family—one where heartsoothing is known and welcomed. My mother would love you, and so would my brothers, and I can help you find a home and a—"

"Why?" she interrupted, scrutinizing him, the sudden depth of his dark eyes and soft line of his lips. "Why do you want me to come?"

His brow crinkled. "Nhika, isn't it obvious?"

The Congmis kept her because they needed her services, but Kochin . . . The two of them had always been push and pull, him keeping her away but always drawn back like gravity. Now he wanted to pull her in, but for what reason? "If this is just another ploy to keep me safe and sequestered away, then, Ven Kochin, I swear—"

Kochin leaned forward and kissed her.

Nhika drew a sharp breath of surprise before she succumbed to it, to his hands on her cheeks and his lips on hers. He must've been soothing her, or maybe she was soothing him; Nhika couldn't tell. Her senses had rewired themselves, his touch overwhelming, and yet she'd never felt more at home in her own body. Kochin drew her closer, a hand moved to her waist, and Nhika came apart at his touch: muscle unwrapping from bone, nerves aflame, lungs bursting. A gesture to leave her breathless followed by the warmth to restore it.

At last he pulled away, though he lingered just a hair's breadth, the space between them like the space between nerve endings: raw and electric. She wanted to kiss him again, but he murmured, "Does that answer your question?"

Nhika nodded, unable to conjure words. The dinghy rocked with the imbalance of their weight.

"I didn't realize I could win arguments by kissing you," he said, giving her a smile as he drew back to arm's length. He thumbed away a strand of her hair. "I want to leave this city, but I don't want to leave you. So, will you come with me?"

This time, she understood. He'd asked her to come not because she was the only other heartsooth, nor because he felt compelled to protect her. He'd asked her to come because he wanted *her*.

Nhika held his gaze as she processed the offer. There was nothing to leave behind—in Theumas, she'd already restarted her life a dozen times over, and the only thing she had of value was the ring she wore around her neck. If she had to do it again, if she were to choose something that might finally stick, then it would be with Kochin.

"Yes," she said, surer than she'd ever been. Adrift on this dinghy with the shadow of Theumas's cityscape far behind them, Nhika felt the bubble of something true and overwhelming: happiness. "I'll come with you."

Kochin smiled, so wide and boyish that she couldn't help but return it. "I was hoping you'd say that."

Then he kissed her again.

— TWENTY-FIVE —

WHEN THEY REACHED THE CONGMIS' PRIVATE graveyard, they found it occupied by an intimate group—the siblings, Trin, Hendon, and a smattering of officials. No police cordon, no press, no aristocratic guests; it would seem the Congmis had heeded the need for discretion.

Trin came to open the gates for them at the bottom of the hill, giving Nhika a stout greeting and Kochin a wary look as he escorted them up the path. There, they met the others at the mausoleum, all dressed conservatively for the occasion.

"There they are," Hendon said, addressing the uniformed officers. "We can begin."

Nhika surveyed those in attendance: a handful of constables; the groundskeeper; a criminalist; and a couple cemetery hands, each equipped with a bag of tools. They all drew closer as Trin swung open the gates of the mausoleum, but Nhika noticed how Kochin lingered back. She tilted her head in question, but he gave her a reassuring smile, just a quirk of his lip to say, *I'll keep my distance.*

"Be our guest," Andao said, sweeping a hand toward the cemetery workers, who then entered the mausoleum to remove Mr. Congmi's body from its crypt.

So the exhumation process went: slowly, awkwardly, and

without any conversation. Everyone stared ahead at the mausoleum's closed gates, hearing some sort of chipping and grunting as the cemetery hands worked to remove the entombed casket.

The last time she'd been in this graveyard had been for the procession, but today was nothing like that—the funeral had been gloomy, but now the sun beat down from a cloudless sky. Before, she had barely been able to think through the fanfare and clamoring of journalists, but now all she had were her thoughts.

There was one more difference: She had felt so small then, seeing this graveyard spanned with the headstones of so many Congmis, an ever-growing lineage immortalized in granite and marble. Now she realized that she didn't need this kind of remembrance in her passing. If all the difference she ever made in this city was not in graveyards nor children, but in the freedom of a single heartsooth, that would suffice.

Maybe, that was all that legacy truly was: remembrance from beyond the grave. It didn't need to be resounding, and it didn't need to be celebrated; it just needed to be. It was the same with heartsoothing, which had died a generation before her, but with her family's escape from Yarong, the legacy lived on in those like her, and like Kochin. A whisper where there had once been a shout, but a voice nonetheless.

And maybe that was enough.

At last, the cemetery workers emerged from the mausoleum, signifying the adjournment of their work with a respectful bow. The criminalist started toward the gates, but Mimi lifted a hand.

"If we may," Mimi began, "could we request time to repay our respects alone?"

The criminalist deferred to them. With a knowing look, Mimi ascended the steps to the mausoleum. Nhika followed.

Trin shut the gates behind them as they entered, leaving only the company of those in conspiracy. Compared to the monument it was on the outside, the mausoleum's inner sanctum felt claustrophobic and colorless, the light coming in dusty shafts from clerestory windows and walls ringed with crypts. There was space left for many generations of Congmi heirs in these walls, with a single casket removed from its slot and sitting open at the center of the mausoleum.

Mimi shuddered, searching for the comfort of her brother's side. "I can't look," she said, her voice small.

At first, no one dared approach the casket. Nhika waited for their approval—the siblings', Trin's, even Hendon's—but when none came, she took it on herself to step forward.

To her surprise, Mr. Congmi did not look much different than he had the last time she'd seen him, perhaps the product of a good embalming and dry grave. The only difference was how everything had shrunken down on itself just a little, cheeks sallow, eyes hollow, and scalp tightening around the hair. Nhika couldn't find it in herself to be disturbed or scared of a corpse; at the moment, she felt nothing but remorse for the act they were going to perform.

With a subtle gesture, she called Kochin to her side. Then he withdrew the bottle and a needle and turned to the siblings.

Mimi had her face turned into her brother's jacket, but Andao gave Kochin a permissive nod. Kochin drew up a healthy dose into the syringe. He moved to inject it into the dwindling muscle of Mr. Congmi's deltoid but stalled, the point of the needle wavering just over waxy skin. When Nhika glanced at his face, the look behind his eyes was haunted. Seeing his repentance, as well as the Congmis' renewed grief, her chest tightened.

Nhika wrapped her fingers around Kochin's hand and, together, they pushed the needle in.

"Just a touch of cyanosis around the lips and a bit of spotting of the skin, and that should be enough," she said. Kochin nodded, doffing his glove to soothe, but a noise from Mimi stilled him.

"Wait," she said, facing the body for the first time. Whatever words she'd prepared left her in an instant as her eyes fell upon her father. The heaviness of the moment seemed to dawn on her in parts: first as pain collapsing her stony expression, then as water welling to her eyes, and finally as the violent tremble of her lip. She soldiered through it to say, "Nhika, can you do it instead?"

"Me?" Nhika shared a look with Kochin, but he didn't object.

"Yes. I don't want—" Mimi swallowed, reworked her words. "I'd rather you do it."

From his stiffness, Nhika could tell Kochin wanted to soothe Mr. Congmi for her sake, but the siblings' preference held highest authority here. With a nod, Nhika drew off her glove. Her fingers hovered over the corpse, unsure where to touch— anywhere was a violation, one she hadn't personally been planning to commit today. But she'd been the one to insist on this plan, and soothing a corpse couldn't be so different from soothing someone living.

When she couldn't decide, Kochin took her wrist in a light grip and guided it down to Mr. Congmi's hands, laced over his chest. The fingers were cold and waxlike, but Nhika fought the urge to draw away.

"Act as though they're alive," Kochin said. "It's easier that way."

Nodding, Nhika rested her hand atop Mr. Congmi's and pushed her influence inside.

There, she found nothing awaited her. No electrical melody, no pulsing waterways, no swelling breath. Just the ghosts of anatomical architecture, bones so brittle she feared her influence might crack them and muscles so sour she puckered on instinct. Nhika fought her way toward his deltoid, trudging through the remains of clotted blood thick with the pungent odor of embalming fluid.

Act as though they're alive. Hard, when this body was so patently dormant, when the processes Nhika relied on so heavily had come to a standstill, the vasculature like an abandoned train station whose empty halls echoed with commuters past.

With much effort, she reached Mr. Congmi's shoulder, biting back bile as the taste of the sancuronium flooded her tongue. It was the one dynamic thing in this body, still suffusing through muscle.

In a live body, if she wanted to expedite this process and circulate the drug through the entire body, she might've depended on the waking functions of the anatomy—the constant circulation of blood, the squeezing of muscles. Now, with her influence in a corpse, that grip she had on blood and muscle felt slack, useless. What's more, empathy with the dead made her feel corpselike herself, limbs numbing and skin bloating and mouth drying; that stone of bile was rising quickly up her throat.

A hand pressed against her shoulder. "Take a step back," came Kochin's voice, as though it hovered just beside her ear. "Breathe."

He was right; she didn't need to be so close. Nhika drew back, remembering how it was to soothe as he did, separate from the body. Her influence yanked from the corpse until she was looking down at the casket from above.

Once she'd reoriented, Nhika could see Mr. Congmi as a whole. There was detail lost in doing so—she could not feel all his ailments and incongruities as if they'd mirrored onto her own body—but she saw him as he was: a dead man under her influence and nothing more.

No longer having to fight the disgust of inlaying herself upon a dead body, Nhika soothed. Because Mr. Congmi had no energy stores readily available, she used only her own. Otherwise, the processes were easy enough, flexing muscles and squeezing the heart, tightening vessels and stippling the skin. Nhika didn't change much—she would not violate the Congmis' father any more than she had to—and it only took a couple minutes once she'd started. By the time she pulled away, shuddering off the last omen of death, Mr. Congmi did not look wholly unchanged. However, another medical examination might find something amiss—enough to begin investigations.

"Are you done?" Mimi asked, voice fragile.

"Yes," Nhika said, drawing her glove back over her hand. For once, she was glad for the confines of silk, something to quiet her gift for a moment. With a note of heartbreak, she could see how, after years of doing this at Dr. Santo's behest, Kochin could learn to hate something that had only ever been beautiful to Nhika.

"Are we ready to hand him over to the medical examiners?" Hendon asked.

"Before we do, may we have a true moment with our father?" Mimi asked. She didn't wait for a response before stepping up to the casket, coaxing Trin and Andao to follow.

The rest of them gave the trio their space, Kochin diverting his eyes as though his audience itself was sacrilege. Nhika couldn't look away, her eyes lingering on the way Trin and Andao interlaced their gloved hands, on the way Mimi fit so perfectly between them. Seeing that unbroken trio now, Nhika wondered why she'd ever thought she could belong among them—they were already so complete. The Congmis had reminded her of what it meant to belong somewhere, but her place was not with them, and Nhika was beginning to understand that.

"Father, if all of Theumas is wrong and an afterlife does exist, forgive us for this," Mimi confided to concrete walls and a solemn audience. "It was always so clear what you lived for—your automatons, your children, your city. We've learned what you died for, as well, exposing your own friend. Now that I know, Father, I promise I won't leave your work unfinished."

Mimi bowed her head in conclusion and Andao and Trin

bent over to whisper some final words of their own, the echo of the mausoleum making their speeches indiscernible. Once they were done, they stepped back from the casket, and Nhika found something new in Mimi's eyes: resolution, as though she'd matured five years in a moment. Perhaps, it was the look of closure.

Having finished their business, they gathered the evidence of their tampering and exited the mausoleum. As they walked down the stairs, Trin appeared at Nhika's side, drawing her attention with a touch on the shoulder.

"I'm sorry," she said on instinct, because she felt like a trespasser here—in Mr. Congmi's body, in the mausoleum, in this entire graveyard.

"Don't apologize," he said. "We've been theorizing about what happened to Mr. Congmi since his death, and you gave us our answer. Perhaps it was an answer we didn't want to hear, but . . . it's an answer. Mimi won't admit it, but she's grateful."

"I didn't mean to unbury their grief along with their father."

"If it's how we get justice, then so be it. The siblings are stronger than they look." Trin watched her out of the corner of his eye, rocking back on his heels. "And it's in both of our interests. This helps you and Mr. Ven, and we'll make sure Dr. Santo sees punishment for what he's done."

"A suitable transaction," Nhika said. That's what her relationship with the Congmis had always been, right? Services for a price—convict their murderer, this time at the cost of fresh bereavement.

"Well, I should hope that it would be more than that. I don't consider you just an accomplice in . . . whatever this is. I consider you a friend." Trin cleared his throat, as though the small admission was too much for him. He glanced at Kochin down the road. "But . . . you're not planning to stay in Theumas, are you?"

She shook her head. "This city has never wanted me."

"I understand. Whatever it is you're looking for, Nhika—I hope you find it. Tonight, when you plant the rest of the sancuronium in Dr. Santo's office, I want to be there to help. A way of saying thank you, and I'm glad you came into our lives, even if you can't stay."

Nhika gave him a wry smile. "Not everyone can be adopted into the wealthiest family in Theumas, can they?"

"No, I suppose not."

Out of the corner of her eye, she found Kochin standing by the gate. She gave Trin a bow in parting, feeling lighter for having talked to him. "I'll see you tonight then."

"Nhika," he said, catching her. "For what it's worth, I didn't think you killed their father. You're soft underneath that dangerous act."

She faked affront. "You wound me, Dep Trin."

With a grin, Trin nodded his farewell and Nhika turned down the path, her eyes lingering on the family for just a moment. This might well be the last time she'd see this company in its entirety like this, as flesh and bone rather than portraits on the front page. She memorized them as they were now: gracious enough to let her back into their lives, if even just for an exhumation.

Nhika joined Kochin at the bottom of the cemetery gates.

He stood outside the fence, hands clasped behind his back as he watched the criminalist begin her work. The pensiveness in his eyes was as deep as the ocean.

"Do you ever think we're the last ones?" he asked in a solemn tone as he surveyed the graveyard. So, the morbid affairs had gotten to him, too.

"The last heartsooths?" she asked.

"Yes."

Nhika shifted her jaw in thought. "I always knew I couldn't be, but it didn't make any difference if I *felt* like I was. What do you think?"

Kochin's brow set with pessimism. "I think it dies with us, our generation."

"How can you be so sure?"

"My grandmother passed the gift to my mother, and my mother to me, but not to my brothers. Who knows if I'll pass it to my children, if I even get that far. So, how could it ever grow stronger? It can only get weaker, and smaller, and further from us. How are we supposed to keep it alive?"

Nhika had often felt the same. Her grandmother would lament that, with no more teachers, the art would die. But ever since she'd met Kochin, heartsoothing had come alive again—captured in rotting journals, exchanged between two schools, warmed by shared experiences. He'd shown her that heartsoothing survived through more than its tenets and rights and teachers; it survived simply through its people. "You live, Kochin. As long as you live, your heartsoothing lives, whatever form that might take. That would be enough."

"And when we're gone?"

"Then we find someone who will remember us as we want to be remembered." Even if heartsoothing was forgotten, its teachers wiped from Theumas and Yarong, some small part of it would exist forever: passed down from mother to daughter, immortalized in small acts of healing, shared with those who'd forgotten. Just like her bone ring, a shard for every heartsooth in her lineage—lost, but never forgotten.

Nhika reached into her shirt and drew out the ring, which she held out to him. She'd never shown it to anyone because no one else could appreciate it, but that was before she'd met Kochin.

"A Yarongese bone ring?" he asked incredulously, eyes rimmed with awe. He cupped it with his palm, inspecting the characters on the inner band. "What does this say?"

"Suonyasan," she responded. "My family name."

"Ah, I remember," he said, his smile soft and voice mesmerized. The sincerity of his gaze was almost too much to look at. She'd never known anyone who could appreciate her as he did. He put into words the nuance of it, something she'd never endeavored to do, because what were words worth if no one could understand them? But now he existed, and as Nhika gazed upon his thoughtful smile, his gloved hands, his dark eyes, she was glad he couldn't soothe her now. If he did, he might notice the soft tremor in her heart that stuttered in time with his breaths. Or, he might catch the redness in her cheeks, stifle those vessels though she might. Maybe, just maybe, he might even feel the heat surfacing on the back of her hand, still burning where he'd once kissed her.

Nhika pulled her gaze toward the pavement. Suddenly, he was at once too close and too far away. How long had she been looking for someone like him? Someone who knew her fears and her joys, as they truly were. Someone who might remember and keep safe her family name, as it truly was. And someone who might deign to keep her close—not as a blood-carver, nor even as a heartsooth, but as Nhika. Just Nhika. It had never been a probable fantasy for her—who would know what she was, and still let her touch them? Hers was not a touch that held, or caressed, or kissed; hers had always been the touch that carved.

But he was the marble that weathered.

When she looked back up at him, the humor had melted away and the line of his smile had softened. He straightened, returning the ring and looking again toward the mausoleum. "Thank you, Nhika. You were right about the loneliness. Before you, I'd never considered there might be a way out of my binds. When I was alone, I just had this . . . hopelessness. There was no sense in tomorrow because Dr. Santo dictated my hours, my days, my life. At some point, I think I resigned myself to it, an indentured life, because even if I was suffering, at least it was just me. If I hurt, or stumbled, or fell; if I didn't want to wake up to another day; if I hated myself at the end of it, then it was just . . . me."

Her heart squeezed as a sedated melancholy touched his expression. He gave her a wan smile, humor belying the grief in his eyes, and she felt tears burn through her nose. He'd put it into words, the feeling that had haunted her for so many years.

For a moment she was eight, surrounded by family, her home whole.

"What I mean to say, Nhika," he continued, "is that you remind me of someone I used to be, someone I was proud of. And you give me hope that I can be him again. I don't know if you understand how much that means to me."

"I do." The words left her tongue in a rush. "Trust me, I do."

With a soft smile, Kochin reached out and took her hand. They wore gloves; the gesture was not a heartsooth one, but a human one—just two lonely people who had been denied the grand promises of their city, so they found meaning in small acts of connection instead.

In the bone ring around her neck.

In the closeness of their bodies.

And in the way he squeezed her fingers just for a pulse, a silent promise that she would never be alone again.

The gesture, however small, was enough. Her chest crushed with a distant, unfamiliar ache. Not pain, not sadness.

Peace, freedom . . .

. . . and that final word she dared not speak aloud.

— TWENTY-SIX —

NIGHT CAME WITH THE LIGHTING OF GAS LAMPS and the hum of incandescent bulbs. On the houseboat, Nhika and Kochin gathered their things—a half-empty bottle of sancuronium and enough equipment to perform the second break-in. Everything that would be evidence, they handled exclusively with gloves.

They made the trip to the Theumas Medical Center on foot. In the darkness, the building held an eerie look, the arched windows too shadowed and the wide doors like those of a prison. She could see that activity still carried on in the adjacent emergency complex at the rear of the medical center, but the front had dimmed with a quietness like death.

There, the lot held only a single autocarriage with darkened windows, but Nhika knew who it belonged to before Trin opened the door. He and Mimi stepped out, and Nhika felt an echo of the past, seeing those two in the autocarriage as it had been when she'd first met them. This time, Mimi was not in white silks but dark ones, and Trin was not so nervous. With his pistol on his hip and thick arms crossed like corded dragons, Trin looked ready.

"I'll enter at the first sign of trouble," he promised, giving them that singular, reliable nod that she'd come to expect.

"Leave nothing to question," Mimi said, an offer of luck.

With murmured affirmations, Nhika and Kochin started toward the medical center, but Mimi caught her sleeve before she could go.

"Nhika," she began, her eyes downcast with something between bashfulness and nervousness. "I wanted to let you know, in case I forget later, that I didn't just come to see things through to the end. I came for you."

Nhika's lips parted with surprise. "For me?"

"To apologize. For . . . everything, really," Mimi said, looking sheepish. "I said a lot of things I regret, and I should never have accused you. But you came back anyway—healed Hendon, too. It's more than we deserved."

"You *do* still plan on paying me when this is over, right?"

Mimi laughed. "I suppose that's due. We'll make sure you're cared for. I want to see you happy. And if that's with him, then so be it. I don't think I can stand to see him again in my life, so before you depart with him, I want to help you find your happy ending, too. As a way of thanks. We won't forget this, Nhika. *I* won't forget you."

Nhika's chest bloomed with something pleasant. This was how it felt, then, to be remembered? Now she understood why the Congmis had claimed their graveyards and erected their mausoleums.

"I won't forget you, either," Nhika promised. And then, whim seized control of her and she placed a palm atop Mimi's head with all the familiarity of a sister. Mimi didn't shy away from the touch; she only beamed.

"How could you?" Mimi simpered. "I'm sure the Congmi name will follow you wherever you flee to in Theumas."

That drew a laugh from Nhika. "Be good to Trin," Nhika said, casting a weary look at the cross-armed bodyguard standing by the autocarriage. "I'll be back soon."

With a wink in parting, she joined Kochin at the medical center. They chose a door that faced the lots and she set to work on it with her lockpicks. With all the practice she'd had these past few weeks, the lock came easily undone. Quietly, they slipped into the building, leaving Mimi and Trin to await them outside.

This door led into the main foyer, vast and empty. Chairs lined the waiting area like gravestones and the arched windows splayed long shafts of moonlight across white tile. Nhika heard the echoic tick of cogwork somewhere down the hall, machines running on command rolls left inside, and had to remind herself that she didn't believe in ghosts. But how many had died within these walls? How many with unfinished business?

"I've never seen this place so empty," Kochin whispered, his breath catching on awe. "It's almost beautiful."

"That wasn't the word I'd have chosen," she said. "Maybe something more like 'creepy.'"

"Scared of ghosts?" he teased.

"Scared of becoming one. Mother knows I won't be allowed in Heaven."

"Not to worry. We can avoid all the surgical wards. Just for you."

"And not for the fact that his office is just upstairs?" she asked. Fourth floor, if she remembered correctly.

"Certainly not." The moonlight caught his boyish grin.

Their footsteps echoed up and down the stairs in the silence. Nhika hadn't remembered the hike to be so long, but every sound became a possible night guard or a lost emergency physician. With such an open, atrial floor plan, Nhika felt vulnerable, her silhouette cast in moonlight every time she rounded a window. But soon, surely, they made it to the fourth floor, where they turned down the hall.

This space afforded them the privacy of walls. Nhika remembered this walk in the daylight, the bustle of secretaries and physicians and researchers. Now it echoed with each footstep, deathly quiet. With its dark lacquered walls and plush carpet, it resembled the inside of a casket. The long hallway unnerved her; she expected a ghostly figure to be standing at the end of it. None materialized before they reached Dr. Santo's office, but she still felt a breath of relief when they stepped inside.

This was a familiar room. Here, with the dark wood and sparse windows, Kochin lit their lamp.

"This way," he said, leading her to the back. They passed the front desk, closets, and examination rooms before they reached an oak door in the back. The painted letters on the frosted window spelled out a lustrous name: SANTO KI SHON.

Kochin tried the handle—locked, but that was to their advantage. Dr. Santo had the only key into the office—not even Kochin had been given one—so anything they left here would incriminate him and him only. They'd chosen the end of the week for their break-in so Dr. Santo wouldn't see his office before the investigators did. Mimi's words played in Nhika's head: *Leave nothing to question.*

They wouldn't.

Nhika squatted by the door and drew out a lockpick. She fiddled with the pins, finding them more numerous than the locks outside, and with less tactile feedback. If only she could soothe metal, this wouldn't be so difficult, but she set to work one tumbler at a time. "This should only take a few minutes."

Kochin nodded, and she could feel his eyes watching her. For some reason, that made her sloppier.

"I'm glad you're here," he murmured, as though talking to himself.

"Actually, I'd love to see you handle these locks without me."

Pin by pin, she jiggled the tumblers into place, until finally the lock slid free beneath her wrench. Straightening, she tried the handle again and the door swung open with ease.

"There," she said, pocketing the picks. "Not so hard."

Kochin didn't say a word as he stepped into the study. It looked like such an unassuming place, just a blocky desk and laden shelves and an arched window at the far back, where one could stand sentinel over the sprawl of the Cat Borough. Nhika had been in many places she didn't belong lately—Dr. Santo's house, a dead man's body—but this felt the most innocuous of them all.

As Kochin busied himself with planting the bottle, Nhika found herself gravitating toward the desk, careful not to touch anything despite her gloves. It was sparse for such a renowned physician; the only things on it were a stack of papers, an inkwell, and another photo of his son.

The boy was slightly older this time, an adolescent, hands folded patiently as his portrait was taken. A newspaper clipping had been stuck into the frame, its headline tragic: HEART TRANSPLANT FAILS, DOCTOR MOURNS BELOVED SON.

"Nhika," Kochin said, calling her attention. He lifted a weathered folder that had been labeled with his own name. "Look at this. It's everything Dr. Santo has against me."

She took Kochin's side, looking at the folder's contents over his shoulder. It was as he'd said: a forged deportation warrant with Auntie Ye's name; a record of a patient who'd died with an autopsy report to suggest a bloodcarver; clandestine photographs of Kochin's barehanded patient visits.

All of it blackmail. All of it waiting to be spent—if not Kochin's mother, then something else, because Dr. Santo never planned on letting his heartsooth go.

"By the Mother," Kochin whispered before closing the file. "It's more than I ever knew."

"We can shred it," she suggested, gesturing to the paper grinder in the back of the office, its mechanical lever jutting from its side.

With a look of surety, Kochin picked the clips from the files and jammed the entire folder in the grinder. As he turned the handle, it ate up the folder with little discretion, shredding photos and chewing ink. With each shrinking inch, Nhika felt her heart lift, until the folder disappeared completely into the machine, nothing more than kindling.

With the sancuronium planted, Kochin extended a hand and, with an eager smile, Nhika took it.

They exited the room and closed the door, locking Dr. Santo's fate in behind it. Relief slid into place in Nhika's chest, her heart finding a contented rhythm to match the sounds of Kochin's slow, cautious breaths.

"It's done," he said, as though the reality of it was just dawning on him. "I'm . . ."

"Free," she finished for him.

"Free," he echoed breathlessly, turning to her. His expression was dipped in hope and mired in doubt, but she laced her gloved fingers in his and squeezed.

He squeezed back.

"Kochin, I . . ." she said, facing him in full. The space between them hung with words unspoken as he turned.

"What?" His expression was expectant.

Nhika didn't know how to describe what they meant to each other—first strangers, then adversaries, then heartsooths. Friendship had come somewhere along the way, and he'd kissed her on idyllic waters, but beyond that? Was there a word to encompass the feeling of seeing herself so completely in his eyes, of being found when she'd resigned herself to waywardness?

She realized there was; she'd just never had the certainty before to say it. With the enormity of their future unfurled before her, the promise of a life with another heartsooth, doubt yielded to faith and Nhika found the bravery to say, "Ven Kochin, I lo—"

The click of a gun.

They both startled, pulling apart. A shadow occupied the end of the hallway, the shining barrel of a pistol catching the glint of silver light. It aimed directly for Kochin's heart. The figure stepped forward into the moonlight, but Nhika already knew who it was. The grim look on Kochin's face revealed that he did, too.

There, blocking the entrance with pistol in hand, was Dr. Santo.

Gloves had never felt so damning before. Her hands burned, wishing to be free from the constraints of silk, to find a home around Dr. Santo's neck. Even then, he kept them at a distance, one meant for the speed of a bullet but not a heartsooth, and he'd evidently come prepared: a scarf tied around his neck, sleeves tucked into his gloves, pants that kissed the ground.

"Kochin," he said, his voice adopting the scolding drawl of a disappointed parent. "I thought you'd learned your lesson."

Kochin edged forward, placing himself between Nhika and the pistol. "Dr. Santo," he began, voice wary, "I've done as you asked. I killed Mr. Congmi. You don't need me anymore."

"Fair enough," Dr. Santo conceded, but the gun didn't lower. "However, do you remember what I said the last time you crossed me?"

Kochin lifted his chin, eyes narrowed. Nhika could tell he didn't want to afford Dr. Santo the satisfaction of an answer, but a jerk of the pistol coaxed it out of him. "You said that I wouldn't be so foolish as to do it again."

"Right," Dr. Santo said, and spread his free hand. "Yet, here we are. And what's more, you've roped in another. Now, just who *are* you, Nhika?" His imperative gaze turned to her, though the gun remained on Kochin. Where was that mentorlike glimmer behind his glasses, the kindness that had drawn her toward his lab in the first place? Where was the Dr. Santo who had made her feel as though she could be someone in high society, something more than a charade?

The patience had been replaced with icy cunning, and the twinkle in his eye with the shine of a barrel. As disgust boiled its way up her throat, she realized the man she'd thought was Dr. Santo had never existed in the first place.

"I'm nobody," she responded, her voice steady. She wondered if their advantage in numbers would be enough to best Dr. Santo, one to distract him and the other to remove a glove and carve. But the gun was level with Kochin's forehead, and an itching trigger finger was faster than a heartsooth.

"Certainly not a nobody, if Kochin has chosen to involve you. Is this some elaborate plan to collect evidence against me?"

"All I want is to leave," Kochin growled. "You've won—I won't tell anyone how you truly transplanted those organs, and you've already murdered your own friend to cover up the crime. I'm just asking for freedom." Nhika heard the crack of desperation in his voice, the fear leaking through.

For a moment, Dr. Santo seemed to consider it, his finger slipping from the trigger. Nhika wondered if it was out of cold calculation or understanding—was there some part of his mask that was real? Some part that cared for Kochin, for the Congmis, for even her?

Then his resolve hardened, fingers tightening around the pistol, and Nhika remembered there were things he cared about more. "Tempting, but you shouldn't take me for a fool."

"I'm not sure what you mean by that." Kochin's tone was steady.

"Don't play coy. I knew something was amiss. Your visit to my house did not go unnoticed. I had to wonder what this was all about, but now that I see you with the Congmis' ward, it's clear enough." He jabbed the pistol forward. "You, Suon Ko Nhika, healed Hendon, he remembered Kochin, and Kochin revealed all. Did I miss anything?"

Nhika shouldn't have been surprised by Dr. Santo's guile; even if he'd lied and murdered to secure his position, he had not become one of Theumas's meritocratic pillars through deception alone. She opened her mouth to rebut him, but Kochin spoke first.

"*I* healed Hendon," Kochin said. Nhika flared her eyes at him, but his intention was clear—he was trying to save her, because the most dangerous thing to be before Dr. Santo was a heartsooth. "I went behind your back. I couldn't live with what you made me do, so I cured his brain injury. When you tried to drug him, I healed him again. Santo, let us go. Leaving more bodies in your wake won't help you."

Dr. Santo roared out a laugh. "Your bodies couldn't hurt. You think anyone will miss you, Kochin? You haven't spoken to your family in years; they probably already think you're dead. And you, Nhika—you said it best yourself. You're nobody."

"He's bluffing, Kochin," Nhika said. "He wouldn't hurt you. He needs his bloodcarver."

"Clever girl," Dr. Santo drawled, tone devoid of true praise. "But, if Kochin is to be believed, and you did not heal Hendon, well then—" He swiveled the gun to her. "That would make you expendable."

Beside her, Kochin tensed and she heard him suck in a sharp breath. This was not the first time Nhika had stood on the other side of a gun, but it was the first time she truly feared for her life.

"Now, Nhika, tell me the truth. Are you a bloodcarver?"

Indecision held her tongue. Admit the truth, and she'd reap the full peril of Dr. Santo's attention. Worse, she feared he'd shoot Kochin, having no need for two heartsooths. Nhika wondered if he already knew, if this was just a test—a cat playing with its prey.

But, say no and get shot where she stood. If he was a smart man, he'd aim for the head. Anywhere else, she might be able to heal it and give Kochin enough time to subdue him. A long shot, sure, but Nhika drew all her courage into her lungs and said, "If I were a bloodcarver, you'd already be dead."

"Let's test that, then, shall we?" Dr. Santo sneered, and Nhika hardly had time to process the words before his finger went to the trigger.

She sucked in a sharp breath, feeling the echo of the gunshot resonating in her chest as she numbed the pain receptors of her skin. Black eclipsed the flash of gunfire in the darkness and Nhika recoiled, waiting for the slice of metal through her heart.

But it never came, and when she looked up, Kochin was standing before her, his back quivering and shoulders collapsed. It took her a long second to realize where the bullet had landed.

Not in her chest, but his.

— TWENTY-SEVEN —

"NO!" NHIKA'S LUNGS EMPTIED OF AIR AS SHE flew forward to catch Kochin. She lowered him in her arms beneath Dr. Santo's impassive gaze. Her breath stuttered at Kochin's pained grimace, hands following his in the dark as they sourced the bullet wound. Immediately, she felt the warmth of blood seep through her gloves. But he wouldn't be able to heal himself—not without an external energy source.

She glared up at Dr. Santo, willing him to fear, to rue, but his eyes held only shrewdness—he cared not who he shot, he was merely assessing if his gambit would pay off or if he'd lose his only bloodcarver.

"Go on," he taunted. "Heal him. You can, can't you?"

Nhika pulled her eyes down to Kochin, and he shook his head imperceptibly. "Don't," he whispered, the word so quiet he might've just mouthed it.

"You'll die," she said, her voice shaking with a sob.

The resignation in his eyes told her he knew that. Maybe he knew even before he took the bullet. "I don't care."

"I do," she replied, shutting her eyes against the welling tears. Tugging off a glove, Nhika bowed over his frame and cupped her fingers around the nape of his neck. There, she sowed her influence, feeling the immediate knife of pain in her lungs, a subdued reflection of his. She quieted that empathy, focusing instead on reconstruction—skin, lung, ribs.

Before she could finish, the click of the gun drew her from her soothing, and when she opened her eyes, the barrel wavered just above her forehead.

"Just as I thought," Dr. Santo huffed. "A full Yarongese. I never figured I could trade up a troublesome half for a real bloodcarver. Aren't I lucky?"

"Let me finish healing him," Nhika pleaded. Kochin's wound was spurting blood, and she could still hear the burble in his breath.

Dr. Santo's expression curled into a cruel grimace. "Step away, Nhika."

"He'll die!" Nhika dredged her voice up from the back of her throat.

"So, now you see what happens to those who cross me."

Kochin's chest shuttered with a pained breath. "Do as he says." His request came out weak, and she only tightened her grip on him.

"Listen to the boy, or I'll give you a different injury to heal," Dr. Santo threatened.

"You wouldn't kill both of us. You need a bloodcarver." As an act of defiance, she craned her neck up to meet the barrel of the gun.

"Oh, but you forget—I don't have to kill you." With only that as warning, Dr. Santo lowered the gun to her shoulder and fired.

The muzzle flashed in the dark. Nhika had no time to numb

her nerves before the bullet sliced cleanly through her frame, too close to her heart. She gasped for air, feeling the rise of blood in her throat and tasting metal on her tongue.

Kochin let out a pained gasp as they fell apart. "Nhika!"

She crumpled backward, falling against the floor and smearing blood as she tried to grapple for balance. Dr. Santo had known exactly where to shoot her to keep her alive but incapacitated. Every alarm in her body hailed her at once: lungs screaming for air, chest pounding with its new puncture, muscles roiling in fiery pain. Black swarmed her vision, and she squeezed her eyes shut, turning her focus inward. Her influence waned with each throbbing heartbeat, but she rushed it toward the site of her wound, taking energy from her liver to restore the tissue, mend the bone, knot the vessels.

She left the wound unfinished, feeling too drained to sew her skin and resigned to letting it clot on its own. Her shoulder ached, her patched heartsoothing rushed and sloppy. This was a wound that would scar. When the red cleared from her vision, Dr. Santo had tied Kochin to the radiator. His gun remained trained on Nhika, finger ready on the trigger.

Nhika didn't doubt he would shoot her again. And again, and again, until he'd sapped every last ounce of her energy, until he'd bled her near death just to keep her on the precipice of life. A harrowing realization came to her, the recognition that Dr. Santo had studied those like her, had read of her limitations and weaknesses. He knew the rules of her heartsoothing and used them against her. And for it, Kochin would die.

"If you kill him, you'll have to kill me, too," Nhika spat. "I'll never work for you. You can't blackmail me, Santo. There's only one thing in this city I care about, and you've just shot him."

Dr. Santo stiffened, mulling over her words. She wondered how far he would go to control her—would he use the siblings against her, the same ones he claimed to love so much? It was almost laughable; all his power lay in the deceit he wielded as a weapon, the gun he brandished as confidence. Beneath it all was just a lonely old man.

"You're right," Dr. Santo said, and the words sowed more dread than triumph. "You know, from the moment I saw you, I always suspected you were a bloodcarver. I puzzled myself into corners trying to figure out what I needed to have you, and now I see. You care for Kochin."

Nhika met Kochin's eyes, finding his expression broken. His chest rose with uneven breaths, hands bound, but he didn't break eye contact.

"I've been looking for a bloodcarver for a long time. A *true* bloodcarver," Dr. Santo continued. "Someone who can do something Kochin was never able to."

She suddenly recalled the Daltan texts in his private study, their headlines, REINCARNER VE MORTS; the pictures on Dr. Santo's desks, a boy taken from him too soon; the incessant search for heartsooths, for the limits of what medicine could do—they were starting to make sense. Mr. Congmi didn't die because he threatened Dr. Santo's research projects. He died because he threatened something Dr. Santo cared about far more.

The corpses, their organs, *something Kochin was never able to do* . . . Nhika realized that Dr. Santo didn't ask Kochin to soothe dead bodies to keep their organs fresh for transplant. In fact, it was never about the transplants—

"You're trying to bring your son back," Nhika whispered, and watched as Dr. Santo froze in surprise. In the silence, she continued, "You've been searching for a heartsooth who can."

Her gaze flicked to Kochin, tied against the radiator, and she saw the same horrified realization creep into his eyes. She needed no other confirmation to know she was right.

Something solemn flashed behind Dr. Santo's glasses; Nhika recognized the same look from the wake—*losing someone slowly*. Except, Dr. Santo didn't believe his son was truly lost, did he?

In the next moment, Dr. Santo's lethal facade returned, and he said, "How observant. Well, this is my proposition. You bring my son back, and I'll let you heal Kochin. The last thing I need a bloodcarver for and the last thing you care about. Never let it be said that I'm not reasonable."

She shared a look with Kochin. They both knew she wouldn't be able to do it—there were limits to heartsoothing, and bringing back the dead was not possible—but she saw no way out of this. Kochin's head moved, an imperceptible shake to tell her *no*, but she couldn't let him die. If anything, she at least had to buy them time. "I'll do it," she said. "Now, let me heal Kochin."

"My son comes first," Dr. Santo said. "Put your gloves back on."

She didn't want to leave Kochin here, bleeding out through a half-sealed wound, but Nhika needed to lower Dr. Santo's guard. She would not be able to save his son—even if it were possible. After healing her shoulder, her liver dwindled toward empty, and Nhika feared that doing anything more might just kill her where the bullet hadn't. But she had few other options.

"Dr. Santo," Kochin rasped, finding his voice. He pulled forward against his restraints, glowering at him with an enmity that could cut steel. "If you so much as lay a finger on her, I'll—"

"You'll what, Kochin?" Dr. Santo dismissed with a flourish of his gun. "If I were you, I'd save my energy. Now, Nhika, are we doing this or not?"

"We are," she said, the dread settling deep into her bones as she pulled on her gloves. Anguish scrawled itself plainly in Kochin's expression, but she gave him a look that held both an apology and a promise. "Take me to him."

— TWENTY-EIGHT —

DR. SANTO TOOK HER OUT OF HIS OFFICE AT gunpoint, then down the stairs. She'd walked this path before; he'd escorted her this way when she'd asked for literature, so she knew their destination to be his lab. Under the threat of a bullet, Nhika numbed herself until she was little more than a walking corpse, body unfeeling as she ambled forward. Her shoulder still oozed, the blood soaking through her gloves and dripping in a steady trail behind them, but who would notice in a hospital?

They reached the double doors of Dr. Santo's lab. Once the gilded gates of opportunity, they were now a hellmouth cast in poor lighting and dim moonlight. He pushed her through and, as the doors swung shut behind her, Nhika felt another ounce of her hope dwindle into dread.

Her fear made mazes of the hallways and prison cells out of examination rooms, but in truth, not much had changed since she'd last seen the space. That surgical automaton still sat behind an operating table, its claws now dormant. And there was the door to the library, where Dr. Santo had once offered her all the knowledge Theumas had to provide.

Instead of those rooms, Dr. Santo took her to a windowless steel door. With the gun still trained on her, he unlocked it and heaved it open to a plain white room. Inside was a row of metal caskets that felt vaguely familiar to Nhika, inset with machinery and wires and bellows. Three of them remained open, revealing a cushioned space inside, room enough for a single supine body.

The last one, at the end of the row, was closed. Through the glass window she saw a face that looked like sculpted porcelain.

Dr. Santo forced her toward the last casket with a gun at her ribs and a gloved hand tight around her injured bicep. His thumb teased her wound. He only loosened his grip to open the casket, first unlatching a series of buckles, then releasing a seal that hissed with the discharge of pressurized air.

The boy inside did not resemble the photos on Dr. Santo's desk. His muscle had all but wasted, leaving only a skeletal frame bound by taut, dry skin. Catheters extended from the casket into a variety of places in the body, powered by bellows to assume the role of circulation.

This was not a boy anymore. It wasn't even a body. To abate her horror, Nhika could only consider it an automaton, with a chassis made not of bronze but bone and functions overtaken by machine. Now more than ever, she prayed there was no afterlife, because Dr. Santo would've doomed his son to suffer in it.

And he was either delusional or desperate if he thought she could possibly bring him back.

"Well?" he said, prompting her with the twitch of his gun. She stepped toward the casket, brow furrowed, and watched as the body pulsed with unnatural movement, lungs swelling with air and tubes bulging beneath the skin.

A sharp pang of sorrow hit her. She remembered their conversations, the newspaper clippings, and saw how Dr. Santo's entire medical empire was founded not for Theumas's technocracy, but for a boy he hadn't been able to save. The irony was that she understood him—maybe better than anyone ever could. She understood him so well that she knew he would never stop trying, because if she truly believed heartsoothing could've brought her family back, she wouldn't have either.

"His name was Leitun, right?" she said softly.

"It doesn't matter to you," Dr. Santo snapped. Briefly, it seemed he would leave it at that. Then, in a grief-choked tone that reminded her of the Dr. Santo she thought she knew, he said, "Yes, it was."

"So, all of this—the killing, the extortion—was for him?"

"Why do we do anything, Ms. Suon, but for the ones we love?"

"What about Mimi and Andao? Trin? Mr. Congmi? Did you not love them?"

"When you lose someone who means the entire world to you, then you'll understand. Not all of us can be so lucky to be born with the gift to bring them back." Rage returned where she'd made room for remorse, and Nhika wanted to tell him that she'd known that loss—more than he could imagine. The thing that divided them was that her losses drove her to heal others, whereas he'd let his consume him. It's what made her the true healer between them. Remembering Kochin and the wound in his chest, Nhika saved her words.

"I'm removing my gloves now," she said. Slowly, with her hands displayed before him, she drew off her gloves and let them fall to the floor with a wet *splat* of blood.

Keeping him in the corner of her eye, she extended a hand toward the body. Nhika didn't want to soothe him; she didn't even want to touch him. Now, with her hands bare, she considered making a try for Dr. Santo, for the thin line of space at his eyes—all the skin she could see on him—but he stood three bounds away. She would never be able to outpace the gun; instead, she'd have to draw him closer.

Act as though they're alive, Kochin had told her. Nhika let out a breath and prepared herself to soothe.

As soon as her influence entered him, Nhika nearly vomited. It was an amalgamation of unnaturalness—all the strange fluids in him, the wires snaking underneath his skin, the decay he'd gone through. The very thought of altering anything here repulsed her.

She kept the body at a distance, soothing the way Kochin did, the way she had at the exhumation. She oriented this boy before her, the rest of the room falling away. White walls folded and collapsed into emptiness, the floor sank into abyssal darkness one tile at a time, and the ceiling peeled back to reveal a vast blankness above.

It was just Nhika and this body. The sounds of the casket dulled to silence and even Dr. Santo's gun felt far, far away.

In this moment, Nhika knew only three things.

The first was that she could never resurrect this corpse no matter how hard she tried, because she hadn't the knowledge, and this corpse resembled a human only in form. The second was that the candle of her energy had dwindled to a stub, and healing anything more might just cost her life. If she had to spend it, she would spend it wisely.

And third, most important of all, was that Dr. Santo had torn apart the city for this one, singular child. Nhika knew Dr. Santo wouldn't let her go even if she could revive the dead, and if she couldn't, he'd look for someone who could. So long as he believed there was a chance to bring his son back, he'd hunt for the heartsooth to do it. Keeping Kochin had never been about the research, the organs, not even the heartsoothing.

It had been about this body. It always had.

So Nhika would destroy it.

Her influence mired itself with the corpse. Wherever it touched, organs burst and bled. Skin bruised, bones embrittled. The corpse came apart under her touch, razed past the threshold of repair, heartsooth or otherwise.

"What are you doing?!" Dr. Santo roared, ripping her away from the body. But the damage had already been done; flesh bloomed green and purple with decayed blood and wires tore loose from papery skin. Dr. Santo howled as he saw the damage, then spun back to face her.

Nhika flew forward at the opportunity, her fingers finding a hold against his face.

Her influence invaded him. It raced to his liver, prepared to steal his stores to replenish her own. She'd only managed to catch a mote before pain erupted across her scalp—not mirrored, but her own. Her influence broke immediately, her soothing a dazed kaleidoscope of color and feeling as she tumbled through anatomy, unable to grab hold of anything solid.

When her senses returned, she found herself on the floor with rivulets of blood messing the side of her face and a swollen lump on her temple where he'd bludgeoned her. The barrel of the gun pressed against her rib cage once more and Dr. Santo wrenched her arms behind her back with a strength unbefitting his body.

"You'll regret this," he promised, lifting her from the ground and dragging her to one of the metal caskets. Her feet tangled themselves as she fought to escape his grip, but he'd already heaved the casket open with his shoulder.

"In," he ordered, and Nhika realized this was a fate worse than death, being forgotten alive in this contraption. He jerked the gun with impatience. "I won't ask again."

Fearing the bullet, she lifted herself in and he slammed the lid atop her. The glass window fogged with her breath, but she could still see his visage looming on the other side, glasses speckled with her blood.

"What are you going to do?" she asked, no longer able to hide the fear in her voice.

"If you won't heal him, I'll have to do it myself," Dr. Santo said, his voice muffled through iron. "I need only test a myth—whether the heart of a bloodcarver can confer the gift, after all."

Mother, he was going to slice her open, take her heart. Nhika screamed, only succeeding in fogging the glass further. But, instead of moving toward her, Dr. Santo latched up her coffin and left the room. Realization was slow to dawn, but when it did, it dragged in horror behind it.

Dr. Santo wasn't going to take her heart. He was going to take Kochin's.

— TWENTY-NINE —

THIS WAS WHAT IT FELT LIKE TO BE BURIED ALIVE.
Eaten by the abyss and choking on recycled air, Nhika screamed
until her lungs grew hoarse. She banged her fists, kicked her
feet, rattled the metal coffin until even the Mother must have
heard her. She prayed for company in this medical center—a
late-night janitor, a passing physician, or even Dr. Santo, so that
she might carve his eyes out of his head.

He planned to cut out Kochin's heart. Nhika wondered if
she would be next, or if she would play as Dr. Santo's new aide,
a bloodcarver pet to kill and heal at his behest. It hardly mattered; in the moment, it wasn't her life she feared for.

"Somebody, please!" she cried, using the limited mobility of
her arms and legs to rattle the lid. She turned on her side, heaving her shoulder against the top. But the latches held, her muscles tired, and Nhika hadn't even strained the metal.

With few options left, Nhika beat her palms against the top of
the casket, screaming till her lungs ran raw.

The screams eventually subsided to whimpers, and then to
a choking sob. She could hardly breathe; Nhika couldn't tell if
it was the claustrophobia, the panic, or the thought of Kochin
on the operating table. Maybe she would die here in the casket,
suffocated. What's worse, she might not be in time to save *him*.

Why? Her arms fell at her sides, joints aching and muscles raw. Why was it that the world insisted she be alone? She'd thought her fate changed when she'd met Kochin, but had that been a cruel tease?

Her tears came undammed. There was no shame in them because she was alone here, because if no one would remember Kochin, then at least she could weep for him. Nhika shrank into herself, wishing the dimensions of the casket would allow her to curl into a ball. For all her heartsoothing, for all the years she'd spent evading death, this seemed an awful lot like fate. It was an intimate form of cruelty; she'd wished for death so many times before, and the Mother had only waited until the moment she needed to live.

An aseptic chill settled in. She felt like a corpse, unfeeling and languid in the coffin. The only warmth came from her tears, welling in the corners of her eyes, but even those turned frigid as they traveled down her cheeks. Colors danced in the darkness, ears ringing in the silence, and Nhika squeezed her eyes closed to quell it all, the rising panic and mounting grief. If Kochin died, it would be her fault. She'd flown him into a thunderstorm on paper wings, quelling his anxieties with whispered assurances. He'd thought he'd pulled her into his tempest when in reality, she'd pulled him into hers. Because no one who'd ever touched her, loved her, cared for her at all, had made it out of her life alive.

A voice. Nhika's eyes snapped open, and she blinked away the lingering tears. She trained her ears, but nothing more came. Had it been the ringing of the silence?

But then: "The blood stops here, Trin."

Mimi. Hope reinvigorated her sore body, and she slammed her palms against the cabinet. "Mimi, I'm here! I'm here!"

More voices, lights, and then a fogged face appeared on the other side of the glass. It was Mimi, unlatching the lid and pushing it open with all her weight. Cold, sanitized air filled her lungs as Nhika rolled out of the coffin, eyes streaked with tears but never so happy to see the two of them.

Trin's eyes bugged at the amount of blood covering her, his lips twisted in discomfort. Her eyes found the pistol at his belt—good. They'd need it.

"What happened?" Mimi asked. "We heard the gunshots, and heavens, Nhika—did he shoot you?"

"I'm all right," she said, though her shoulder and skull throbbed with every heartbeat. "Kochin's in the office. He's going to die without my help." She was already headed toward the door when Mimi caught her wrist.

"He's not there. We checked. There's nothing there but blood."

Nhika halted, horror coming like a slow dawn. If Dr. Santo had already moved him, that meant . . . "The operating rooms. Where are the operating rooms?"

Trin jerked his head down the hall. "Follow me."

They rushed through empty halls, toward the section of Dr. Santo's lab that housed his operating suites. Nhika cared little about who might find her now. Let them see her bloodied robe, her gritty determination, her culminating wrath. Let them try to stop her.

They turned the corner and Nhika knew this dark, ghostly corridor to be the surgical ward. There, at the far end, was a light.

"Trin, is your pistol loaded?"

He nodded.

"Call him out at gunpoint. Distract him and I'll soothe him." Now, *soothe* seemed too kind a word. No, she wanted to rend him piece from piece, grind his bones to dust and ignite every nerve in his body. After she finished carving, not even vultures would recognize him as carrion.

As they approached, she could hear the grind of a bone saw, smell the burnt tang of its dust. Disgust rose in her throat, and she swallowed the sour bile, focusing instead on the shadows playing in the light. Dr. Santo's shadow splayed across the far wall, stretched and monstrous, but she couldn't see Kochin.

Nhika sucked in a breath, dipping into the cover of the adjacent room and concealing herself behind a wall. She waited for Trin, who drew his pistol and aimed it down the hallway. His voice echoed in the emptiness of the surgical ward as he called out, "Dr. Santo! Show yourself."

The shadows stilled, then shrank. Their edges crystallized and Dr. Santo's silhouette took shape as he approached the threshold of the operating room, until Nhika could see him blocking the entrance. Her breath hitched with anticipation, fingers aching for vengeance. She thirsted to curl them around his neck, to choke him from the inside out. And she would.

Dr. Santo stepped into the hall, garbed in a bloodied brown apron with a pistol in hand. At the sight of Trin, he raised his aim until they'd locked each other. Nhika coaxed him closer with a prayer, waiting for him to draw within her range. But he remained fixed in his spot, looking calmer behind the barrel than a doctor should've.

"So, the secret's out, isn't it," he muttered, voice muffled by a surgical mask.

"Dr. Santo," Mimi snarled, fierce for her position behind gunpoint. "A part of me wanted to believe you, up until the very end. I couldn't fathom that you could help us plan our funeral and find our murderer when it was *you*, all along, the man we were looking for. How could you do that to us?"

"Leave," he warned, his voice holding genuine concern—for Mimi or for his crime, Nhika wasn't sure. "You have no idea what's at stake."

"If it was all a lie, all that you've done for us, then tell me at least one truth," Mimi said. "Why did you kill my father?"

Arm outstretched, pistol unwavering, Dr. Santo said, "Because he didn't know when to look the other way for the sake of a friend. And neither, it seems, do his children."

Taking that as her cue, Nhika leaped from the curtains and diverted Dr. Santo's wrist. A bullet fired into the ceiling, and then she was grappling for the gun, hands slipping against his gloves, slick with blood, and palms struggling to find skin underneath his layers.

He threw his arm out in an arc and pain bloomed across her chest. The surgical light was enough to catch the shine of the surgeon's knife in his hand, and Nhika numbed those receptors, leaving nothing but a lingering warmth on her skin and tightness in her chest.

He drove forward with the scalpel and she caught his arm. They were stuck in a lock, Nhika's hands shaking as one pinned Dr. Santo's gun and the other his scalpel. The knife drew closer to her gut; her fingers tightened against slipping rubber. Nhika gritted her teeth as she glared at him, finding the only exposed strip of skin on him to be his face above the surgical mask.

Her grip loosened on his pistol hand and she felt him angling his wrist. The barrel curved toward her, dangerously close, and Nhika drew in a sharp breath at the expectation of a bullet.

"Nhika!" Trin called, and she turned her head just in time to see the flash of his barrel.

Trin, who had wielded that pistol so many times as a threat but never before pulled the trigger, did so now.

And it was a beautiful shot, passing her as it entered Dr. Santo's leg and escaped cleanly out the other side. Trin did not miss.

With an outraged cry, Dr. Santo collapsed, clutching his thigh. Viper fast, Nhika's hand shot out and latched itself onto his face.

Skin. With it, her influence exploded across his body. The dim lights of the medical center fell away, a world turned inside out as she carved. Nhika wrested control of his hands, squeezing extensor muscles until both the scalpel and the gun fell from his grip. Something within him fought her for control, not an influence but the absoluteness of his will, and Nhika had never felt so much a trespasser in a body than now, when the body fought her back.

But she forged forward: teeth gritted, fingers curled, brow

set. For Kochin, and the Congmis, and for herself—because Dr. Santo had razed and killed and defiled just to control a bloodcarver, so she would show him what it meant to truly have one.

Dr. Santo's will broke like shattered glass and she fell into the full dominion of his anatomy. Her influence tumbled forward into his chest, the hollow of his rib cage, finding his heart locked between two lungs. Its muscle pulsed with vigor and all she had to do to kill him was reach up to that line of influence, the one that diffused electricity around the heart, and disrupt it. Nhika extended her influence, curled it around his heart.

And paused.

Here, suspended in his thoracic cavity, Nhika could almost forget who it was she carved. His heart beat the same as any other, its cadence suddenly so fragile and mortal, and Nhika remembered when she'd last been in this position: with Kochin, a knife in his side and a hand around his neck, before she ever knew what he was. Back then, he'd fought against her, not so he might live, but so she wouldn't have to defile her gift by taking a life.

Nhika would not let Dr. Santo, in his last act of life, defile her gift now.

She drew back from his body and into her own. As if she'd taken all his energy stores, Dr. Santo slumped to the ground, leg still bleeding, as Trin arrived to apprehend him.

"Nhika, you're hurt," Mimi fretted, wide-eyed, as she stared at Nhika's stomach.

With a shake of her head, Nhika dismissed her concern.

"Find a telephone. Call the constabulary. Get Dr. Santo out of here," she managed, squeezing a hand over her abdomen and finding it warm with blood.

"Come with us—you need to see a doctor."

Nhika shook her head. "Not now."

She turned to leave, but Mimi caught her sleeve. "*Please*, Nhika, you're hurt."

Nhika paused, feeling the pain prickle under her skin, muted. She looked at Mimi and Trin, at Dr. Santo between them—no more lies, no more weapons, just a doctor whose will she had broken. If she left with them now, the terror of this night could end, but she only shook her head. "Leave, Mimi. Find your justice."

Nhika needed to find Kochin.

With looks of acceptance, Mimi and Trin pulled Dr. Santo away while Nhika ambled toward the operating room. There was little pain, but her body still reminded her it was dying. She left the wounds as they were, her pounding skull and bleeding abdomen; Nhika lacked the energy to heal herself now.

Her throat closed when she saw Kochin. Dr. Santo had strapped him to the operating table, pinned by leather restraints. The operation had already begun, and tears burned at the thought of being too late.

He stirred when she neared, giving his first sign of life: a slow blink, wide eyes trembling with subdued panic, and then an anguished smile. There he was, shirt torn open and chest bloody, and he was *smiling*. She wept, her emotions a disorderly mess of fear and relief and panic and urgency. He was here;

she'd come in time. But his wounds were deep, and her energy was petering out, and for all the lives she'd saved before, she might not be able to save this one.

"Nhika." His hand lifted, but fell again once it met the resistance of the restraints.

"You're alive," she breathed, then rushed to him, unbuckling straps and joining him on the table, where she pulled him into her arms. Her hands were wet with blood, either his or hers, and she saw the raw damage of the gunshot, still leaking blood into his open chest.

"It's okay. I don't feel a thing," he said. Why did he say that as if they were his last words? Tears blurred her vision as she placed a hand against his chest.

"I can heal this," she said, palm plastered over the wound.

Arm trembling, he lifted his hand to her cheek and thumbed away a tear. She caught his hand, holding it there, just to feel that warmth a final time.

"This isn't your fault," he said, just a whisper, as though he were already fading away. But it was her fault. She was too late; there was too much to heal, too little energy. She herself was dying, though her body knew better than to remind her now. Everything she touched died; whenever she got involved, she lost it all. But Kochin was hope after a flame snuffed out. She wouldn't survive healing him, but she wasn't sure she would survive losing him, either.

As she bowed her head, something slipped out from underneath her shirt. It was her bone ring, yanking at the end of its string and catching the glare of the surgical lights. Through the fog of her fatigue, she saw the bone shards aligned along the band, the crack that threaded through them. She saw the space left for her grandmother, for herself, for the heartsooths after them. She saw the three characters etched on the inside, *Suonyasan*, a name that yearned to be remembered.

And she realized, suddenly, and with perfect clarity, what she had to do.

Her forebears had passed heartsoothing on to her grandmother. Her grandmother had passed it on to her. Now she would pass it on to Kochin—the only person who would know what it meant, what it was worth.

Let him have her heartsoothing, which had saved Hendon; which had defeated Dr. Santo; in all its forms, with all its wonders, which she'd been granted for a singular purpose: to *heal*.

In her final act of heartsoothing, that was exactly what she would do.

"Kochin," she exhaled. "I love you."

She knew he wouldn't accept what she was about to do, so she distracted him the only way she knew how—Nhika bent over and kissed him.

With the finality of someone accepting his end, Kochin rose to meet her. As their lips met, as she flattened her palm against his wound, heat burst forth from her abdomen like a star born within her. She funneled that heat into him, at the juncture of their lips and her palm, a flood of life wherever their skin touched. Her influence seeped into him like sunlight, smoothing his fractured ribs, stitching up burst vessels, making his lungs whole again.

His eyes flared when he understood what she was doing. Kochin pulled away from the kiss, his breath sharp, but she kept her palm planted against his chest. From that contact, she seeded growth, drawing from her muscles to sew up his skin.

"Nhika, no," he gasped, finding voice in his lungs again. Renewed, he sat up, pulling her into his arms and wincing at the motion. "*Stop!*"

But she wasn't done. She'd sealed his body back together, but Dr. Santo had made a mess of his core, lungs askew and organs bruised. Pain flared up in Nhika's own anatomy as her hold on herself slipped; her abdomen flashed in agony where Dr. Santo had opened it, the injury loud after she'd silenced it for so long. She ignored the burning that spread up her legs, starved of their energy. Ignored how her vision swarmed with spots, shadows over her retinas. Ignored the dryness of her tongue, thirsting for water.

Nhika fell into his arms, limbs losing strength. She felt her heartbeat in her neck, her chest pounding as though preparing to burst. But she kept soothing, even as she felt Kochin rise to fight her. Their influences warred, entangled and inseparable, until at last hers won out.

"Don't fight, Kochin," she whispered, but he only shook his head. "Your heartsoothing. It's yours again, to be whatever it is you want it to be."

That, she realized, was her legacy: a gift to the ones after, the ones she cared for.

Nhika laid herself into his bones, his muscles, his heart. Soon, there was nothing left to her that wasn't Kochin's as well, nothing but an empty vessel and a withered liver. He gathered her close and, through the blurriness of her vision, she saw that he was crying.

"There," she said at last, her voice a rasp. "Now you'll have it all. Peace, freedom . . ." Nhika lost the energy to complete the sentence.

"Please, don't leave me," he begged, anguish cracking his words. He wrapped her hand in his, brought her knuckles to his lips, planted a kiss.

She couldn't stay, but that didn't mean she was leaving him. Nhika had never known what to do with her damned empathy organ, figuring it'd be the death of her. Well, if that was to be the case, then Kochin could have it. He could have it all, her wretched little heart.

Her vision blackened. Wakefulness tapered. Pain bloomed. With the last of her waning strength, she moved Kochin's hand to the ring around her neck, curled his fingers around it. In his embrace, her world melted away at the edges and her breathing slowed, but Nhika only smiled.

Because she'd found it, at long last. The place where she belonged.

⸺ EPILOGUE ⸺

SO WENT THE STORY OF THE MOTHER AND THE Trickster Fox: There came a fox who'd observed the Mother's sacred gift and decided to attempt it for himself. Without the Mother to teach him, his heartsoothing manifested not as healing but as shape-shifting, a tool he used to walk among humans as one of their own.

When the Mother learned of how he had profaned her gift, using it not to heal but to beguile, she grew incensed. As his punishment, she carved away the thing he cared for the most: his nine-fold tail, the plumage that set him apart from all the other beasts, and cursed him to forever flee from humans.

But Kochin had never seen the fox as a villain. He saw the fox as one who could not use the Mother's gift as others could, so he had to find his own way. Therefore, his punishment was never a victory to Kochin, but a warning from a goddess he didn't believe in.

Perhaps he should've listened.

If he had, maybe he wouldn't be standing here before Nhika's tombstone, living on in her stead. Her last words replayed in his mind in an agonizing melody: *Peace, freedom* . . .

Now he carried her as a part of himself, carried her youth in each stride and her laughter on every breath. Nhika was there in the bone ring around his finger, in the scar that split his chest from sternal notch to solar plexus. If he focused, he could even imagine her warmth beside him, both of them surveying her empty grave.

"A granite headstone?" she would've said. "I thought I'd be worth marble, at least."

"Well, the venue is nice," he reasoned, sweeping a gaze around the empty graveyard. It was the Congmi family's own cemetery, where the siblings had gotten her an honorary headstone, though her details were few. SUON KO NHIKA in all capitals, engraved with the image of an anatomical heart. They had never consulted him about the familial name, had never thought to ask if she truly had one. But the grave was only ceremonial; no body lay beneath the dirt.

A throat cleared behind him and he turned, the image of Nhika dashed. It was Andao, Mimi, and Trin, all in black attire. Mimi held a bountiful bouquet in her arms, chrysanthemums blooming white and yellow.

"I'm sorry," Mimi said, diverting her eyes toward the ground. "We came to pay respects. We didn't realize—"

"It's all right," Kochin said, making space for them. He stood to the side as they left the bouquet atop her headstone. Mimi placed her palms together, murmuring a quiet prayer— to whom, Kochin wondered, when Theumans worshipped no god?

They whispered their respects, too quiet for Kochin to hear, before straightening. He watched them out of the corner of his eye, his expression neutral.

"We owe a lot to her," Mimi said, and Kochin took a moment to realize he was being addressed.

He nodded. "Me too." *Peace, freedom* . . .

"We came to tell her the good news," she continued, her voice edging on hope. "Dr. Santo was sentenced this morning. For life."

Kochin nodded once. "So, he's finally seen justice for his crimes." Except . . . not all of them. Theumas would never know all that Kochin had lost that night.

"You had plans with her, right?" Mimi asked. The words were innocent, but they drove a knife through his heart.

"Yes," he responded curtly.

"I'm sorry," Mimi said again, as if she knew nothing else to say. "Now that she's gone, will you stay in the city?"

He sensed the true question behind her words. "I'll leave your lives," he assured her. And then? *Peace, freedom* . . .

He'd lost Nhika, but she wasn't gone. In all of heartsoothing, there were known taboos. He'd already broken many of them, using his art to injure and disable, but there was one he had yet to attempt. One that not even Dr. Santo had been able to achieve.

Bringing back the dead.

Most would tell him it was impossible, that even heartsoothing couldn't breathe life into something that had gone. But all taboos had pretense; he'd learn how to do it, even if he had to search every corner of the city for the answer. Even if he had to raze Theumas down to its roots.

"What will you do?" Mimi asked, drawing him back to the cemetery.

"I'm going home," he said, but that was only half the truth.

Kochin stared at the empty grave, his fist tightening with resolve. The granite headstone teased him, the false name an omen. Because she wasn't really gone, was she? With heartsoothing, she'd given him her life.

And with heartsoothing, he was going to bring her back.

ACKNOWLEDGMENTS

I started *The Last Bloodcarver* during a time when I felt lost; finishing it now, I feel found. Innumerable people have been monumental to the life it has now, not only those who worked directly in making this book take shape, but also those who have supported me along the way.

I'd firstly like to thank my editors. Emilia Sowersby, Emily Feinberg, and Mariam Meshmesh; you were the editorial team to end all editorial teams. Thank you for elevating this story to its fullest potential.

Thank you to everyone from Roaring Brook who helped this book reach publication. To Mia Moran, Emily Stone, Claire Maby, and Katy Miller, thank you for your eye for detail. I've learned grammar from my copy edits. To Meg Sayre, Mallory Grigg, and cover artist Yoshi Yoshitani, I cannot thank you all enough for bringing heartsoothing to life on that cover, more beautiful than my words can express. To Celeste Cass; Jennifer Healey; Connie Hsu; Allison Verost; my sales team; my publicist, Morgan Rath; those who worked on subrights—Kristin Dulaney, Kaitlin Loss, Jordan Winch—and everyone else working behind the scenes to help me realize my vision, you have my eternal gratitude.

Everyone at BookEnds but especially Ramona Pina, thank

you for believing in this book's potential and treating it with such care and diligence.

To my writing community: Mia, pharmaceutical encyclopedia and semantics expert, I attribute all the finer parts of this novel to you. Selena, you read this story in its roughest shape, and yet still believed in it. Elise, Emma, Trinity, Tiffany, Sarah—I could not ask for better friends and readers. And of course, thank you to all the mentors I've found in the writing community along the way.

To old high school teachers, who saw my spark even back then and fostered it: VJ Sathyaraj, thank you for inspiring my love for reading. Debby Schauffler, thank you for cultivating my love for writing.

To my dear friends: Evan, Lei, Giorgio, Ben, thank you for hyping me up through every step in the process. Melanie, Winlyn, Kryss, Sydney, Denae, thank you for being the first to celebrate any good news I shared.

Lastly, thank you to the most important figures in my life, my family. You may all see some part of yourselves in these pages. Brendan, I wouldn't be the person I am today without following your example. Cameron, you inspire me more than you know. Caiden, your unending enthusiasm and support keep me going. I'm immensely grateful for you three.

Charles, I could not have written this book without you in my life. You celebrated my every high and consoled me through every low. You are my heartsooth.

Most importantly, thank you to my mom, my dad, and my bà ngoại. I know I gave you express instructions not to read this book, but it was written in your honor. Thank you for raising me to be the woman I am today. I hope it's not conceited to say that I think you all did a mighty fine job.

Finally, to my readers: I hope you all find yourselves in these pages.